BOOK 4 IN THE SHADOW SWORD SERIES

THE SWORD AND ITS WOMAN

S.J. HARTLAND

Dark Blade Publishing

ROHANE

She watched herself kill, watched her sword rip limbs from bodies and sever heads from torsos. Savagely, she cut a path through figures on the battlefield, the torn bodies of wounded and dying warriors piled in her wake. Steel rose and fell, showering blood and shards of bone, the blade hungry for death. Yet its pitiless reaping was apart from her.

Later, she would pay for that. When the guilt came. When it took her over and she wept, her tears falling into the earth, into the blood. But for now, there was no guilt, only ghouls to cleave in a delicious, murderous wave.

Sometimes she wished the berserker fever that flamed through her limbs, the darkness that consumed her will, would never end. Then there would be no pain, no remorse, only the intoxicating scent of blood. A call to chaos. A summoning to bring death.

But as it always did, the fever burned out too fast, that bright, sharp burst of blind strength and blank rage draining away like rainwater after a storm. Rohane's knees folded. Her breath racketed in her breast. Her vision blurred then cruelly sharpened on the carnage she had so savagely wrought. Dismembered bodies lay heaped in ragged lumps. Wounded men groaned as they crawled away. Already black wings circled, scavengers ready to feast upon her butchery.

Among the dead, a figure lay like a sleeping child, one hand curled softly. A shudder of sorrow and despair crept down Rohane's spine. *Not real,* she told herself. *She* was never real. Only a shadow, a shade, the embodiment of Rohane's guilt.

Tears wetting her cheeks, she stretched her hand towards the beloved face. Just as Rohane touched her, the woman disappeared. In her place, there were only dead strangers, only dead men and ghouls in an ugly tangle of corpses, their staring eyes accusing.

You killed us. Just like you killed her. You're a monster.

A hand fell on her shoulder. Rohane sprang to her feet, grasping her blade as she turned. A woman flung up her gauntleted arm. "It's me, you crazy fool."

Rohane blinked rapidly. She snatched a breath. "You took me by surprise, Persia."

The battale captain scowled. "I thought the blood fever gone from you."

Rohane shoved her sword into her belt. "It's gone."

Persia swept a gaze over the field of death, where Quisnaf warriors prowled, driving swords into the throats of men beyond help or ruthlessly cutting down ghouls attempting to flee.

Other warriors dragged men likely to survive their wounds towards a huddle of prisoners so healers could tend to them. Those who'd surrendered knelt in the churned mud and blood, fingers entwined behind their heads as they glared at watchful guards.

"You must have killed fifty or more." Persia's voice held awe but also fear. Once that fear—the way her warrior sisters shrank away when she passed—would have cut Rohane with hurt and resentment. Now, she shrugged. Her curse was penance. It must be accepted. It must be endured.

"It is a terrible thing, this berserker rage." Persia scratched at her scalp beneath her helm. "Perhaps I was wrong to make use of you. You are a valuable weapon, but you are not here to fight, after all."

Rohane scuffed dirt with the toe of her boot. "I can both fight and do the will of the blood keepers," she muttered. "Should I sit and plait my hair while my sisters fight and die? I could not. But now the battle is won, with your permission, I will fetch the man I was sent to retrieve."

Persia looked past her to the aftermath of battle, drumming her fingers against her weapons belt. Rohane understood her restlessness. Nothing was more unsettling than a victory. A good captain always reflected upon not only defeat but also success. To simply overcome an enemy was satisfying, but every Quisnaf commander knew it was preferable— and more profitable—to force an enemy to yield.

As a young warrior, Rohane had mistakenly thought Persia the most officious of the four Quisnaf battale captains. Now she understood Persia was disciplined, that she'd adopted a strict code to maintain honour even in battle.

"I'll assign warriors to help you," Persia said.

Rohane shook her head. "Roaran assured the Quisnaf council this man will surrender willingly."

"He's a bladesman. Twice now, he's eluded us. He might lose his nerve and run again."

"You don't think I can take one man?" Rohane screwed up her face in irritation. "I've never failed. As a retrieval captain, I have a perfect record. No man has eluded me."

Persia shrugged. "Nevertheless, you'll accept my offer of warriors." Unexpectedly, she reached to flick Rohane's hair from her eyes. The battale captain's lips curved in a faint smile. "He shall certainly run if he sees you now. Your clothes are blood soaked. Your hair matted with bone fragments. You look like a reaper of the dead."

Rohane brushed away the other woman's hand. "What do I care how I look? Am I a pampered breeder or a scribe spending my days with pen and parchment?" Scoffing, she again kicked at the dirt. "With your permission, *Captain*, I'll ride for the castle and Val Arques Caelan. Heaven help them if they deny me my target."

VAL ARQUES

Val trudged at the end of a rope looped about a saddle, his wrists bound. For all his nervous exhaustion, he held his body with stiff control, his chin tilted defiantly. He might be a prisoner, but the Quisnaf would never see him bowed or diminished.

Angrily, Val eyed his captor, resentful she had trussed him to her saddle like a beast led to market. "The ropes aren't necessary," he hissed in indignant Telorian. "I gave my word to go with you."

The rider ignored him. The only sign she had even heard was a slight twitch of a muscle in her jaw. Despite the weight of the sword and bow slung over muscular shoulders, she sat tall in the saddle. A sweep of light-brown hair tumbled down her back, knotted in a strip of scarlet velvet he would like to tighten around her neck.

At first glance, she was young but not quite beautiful. Her lips, curved upwards, were overly generous. Her expression was stern and unyielding, like a scolding nursemaid's.

Yet at a second glance, his gaze lingered. Perhaps it was how she held herself proudly, her head high as though to challenge the gods to fault her. Perhaps it was the hint of resolved courage in her eyes, their colour darker than her hair. Or perhaps it was her aloof, contained disinterest.

At a burst of laughter, Val glanced over his shoulder at riders herding weary men roped together in a straggling line. They must feel as wretched as him, more so, given they were unwilling captives taken after the battle.

Not watching his feet, Val stumbled on the dark trail through thick-trunked trees. Branches swept low, heavy with blossoms that perfumed the night air. Jasmine, maybe. On other nights, he might have delighted in its sweetness, but nothing pleased him in this moment. Ferns brushing the top of his boots irritated him. Welling shadows groped with menace. A bird's cry taunted him for his helplessness.

He considered his sword poking from his captor's saddlebag, just one lunge away. Even with bound hands, he might grab it and break free. Would he? He had given Roaran his word to surrender himself, yet the prideful part of him needed to know he could escape.

He twisted his chafed wrists and kicked a stone, punishing it for his predicament. Restraints, to be subject to another's will, exposed his inner wounds, his anger at his powerlessness. Throwing back his head, Val shouted, a wordless cry of helpless frustration.

The rider looked over her shoulder. "Calm yourself," she said in near-perfect Telorian.

"Why should I?" he snapped.

"Otherwise, my sisters will demand I gag you."

No! It was shameful enough stumbling after a horse, bound. But gagged? Val took a slow breath. *Keep control. Think it through.* Of course, the Quisnaf did not trust him. He should expect ropes and commands. But that undercurrent of unease would not go away. How would his captors treat him? Kindly? Harshly? He was desperate for reassurance, to banish the nerves in his belly and understand what he faced.

"Do you have a name?" he called in her tongue.

She turned her head, one brow arched. "You speak Quisnaf?"

"I do."

"Useful to know. I shall be careful not to plot when you're around. You can address me as Captain."

"Captain what?"

When she did not answer, Val muttered, "Captain Grumpy then."

He trudged on. Time stretched like an age. Val wanted this journey done with, to be at once in Quisnaf, where he could stare unblinking at his fate and accept it. But before him was a long journey by sea then perhaps a trek overland to the famed city of caves.

At last, they reached a wall of spiked stakes protecting a clearing of canvas tents and cook fires. As the line of riders and their captives appeared, sentries at a wooden gate snapped to attention.

Val's feet dragged. Scowling, the captain turned her head and tugged at the rope.

He stumbled. "All right," he muttered. "All right. I've learnt my lesson, Captain Grumpy."

For a moment before she looked away, he was almost certain she grinned.

She led him through the camp to a large tent. A young woman with a homely face and fair hair caught up in a bob came forward to take the captain's horse. The newcomer threw Val a sneering glance. "That's him, then?"

"See to my horse, Mel. I'll see to our guest." The captain dismounted. She drew Val's sword from the saddlebag and passed it to the young woman. "Here, take good care of this. Oh, a warning. He speaks Quisnaf."

Unimpressed, the young woman sniffed and strutted off with both horse and sword.

The captain untied her end of the rope. "Walk."

At even this simple command, Val bristled. He stood his ground. His captor jerked the rope. "Don't try my patience on our first day of acquaintance. I might make a quick judgement about you."

"Like what?"

She shrugged. "That you're stubborn and wilful. That sort of thing."

Val forced a bitter laugh. "That would be the truth."

"A man who knows himself." She turned away, assuming he would follow.

With a heavy sigh, he strode after her to a tent, brushing through the flaps in her wake.

The captain gestured at a thin pallet unrolled on the ground. "We have a long walk at dawn. You will sleep."

At yet another command, he glared.

The woman slid her hands to her hips. "Let's be clear from the start. The rules are simple. You obey, or someone makes you obey. Do you understand?"

"Oh, I understand all right. It's just those rules don't appeal to me particularly."

"Then you will find Quisnaf an unpleasant place. Shall I rephrase my order?" She raised her eyebrows, her face impassive. "You must be tired. If it would please you, I would be glad if you would sit."

"Oh, ha ha." Val huffed.

"Please." She gestured at the pallet.

Val sank down. In truth, he was wrung out. His wrists, shoulders, and back ached, and his inner turmoil, that constant battering of thought and imagination, exhausted him. So much had happened in the past few hours. He had watched ghouls butcher Roaran Caelan on a wheel. He had thought he would watch Alecc die. All because of Genya. Despite her change of heart, his ward's betrayal still shocked him.

He held out his wrists. "I gave my word to go with you."

The captain dropped the sack containing his meagre possessions beside the pallet. "You did not give your word to me."

"Then ask me."

She hesitated. "Very well. If you give me your word you won't try to leave—"

"You have my word."

For a moment, she stared at him. Then she nodded and stooped to cut his hands free. Val rubbed his wrists, sighed, and lay back.

"It's not long until dawn," she said. "Get what sleep you can. It will be a tiring day."

Val hardly heard her. He fell at once towards sleep.

ROHANE

Rohane expected Persia's summons. She did not resent it. The battale captain had a right to know exactly what went on in her camp. But Persia believed in rules—and Rohane liked to break them.

Weary, wanting the day done, she trailed after Persia's girl, a sullen, pale-cheeked creature of dubious blood called Dagmar. Dreary Dagmar, some of the younger warriors called her. Given her washed-out hair and bony face, she might be of Venivan heritage. Strange how those sharp Venivan cheekbones carved some faces elegantly, creating a palate for beautiful eyes and lips. In others, like this slender warrior-to-be, those same bones looked misplaced and gaunt.

Well before they reached Persia's tent, Rohane heard Marlisa's exuberant laughter. It rolled with careless abandon, much like the woman herself. When Persia's lieutenant came into sight, Marlisa was sprawled on her elbows, legs extended, at the centre of a group of young warriors drinking about a cook fire. She brushed a few strands of blonde hair from her forehead and grinned at Rohane. "She's within."

Rohane nodded. She shouldered past a scowling Dagmar into a tent larger than the others.

From a stool behind a table, Persia peered up. Lamplight glowed on loosened hair the colour of honey. Her expression held neither pleasure nor displeasure. "Well?"

Rohane disliked the blunt demand. The battale captain used words like weapons; they either nicked like thin knife cuts or cleaved like a swinging sword.

"'Well' what, Captain?"

Persia's mouth tightened. "I am weary. You are weary. Neither of us shall sleep tonight. So let's not draw out this conversation. Tell me about *him*."

Rohane lifted and dropped her sore shoulders. "He submitted willingly enough, but there's defiance in his eyes."

"Is he contained? Must I take extra precautions? I saw ropes about his hands but no shackles. Why? I trust you left him in irons. I have no taste for a hunt tonight."

"My girl is watching him. I left him sleeping. Untethered."

"What!" Persia shot to her feet and rounded the table to confront Rohane. "Do you fail to understand the council is in a lather about this man?"

Rohane did not recoil. She was at least as tall as Persia and just as irritable. She would not be intimidated. "He gave me his word—"

"Word?" Persia cut her off. "Of a Telorian? I want him restrained, *Captain,* and not just with rope. With chain. And guarded every moment."

"I know what I'm about."

"Do you?" Persia's enraged breaths heated Rohane's cheeks.

Rohane resisted a longing to shove the other woman away. "I'm good at what I do, Persia. The council wants this man. They shall have him."

Persia's stare dwelled upon Rohane for a long moment. Then she sighed. "By the goddess, Rohane," she murmured. "He's not as I expected. I was told a bladesman. I imagined the usual broad-shouldered brute. He certainly has a warrior's form. But what bladesman looks like that?"

"You mean his physical beauty?"

Persia tongued cracked lips. "It's said these Caelan princes are striking, but—" She broke off with a self-mocking laugh. "Listen to me. I'll quote poetry next, and you'll think I've lost my wits. It's just for a moment when I looked upon Val Arques, it took me back to my childhood when I first glimpsed the seer king."

"Roaran?"

Persia nodded. "I cannot forget him. Power rolled off Roaran like waves over a reef. And those eyes. The strangest blue, an impossible colour, as though dark-blue fires shimmered deep within."

Poetic, indeed. "The old ones speak of a ghosting. It comes upon those who live too close to the otherworld."

"How can he be dead? It seems impossible."

"It is certainly a waste of Caelan blood."

"Tragic." Persia shook herself. "But enough romantic nonsense. This man we are bid deliver to the council has no magic, by all accounts."

"So it is said."

"But from the size of him, he'll possess formidable strength. Skill with the blade, too, if the stories are to be believed. I want him chained, Rohane, wrists and ankles both. I don't care if he can't walk… put him in one of the carts with the wounded."

"You must trust me to do my job," Rohane said.

"No, I insist you take no risks, Captain."

Rohane huffed out a breath, impatient that Persia required tedious explanations. "No action of mine is careless. I deliberately chose ropes and forced him to walk beside my horse. Tomorrow, he will also walk. There is a reason for it."

"How so?"

"He passed out, exhausted, just now. Tomorrow night will be the same. He must worry about putting one step after the other, never slipping. It allows no time for thoughts to ferment, for him to lose his nerve, to wish he had not agreed to Roaran's request, to plot his escape."

"But unbound?"

"He must come to see me as someone he can bargain with. I sought his word tonight, and if he does not break it, he is rewarded. If he disappoints me, he is punished. Reward and punishment. You understand this. It is the Quisnaf way, after all."

"So it is. Go on."

"Later, I will ask other things of him, things he will not like, things he will buck against. But he is more likely to submit if he trusts me, trusts I do not ask without reason."

Persia's stare held on Rohane's face. "You're already training him, preparing him for his life in Quisnaf. Why, Captain." The thinnest of smiles flitted across her face. "You're far more devious than I thought."

"From you, that's a compliment," Rohane said.

GENYA

"He wasn't there," Genya muttered. "Not where I left him." Shoulders tight, she followed Alecc through the underground passages beneath the hall. He carried keys on an iron ring, his steps brisk.

"Someone found him then. They'll have brought Dannon to the castle."

"No one has seen him."

Water rushed behind the walls. Damp, cold air brushed Genya's neck. The tunnel smelt of moist earth, though the faintest odour of roasting meat also wafted down the stairs from the kitchens. Life at Vraymorg went on. Cooking, eating, and sleeping. It was only she who was paralysed. Numb. Val had abandoned her. Now Dannon was missing, gone from the hunting lodge where she had left him. No evidence that he had been there remained, not even a bloodied cloth. One of Felix's men must have found him. He had to be in the prisons. He *had* to be.

Alecc stooped to unlock a cell door. Cries of alarm broke out within. When the door swung open, men and women huddling near the far wall shrank back. Genya peered at them hard, desperate to find Dannon. But he was not among the captives.

"You're free," Alecc said simply.

A silence held, as if the prisoners struggled to take in his words. "Go," Alecc said.

For a moment, they still looked afraid and bewildered. Then slowly, some staggered up, whispering to their companions or helping others rise.

Genya caught Alecc's arm. "You don't know that all of them were wrongfully imprisoned. Some might be in here for good reason."

"The guards say Felix imprisoned those who opposed his alliance with Archanin," Alecc said calmly. "Anyone Felix locked up, I'd be inclined to let loose. Out of sheer bloody-mindedness if nothing else."

Genya shifted her weight uncomfortably. Felix's loyalties had briefly been hers. She had believed Archanin's lies, believed that only the ghoul god loved her.

Sorrow once more turned over in her gut. She had brought about all that she'd feared. Val despised her. Her companions watched her with suspicious glances. Except for Alecc. There was a pragmatism to him she hadn't expected. How much had it hurt him, though, that his father had chosen to save someone else over his own son?

"Take the stairs to the hall," Alecc told the prisoners. "The steward will see to your needs. If you're hurt or ill, a healer will tend to you."

The captives shuffled towards the door. Alecc stepped aside to let them pass. At the odour of unwashed bodies, Genya wrinkled her nose. "Was there a man with you?" she begged of those closest. "His name is Dannon. He would have been badly hurt."

Some shook their heads. A few looked at her with sympathy. Genya swallowed, her throat dry. Dannon had been wounded, unconscious. He hadn't wandered or even crawled off. Someone had taken him away. But if he wasn't here, where was he?

"How is this possible?" A man paused beside Alecc. "Has the Lord Felix had a change of heart?"

"Felix no longer rules in Vraymorg," Alecc said stiffly.

Some prisoners gasped in surprise. Others exchanged startled looks.

"Then who…" a woman started.

"This castle is under my protection," Alecc said.

From another, the words might have sounded pompous. But in those few hours since a Quisnaf army had destroyed Archanin's army, in those few hours since a death rider had taken the body of Roaran Caelan into the mist, a change had come over Alecc.

She watched him offering words of reassurance, clasping the hands of those who gripped his arm, his head high. The boy who had hurled mud at her in the forest was gone. In his place was the son of a queen, the son of a great lord of Telor.

"Where is Felix?" another prisoner asked. "Is he dead?"

"He is on the run," Alecc said. "But he will answer for his crimes."

More murmurs and whispers broke out. An old man, his shirt stained with blood, grasped Alecc's hand. "Bless you."

Alecc nodded grimly. "Can you find your way to the hall?"

With a nod, the old man staggered up the stairs.

Alecc lowered his voice to Genya. "I hoped Dannon had been recaptured and imprisoned here. Could he have woken and wandered off, confused?"

Genya curled a fist. "He was too ill to move."

A man with dirty greying hair limped closer. "You're his son," he said, his voice breathless with awe. "Val's son."

Alecc considered the man kindly. "I am Alecc Caelan. I am indeed the son of the former lord of this castle."

Those who were closest turned their heads. Genya nodded. It was useful if word got about the castle so others could testify who Alecc was.

"I remember the day Queen Rozenn came to this castle." The old man's eyes misted with memory. "I remember her walking the corridors, her feet bare. It was a dismal, cold night, like so many are in the Mountains. She carried a candle…" His voice fell away. A flush rose into his jaw. "Forgive me. I have spoken out of turn."

"Who are you?" Alecc asked.

"My lord, I am Ewen. I faithfully served your father for many years."

"Felix told my father you were dead."

"Felix." The servant spat at the ground. "The deceiver. He opened the gates to Archanin. When some of us protested, he threw us in the cells." Ewen shivered.

Guilt lumped in Genya's gut. When she and Kaell had entered the castle through these tunnels, she had told him she would free those in the cells. She hadn't. Instead, she had freed Dannon then followed Kaell to Archanin's chambers and helped the ghoul god capture him.

"Is he here?" the old man asked. "Val?"

Alecc bit his bottom lip. Reluctantly, he said, "He was here. But he is gone again."

"Gone," Ewen muttered.

Alecc touched Ewen's back lightly. "Let me help you to the hall. When you've eaten and rested, we'll talk." He glanced at Genya. "I've sent messengers to the nobles of the Mountains. They're coming. They'll meet here."

Genya's back stiffened. The Mountains lords would hear what had happened at Vraymorg. They would hear not only of Felix's treachery but of hers as well. It hardly mattered that Archanin was dead. The stain of her betrayal lingered.

Gendrick, too, had sided with Archanin. Redemption lay in taking him down, in putting Alecc on the throne and deposing Gendrick Caelan.

"I shouldn't be there," she said slowly. "I must search for Dannon."

Alecc put his hands on her shoulders. "I want you there."

Genya laughed bitterly. "You're the only one."

"I have to persuade men I've never met, hard lords and ladies of a hard land, to follow me into battle against Gendrick. You're Roaran Caelan's daughter. If you're with me, then who can be against me?" He paused, looking her in the eye. "I need you."

Genya stood undecided, an uncomfortable pricking at the back of her eyelids. "I'll be at your side."

VAL ARQUES

A palm clamped his mouth. Val jolted awake, confused. He flailed beneath the restrictive hand, searching the gloom to see who restrained him.

"Shhh. It's only me." A figure removed their hand.

Val blinked, still struggling to identify who crouched by the bed. The moons waned outside, the predawn light ashen. "Who?"

"It's Kaell. You're not bound? Good. We must move quickly. Stay silent."

"Kaell, you can't be here." Val rubbed his eyes. Sleep still bewitched him with strangeness, a dulled sense that this wasn't real.

"I'm here to save you."

Alarmed, Val grasped Kaell's arm. If the Quisnaf found him here… "Get away from this camp. At once."

"Not without you." Kaell laughed softly. "Not after all my trouble to sneak in."

"You don't understand. I promised to go with them."

"I heard what you told me. But you can't mean it. Val, they're Quisnaf. I know what they'll do to you. It's a fate you wouldn't wish on your enemies. You must leave with me—"

He broke off at a sound. Backlit by the waning moon, a shape loomed in the tent entrance. Kaell shot up, groping for his blade.

A figure lunged at him. A sword hilt cracked on bone. Kaell grunted then collapsed in a huddle.

Val surged to his feet. A lamp flickered to life. Three women filled the tent.

"On your knees." The Quisnaf captain poked steel at him.

Val hesitated.

The two women with her moved in quickly, pushing him down. The captain nudged Kaell with a boot. He didn't stir. At her gesture, her companions dropped Val and dragged Kaell, insensible and unmoving, from the tent, his heels rutting grass.

"What's happening?" Val demanded. "Where are they taking... her?"

In the lamplight, the captain's dark gaze hung on his face. She tapped her sword on the ground. "You disappoint me. You gave me your word."

"What? No, whatever you think, it's wrong. They—she followed me, believing I was in trouble. Please don't hurt her. She only wanted to help me."

"She came to free you." Her tone was as unrelenting and cold as iron.

"I refused to go with her," Val shouted, mutinous. "I gave my word to Roaran. Then to you. Listen to me. This isn't what you think. She didn't understand. Just let her go."

The tent flap shifted. Mel looked in. "Rohane? You need help?"

Rohane. Val distantly stored the name. Captain Grumpy was more apt.

Rohane's gaze still remained on Val. Then her hunched shoulders relaxed. "No."

Mel nodded and disappeared.

"Kate," Val said, remembering the name Kaell used with strangers. "What will you do with her?"

"That's to be seen." Rohane brushed the flap aside and peered at the camp. "It's nearly morning. Best get ready."

Dawn's rose rimmed the horizon beyond the mass of trees. The air was already warm, the grass wet with dew. The camp bustled with movement and noise. Women dismantled tents, loaded pack horses and wagons, and stamped out fires. Armed warriors shook chained captives awake.

Val's belly growled, but no one offered him food. Instead, Rohane waved coiled rope at him. He huffed a breath. "I gave my word. Isn't that worth something?"

"It is worth everything... and costs everything if you break it. Remember that, Telorian."

Val folded his arms. "Well, then."

"I am required to take precautions with valuable property."

"Property?"

"Wrists together."

"No."

She sighed and gestured at armed riders clustering outside the enclosure. "You're outnumbered, Telorian. You cannot win a battle of resistance, not today."

Val wanted to yell in frustration, to rant against his defencelessness. But it would gain him nothing. Banishing his pride, he ungraciously shoved his hands at her.

Once she had bound him and tied the other end of the rope to her saddle, Rohane urged her horse forward into the stream of carts, covered wagons, and riders. Other mounted warriors fell in about a straggling line of hollow-eyed men restrained by chains.

Val searched in vain for Kaell. "My friend—"

"Safe," Rohane said. "Now walk."

Near noon, when the long column of riders, drays, and prisoners halted, Rohane slid off her horse. She passed Val a waterskin. He gulped water quickly then wiped his mouth on a sleeve. "Kate. I don't see her. Just tell me she's alive."

Rohane's dark gaze flickered over him. "She's in a cart. I hit her harder than I intended. I'm sorry for it."

He studied her face, seeing only sincerity.

"But why bring her? Do you mean she's a captive like them?" Val nodded towards the shackled men. Barely contained anger thickened his tone. "No, you can't do that."

Her mouth hardened. "She stole into our camp, knocked out a sentry, and tried to free you. What do you expect us to do? Give her a kiss and a bunch of flowers? Scold her like a naughty child? She shall be taken to Quisnaf to answer for her rashness."

Val growled. "I agreed to go with you. Kate did not. You have no right to just swoop a woman up because she tried to help me. By The Three, only a day ago, she fought with you. *With you.*"

Rohane gripped her reins with a calloused hand. "I will not argue our ways with an outsider." She put a foot into the stirrup, then paused, turning back. "Fought with us? Quickly. Tell me more of this Kate."

"Why?"

"It may save her life."

He stared in disbelief. "You're not serious. You mean to kill her?"

"The Quisnaf harshly judge any interference with prisoners. But if I can convince my commander this captive has worth, they may let the blood keepers assess her."

Blood keepers. The words sparked a distant memory. "She is a bladeswoman," Val offered eagerly. "One of Roaran's brotherhood, chosen." He cast another desperate look behind. Which cart? Could he find Kaell and free him? Perhaps tonight, when Rohane untied him.

"Roaran's chosen," Rohane's gaze sharpened on Val. "She is a good bladeswoman?"

"The best."

Rohane dropped the reins. "Do not move. I'll speak with Persia."

She strode towards a group of Quisnaf warriors about a tall, singular woman with blonde hair caught up in a ponytail. The woman wore a steel skullcap with guards covering her cheeks and nose. There was something stark, blunt, and frightening about the contrast between that armour and her bobbed hair that he could not quite grasp.

Rohane touched a hand to her brow. Val couldn't hear what was said, but the other warriors slid glances his way. The steel-clad woman drew one of her companions aside, exchanged quick words, and sent her off.

Rohane turned and walked back to Val. At his expectant look, she grinned. For a moment, she seemed less stern, younger too.

He wondered at her age. In Telor, an exceptional captain might be twenty-three or twenty-four, but most were older, not only experienced in battle but of an age to know themselves, so they could lead and understand others. Roaran had been named a Serravan captain at just nineteen, the youngest for a generation.

Unexpected sorrow flooded him. He didn't want to think about Roaran—because then he'd think about Genya. And he wasn't ready to do that. Not yet.

"Your friend will be all right." Rohane threw up a hand to silence his questions. "No. Get ready to move. I'll lengthen the rope so you can use the bushes before we start off. But don't wander too far."

"Who was that woman?"

"The battale captain, Persia." Rohane paused as though considering how much to say. "She was once my captain, and I know her for a fierce and loyal warrior of Quisnaf." She barked a laugh. "She would broker no nonsense or talk from you. Be mindful."

⁕

As dusk gathered, the riders descended a steep track onto flat grassland. The wind fell silent in gloaming light. An early moon crept between distant peaks at their backs.

When Persia called a halt, Val sank to the ground and rested his head on his raised knees. His body was fit and strong, but he was accustomed to long days in the saddle, not long days trudging at the end of a rope.

Hungry, tired, and already fed-up, he groaned. His shoulder muscles were cramped; his blistered feet ached. He longed to wash. Other Telorians thought Isles folk soft because they bathed daily. But a bath soothed troubles and renewed a sagging will like nothing else.

Warriors in padded jerkins or light leather armour dismounted around him. Servants in loose tunics over pants took their horses. Others began erecting tents and starting cook fires. Guards with spears secured captives.

Rohane reached down to draw him to his feet. She untied the rope and led him to her tent. Inside, Mel flapped out blankets and garments. She curled a lip at Val then bowed her head to the captain. "After the shenanigans at dawn, Persia wants him in irons. Marlisa brought the message to say you're to secure him at once."

"Oh, that's where you've been?" Rohane cocked an eyebrow. "Gossiping with Marlisa? Bring food."

Mel sniffed, nodded curtly, and disappeared.

At Rohane's gesture, Val sank onto the pallet, too weary to argue. "I worked out why I must walk." He tossed her a half-hearted grin. "So I collapse exhausted and give you no trouble."

"Clever boy," she mocked, but without malice. "There's a little more to it, of course. There's always more to it in Quisnaf. Ours is an ordered society. It is all about rules, about discipline, about structure. There is a way things are done, a way they are always done."

"About Kate—" he tried again.

Rohane grimaced. "Enough. I mean it." She stripped off her weapons belt and stretched her neck. She was tall for a woman, though perhaps not for a Quisnaf warrior—heavily muscled in the shoulders but with a shapely waist and bosom. Given she carried both a bow and sword, he wondered which weapon she favoured.

"Let me offer you a word of advice," she said. "Lower your eyes if you see a Quisnaf warrior. Most will whip you if you brazenly inspect them the way you just did me."

"But not you?"

"I'm accustomed to men unfamiliar with our ways." She crouched to free his hands. "No trouble. No wandering to find this Kate. I choose to trust you." She gave him a look. *Break my trust once, and that's it,* that look said. *No second chance.*

The girl returned with a bowl, bread, and a wineskin.

"For him, Mel." Rohane tossed her head in Val's direction.

Mel shoved the bowl and damper at Val. He took it. The bowl held pottage with some sort of meat in it, maybe goat, he guessed from the smell. With no fork or spoon, he used the thick slab of unbuttered damper to soak up the liquid.

"I'll eat later," Rohane said. "Is that wine?" She grabbed the skin from Mel and gulped.

"You must sleep. You didn't sleep last night," Mel said.

Rohane touched the girl's arm. "You take good care of me, Mel."

"Someone has to," Mel grumbled. Then she shot Val another glare and flounced out.

Rohane yawned. "There's a bucket. Then sleep. We leave at first light."

"I'm to take the pallet again? What about you?"

"I prefer to rest curled in my cloak." True to her word, she lay on the grass near the tent opening, wrapped her cloak about her chest, and shut her eyes.

Val stretched out, his hands cushioning his head. He had to stay awake until the camp quietened, then he would find Kate. But almost at once, worn out by the long trek, he plunged into a dreamless sleep until Rohane shook him awake at dawn.

By midmorning, the leaden sky closed over with clouds. Drizzling rain fell. It trickled down Val's neck, soaking his tunic. His toes squelched in wet boots. It was a miserable day to stumble along behind a horse, wet rope chaffing his wrists.

The journey, though slowed by the cold rain and treacherous muddy ground, was not long. At midday, they cleared a ridge, and the sea stretched like grey velvet below. Islands blinked through shifting clouds, their stark rock freckled against the horizon.

The riders halted, huddling in cloaks, as Persia studied a map. At her command, the Quisnaf host followed a cliff path, at last descending towards a sheltered cove. A fleet of ships—long, sleek black-hulled vessels with Venivan square rigging—sat at anchor. Two were moored to a jetty near a smattering of huts.

"Persia wants him in irons." Mel urged her horse closer to Rohane's. "She sent me to tell you again. She's edgy after the incident in the tent the other morning."

"I'll do what I've always done," Rohane said.

The track down was steep and uneven. Val slipped often. Once, he skidded to his knees.

The captain looked back. "Careful." She lengthened the rope.

"I'm all right." Val regained his footing, cursing his clumsiness. Call it pride, foolish maybe, but he would not let the Quisnaf see him bend his neck or even stumble.

They reached a cobbled road winding through a village of wooden huts and pens for goats and chickens sprawled about the bay. Among the black-hulled Venivan ships, fishing boats bobbed on flat water beneath the iron sky. Circling gulls cawed. Scents of sea and brine swirled.

Persia and a second warrior dismounted. Leaving their horses with grooms, they trod onto a harbour boardwalk towards the village. Curious townsfolk emerged from houses.

Three men approached the Quisnaf women, bowing. Words flowed, pleasant words from the broad grins. Persia passed the men a bag that might have held gold or coins. The men nodded, smiling and gesturing towards the ships.

Rohane slipped off her horse. Her boots and pants were splashed with mud. She showed little interest in what unfolded, her gaze drifting across the rolling grey waves.

"Where are we?"

"Never you mind." She snapped the words like a mantra then seemed to reconsider. "An Isles fishing village. It is quiet, remote, and the villagers watch our ships just so long as we do not intend to act against their lords and king. Your lord suggested this place."

"My lord?"

She peered at him in surprise. "Roaran Caelan. Who do you think I meant?"

He wasn't my lord, he might have answered. *It wasn't until the end that I even trusted him.* But Val said nothing. They were hardly friends sharing confidences.

Rohane's stare still fell into the distance. "Strange how different the light is in Telor. Softer. The sun burns bright in Quisnaf, harsh like the desert that surrounds us. I am not sure which I prefer."

"The light is more intense in the Isles than the rest of Telor."

She stirred from her reverie. "Where is Mel?" She looked around just as the battale captain Persia stomped up, scowling.

"Why have you disobeyed my orders, Rohane? Have you no sense? Get chains on him. Now."

Val started to protest, dread churning in his belly. "There's no need."

Persia looked through him. "I thought you knew what you were about, Rohane. In this at least. I'd heard good reports. But now you are wilfully ignoring my commands."

Rohane stubbornly tilted her chin. "The path down was treacherous in the wet. I could not risk damaging him."

Persia was already moving away. She called over her shoulder. "Just get him on board. *You know who* waits in the main cabin."

You know who? Val raised an eyebrow at Rohane. "That sounds ominous."

She did not answer, only frowned at the turmoil of bodies, carts, carriages, and horses. "Mel. Curse it, girl, where are you?" She lifted her voice. "Mel?"

The young woman arrived in a hurry. "My captain?"

"Bring his things, his sword. But first, see to my horse. You know what to do."

Rohane led Val onto the jetty towards one of the black-hulled ships. Water lapped boards. The air stank of raw fish, heat, and horseflesh. Excited gulls shrieked as they dived for food scraps.

At the sight of the ship's gangplank, fear rushed him. The vessel would take him far from his homeland, to a city where he had no rights, where he was powerless. Val pulled up. "I don't know. I don't think I can do this."

"Be easy. Nothing is as bleak as it seems."

Two armed women stopped. "You all right, Captain? Need a hand getting him on board?"

"No."

Val's pride again reared up. He would not be dragged or forced at sword point. He would walk. At Rohane's gesture, he strode up the plank and clambered on board. Silently, he seethed at his lack of control, at how he must accept her commands. And always the thought nagged: this was his life now. He must learn to accept it.

The ship rocked gently. Masts creaked; furled sails rippled against their ropes. The wind was soft as though drizzling rain strangled its voice. Val shook droplets from his brow.

"This way." Rohane led him down steps into a cramped passage below deck. Light flickered somewhere ahead. In the enclosed space, the odours of stale sweat from his body and damp cloth assaulted his nostrils.

Rohane bid him stop before a door. She rapped its wood. A woman called in the Quisnaf tongue, "Who is it?"

"Rohane."

"Well, come in, child. Do you have him?" Steps closed on the door, then it creaked open. A woman inspected Val with eyes as grey as her wavy hair. It was cut to the shoulders and shaped a face that might have once been handsome rather than pretty.

The cabin at the woman's back was large and wood-panelled, luxuriously furnished with a built-in bed, a table, stools, a divan, and cushions. A rug covered the wooden floor, and a large window was shuttered against the sea breeze and drizzling rain.

"Let me look at him." The woman's voice was brisk.

Rohane's breath warmed his ear. "Stand still, Telorian. Say nothing. Do nothing."

Another order. To check his resentment, he drew in a slow breath. *Pick your fights, but don't pick all of them.* Over and over, he had told Kaell this.

Oh, gods, Kaell. Misery swooped in his belly. Would Kaell be all right? Val had to free him then convince him to stay away. And what of Genya? He did not want to hold on to his anger at her, but nor was he ready to let it go.

The older woman circled him. He caught a faint hint of her perfume—citrus and sandalwood.

"My, my," she pronounced. "What a striking man. Physically excellent. He is taller than even you, Rohane." Her laugh was low and throaty. "Though he bristles with defiance."

"Councillor, a warning. He speaks our tongue."

"I assumed as much."

Slowly, in response to her probing inspection, Val lifted his gaze to the stranger.

"Now that is a brazen look." The woman laughed. "He is true to his reputation."

"I am sorry, Councillor," Rohane said. "Before we reach Quisnaf, I will instruct him on obedience. If this rebellion continues, I will break him on the flogging post."

"I sometimes forget how young you are, Rohane." The older woman smiled indulgently. "You must learn patience. He is a lord of his land, born a prince of the Isles. To break such a man on the flogging post on this ship—or worse, to break him in Quisnaf—would be a pity."

"I'm right here," Val growled.

Rohane backhanded him across the face so hard, his head spun back. At a spurt of anger, he almost stormed to his feet. "You'll regret that," he growled.

"Promises, promises." Her hand nudged her hilt.

"Rohane." The older woman's single word held disappointment, an admonishment.

The captain's cheeks flamed.

"I apologise for our rudeness, Val Arques," the councillor said, gesturing that they should move farther into the room. "It is not that we are ignoring you. It is more that we are unaccustomed to men from other lands speaking our tongue. Rohane, your knife." She held out her hand. Rohane surrendered her blade. The councillor freed Val's wrists. "You may stand, Val Arques Caelan." As he rose, she passed another appraising look over him. "You're wet. Rohane, find him cloth and dry clothes."

With a sniff of disgust, Rohane crossed to a chest, flung back the lid, and rustled about. She drew out a tunic and pants and shoved them at Val.

"Go and change." The councillor nodded towards the back of the room. "We won't look. I promise."

At the glint of mischief in her eyes, Val threw her a doubtful glance. He took his new garments and disrobed as far from them as possible. Once dressed, he walked back and tauntingly thrust his wet garments at Rohane.

Rohane dropped his clothes on the floor. "What am I? Your slave?"

The older woman flicked a hand. "My servant will see to them." She poured wine and pressed a cup into Val's hands. "It's Cahirean. Delicious. It smells of berries with a hint of pepper."

"Who are you?" Val blurted.

Rohane's brows drew down hard. "You do not question her. You show respect. I don't care if you're king of Telor or the Emperor of Everything. This is Samantha, Daughter of Maud, Councillor of Quisnaf. You will address her properly as 'councillor.'"

Val returned Rohane's glare. Once or twice on their journey, he'd glimpsed hints of humour in her manner. Now a rigid mask of duty had come down.

"Come and talk with me, Val Arques." Samantha sat upon the divan below the window and patted the cushion beside her. "Don't mind Rohane. She only pretends to be severe."

"Councillor!" Rohane's tone held shock. "Once you've questioned him, Persia wants him restrained. Below."

Grinning at Rohane with malicious pleasure, Val sat.

Samantha poured herself a cup of wine. "You are a good retriever, Rohane, but we treat guests differently to captives."

"I know this," Rohane muttered.

"Your part is done for tonight," Samantha said. "He is under my protection for now."

Rohane studied her boots as though to hide displeasure. "The council bid me keep a very close watch on him until we reach Quisnaf. Persia wants him locked below."

"He'll sleep here. You will, too, so you can watch him."

Val slid a look at the bed. Embarrassed, he coughed.

"Oh, I wish I were young enough to invite you into my bed." Samantha offered him a wicked grin. "You may sleep upon the divan. Rohane will take the floor. She prefers it. Though I think she pretends so to anger me. She is perverse in her way."

Val wondered at their relationship. The familiar yet caustic undercurrent hinted at more than councillor and captain.

Rohane slid her hands to her hips. "I take the floor because I am required to sleep near the man I guard."

"Yes, yes. It is always about duty with you. I excuse you from your duty." Samantha waved a hand again. "Go. Enjoy yourself. I am not so old that I do not remember the celebrations after a battle. Though, find Persia for me, will you? Tell her I will speak with her once we sail."

"The battale captain is busy." Rohane's tone was sharp.

"Indeed, she is always busy. Just as you are always difficult."

Her face stormy, Rohane bowed then retreated briskly, her sword slapping her back. Val could not help but admire the crafted hilt. If he wasn't mistaken, the design suggested the blade might be Seithin steel. *Well, well.*

Once the door thumped shut, Samantha turned to Val with a disarming smile. "Good. Now we will talk. I want to hear all about you, Val Arques Caelan."

⁓ ∞⟡∞ ⁓

They fell into talk, stilted and uncomfortable at first. He commended Samantha on her Telorian; she replied with a laugh that his Quisnaf was outdated. Old-fashioned. Gradually, though, they grew easier with each other, discussing the Mountains, the Varee, and even Val's time in the Icelands.

"Judith Damadar was a lovely girl." Samantha's eyes misted with memory. "Though she quickly learned how to make a man gasp with pleasure, she retained a sort of hopeful sweetness."

Val blushed, but Samantha did not see it. "Rohane called you a councillor. That sounds impressive."

"It's one of my titles," Samantha said. "Another is Protector of Men."

"Oh," Val said.

"That means your well-being, your... safety, concerns me deeply."

"Oh."

Samantha poured more wine for them both. "You look displeased."

He sifted his disquiet. Protector of Men might sound benevolent, but it was also patronising. It belittled. A warrior could protect himself. "Does that mean I have rights?"

She hesitated. "Very few."

"Oh," Val said.

For a long moment, all that sat between them was the lap and gurgle of waves against the ship and a distant creaking. Furled sails rippled in a breeze.

"It does mean if you have a complaint, I will listen. I will investigate if necessary, especially if you have at least two witnesses to any ill-treatment."

Val thought that through. "Huh. 'You'll need two witnesses' sounds like 'Don't bother to complain.'"

"It's not quite that unfair. There is a complex body of law in Quisnaf." Samantha sighed. "I intended to put you at ease, not stir alarm. Let us talk of other matters."

"My friend. Kate. She's with the other prisoners, but she doesn't belong there. She fought with Roaran's brotherhood."

"I'll ask Persia," Samantha said.

Another silence fell. Samantha stared out the window. Frowning, she clasped her hands in her lap. "I should like to ask you about Roaran Caelan," she said after a long moment. "Persia has told me certain things, but you were there." She paused to study his face. "If it is not too painful, will you tell me how he died?"

Val closed his eyes briefly. What had unfolded in the hall at Vraymorg was never far from his thoughts. "The ghoul god Archanin butchered Roaran on a wheel. It was horrific, brutal. Vicious."

He told her of how Genya had turned on Archanin, how she had sacrificed a dying Roaran so that Archanin could be killed with a Seithin temple knife. Samantha listened quietly, saying little.

When Samantha retreated to her work, Val stretched out upon the divan. Aided by the Cahirean wine, the sultry heat, and salty air, sleep came quickly. If he dreamt, his dreams vanished like mist as soon as he woke.

Val uncurled his cramped limbs. A girl entered the cabin to light a lantern swinging from a ceiling beam, then she departed. He lay still, content to drowsily stare into the gathering darkness, to listen to pattering rain, cocooned in that comfortable room. It was as though his dread and fear waited outside the door. But here, in this moment, nothing could touch him.

Soon, sounds intruded from the deck: raised voices, a chink of glass, and a smattering of laughter. Val sat up and yawned.

"You're awake?" Samantha looked up from the table, scrolls spilled about her. A guttering candle half shadowed her face.

"I slept like a rock. The wine, I think."

"Or the sea air? Are you a good sailor?"

"I am content on a ship."

She nodded. "The people of the Isles are, as they say, sons and daughters of the sea. Well, the ship's captain promises a smooth passage."

And then? He needed to know, to understand. "I have questions, Councillor."

"Yes, of course. Ask them. I am to instruct you."

Val cleared his throat. "What exactly happens once we land?"

"We'll put ashore to the south of Vene if the tides are right. Then it is a matter of a few hours' march to the City of Caves."

"And then?"

"Ah, you mean what happens to you?" Her expression softened. "You will be brought before the council. They will examine you."

The back of Val's neck prickled. "Examine?"

"They will question you, seek your oath to obey. Then a healer will make certain you are without flaw, physically. There is a way to these matters. A tradition, if you like."

Without flaw? What would the healer make of the knotted scars whitening his wrists? Though that was not so much a physical wound as a wound deep within his spirit.

Forgive yourself. Heath's voice drifted from the past. *If I could give you one gift, Val...*

"Let me assure you of this," Samantha said. "While you are our 'guest,' the Quisnaf will not treat you harshly. *Guest* is not just a polite word. It is your position in Quisnaf. I know I said you have few rights, but a guest has certain privileges, freedoms even. Unless..."

"Unless?"

"Unless you break our laws as they apply to guests."

"I see. And I shall learn of these laws..."

"Once in Quisnaf, the council will name a guardian to guide and protect you."

"I can protect myself," he muttered.

"Quisnaf is a dangerous place for a man." Samantha sat back. "You will not be restrained, but you cannot walk freely unless with your guardian, a captain, or a councillor."

"I cannot be alone?"

"Not outside your room. Protected, you may wander as you please."

"There's that word again." Val laughed coldly. "I am a bladesman, not a child."

Samantha considered him. "And it hurts your pride to think you may have to rely on another to keep you safe. You are entering a perilous world, Val Arques. Men are a currency of sorts in Quisnaf. That is a polite way of putting it. Without protection, you would be an object of pursuit. Do you understand?"

"I'm beginning to. I don't like the sound of it."

"The council, and I, as Protector of Men, will ensure nothing happens to you. However, never forget ours is an ordered society. Hierarchical. Everyone knows their place. Our courts deal harshly with anyone who breaks the laws or strays from that place. My advice is to learn your place—then accept it."

Glass shattered. A woman laughed, joined by others. A tumult of sounds now carried from deck: thumps, bangs, scuffling, hurrying steps, and raised voices.

"What's happening?"

"Oh, that?" Samantha shrugged and returned to her books. "A celebration. Because they've escaped death, warriors fight then feast and drink and squabble and paw men."

"Paw men?"

She did not look up. "The nonsense has started early. It is well you do not leave the cabin. Any man is fair game tonight."

Val frowned. *Fair game?* "Do you mean—" He could not quite say it.

"When they're drunker, they'll stagger down to the hold and drag a few captives up onto deck. The handsome ones. They'll invite these men to celebrate with them."

Shocked, Val stormed to his feet. "That defies decency."

Samantha arched a brow. "And what Telorian soldiers do when they take a town or castle is different?"

"I forbade such behaviour among my soldiers." Val clenched a fist. "My friend Kate is a prisoner. What happens to her amidst all the debauchery?"

"I said I would ask after her," Samantha soothed. "You will do nothing. You will not leave this room. Not tonight or any other night when drunken warriors prowl."

"I can't sit here while she's in danger—"

"So you'll storm onto deck and fight an entire Quisnaf battale?" Samantha frowned. "Though, such recklessness is in character from what I've read. Must I call the guards to restrain you?"

"No," Val muttered, sullen. To collapse his anger, he slowly unclenched his hand. Reluctantly he sat, thinking hard. Rohane had mentioned imprisoning him below. Kaell was likely there, if he was even on this ship.

He leaned back against cushions. Sounds of feasting carried from the deck. A woman broke into a drunken song. Ribald cheers rang out.

A servant brought stewed fish and more wine. Samantha invited him to join her at the table. The girl filled their glasses from a pewter jug then withdrew.

"When do we sail?"

"I am told the tide will cover the reefs just after midnight. Are you in a hurry to reach your new home?" Samantha looked amused.

"It's not that. It's just… I hate this uncertainty. I need to know what I must face."

Her eyes rested thoughtfully on him. "You are a man who confronts life as you might confront an enemy on the battlefield. Like a necessary evil?"

"If you like."

"But what of the journey, Val Arques? Not everything in life is a destination."

"Journeys make me restless."

The councillor sipped wine and considered him. "I sense you understand yourself. How few of us can say that? I hope we find time upon occasion in Quisnaf to talk. But you must be tired. And I must read this nonsense." She swept a hand at the papers. "Tonight."

Val recognised a dismissal, though presented softly. He retreated to the couch, to think and plot.

❧

Through low-lidded eyes, he watched Samantha fill then refill her wine glass as she read. A new candle burned low. At long last, her eyelids drooped. Her head sank onto her arms.

Quietly, Val rose, slipped a knife from the tray into his pocket, and tiptoed to the door. It opened into the unlit passage. He groped his way towards the stairs.

A man screamed. Hairs stood up along his arms. The pitiful sound, the cry of someone in pain, came from behind a second door. Val paused to listen. "More of the poppy," a woman snapped. "Quickly now. It's all I can do for him."

Who was in the room? A wounded man, but why keep him apart? With a shrug, Val moved on. He must find Kaell, not linger at doors, wondering about strangers.

The stairs led to the deck. He retraced his path to a wooden hatch at the far end. It scraped open onto another set of steps leading lower. Watchful for guards, Val crept down into a gloomy, long hold. The anchored ship rocked gently.

Light from a single lantern swaying from a beam fell upon hollow-eyed men chained by neck rings to wall brackets. Most sat in straw with their knees drawn up or their backs against the hull, their faces resigned. Some curled to sleep, their chains clinking softly when they moved.

"Here, this hatch is open," a woman said. Light glinted from above.

Val dropped into the murk beside the stairs. Two women clattered noisily down the steps. They carried steel, their gaits unsteady. A girl with a lamp tiptoed behind.

Metal clanked as prisoners recoiled. Some hissed. A man with light-brown hair shouted, "What did you do with Nicca? Where is he?"

One of the women stopped. "You're about to find out. He'll do."

The man tried to throw himself at her only for the iron collar to jerk him back. The woman thrust her sword to his throat. "Still. This won't hurt at all. Not a bit."

The girl stepped in with keys to unlock the band. Released, the man sprawled in the straw. The woman hauled him up, her sword prodding his side.

"Another?" Her companion walked the length of the hold, inspecting captives. The girl hurried behind with the lamp and keys. "Where's the handsome one from the cart?"

"Not him." Her companion laughed harshly. "He's claimed for later."

"By whom?"

"Guess."

"Persia?"

"No. And not Marlisa. Try again."

They laughed together. "She has a good eye, I'll give her that." The first woman walked back slowly. Then she stopped and jabbed a finger. "This one's pleasing." She poked steel at a crouching man.

The girl rushed to release the iron collar.

"He's barely a boy," someone drawled.

Val stiffened, recognising Kaell's voice. "Let him be."

The Quisnaf woman kicked at him. Val could not see Kaell, but he heard him grunt.

"You will speak only when asked," the woman said.

She leaned in to grab her initial target. Val glimpsed an unshaven, frightened face framed by wavy brown hair as the Quisnaf woman shoved a man forward, her sword digging into the small of his back. "Walk."

The women forced the two men up the stairs. The hatch thudded shut. Gradually, their footsteps and laughter faded. The ship lurched with a violent creak. Oars slapped waves. Val recognised the sounds of boats towing the vessel towards deeper water.

He slipped out and along the line of captives. Startled men peered up. Voices clamoured for his attention.

"Help me," one whispered in Telorian. "Help us."

Their whispers turned to shouts. Hands groped at his legs. Val shook them off. "Quiet. You'll bring the guards. I'll be back."

He found Kaell sprawled against the wall. Cloth bandaged his head and brow. His lip was bloody. He grinned at Val. "Took your time."

"You don't look so good," Val said.

Kaell touched the bandage. "My head aches. I was sick as a dog yesterday. Dizzy, retching. Remind me to thank whoever hit me sometime."

Val crouched to jiggle the knife tip in the collar lock, his fingers slipping in his desperation. He had to act quickly. The ship was headed out to sea.

Voices boiled about him, men pleading for help, others thumping their boots against the floor. The noise would soon draw a guard.

He twisted the blade this way and that. It was clumsy work, but eventually, he slipped the lock. Kaell ripped the band off and rubbed his throat. "What now? The ship has sailed."

"Only just. This way."

Val led him to the stairs. A man grabbed his ankle. "What's so special about her? Free us too." The others picked up the cry: "Free us."

Val tugged his leg clear. "Here. Save yourselves." He dropped the knife. The captive scrabbled for it as Val and Kaell slipped upstairs into the passage. The deck hatch flew back. Both men dropped into the shadows. A woman rushed towards the hold, sword drawn, shouting for quiet.

When she disappeared into the hold, he and Kaell climbed onto the deck.

Rain no longer fell, but thin mist wisped. Strands of moonlight frosted a gently tumbling sea. Hulking cliffs rose beside the ship as though it ploughed through a watery valley. A distant hum of waves over reefs was barely an undercurrent to riotous shouting and laughter.

In the bow, a knot of warriors drank and boasted of deeds in the battle against the ghouls and Varee. Some swayed drunkenly. A pack of women circled one of the men from the hold. A handful of sailors watched from a distance, unalarmed, as though accustomed to these excesses.

Kaell shook his head. "If you're a man, it's a good night to have warts and an ugly face."

Val and Kaell crept around the wheelhouse onto the port side. Unlike the main deck, it was deserted. Only the echoes of laughter pierced the salty air.

From the stern, the sea stretched before them, unbroken but for a few islands like black ridged spines on the horizon. The ship crossed the mouth of the bay, now under sail. Within the creeping mist, Val glimpsed other vessels.

"You'll have to swim."

Kaell grinned and tore off his boots. "It'll be like a quick dip in a warm bath. Are you coming? Boots off, or you'll sink."

"I can't."

Kaell arched a brow. "I assume you don't mean you can't swim?" He dragged his fingers through his dark fringe. "Regardless of what you did to him, this is a hellish way to pay. Roaran would know what they want of you. He wouldn't ask this of anyone."

Roaran would. He had given Val a choice, but he knew.

Kaell gripped Val's arm. "It's not too late. We can swim to shore, both of us. They won't come after you, not now they're under sail. You can be safe."

"I gave my word. I understood what it meant."

"I can't leave you. Not now when we've finally found each other again. When we've come to… understand each other."

"You have to let me go."

Kaell's grip tightened. He searched Val's face. "I should force you for your own good."

Val laughed mordantly. "This day was long coming. The Quisnaf searched for me for centuries. Twice, they nearly had me. I can't run anymore. I wouldn't if I could, because my word has to mean something."

"Your word to a dead man," Kaell said softly.

"Even so. I'll go with them willingly. They'll not treat me badly."

"You don't know that. I've heard terrible things. Come with me, my lord."

Val put his hands on Kaell's shoulders. "This isn't our time. Things have to happen before we can be together."

"Then when is our time? There's always something. Spells, the Damadars, Roaran. Something that keeps us apart."

"I don't have an answer for you. I only know that I have to do this." He paused. "Watch over Genya, will you?" Her name tasted bitter on his tongue. "Go, please. I can only do this if I know you're safe."

"I'll come for you," Kaell said. "I'll find you." He drew Val into an awkward hug then turned away abruptly. He climbed onto the rail and dived into the water with a splash. At once, he surfaced, lifted a hand, then struck out towards shore.

Val watched until the darkness swallowed Kaell. Loneliness rushed him. He was friendless, wholly alone, on a ship sailing for a strange land. He had told Samantha he wanted to confront his fate. But what if his courage failed?

"She's safe then?"

Val spun. His hand fell to his empty sword belt.

"Your lover. She's made it to shore?" Rohane sat with her back to a wall, her hands wrapped about her drawn-up knees. A bow and a spilled quiver of arrows rested beside her. An empty flagon rocked on the deck.

"How long have you been sitting there?"

"A while." She yawned. "It's peaceful listening to the waves. Listening to her bold attempts at persuasion, your noble words about promises."

"What? Not celebrating?" He mocked. "No taste for a bit of groping?"

"How moral and righteous you are. A victory is a victory, after all. And we took valuable captives who'll fetch gold in the Venivan markets because they're warriors, but better than that, they're Telorian warriors and just that bit exotic. That's cause enough for a little riotous behaviour."

"What I just saw disgusts me."

"I hope you're just as disgusted when your warriors take a town in battle and celebrate by raping the women and killing the men."

"I don't permit it. I've executed those who disobey me."

Her look sharpened on his face. "Well, well," she said softly. "You surprise me."

"Just as you surprise me. Drinking alone in the dark rather than enjoying the sick pleasures of the flesh. I suppose you'll tell me it's not to your taste."

Rohane laughed. "Don't get me wrong, Telorian. I'm as bad as any of them. I just don't like to share a man. I had one in mind. I was about to wander down to the hold and take him off somewhere quiet—if he proved willing. Note that last bit, Telorian."

"Well, don't let me stop you."

Her eyes gleamed with mischief. She swept up the bow, stood, and joined him at the rail. "More entertaining listening to you and your lover."

"She's not my lover."

"Oh? Are you sure? 'This isn't our time.' 'When we've just found each other again.' The sort of things lovers say to each other."

"Kate's like a daughter to me."

"Ah." Frowning, she stared over the water as if absorbing what this meant.

Val eyed the bow. "Why not shoot her to stop her escaping?"

"Why not, indeed? Duty requires I do that. Captives who attempt to escape are either killed or whipped—as an example to the rest."

"Not skilled enough to take the shot in the moonlight?"

Her lips twitched with savage amusement. "I could make that shot, Telorian. At best, I would kill her. At worst, wound her. Then she'd drown. Either way, that's my duty done."

"But you didn't."

"No." She gripped the rail. "I thought, 'Why waste a life simply because it is the law?'"

He gave her a second look. "You're a strange woman. For someone Quisnaf born."

She shrugged coolly. "Is that a compliment? The question is what this strange woman should do with you, Telorian. You're not meant to wander. Especially tonight. My sisters might scoop you up and have their wicked way with you."

Val bared his teeth. "Let them try."

"Ah, that's better."

"What?"

"You almost had me fooled, all this righteous outrage. I might begin to think you're a decent man. When in fact, all you are is a warrior at best and a murderer at worst."

He faced her, astonished. "Murderer?"

Rohane fingered the knife in her belt. She looked past him into the sea mist. A rising wind lifted Val's fringe as the ship ploughed through the swell beyond the sheltered bay.

"Matilda was my friend," Rohane said quietly. "A mentor of sorts."

For a moment, Val was lost. Then he remembered the two warriors sent to the Icelands to escort him to Quisnaf. "I see," he said sombrely.

"Matilda and Morgan never returned from the Icelands." She paused. Turning, she put her back to the ship's side. "Did you kill them?"

Memories tore at him. Snow, icy air, an enspelled bracelet's cold metal on his arm, the clank of blades as Morgan fought an intruder, someone who had come in the night.

Kaell.

Val pressed his hands into the rail. "I didn't hurt Matilda or Morgan."

"Do you know who did?"

His pulse kicked up in alarm. The last he had seen of the two Quisnaf women was in a cave, ropes about their hands. But Kaell had told him he'd left the women a knife so they could get free. He had to believe Kaell had told him the truth.

Rohane sighed. Her fingers fell away from her knife. "You'd best think of an answer to give the council by the time we reach Quisnaf."

"The last time I saw both Matilda and Morgan, they were alive."

"So you say." She took his elbow. "Best return you to the dragon."

Val shook off her grip. "I'm not a child. Nor will I be led about like a prisoner."

"But you are proud, I think." Rohane grinned. Then with deliberate insincerity, she said, "Come with me, please, Telorian. I wish only to protect you. It is dangerous for a man to roam this ship tonight."

He gave an equally insincere bow. "After you. But why is the councillor a dragon? I thought she was gracious. She's certainly kinder than you. Better company, too." With heavy steps, he followed Rohane back towards the wheelhouse.

"In my experience, the ones with honeyed tongues are the most dangerous—" Rohane drew up. Two women staggered around the corner. At the sight of Rohane and Val, they stopped.

"By Cyrah, he's pretty." One started to circle Val. "Let's take him back to the others."

"Let's not." Rohane shoved the woman. She stepped between Val and the newcomers, her fingers curled about her sword hilt, her teeth bared in a grimace. "Just back off."

Val huffed indignantly. "I don't need you to defend me."

"You're not armed, you proud fool."

The first woman sneered. "Who are you to tell us what to do?" She leaned forward to peer at Rohane. Her hand rose to her mouth. "My apologies, Captain. I didn't recognise you. Who is this with you?"

"This man is under my protection."

"Oh, protection, is it?" The second leered at Val.

"Step away," Rohane said. "This man is a guest."

"Let's take him off her," the second woman said. "She's not our captain."

"Shut up, fool. You're drunk," the first hissed. She dipped her head to Rohane and dragged her complaining companion away.

Val fisted his hands. "How dare you do that! I am well able to protect myself. And you, if it comes to trouble."

"Let go of that pride, Telorian," Rohane said. "I have no doubt you're formidable with steel in your hand. But unarmed, you're at risk. Come below, where it's safer."

Val considered her. She seemed calm, hardly troubled by the encounter.

"That warrior backed off quickly when she saw who you are. What was that? Respect?"

She nibbled her lip. Then reluctantly, she said, "They fear me."

"Why?"

"They think I'm cursed."

"Why would they think that?"

She turned slightly so her face fell into shadow. Her shoulders hunched. In the silence between them, sails rippled in the breeze. The ship plunged through black waters.

"Why would they think that?" Val asked again.

Rohane sighed deeply. In a voice stripped of all emotion, she said, "Because I am."

❦

Persia jabbed a finger at Val. "He helped a prisoner escape. If that's not bad enough, he left a knife in the hold, so four others managed to get free. We recaptured them, but I will have to whip the fools in the morning as a warning to the rest."

"If anyone is to blame, it's me." Samantha glanced at Val, her mouth tight with disappointment. "I fell asleep without locking the door. Did you retrieve the captive?"

"She's gone," Rohane said. "No sign of her."

"How could he just wander about the ship?" Persia whirled on Rohane. "I told you to restrain him. Where were you? Why was your valuable prisoner free to creep about, releasing captives? Do not deny it was him."

"It was me," Val said. "Kate is like a daughter to me. I freed her. I'd do it again."

Persia refused to look at him. "Instruct him he does not speak to me. I am addressing you, Huntress."

Samantha moved between them, her arms extended. "Persia, please. You made your point. It's my fault he went roaming."

"Oh, she made her point, all right." Rohane thrust her hands to her waist, her face hard. "She thinks I can't do my job."

"Well, can you?" The battale captain's cold blue eyes bulged. "You should have remained a warrior, Ronnie. You were good at that. Killing, I mean. One might even say that death follows you around."

A stillness fell, uncomfortable and charged with an undercurrent of meaning Val could not unravel. A slow blush fired Rohane's cheeks. The councillor studied the ground.

"That's unfair," Rohane muttered. "You know it's unfair. Cruel, even."

"Cruel?" Persia echoed. "I know who I am, Ronnie. I know what my duty is. Can you say the same?"

"I know my duty," Rohane said crossly.

Samantha whipped up a hand. "I took charge of Val Arques tonight, Persia. I commanded Rohane to join her sisters in celebration, to put aside duty for a few hours."

"She did not join her sisters. Such sordid matters of the flesh are beneath her. It is her father in her, no doubt."

Rohane glared. "You go too far."

"Rohane is right." Samantha made a cutting gesture. "You cannot blame Rohane for another's… mistakes. Shall we return to the problem, Captain?'

"As you say." Persia looked unrepentant. "I want the problem chained—in the hold, where he can't cause trouble."

"I will instruct him further on our laws, Captain," Samantha said. "He will give no more trouble."

"And again, I am right here," Val complained.

This time, the battale captain whirled. Her hand rose to strike him. Instinctively, he blocked the blow with his arm. Persia's fingers fell to her sheathed blade. Her blue eyes flared with anger. She half drew the sword, only to jam it back. Val knew a fleeting moment of respect for her control.

Lips pressed tight, Persia turned once more to Rohane. "You'd best teach him his place, Huntress, before we reach Quisnaf. Or I will. I'm set to flog four captives in the morning. Why not another?"

Both women glared at each other. Samantha interceded. "Persia, a moment of your time."

The battale captain shrugged impatiently. "To what point? I know all I need to know."

"Clearly you do not know enough." Samantha drew the other woman aside.

"How dare she!" Rohane muttered. "I am good at what I do. For two years now, I've brought back every man the council sent me to retrieve. I've not failed yet. She should remember that." She stopped and glanced at him sideways. A flush rose in her throat.

Val watched the conversation between Samantha and Persia unfold with gestures and sharp nods. "What do you think the councillor is saying?"

"She is likely explaining you are special," Rohane said.

Val threw her a guileless grin. "I am special."

"Especially tiresome. Especially disobedient. Especially a pain in my neck."

Samantha and the battale captain joined them.

Persia glared at Val. "You, Telorian."

"Are you addressing me? I'm honoured."

Persia ignored his nonsense. "The councillor assures me you won't leave this room unless accompanied by either Rohane or herself. She says you will behave."

Samantha looked at him with a wide-eyed expression of benevolence. Val sensed a keen intelligence at work. He would have to be careful around her. How easily she'd lulled him that afternoon. Her interest in him had seemed genuine. He'd liked her, enjoyed her company.

As Lord of the Mountains, as a young man in the Isles, he'd known other charming, perceptive, and disarming courtiers. Unlike some intent on manipulation, he sensed Samantha bore him no malice. But he must never forget she was Quisnaf, and not only that, a councillor, a powerful woman with the ability to carve his fate.

Protector of Men. A sickening title.

"And in return, I must have your promise, Val Arques." Samantha touched his arm gently. "You will remain in this cabin until I say otherwise. I trust your word means something?"

She had backed him into a corner. Val sighed heavily. "I will not leave this cabin unless accompanied."

"I will hold you to that, Councillor," Persia said. Val noted she did not accept his oath. Only the vow of a Quisnaf woman mattered. "If he so much as sneezes without permission, I'll whip him, and he'll spend the rest of the journey in irons."

"Charming," Val said.

GENYA

Raised voices echoed within the hall's stone walls. At the far end, Alecc and Nicky stood arguing, their bodies stiff, their gestures sharp.

Beneath Genya's feet, fresh rushes covered the floor. Servants had set up new trestle tables and replaced both the lamps swinging from rafters and the candles in crevices. Nothing was permitted to be the same. Alecc had ordered every stool, table, and cloth to be taken out and burned. The floors and walls had been scrubbed. Yet Genya had only to shut her eyes, and she could picture Roaran on that wheel, his wrecked body bloody and viciously torn, his dying breaths laboured.

Forcing away the image, she strode towards the two men, the sword clipped to her belt slapping her thigh. Pale sunlight bled through windows but did not warm the stone. Though summer lingered, she pulled her fur-lined cloak tight to shut out a cold draught.

"I thought to find his body in the crypt," Alecc was saying, his voice indignant. "Now I learn you handed him over, just like that?"

"I handed over a corpse. Roaran is dead." Nicky winced as if fighting a shudder. "No one can hurt him anymore."

"He belongs here. If a sorcerer or sorceress should get hold of his body, who knows what use they might make of it," Alecc said. "My mother told me horrendous stories about the magic of necromancers."

"Can they revive him?" Genya interrupted. "The death riders who took Roaran?" Should she have tried? Could she have revived Roaran as she had a boy so long ago? A single image flashed in her mind of the young man she had brutally killed then restored to life because of her death rider blood.

Both men turned to stare at her.

"I do not think so, Genya," Nicky said sadly. "Roaran was killed by four Seithin temple knives."

"Then why did they want his body?"

Nicky shook his head. "I don't know. It just seemed to me he belonged with them."

Alecc touched her shoulder. "Still no sign of Dannon?"

"None." Miserable, Genya dropped her head. "I can't find him."

She had searched and searched, raked the forest, looking for tracks. But Dannon was gone, and with his absence, her world had disintegrated. Val had left with the Quisnaf, a prisoner. Now her lover had disappeared. Yet did she deserve anything less?

"We'll find him, Genya," Alecc said. "Someone must have seen something."

"What if it's the Varee?" Genya shuddered. "They think he's a traitor. They'll kill him."

"They'd not stay quiet about capturing him," Alecc said. "That there's no body means there's hope."

The doors to the hall banged open. A whip of wind iced Genya's neck. A number of men and a few women strode in: the lords and ladies of the Mountains and their retainers, summoned by Alecc to Vraymorg.

Alecc went to greet them. Nicky joined Genya. "Something you should know," he muttered, his eyes on the newcomers.

"Please. No more bad news."

Nicky shrugged. "I can't say this is good or bad. Kaell's back.

Turned up a few hours ago. Barefoot, sneezing, weary."

"Where'd he been?"

"Went after Val. He's quite the story to tell. When you're ready." He turned to face her, his expression one of concern. "Gen, about Val—"

"Don't." She backed up a step, her palm raised. "I can't."

"Talk to Kaell. Maybe it will help."

Genya hid a sneer. She had no desire to seek consolation or comfort from Kaell. Kaell whom Val had hugged hard. Kaell who Val had spoken to kindly, fondly, when he had only bitterness for her.

The hall filled up. Men and a women took their places on benches before a raised dais, their retainers dismissed to the entrance chamber.

Alecc brought two strangers to Genya. "This is Lord Drystan. And Greyson, the Lord of Stonecliff." He gestured at each man in turn. "This is Genya Caelan. Roaran Caelan's daughter."

"You're real?" asked Lord Drystan, the younger of the two. His plump-cheeked face lit up in delight. "There have been rumours, but there are always rumours in the Mountains."

The other man glared. "How do we know you're Roaran's daughter?"

Alecc's lips compressed to a thin line. "Roaran acknowledged Genya," he said tersely. "Really, my lord, your question is out of line."

"Is it," the Lord of Stonecliff said flatly.

Genya met his glower. His face was hard and chiselled by the elements, at odds with a lush sweep of dark-brown hair tied back in a thong.

"My lords," Alecc lifted his voice. "If we could convene."

"What's this about, boy?" another man called. "What gives you the right to summon the Mountain lords?"

"You're Eirean, one of the border lords," Alecc replied. "My mother spoke of you. She called you one of the most courageous warriors she had seen, but if you should be a little less principled, she said, you would fight fewer duels."

Alecc's boldness surprised Genya. But Eirean slapped his thigh and laughed. "Your mother is a sharp woman."

"Eirean's point still stands," Greyson snapped.

Bad-tempered, sharp-faced man. Genya disliked him already.

"We are called together by children. Children." Greyson sneered first at Alecc then at Genya.

"Alecc is a warrior of the Sword Brotherhood." Genya let her voice carry. "The brotherhood called together by Roaran Caelan. My father."

A low rumble of voices picked up about the hall.

"That makes him a warrior, not Lord of the Mountains," Greyson said, still in that jeering tone.

"Let's hear the lad out," Eirean said.

Alecc nodded. He took the steps to the platform and threw himself into a chair. Nicky took his place behind him, his hand on his sword hilt. Genya followed. She stood at Alecc's shoulder, watchful. Greyson and the plump-cheeked Lord Drystan sat with the others.

"You're quick to take the former lord's place on that dais, but we've no proof you're Vraymorg's son," someone called. "The former Lord of Vraymorg, I mean."

"My lords, if I may speak?"

Heads turned. Ewen appeared in the doorway. With the aid of a stick, he hobbled between the benches to come to a stop before the gathered lords.

"I remember you," Greyson said slowly. "You served both Felix Hillborn and the former Lord of Vraymorg, this man they're now calling Val Arques Caelan."

Ewen inclined his head. "My lord. And now I serve Val's son."

"This boy?" Eirean frowned. "Are you certain?"

"I am certain. I do not wish to be indelicate, but I remember when the Queen of Cahir came to this very castle and where she spent the night. My lord, Val Arques, who you knew as the Lord of Vraymorg, told me the queen had named Alecc as his son."

"But what of Gendrick Caelan?"

"He is not my father." Alecc thrust out his chin. "My mother admitted the truth to the king. Gendrick threw me in a cell in the hope I would grow sick and die."

Shocked voices rippled.

Eirean was on his feet. "Is there nothing written? Proof in Vraymorg's hand?"

"My lord," Ewen said quietly. "Do you know me as a truthful man?"

Eirean frowned. "Yes."

"Then please accept I am telling you what Vraymorg confided. That Alecc is his son."

"Where is the former lord of Vraymorg?" another lord asked. "Why can't he speak for himself?"

Alecc gripped the chair arms. "He is on a journey. It is because of a vow he swore to Roaran."

Again, mutters ran through the hall.

"This is nonsense." Greyson flicked his hand. "We're to accept this boy as Lord of the Mountains on a servant's word?"

"A loyal servant," Eirean cautioned.

Genya could stay quiet no longer. "You have Alecc's word, too. And I am sure the Queen of Cahir would confirm that Vraymorg is Alecc's father."

Greyson turned a cold look upon her. "The Queen of Cahir has long sought to extend her power into the Mountains. This is just her latest scheme to broaden her influence."

"Do you doubt my word?" Alecc asked quietly.

"Why should I trust the word of some Cahirean bastard? All Cahireans are liars and have no honour."

"You go too far," Genya snarled, starting forward.

Nicky grabbed her shoulder to pull her back. "Whatever you're intending, don't."

She pulled free. "There's only one language a man like this understands."

"Genya—"

She trod down the stairs.

Greyson was on his feet, his fingers hovering near his sword hilt. "What is this?"

"You insulted my king," Genya said. How she longed for a fight. No, how she longed to fight *him*, to wipe his sour expression off his face. The tension of the past few days, her fears for Dannon, her anger at Val, all coiled within her, demanding release.

"King?" His sneer returned.

"Yes, my king. You will take back your insults."

"And you're what? His protector?"

Genya ripped out her sword, its screech against leather satisfying. Hot blood pumped through her body. With cries of consternation, the other lords scraped back the benches and cleared out of her way.

Unhurriedly, Greyson freed his blade. "You're going to be sorry you opened your insolent mouth, girl. Even sorrier you drew that sword."

"Genya—" Nicky cautioned irritably. "This is not how the daughter of a king behaves."

"It's how *this* daughter of a king behaves." She circled, watching Greyson. On the edge of her vision, she glimpsed Alecc leaning forward, his fingers still curled about the chair arms. His gaze held satisfaction and something else she could not decipher.

"Let's see how the daughter of a king bleeds," Greyson taunted.

He struck at her lazily. Genya parried, her riposte low. Still smirking, Greyson swept it aside. When she was younger, his derision would have stirred up her anger, her recklessness. But now she coolly, deliberately tested his skill with different patterns, careful to disguise what she was about.

Val taught me this. Sadness tugged in her gut. Pushing it aside, she countered the battering cuts and thrusts as Greyson roared and unleashed an onslaught of steel. Expertly, she kept him out then answered with a furious assault, her sword quick-fire in her hands.

As Genya and Greyson circled or lunged, their strokes vicious and deadly, the other lords ringed them loosely, muttering or gasping at every brutal exchange. Cut. Thrust. Hack.

Just when Genya thought she had Greyson's rhythm, the lord leapt at her with a bloodthirsty cry, his sword swinging. Without giving up ground, Genya swept up iron, blocking the assault. She shoved him off with a hard shoulder.

"Kneel," she hissed. "Offer your allegiance to your lord and king."

Scoffing, he recovered his balance and came for her once more, hewing at her head. She ducked. He thrust deep. She backed up fast, catching the blade as late as she dared.

They traded blows in a flurry of iron, their breaths sharp, sweat plastering her tunic to her back, chasing each other around the benches. Genya used what was in the hall, at times jumping onto a table then leaping off with a downward smash, at other times vaulting a bench to attack Greyson from a different angle.

"Kneel," she demanded again when their blades caught, jamming them close together.

"Bleed," Greyson shouted, hacking at her ribs.

Genya retreated quickly, her blade extended. He tried to take control of it, sliding the edge along until his guard locked. With ghoul strength, Genya yanked her weapon free. She threw out a shallow jab, a feint, then slipped her blade beneath his when he crashed steel laterally. The tip caught his hip. Blood pooled upon his tunic. Enraged, he howled, coming at her hard with hefty blows. Genya skipped away. He chased her.

Letting him draw close, she loosed a series of thrusts, a sequence where she anticipated his reaction to each stroke, how he would parry, how he'd riposte. Each carefully planned attack, each defensive action was designed to draw a particular reaction. She went through the sequence in order at rapid speed. Until the last.

Abruptly, she changed the rhythm, her blade flashing as she threw out a feint, cutting over the top of his rushed parry and driving her sword into his shoulder. For a single moment when pain distracted him, Genya kicked a bench. It slammed into his legs, knocking him off his feet. At once, she pounced, her blade to the throat of the fallen man. "Are you ready to kneel, or do you need further persuasion?"

He glared at her with hate-filled eyes. Genya ground the tip slightly into his soft flesh. A spot of blood appeared. The Mountains nobles murmured. Some shook their heads.

Though clenched teeth, Greyson muttered, "I'll kneel."

Genya drew back her sword. She stepped away, her gaze sweeping across the gathered nobles before resting on Alecc. He still sat forward on his chair, a gleam in his eyes.

To her, he nodded. Then he rose and clapped his hands, calling servants to him. "Lord Greyson needs a healer. Please help him to his room."

❦

Argument raged for several hours, until late into the night. Alecc allowed every man or woman present to have their say.

"There are ghoul strongholds near my lands," one young lord said. "All this talk of how Archanin's followers offer up their blood is nonsense. *Offer*." He scoffed. "Villagers go missing, and my sheriffs can't do a thing."

"We take the fight to them," Alecc said. "We bring down every ghoul castle. We destroy them."

"How?" Eirean asked.

"We use Roaran's idea of the Sword Brotherhood, only on a bigger scale. We raise an army."

"It won't be enough," Lord Drystan said. "These ghoul strongholds are heavily protected."

"And don't forget, my lord," Eirean said. "Gendrick Caelan will soon learn what unfolded here. He can't stand by and let you declare yourself king of Telor. He must answer that with force."

"Let him come," Alecc said. "His won't be the first force shattered upon these mountains."

Eirean spread his arms. "The Mountains cannot stand alone against the rest of Telor. Gendrick will overwhelm us."

Alecc slid Genya a look. "Not if we have magic on our side."

⁓ ∞⦙∞ ⁓

As the lords and ladies wandered off to their beds, led by servants carrying candles on holders, Genya confronted Alecc.

"What magic?" she demanded angrily. "If you think I know more than how to cast a few simple spells—"

"You'll learn." Alecc slid Nicky a look.

The other man nodded slightly. "You have Roaran's blood," Nicky said. "You just need instruction."

Genya dropped her hands to her hips. "Instruction?"

"My mother," Alecc said.

Genya scoffed. "What are you talking about? Your mother is in Dal-Kanu or Tide's End. At Gendrick's side."

Alecc grinned wearily. "I have a plan."

DANNON

Like faraway music, voices faded in and out. Hands lifted him, carried him. He wanted to beg them to leave him be, to explain that it hurt to move, but only a scratching noise came out of his throat. Sounds blurred: footsteps, murmurs, cloth slapping on a post.

Most of the time, he drifted in dreams as poppy juice took away the pain and carried him into gentle slumber. Until the pain returned like a hunting beast, sniffing the scent of weakness.

Dannon woke shouting, in blackness. Blindly, he tore at his eyes. Someone grasped his arms, wrenching them down. "Hush," a woman said in stumbling Telorian. "It's all right. You're all right."

"I can't see," he said, his voice rising in panic. "I can't see."

"Your eyes are bandaged," the woman said. "I've tried to save them. Don't touch them, or you'll undo my work."

Dannon's breaths racketed out. "Will I be blind?"

She sighed heavily. "I hope not. Now lie still. You're badly hurt."

Dannon sank back onto pillows. He was on a bed of sorts, but the room was not steady. It rocked beneath him. Beneath the edge of the bandages, he glimpsed streaked sunlight. The woman leaned over him, her hands upon his naked body. She wore no perfume, but her hair and skin smelt fresh and clean.

"Where… Where am I?" His thoughts were dull, his body a ruin of bruises and aches.

"You're on a ship." The woman pressed a cup to his lips.

Dannon recognised the scent and the taste of poppy juice mingled with wine.

"Ship," he repeated, unable to take that in. "A ship." He listened to waves battering boards, to creaking timber, and to someone's rasping breaths that he didn't immediately recognise as his. The air smelt warm and salty. A thin coverlet prickled against his skin.

The woman patted his arm. "I thought I'd lost you. The fever, the broken bones. The other… injuries. Somehow, you held on."

"I'm stubborn," Dannon wheezed. A warmth moved through him, the pain retreating as the poppy juice took over his body. "Even about death."

"So I see."

"Who are you? What ship is this?"

"I'm Elena. No more talking. Sleep."

Dannon obeyed willingly.

Later, he floated to wakefulness, squinting into too-bright sunlight. Carefully, he groped at his face. The bandages were gone, but his eyes watered, and his eyelids were painful to touch.

A woman sat on a stool by the bed. Her gaze fell somewhere distant, her smile gentle, as though she remembered something pleasant. Dannon stared at her for a moment. Hers was a wholesome, shining face. Her skin was sun bronzed, her pale hair wisping where it escaped from a single long plait that trailed like a tail over her shoulder and down onto her breast. She was not quite pretty, but there was a sweetness to her gently parted lips and a pleasing serenity to her smile.

Dannon moved slightly.

The woman stirred. "Back with me? Are you in pain?"

"Maybe a little." His shoulder throbbed. Aches in his chest, his thigh, his arm, even his ankle were dull and persistent, but not the sharp, stabbing pain that drew his screams. "Are you... Are you Elena? I remember an Elena."

"I am." Rising, she carefully pulled back the silken coverlet.

Dannon shivered slightly as the sea breeze, briny and fresh, through a window caressed his bare flesh. He glanced about at the small cabin. It was furnished with the cot he lay upon, a table, a stool, and rolled-up bedding on the floor. A ship, she had said. How had he come to be here?

Elena began to prod and squeeze his body. When he winced, her brows knotted, and she nodded as though keeping a record in her mind of which wounds still hurt.

"I think tomorrow I shall try to get you up," she said. "There's a rattle in your chest I don't like. But now." A bright smile unfolded as she wrinkled her nose. "A bath."

Dannon watched her move about the cabin, gathering a bowl, cloth, and soap, humming. "What sort of ship is this?"

Elena placed the bowl on the stool. "It is a Venivan ship."

Dannon frowned. "Then... Then you're Venivan?"

Elena laughed. "No. I am Quisnaf. You are a guest of the Quisnaf."

Guest. Quisnaf. Bewilderment drummed through him. That made no sense. What would the Quisnaf want with him? The last he remembered before the ship was a ruin in the forest and Genya whispering words that made no sense.

"I don't understand." He tried to rise, only for Elena to push him down gently. "What do you want from me? What happened in Telor? Are they safe? Roaran, the Brotherhood."

Genya. Oh, gods, Genya.

"Be easy. Samantha will explain soon."

"Samantha?" Again, he attempted to sit up, only to sink down in exhaustion.

Ignoring the question, Elena sponged him with wet cloth. "I'm not hurting you?"

"I can't be here," Dannon muttered. "I need to know what happened in Telor. Are my friends safe? What of Roaran? Archanin? What of Roaran's daughter?"

"Archanin is dead. We—the Quisnaf, I mean—fought with Roaran's brotherhood to defeat his ghoul army."

"What?" He clutched at her arm.

"I've said more than I should." Elena removed his arm and finished washing him. She dried him with another cloth and took away the bowl. Then she helped him sit up, his back to the wall, before bringing a bowl of cold soup. "Can you feed yourself?"

Dannon nodded and took the bowl from her. He took a mouthful. Flavours swirled in his mouth. *Fish? Potato. Some sort of bean.* The soup's texture was thick against his tongue.

When he had eaten, Elena nodded, removed the bowl, and returned with a cup. "Poppy juice, but just a little. I must wean you off it."

"I don't need it." Dannon remembered the men who craved the brew, how the Varee used it as a weapon to control recruits or prisoners. "Won't you tell me how Archanin died? I need to know who lived and died. I need to understand why I'm on this ship."

Elena offered the cup again. "You have no pain?"

"An ache here or there. My head pounds. The worst is the ship's movement. It makes me queasy."

Elena pressed the cup into his hands. "Just a little. For now, it is necessary. For the headache. Please trust me."

He wanted to. Her expression held warmth and sincerity. But this was a Quisnaf woman he'd just met. "Very well." Dannon sipped.

"You've done well." Elena seemed genuinely pleased. "Tomorrow, I'll help you rise, walk you about. We'll find something for you to wear. Then Samantha will talk to you."

"Samantha," he echoed. "That name again. Will she have answers?"

Elena replied, but Dannon did not hear her. He'd already drifted towards sleep.

VAL ARQUES

Before taking him onto the deck, Rohane always knocked at the door to the other cabin and whispered with someone within. Val never heard what was said, but the Quisnaf captain's expression was guarded when she ushered him up the ship's starboard side.

Val would lean his elbows on the rails and sigh with pleasure at the warmth of the sun on his face, watching the barren wastelands around the far distant ruins of Seithin hulk and flatten into forest-tipped mountains and verdant valleys.

A salty wind filled sails but barely cooled his damp skin as the fleet ploughed through deep, sleek green water. Sometimes, the fleet's ships were close together; sometimes, they were spread across the sea.

Two weeks into the journey, Veniva sprawled to the southeast, a lush land of blossoms and thick rainforests of ferns, vines, and strangler figs. It grew hotter, the sun relentless, the cabin airless. Samantha declared Val could sleep on deck but beneath Rohane's watchful gaze.

One night, neither able to sleep in the sultry heat, he and Rohane found themselves talking. She asked him, as Samantha had, to describe the night Roaran had died.

"I'm named for him," she said, as if in explanation for her curiosity.

"You are?"

"Roaran spent many periods in Quisnaf over the years. It was a refuge for him." She hesitated. "Will you tell me how he died?"

"You weren't told?"

"Some of it. Persia met with Nicholas Saltman before we set sail. He told her a death rider came for Roaran's body. Did you know?"

"I didn't." Val curled an arm beneath his head, gazing up at the stars in an endless sky of black. "It's not an easy story. What happened that night was horrendous."

"I should like to hear it. If you can tell it."

He began to speak. The words were as hard to find as they had been when he'd told Samantha what occurred at Vraymorg. Often, he paused, his throat tight. Nor did he tell all of it. Of Genya, he said as little as possible.

"So Archanin forced you to choose?" Rohane puzzled that out. She sat with her back to the rails, her sword resting on her lap. "I should not have been able to. Not between two people I love."

He glanced at her. "Who do you love, Rohane?"

When she did not answer, he looked harder at her. Rohane's gaze was upon the darkling sea, as if her thoughts were faraway. Then she shivered. "I don't know anymore."

"Why is that?" He frowned, thinking about her words from that first night on board the ship. "Because you're cursed?"

"Those I love die," Rohane said, her tone flat and empty.

"Those I love, I hurt," Val said.

She turned her head slightly to stare at him. "Then you, too, are cursed."

"I suppose that is like a curse. Why do you say you are cursed? Because people close to you die?"

Again, her eyes settled upon the horizon. Then in a quiet voice, she said, "There's a rage that comes over me. When I fight. It's in my blood." She paused. "Sometimes I can't control it. Once—" Her lip trembled. "Once I hurt someone. Oh, goddess, I didn't mean to."

"I'm sorry."

Rohane shook her head. "It was a long time ago."

"We could have done with you in the fight against Archanin."

"I was there. I killed my share of ghouls."

"That awful night comes to me in nightmares," Val said slowly. "I hear myself shouting Kaell's name. I can see Alecc. I feel his loss like a sword cut. Then I wake up."

"Wake and find everything is all right?"

"Nothing is all right. Nor, I think, shall it be all right again."

"It was never right," Rohane said.

DANNON

At Elena's insistence, Dannon rolled to the edge of the bed. Grasping his belly, he swung his legs to the floor. Elena took his weight as he tried to rise. Pain scorched like flaming lightning across his groin. Gasping, wincing, Dannon choked back a scream.

"Try again," Elena said.

Dannon breathed through the pain. Slowly, it eased to a throb. He nodded. Elena helped him up. He stood, stoop shouldered, bent at the waist. When he tried to straighten, another rip of pain took him over. *Breathe. Breathe.* It retreated. Dannon tried a step then another.

Elena held his arm. "That's good."

He managed to walk to the door then stumbled back to the bed. "What's wrong with me?" he muttered. "I'm so weak. I've never been this weak."

"Quisnaf wasn't built in a day," she said. "Let's find you a nightshirt. You can't wander about naked."

Dannon hadn't even noticed.

As his broken body slowly mended, Dannon lay upon his sickbed, thinking. He slowly grew angrier and angrier. Yes, he was grateful that Elena had tended to his wounds, but the Quisnaf had no right to take him aboard their vessel.

"Be patient," Elena replied to his questions. "Samantha will talk to you soon."

It must have been two weeks into the journey when a woman came to the cabin. At her appearance, Elena dipped her head and muttered in Quisnaf. Dannon dragged himself up on the pillows. Elena's deference suggested the newcomer was someone important.

The woman approached the bed. She was perhaps sixty, with carefully coiffed greying hair and intelligent, sharp eyes that passed over him with interest. Dannon pressed his back to the wall as Elena moved the stool to the bed. The woman sat, flicked a hand, and rapped a command in the Quisnaf tongue.

Elena bowed her head again and retreated, her gown sweeping the wooden floor. Uneasily, Dannon watched her leave. The room seemed empty, colder. Elena was so nurturing, her very presence comforted him.

Folding his arms across his nightshirt, he fixed the older woman with a stare. "You must be Samantha."

"I am." Effortlessly, she switched to flawless Telorian. "I thought it time we met."

"Our meeting, in fact, is overdue. Why am I on your ship?"

"Elena says you are no longer likely to die. A week or so ago, we weren't sure. How do you feel?"

"Still weak." He managed a grin. "The ship's roll makes my belly churn, but Elena calls me a sook. She says if I truly suffered, I would be on my knees retching."

"You're not accustomed to the sea?"

"It is my first time on a vessel," he admitted. "I lived most of my life in the Mountains, beyond the gorge." Would that mean anything to her? He suspected she was well educated. She certainly spoke near perfect Telorian.

"Most of your life?" Samantha lifted an eyebrow.

"I was born in Cahir, in a village outside Isamasalle." Dannon wasn't sure why he told her so much. Perhaps after weeks in this cabin, he craved company.

"Ah." She tilted her head, considering him. "You do look Cahirean. How does a Cahirean from a village outside Isamasalle end up beyond the gorge?"

He shrugged.

"A long story?" Samantha laughed. "Perhaps one day, you'll tell me. But that's not why I'm here."

"What happened in Telor?" Dannon leaned forward. "Ghouls, Archanin took the castle. Are my friends alive?"

"Some of them." She sighed. "I shall tell you what you need to know. Archanin is defeated, dead. Slain by a girl with Roaran Caelan's blood."

Dannon released a held breath. "Thank the gods. Then she, the girl… she lives?"

Samantha glanced at him speculatively. "As far as we know. A boy is proclaimed king of the Mountains. The fight against ghouls goes on. Some of the Brotherhood survived; some did not."

"Who?" he growled. "Tell me."

"Archanin executed some. Others survived. I do not know names." She paused. "I am sorry to tell you that Roaran Caelan is dead."

Coldness creased his spine. Shocked, Dannon could only stare at her. "Roaran," he stammered at last. "Dead? No. No."

"I am sorry to bring you such ill tidings."

Dannon shook his head in disbelief. Roaran had been so certain, so powerful, so glorious. He could not be dead. He could not. "How did it happen?"

She rose to depart. "Perhaps I should leave you alone with your thoughts."

"No, wait." He frowned. "Tell me why I'm here. Tell me what you intend to do with me."

Samantha sat down again. "We found you badly hurt and dying, in a ruin in the forest near the fortress of Vraymorg. We brought you with us. Elena tended to you constantly. She did not think you would live. But the goddess spared you."

Dannon shook his head, trying to make sense of that. "You tended to my wounds. I'm grateful. But why help a stranger?"

Samantha's gaze did not move from his face. "Because you have value."

He laughed bitterly. "I am a warrior but little else. I am not wellborn. I am not wealthy. I am nothing more than an outlaw and scoundrel." They could not know the truth about him, about his mother. That secret was locked in the past.

"Ah, but you are loved, I think."

"I... What? I still don't understand."

Samantha got to her feet. "That will do for now. We'll talk more when we reach Quisnaf."

"What?" Dannon's spine stiffened. "You're taking me to Quisnaf?"

"What do you think we intended? Mend your body then drop you in the sea?" She moved towards the door.

"I thought... I thought maybe you'd leave me in Veniva or something. Oh, gods." He shuddered. "It's true then? What they say about Quisnaf? You enslave men for breeding purposes? But I am no one." An image flashed in his mind of his mother's face. Dannon's cheeks flamed. The Quisnaf must not discover who she had been.

Samantha paused, her hand on the door latch. "Let me put your mind at rest. We do not want anything from you. We simply need you to be in Quisnaf. That is all."

"That makes no sense."

She threw him an enigmatic smile. "Then it is something for you to ponder as you lie here. A puzzle, a riddle. Think upon it, and we'll talk in Quisnaf."

KAELL

He found Nicky in the gloomy crypt before one of the stone sarcophaguses. Light spilled from a single torch in a sconce in the passage beyond the central chamber, shadowing Nicky's face. At Kaell's approach, he did not move.

"He should have been here," Nicky said without turning. "Alecc is right. I should never have surrendered Roaran to that death rider."

"You did what you thought was right—" Kaell broke off, listening.

A sound came again, a soft scuff of a boot on the stone floor. In the passage, torchlight bobbed. Someone took another cautious step. A whisper echoed in the emptiness. "He should be here. I followed him to the entrance."

The light filled the entrance to the tomb's sanctum. Then a group of men burst into the chamber. Each carried a sword.

"Grab him." Lord Stonecliff jabbed a finger at Kaell. The men at his back started forward, their weapons levelled. Both Kaell and Nicky drew their blades.

"Wait up here," Nicky said. "What's this about?"

Stonecliff's arm shook as he pointed. "Just keep out of this, Saltman. Let us take the half ghoul, and that will be an end to it."

Nicky slitted his eyes. "Take the half ghoul and do what? No, I don't think so. You'll have to come through me to get to him."

Kaell glanced at his companion. Nicky's face was resolute, his expression as hard as flint. Uneasily, he looked at the approaching men. Someone had told Stonecliff what he was. Had they also told him *who* he was?

"Step aside," one of the men with Stonecliff growled. "We're not fighting beside a half ghoul. The only good ghoul is a dead ghoul."

The men started to fan out to ring Kaell and Nicky.

"Step back," Nicky hissed. "This is your last warning."

"Or what?" Stonecliff thrust his chin upwards. He looked grey and ill, as if his wounds bothered him. In that moment, Kaell thought he could do with Genya's help to teach this bitter man another lesson. He turned slightly, watching the circling men. There were five of them. He could deal with five, but not killing them would take skill and care.

"What are you waiting for?" Stonecliff screamed. "Grab him. Let's build a pyre and finish what Cathmor intended all those years ago."

Kaell could not hold back a shudder. The stake, the fire roaring up about him, still filled his nightmares. If not for his lord, he would have burned. If not for Heath Damadar. The young Icelord had changed sides and led the Icelands warriors against Cathmor, the former king.

"Grab him!" Stonecliff yelled again.

With a bellow, the five men attacked at once, their swords swinging. Kaell blocked a slash coming for his neck, shoving the assailant back with a shoulder. At his side, Nicky held out a blow from another, his riposte nearly spearing a man in the side. Another man launched at Kaell. Their swords met in a mighty clash. Nicky forced another to retreat, the clang of their blades echoing about the chamber.

"What by all the gods goes on here?" A voice carried above the shriek and grinding of swords. Alecc stood at the tomb's entrance, a bunch of armed Mountains warriors with him.

"Put your swords down," he shouted. "Now."

Doubtful men looked at him then looked at the warriors. One by one, they put their blades on the floor.

Alecc advanced on Stonecliff. "What exactly are you about, my lord?"

Stonecliff dropped his hands to his hips. He sneered. "Ridding you of a ghoul. Don't get in my way, boy."

Alecc's jaw shifted. Torchlight caught a glint of anger in his eyes. "Kaell's under my protection."

"Kaell," Stonecliff spluttered. "Then it's true what I heard. He's unnatural. A sickness we have to wipe out."

Kaell swallowed. A bonded warrior who had become a ghoul, with ghoul appetites, was indeed a perversion, a depravity. He could not blame Stonecliff for his disgust.

"You know nothing of him," Alecc said. "You know nothing of what befell him. But let me be clear. Kaell is part of Roaran's brotherhood. He fought with us to defeat Archanin."

Kaell glanced at Alecc gratefully. In that moment, despite his lord's absence, he felt less alone.

"I'm not fighting beside a ghoul," Stonecliff muttered.

"Then you fight alone," Alecc said.

"What?" Stonecliff screwed up his face.

"In a year from now, every ghoul stronghold in the Mountains will fall," Alecc said. "I swear it by the gods, by Khir himself."

Stonecliff sneered again. "Big words from a child."

Nicky shoved forward, bringing his face close to the lord's. "He's the son of a great lord of Telor. The son of a queen."

"A Cahirean. A half-breed."

"I will bring down every ghoul stronghold," Alecc said again, his voice steel. "The question is, my lord, are you with me or against me? And before you answer me, ponder this."

"Ponder what?" Stonecliff muttered. "Whether you're old enough to shave?"

The men with him laughed.

Alecc did not react. Coolly, he said, "Ponder what your reputation will be in the Mountains when every other lord and lady learns you turned your back and refused to fight. Why—" Alecc spread his arms. "Some might even think you a coward."

Stonecliff's face reddened. "I'm no coward."

"Then prove it," Alecc said. "Help me bring down every ghoul. Show your people you are not afraid."

Stonecliff stared at him, a pulse fluttering in his throat. Kaell watched him. He could see the reluctance in him, the desire to turn his back, to jeer and storm off. But for a man like this, reputation was all. Alecc had chosen the right words. If Stonecliff did not act, it would seem as if a child had done what he could not. Or would not.

"Are you with me, my lord?"

The other man huffed a breath. Reluctantly, he muttered gruffly, "I'm with you."

VAL ARQUES

T heir ship yawed and creaked after its companions into a bay. Val glimpsed Vene's distant towers glittering golden in the sunlight amid rich, green troughs of gardens. The walled stone city always smelt sweet, or so Rohane said. She told him storms swept in from the sea each evening and dumped torrents of rain on palm trees, frangipanis, and giant crimson bougainvillea. In their wake, the air steamed with heady perfumes.

The heat, the storms reminded him of Isles summers. Sadness and longing tore through him. Would he see Telor again? No—it was useless to dwell on such thoughts. A warrior must accept what was to come without expectation. He must lock the past away and face the moment at hand without wallowing in regret.

Vessels crowded the seaway to Vene. Some were exotic ships with two decks, monstrous rigging, and billowing sails. Others were humble fishing boats with eyes painted on their hulls. Vene heralded the way to the Ice Sea. Once the treacherous passage had been thought impassable, but now, those brave or reckless enough might risk the storms to reach the Circle Kingdoms and beyond.

"Veniva is at war." Rohane appeared at his shoulder. "I don't remember a time when that was not so."

"A deliberate strategy by its kings, perhaps?"

73

She turned to stare at him. "Oh, clever boy."

As a child, Val had learnt southern invaders with blond hair and blue eyes had settled these lands. But they'd brought with them a curse. Too few women were born in Veniva and too many men. How better to quell the restlessness of such a mismatch but through the distraction of war—continual war, with the promise of plunder, particularly slaves.

"Do you know Vene well?"

She rested her hands on the rails. Sweat glistened on her neck. Locks of damp hair framed her sun-browned face. "I know it very well. I am, after all, half Venivan."

"Ah. That's what Persia meant."

"What?"

"When she tried to unsettle you with talk of your father."

She bristled. "That's none of your business."

Clearly, he'd spoken out of turn, lulled by her relaxed manner. Whatever wounded her, it was not his place to enflame it. Val had too many scars of his own, uncomfortable deeds and memories he would keep to himself.

Over the journey, they had fallen into a pattern of surprisingly companionable conversations that ended in arguments as though each needed reminding they were not friends.

"You must have had brothers," he'd complained once. "You injure me with words like a sibling."

"You say the most stupid things," she had snapped.

Val had grown accustomed to her changing moods: calm one minute, irritable the next. It hardly bothered him. Val liked rough edges in a woman. And Rohane had edges. Prickly edges that interested him.

But once they reached Quisnaf, Rohane would be rid of him, her duty done. The council would appoint a guardian to guide him. Control him, more like. Gods, he hoped it wasn't someone like Persia.

"How far to Quisnaf?"

"A few hours if the wind holds up." Rohane flicked at a fly humming near her nose. It turned its attention to him.

Val waved it away. "Go bother Rohane."

"Don't send your flies my way."

"It's a Quisnaf fly. You can tell because it's so prickly."

She laughed, her ill-humour of a moment ago forgotten. It was a carefree sound. In moments when they seemed easy with each other, Val liked her. The other Rohane—the stern, dutiful huntress—he wasn't sure about.

He flapped his tunic to cool his body. What he wouldn't do for a bath. "The sea looks temptingly cold."

"Please don't jump overboard. I'd hate to waste an arrow shooting you."

"You'd shoot me?"

She grinned. "As much as it would give me pleasure, we'd have to row after you and scoop you up from the waves. Like a big fish. Persia would love that. She's itching to dress you in irons."

"I would look very pretty in irons. But it's far too hot." He thought guiltily of the men sweltering in the hold.

She didn't answer. Her face shadowed.

"What? You have that look, like you don't want to tell me something."

"Why should I tell you anything, Telorian?"

"I shall pester you until you do. Like the fly. I can be very annoying."

"You have your moments. All of them bad." She peered along the deck. "There's Persia. I must speak to her. You stay here and don't annoy anyone. Even the fly."

Val stared out over the deep-emerald sea towards the famed city. His stomach roiled with nerves. Very soon, he would see Quisnaf, his new home. He would learn his place in it.

He tried to turn his mind from his near fate, but into the void, more troubling thoughts intruded. *Genya.* She had proved too much like Roaran, prepared to sacrifice others for some nebulous greater good. If she had trusted him, come to him with her doubts, he would have helped her. Instead, she had chosen a ruthless path that had cost Roaran humiliation, pain, and death.

He shut his eyes, unable to banish the memory of Genya running after him as he had surrendered himself to Rohane. He could hear the disbelief, the hurt in his ward's voice.

A woman joined him at the rails. Val snapped open his eyes to glance at her. Then he looked again, surprised.

"You," he said.

The past roared back. In that instant, he could see once more a shabby hut in the forest near Vraymorg. He had never learnt her name, but this woman had shackled him to a post and forced a potion upon him. She was older than he remembered, her face lined and her waist thicker, but it was her.

She flicked auburn hair over her shoulder and smiled viciously. The swirling tattoo on her upper arm was golden in the sunlight. "So Rohane succeeds where all other retrievers failed." Her tone was bitter. "Oh, hail the golden one."

"What do you want?" Val asked cautiously.

"Just renewing our acquaintance. We had a moment, I think, in that hut." She put her hand on his arm.

Val recoiled. "Don't touch me."

She laughed coolly. "What do you think is going to happen to you in Quisnaf, Val Arques? Are you so naïve, you haven't worked out what they want you for?"

"The councillor mentioned 'blood keepers.'" He swallowed.

"I suppose the councillor told you you'd be treated fairly or even kindly. Ha. You're breeding stock, Telorian. The moment you step off this ship, you'll be confined to some small room for the rest of your life, visited by women chosen by the blood keepers."

"Why are you telling me this?"

She shrugged. "Someone should let you know the truth— before it's too late. Or perhaps you're content going to such a fate like a sacrificial lamb. If it were me, I'd run."

Unexpectedly, she grabbed his hand. The heat of her touch burned through him. His mind blanked. He was aware only of her words, softly needling, persuading, compelling.

"So why don't you run?" With a mocking smile, she moved away.

Val pressed his palms into the rails. At the prospect of captivity, overwhelming fear lanced him. What if Samantha had lied to him? Had she told him platitudes to keep him under control?

So why don't you run?

Panic building in him, he glanced at the shore below the city. It was only a short distance away. If he could make his way to Vene, he could lose himself in its streets, even find a way back to Telor.

Val climbed onto the railing. Without a backwards glance, he dived into the sea.

ROHANE

"He's overboard."

At the shout, Rohane spun. She hurried to the rails. The wretched Telorian was in the water, striking out for the shore with quick strokes.

A warrior rushed to the side, her crossbow levelled. She nocked a bolt. Before Rohane could react, the woman fired. The bolt flew towards Val, skimming the waves inches from him.

Rohane pushed the bow down. "Stop."

"But, Captain—"

"Not this one."

A group of warriors reached Rohane.

"We take the boat," she ordered, already moving. Women followed her. One threw a rope ladder over the side towards the rowboat tied at the back of the ship.

Rohane climbed into the boat after a handful of other warriors. Two took up the oars. Rohane sat in the bow, watching Val anxiously. He had hit trouble. A current had swept him up and was dragging him farther out to sea.

"He's in a rip," Rohane muttered. "Row harder."

The craft plunged through the waves towards the struggling swimmer. "Don't fight it," Rohane yelled as the boat reached him.

Val's strength was fading fast. She reached down a hand. "Get in the boat."

He tried to swim away. A shape darkened the water.

"Shark," a warrior shouted, pointing.

Alarm tore through Rohane. "Shark!" she yelled. "Get in the boat."

Val glanced back. The shape darted past him. He gasped. The boat again drew alongside. Two women grabbed him, hauling him in. This time, he didn't resist. They dumped him at their feet. He lay panting.

"Goddess," Rohane breathed.

Two fins now circled the boat. When something bumped the side, one of the women shot Rohane a panicked look.

"We're safe," Rohane said.

They rowed back to the ship. In its hollow, Val pushed up onto his knees. Rohane eyed him angrily. "Fool," she muttered. "They call this Shark Bay. You could have been killed."

He didn't say anything, only looked down.

Rohane sat back, shivering. What if he had been hurt? Oh, goddess, the council would have demoted her, even banished her, for such a failure. But that wasn't why her gut was in turmoil. No, not that at all. She frowned, surprised to realise her fears weren't for herself. She had been afraid for Val. *Afraid.* Why? Did she even like him? Had she become fond of an irritating Telorian? The goddess take her for her foolishness. Anything between them would be forbidden. And Rohane knew she was destined to be alone. What she had told Val that night on the deck was true: anyone she loved died.

Another shiver ran through her. *See this through. Get him safely to Quisnaf. Then move on.* She would be back to her duty as retrieval captain and would soon forget the Telorian.

Doubtfully, she eyed him. "What spooked you? Was it Branwyn? What did she say?"

"Branwyn," he repeated, frowning. "Is that her name?"

Rohane grabbed his shoulder. "She said something. What?"

He frowned as if puzzled. "My mind blanked. I don't know why. She told me to run."

"And you just did as she said?" Rohane sat back, incredulous. Branwyn was untrustworthy, manipulative, and bitter. Rohane glanced at her companions. This wasn't the time to list the other woman's faults. Later, when she was alone with the Telorian, she would warn him about Branwyn.

They reached the ship and climbed the rope ladder onto the deck. Rohane peered at the horizon. A storm brewed at their backs. The air smelt of rain and stirred dust. At once, Persia came forward with two warriors. They took hold of Val, snapping iron about his wrists. His strength gone, he barely struggled as they bore him off.

Rohane was about to follow when Persia grabbed her arm. "I told you to keep better control of him."

"I was expecting this," Rohane muttered. "Just not so soon."

Persia's mouth slitted angrily. "What's this you're saying? If you expected it, then why didn't you stop him?" Without waiting for an answer, she turned away.

Rohane trod after her to the councillor's cabin. There, at Persia's command, the guards dumped Val on his knees before Samantha. The councillor passed a cool gaze over him then lifted her eyes to Rohane, a question in them.

"He went for a swim," Rohane said. "Branwyn said something that scared him."

Samantha turned her back. She poured wine into a cup. Rohane glimpsed her add something from a small sachet. Turning, the councillor pressed the cup into Val's hands. He shook his head firmly. The guards pounced. One held his head, forcing his jaw open. The other grabbed the cup and tipped it down his throat. Almost at once, his eyes glazed. He blinked rapidly as if fighting off sleep. When the guard let him go, he slumped to the cabin floor.

"Keep him sedated," Persia instructed, "until we have him in Quisnaf."

VAL ARQUES

Wooden wheels bumping over a dirt track woke him. Straw prickled his back. He was in no pain and in very little discomfort apart from an ache in his bruised wrists where fetters bit. A blindfold shut out light. Panic tightened his throat.

"I can't see," he muttered.

"Be calm." Rohane was beside him. "We're entering Quisnaf."

Sounds blurred about him. Thunder rumbled. Chains rattled. Reluctant, shuffling footsteps padded over the ground. A whip cracked. In air steamy with heat, Val's skin was moist and his mouth dry.

"Is there water?"

Rohane pressed a skin to his lips. As he drank, Val gathered his thoughts. *We're entering Quisnaf.* Dread stirred in his belly, ready to overwhelm him with dark imaginings. He clamped it down. *No. Do not look ahead. Concentrate only on what is happening now.*

"From here, we walk." Rohane helped him climb from the cart.

"Where are we, exactly? What's ahead?"

"Before me are stone arches leading to a long verdant valley. But for this narrow gated opening, steep mountains loom on all sides. If you listen hard, you'll hear the rush of water from the river that runs through this valley. There are gardens, wonderful scented gardens, which you'll see soon. Quisnaf is beautiful."

Val shivered. "But… the caves?"

She rested warm fingers on his arm. "The ancient City of Caves sprawls within the mountains about this valley. Walls of caves that worm like fingers everywhere, into caverns so tall you cannot see the roof, to shallow passages, to halls and chambers of all description, carved from rock. Other parts of the city are built into the cliffs. At night, with every torch and candle lit, it's as though walls of fairy lights climb into the sky."

"A city of caves. Like the Damadar city."

"Theirs was, in fact, based upon Quisnaf. Some Damadar lord turned up centuries ago, seeking knowledge of magic. He returned and modelled his city on ours." She took his arm. "Are you ready?"

Val gave a curt nod. Whatever lay ahead, he had to face it. He had to do as he always did: Bury the past. Do not dwell on the future. Deal with the present.

Rohane led him forward. Aware of others around him, of their laughter, their booted steps, he focused on putting one foot after the other.

A shadow fell from above. Val guessed Rohane had led him beneath stone arches. Then a roar of sound struck him as though they'd burst into an amphitheatre. Shouts and cheers rang out. Drumbeats thudded up through his boots and into his spine. Children's giggles rang without malice as they might in any town in Telor. Trumpets blared, their notes as clear as ice.

"What's all the noise?"

"A jubilant crowd gathers, rows deep. Guards, seers, clerks, priestesses, traders, healers, servants, everyone has rushed out at news two battales return. A bustling throng lines the valley, cheering their victorious warriors, gaping at captives."

Val swallowed hard, his breath racketing against his ribs. To rally his spirit, he squared his shoulders. If they must stare, then at least let them see a Telorian warrior, unbowed and unbroken. But he could not banish the fear clenching his throat nor silence a voice whispering that he was alone among enemies. Enemies who'd sought him for centuries.

The shouting died to a murmur. Val's footsteps faltered. Rohane's grip tightened. "Stop. Wait."

A hush closed with expectation. A woman began to speak. It was an imperious voice, her words very formal, a structured form of Quisnaf Val hardly understood. He snatched at familiar words. "Prince... Telor... long search."

Then cheers erupted as if the woman had enflamed the crowd with a gesture. Feet stamped. A trumpeter blasted a note.

Hands groped at him. Val fought them, terrified they sought to pull him down and into the mob. Instead, they shoved him against something hard like a timber stake. In an instant, thick rope bound him to it.

Shocked, Val struggled. A tumult of shouts and jeers rolled over him and through him.

Rohane whispered, "Calm, calm. It is for show only."

"What's happening?"

"Boring speeches. Our brave warriors, blah, blah. You'll soon wish you can't hear as well as not see." She yawned audibly.

Her irreverence snapped him back from black thoughts. Val knew a moment of gratitude that she bothered to distract him with humour.

The same woman addressed the crowd again. Val gave up trying to follow the words. Closing his eyes, he let them wash over him.

Then a sound came to him—a whirring then a thump. Shouts broke out.

"Who was that?" someone cried. "Where did it come from?"

A tumult of noise rolled over Val. Running steps, more cries. Someone brushed against him, moving fast.

"The shot came from over there. Get them. Stop them."

Shot. Val shuddered. Alarmed, unable to understand what was unfolding, he struggled against his bonds.

Footsteps approached. The faint perfume of lilacs reached him. The woman said, "Get him away, Rohane. Quickly. There's danger."

"Are you unharmed, Blaire?" Rohane asked. "That arrow was meant for you."

"What's happening?" Val asked. "Are we under attack?"

"It's not the first time. My guards will search out the would-be assassin," the newcomer said.

"What's going on, Blaire? Who would be so audacious as to come after you at a celebration?"

"Just do your job, Rohane. We'll talk tonight."

Cloth brushed Val's hip as the ropes fell away.

"Come with me." Rohane urgently drew him forward.

The noise of unrest, raised voices, and fast-moving feet rioted about them. Stunned to docility, Val went with her.

"Will you explain?" he asked. "Someone tried to kill this Blaire you were talking to?"

"Not now." Rohane's voice was low. "Just know that since Blaire came to power, Quisnaf has become a dangerous place. Stay close."

The uproar fell into the distance. The ground beneath his feet was hard but smooth. Then the light faded. The coldness of stone pressed upon him like a tomb. Val badly wanted to rip off the blindfold as though just seeing would banish his fears. Every step took him farther away from what he knew and understood, to a strange world where his fate was uncertain and terrifying.

For this, surely, was the heart of Quisnaf, a legendary city of black caverns and passages ribboned beneath the mountains all the way to the sea. Val had heard stories that some chambers had lain untouched for centuries, brimming with dust. No prisoner dared escape through the caverns and risk drowning in these dust pools.

They walked on, their footsteps echoing in the quiet. The deepening chill knifed his skin. Every now and then, he heard snatches of misplaced sounds—murmurs or fragmented laughter that drifted eerily as though they came from far away. Other times, he heard very little, only the wind and its whisper.

At last, Rohane bid him stop. Creaking wood scraped over rock. Heat and damp blasted Val's face.

"Who's there?" a woman challenged. "Show yourself."

"It is Rohane, huntress and retrieval captain. Step aside."

"Captain, how may I assist you?"

"You can leave," Rohane said. "Everyone out. I want this place to myself."

Outraged gasps broke out.

"Leave. I won't ask again."

Figures brushed past Val. Scurrying footsteps clattered then faded away. Someone paused. A woman said, "You'll answer for this."

"Off you go, then. Find someone to complain to."

With a sniff, the woman moved on.

Rohane led Val forward. She pulled off the blindfold and released his hands.

Val blinked into soft, flickering light. He stood in a chamber hewn from rock. Steam misted about a pool of dark water cut into stone. Frescoes of naked men and women bathing brightened the walls. Rose-scented candles flickered from alcoves containing shelves lined with folded cloths. The room was pleasantly hot. Moisture beaded on both his throat and brow.

"Be quick. This breaks the rules. I'm meant to lock you up at once." She nudged him. "Bathe. There's soap and cloth on the side."

"Rohane, well, well." A man sprawled lazily in the shadowy water, his arms stretched along the pool's rim.

Rohane groped for her blade. Then her hand fell away. She scowled. "Eamon. Why are you here?"

"In my profession, it can be hard to find a moment alone." There was a taunting edge to his voice, as if he challenged her.

"I want you gone," Rohane snapped. "At once."

With deliberate slowness, the man waded to the side. Elegantly, he emerged, completely naked, and shook his head amid a spray of water droplets.

He was not a youth, perhaps thirty-five or thirty-six, though his body was nothing but muscle, and he possessed the poise of a dancer. In the poor light, it was impossible to tell if his wet hair plastered against his cheeks was dark, but the way the candlelight hit it, Val guessed it was light brown.

"A slug would move faster." Rohane watched the man with distaste. "I think I told you to leave."

The man reached for a cloth, brazenly slow. His gaze fell on Val. He edged up a brow. "So, this is him?"

"This is who exactly?" Rohane shoved her hands to her hips.

"The Telorian." Eamon gave a careless laugh. "Don't look at me like that, Rohane. You know I hear things, that women tell me things. Councillors even."

A muscle twitched in Rohane's jaw. "You're shameless. Cover yourself and leave."

His grin widened. He sauntered to Val and half circled him. Val glared.

"Don't stop on my account," Eamon said. "The water is all yours."

"When you're gone, Eamon," Rohane seethed. "Just leave."

"There's no need." Val stripped off his garments, leaving them in an untidy puddle. Nudity, even public nudity, was commonplace in baths in the Isles. And he was impatient to at last bathe.

Eamon wandered over to a bench. He wrapped a towel about his waist and sat. "He's extraordinary, Rohane. What money I could make with such a man."

"You're despicable," she muttered.

"So despicable, you once couldn't get enough of me. Do you remember that first time your battle sister brought you to me? You were so nervous, you couldn't even look at me. When I kissed you, you trembled. But you learnt fast."

Val turned abruptly, his eyes low-lidded. "Your words are uncalled for."

"I don't need you to defend me." Rohane's cheeks flushed. She faced Eamon. "Leave. Or I'll drown you in one of the pools you're so fond of."

Smiling, Eamon held up his hands in surrender then gathered a pile of discarded garments and trod to the door. "Another time, Rohane, my sweet."

Rohane scowled after him. When the door clanked at his back, she turned again to Val. "Well? Are you from the same slug family as him? Get in."

Val took the rock steps that led down into the pool and sank into the hot water. Tension seeped from his cramped muscles. He sighed deeply.

"Why is this against the rules?" he called to Rohane, who stood with her back to the wall, arms folded, her gaze averted.

"I have no right to send away the attendants. But I sought to spare you their pawing hands, as you might see it."

Val shrugged. "I'm accustomed to women bathing me."

Rohane began to laugh.

"What's so funny?"

"Bathing captives or guests is a menial task. Unless you are taken to the temple baths, where initiates ceremonially wash you, no Quisnaf woman would do it."

"Oh." Val groped for a cake of soap on the pool's rim. His fingers brushed metal rings in the rock. Guessing their purpose, he suppressed a shiver and lathered his hair and body. A sweet scent rose off the water, a potpourri of lavender, roses, and tangerine.

"Quickly. That attendant will whinge to someone. Some bureaucrat will come to scold me about rules."

"I begin to think you are a rebel."

"Me?" Rohane clasped her hand to her breast. "I'm the most officious captain in Quisnaf. Didn't you hear the councillor? It is all about duty with me."

"What's the nature of your relationship with Samantha?" He was curious, sensing an unspoken bond. "You bicker as though tied to each other by more than duty."

"None of your business." Rohane stopped him with a gesture. Again, he had misread her. Rohane's banter was no invitation to confidences. "Time to get out. Unless you want some male slave to put his hands all over you. They might enjoy it, but I doubt you will."

"I might," Val teased. "You know what they say about Isles men. Lusty libertines, the lot of us."

He ducked his head beneath the water to rinse his hair. When he rose and climbed out, droplets streaming from his body, Rohane did not bother to look away. She raised an eyebrow, her lips forming an appreciative smile.

"Ah, cloth?"

"What do you think I am? A bath slave?"

"Ah…" Val stood in puddling water, his skin glistening.

"I'm joking." She moved away through the steam then returned with a cloth, comb, and new garments. Val rubbed himself down, dried his hair, and dragged the comb through damp, curling locks.

Despite the danger of the attack at the ceremony, his heart felt lighter. Bathing enlivened his spirits. He began to hum as he dressed. The garments were simple but comfortable: dark pants that tied at the waist and a sleeveless silk tunic.

He waved the tunic at Rohane. "Half of this is missing."

"At least you have half." Rohane thrust his boots at him. "Let me look at you, libertine," she said when he was dressed.

"Like this?" He gave a mock whirl.

The doors flew back. A woman stormed through. She wore a short robe and sandals with ties that curled up her calves. Two men crept behind her, eyes wide.

"What is going on here?" A hard look swept from Val to Rohane. The woman's eyebrows shot up. "Captain, this is irregular. Even you can't come in here and order everyone out."

"This man is a *guest*," Rohane said.

"That is no excuse," the woman complained peevishly. "You warriors always think you are above the rules. You are not."

"I had little time. The council wants to talk with the guest."

"The council..." The woman shifted her weight, uncomfortable. "Just make sure it doesn't happen again." She turned an appraising eye on Val. "Oh, by Cyrah, no. That beard must come off."

Val's fingers strayed to his chin. He preferred a day's stubble. A lifetime ago, Ewen had even teased him about his vanity over his facial hair.

Rohane waved a hand, disinterested. "Very well. Do it. Quickly."

The woman barked commands. The bath slaves flustered about. One came for Val, demanding he sit. He did so and bared his throat for the knife. To Rohane, the woman asked, "How close?"

"I like thin bristle," Val said.

Rohane nodded.

The attendant took up the knife. When he was finished, Val ran his fingers over his jaw, pleased at the stubble.

"Time to go." At Rohane's gesture, he rose and followed her to the door.

"Do you need help with him?" The woman glanced warily at Val. "There are guards outside."

"Do I need help with you, Telorian?" Rohane scooped up the iron bands with their short length of chain and jangled them in front of him. She was wide-eyed with mischief.

Behind her, the bath attendants gawked with interest. Val held out his wrists. Rohane snapped iron in place then blindfolded him again.

"That's as well." The woman sounded relieved. "Do not break the rules again."

They walked through more passages, lit irregularly by torches. "Straight ahead," Rohane ordered. "Watch your feet."

Val pushed down a stubborn need to disobey, a desire to run. Where would he go, anyway? He would only lurch about in the darkness until the guards retrieved him.

At last, she paused. A key rattled. A door squeaked. She gave him a little push. He stumbled forward then stood deceptively placidly as she released the shackles and removed the blindfold.

Val peered about. The room was a tiny cell with cushions heaped on the floor, a bucket, a candle, and a jug of water. Cool air struck his face through a slanted vent cut into the rock, its opening covered by some sort of netting. It was not large enough, though, for even a child to pass through.

"This is it? You're going to imprison me in a room I can hardly turn around in?" He let her hear his anger. The chamber's meagre size showed his worth. It was a space for someone little valued.

Rohane yawned. "Settle down. This is just to contain you for tonight. After tomorrow, you'll be taken somewhere more befitting an irritating, troublesome Isles lord."

"Oh, ha ha. So, when does the council examine me, as you put it?"

"Tomorrow. Sleep now. I'll be outside."

"You're going to keep watch at my door? How sweet."

She shrugged. "Until I sit you before the council, I am responsible for you."

"What if I have nightmares? Will you stroke my hair and hug me to your breast?"

Solemnly, she replied, "I'll slap you about until you wake. Val—" She frowned. Both knew his nonsense was a poor attempt to cloak his unease.

"What?"

"Just... Just be careful."

"Watch out, Rohane. Your shield is slipping. I'm beginning to think you care."

"I care about doing my job, Telorian."

Val swallowed. "Who is responsible for me once the council...

talks to me?"

"The joy of your continuous company, of suffering your sarcastic wit, of dealing with your stubborn inability to heed a simple command, fortunately passes to someone else. A guardian. Oh, don't look worried. She'll be much nicer than me."

"I don't want nice. I like your rough edges."

"If that's a compliment, then I would hate us to be enemies."

"Are we enemies, Rohane?"

Rohane unfolded a thin smile. "I don't have friends, Val." She turned for the door. A key jangled as the lock ground into place.

ROHANE

Rohane strode through rock-walled passages towards the council chamber, shivering at a breeze ghosting at the back of her neck. In the gloom, the eeriness clinging to the caverns and tunnels was so thick, she could surely slice it with the jewelled knife in her belt. Uneasily, she sought the ordinary: the crackle of flames in wall sconces, the distant rumble of guards' voices, the wind sighing through the valley.

At a sound behind her, a stealthy footstep, she whirled. Through swirling smoke from torches down an adjacent passage, a shape flitted.

Rohane groped for her knife. "Who goes there?"

Whoever it was stilled then fled. "Halt," Rohane shouted. "Whoever you are, stop."

She broke into a run, chasing the figure down the passage. But when she reached a corner, no one was in sight. Rohane drew up, frowning.

"You won't find them."

Rohane turned. The Quisnaf Regenta stood peering at the wall where Rohane had first glimpsed the figure. Rohane joined her. When she saw what her queen was looking at, she gasped.

"Who's behind this, Blaire?"

Blaire grabbed a torch and held it close to a symbol written in red. Beneath a dagger and a water droplet representing purity were the words "The Order has risen."

Rohane touched a finger to wet stone. "Blood." Her tone shrilled. "This is treason." Outraged, she glanced down the passage where the figure had disappeared.

Body rigid, Blaire stared at the symbol. Torchlight struck her pale hair. Her hair was like a silver cloud about her coldly perfect face.

"There have been others." Blaire shivered. "Symbols like this or sometimes just words. 'The Order is coming. The Order watches. All power to Quisnaf.'"

"What? First someone looses an arrow at you, and now this. When did it start?"

"Soon after you left for Telor. I've tried to keep it quiet." Blaire tongued her lips. "Had the signs covered. There's enough tension as it is."

"Because of the new laws you've introduced? The changes?"

The Regenta shrugged. "Many believe my reforms weaken Quisnaf. They don't understand." She fisted her hands. "We are formidable enough, strong enough to show compassion, to bend a little. We have no need to be cruel, and many of our rules—archaic rules—*are* cruel."

"They will accept change in time."

"Unity. Duty. Vigilance." Blaire shook her head. "The bywords of Quisnaf. Three words meant to resonate deep within a Quisnaf woman's soul."

Rohane nodded. The words were meant to rally sagging shoulders and wills, to enflame minds and spirits like drumbeats before battle. Yet when Rohane mouthed these words, she felt nothing.

"Why these words?" she muttered. "Why didn't the first council choose strength or loyalty or justice as their call? Valour. Defiance. Humility." She paused. "Vengeance."

"Sometimes I think Quisnaf is built on vengeance," Blaire said. "Because that is what simmers beneath our order. Beneath our stringent, defined roles and expectations. Beneath our centuries-old hierarchy." She lifted her eyes to the bloody words. "Sometimes I want to rail against that hierarchy and my place in it."

"But you will not."

Blaire smiled bitterly. "I will not. Nor will you. Both of us are too well trained. Such thoughts are idle and foolish, a dream that exists only beyond the harsh realities of our life." She touched Rohane's arm. "You were making your way to the council chamber? Walk with me."

They strode on together. Blaire seemed lost in thought. Rohane, though, glanced over her shoulder, thinking she heard a whisper. Yet beneath the tap of their footsteps, only a heavy silence cloaked the torch-lit passage.

When Rohane paused for a third time, Blaire asked, "What do you hear?"

"An echo of the past." The caverns of Quisnaf groaned and creaked with tradition. The City of Caves was nothing if not its history, its rules, and its disciplines. Its symbols. Its dictums.

Blaire's gaze stole back along the passage. "I hear an echo of my mother's voice. 'Do not forget, Blaire, power requires discipline. Without discipline, without structure, without law, there can be no Quisnaf, Blaire.'"

Rohane laughed. "'You are born to duty, Blaire.' I heard her say that more than once. 'You must seize it as you might a sword.'"

"What are we if not dutiful, Blaire? Blah, blah, blah." The Regenta's hands curled about the hilt of her belted blade. "I wish my mother's ghost stirred, Rohane, so I could explain why the law must change. But there is no one there. Only my conscience, too well disciplined by a mother who knew only what was, what must be, and not what might be."

"Blaire." Rohane faced her. "The Order. That's serious. The last time the Order stirred, centuries ago, it was a portent of rebellion.

This is a direct challenge to you, to the council. Who? Who would dare do this?"

Again, Blaire shrugged.

Rohane seized a breath. "I know you don't want to hear it, but would *she*?"

"No."

"Blaire—"

"No." Blaire's tone was as cold and unbendable as iron. "Not her. For all that sits between us, she would never raise a hand against me."

"You can't know that. She's ruthless. Powerful. And she hates you."

"We were friends. Once. That still means something." Blaire began to walk on, shoulders up. Rohane sighed then followed.

Outside the council chambers, guards dipped their heads and swung open huge bronzed doors. Blaire bent her head to whisper to one, pointing back. The guard nodded and took off down the passage.

Rohane strode into the chamber after Blaire. The Regenta's leather sandals squeaked across the mosaic floor. A menagerie of scents wafted in the air. The beeswax candles, smoke from lamps, the frankincense, and rose perfumes the waiting women wore were all pleasant enough.

At Blaire's appearance, voices hushed. A knot of women broke apart. Samantha nodded at Rohane.

The high priestess Sorcha swept Blaire a low bow. "Regenta." Her slate eyes flickered to the door. "Where is your guard?"

"I do not like eyes upon me everywhere."

"You shall like death less," Sorcha snapped. "You may think the Order subdued, but its acolytes merely retreated to the shadows, awaiting their chance to strike."

"There is another sign in the passage just now."

"What?" Sorcha slid her hands to her hips. "They grow more daring."

"I am not afraid."

"Then I am afraid for you," Sorcha said, her expression grave. She turned away.

"Dear Sorcha," Blaire said softly to Rohane. "Always so fierce. Another who serves the goddess without a blink of doubt."

Rohane cast a gaze about the pillared chamber carved by slaves into the very heart of the mountain. It was a functional room, unlike many in Quisnaf that were beautiful and elegant with soft wall hangings and rugs. A martial state that valued beautiful things, lovely possessions was a contradiction, surely. A warrior might be commended for her swinging blonde hair as well as her valour.

Beauty and strength thrived together. No one questioned it because that was how it always had been. How it would remain.

A sweating guardswoman ran in. Seeing Blaire, her expression softened to relief. "My queen." The young woman dropped to one knee, still breathing hard.

Blaire waved the guard up. "It's very childish to delight in eluding my personal guards," she confided to Rohane. "Another failing, no doubt, as my mother might say. To be corrected, along with all my other failings."

She took her seat at a long wooden table. Chairs scraped on tiles as the most powerful women of Quisnaf sat around her. Powerful, sharp-witted, cunning, and wellborn—those were the hallmarks of the members of the Quisnaf council. Rohane hoped never to join them.

She put her back to the wall, watching how the Regenta carefully did not look at the one empty chair. Rohane, though, winced. That chair represented betrayal. It represented what Blaire had valued and lost—friendship, love, and hope. If she could not have those things, Blaire had once declared, then she must find something to take their place. Duty. Achievement. Control.

Blaire clasped her hands on the table. A woman moved silently between the councillors, pouring wine. When the woman had left the chamber, Blaire leaned forward. "It is a fateful day."

"Praise the goddess." Sorcha carved a sign in the air.

"He is at last taken and within our walls," an older councillor called Aine said.

An excited murmur rose up. Some councillors nodded.

Thoughtful, Blaire tapped her fingers on the table. "He eluded the goddess for too long. Centuries. But she shall have him. The blood keepers will complete the charts."

"Give him to me."

A woman appeared in the doorway. Her voice was harsh and rasping, almost a hiss. Faces turned. To Rohane, it was as if the room leeched of colour and light.

The high sorceress Sisilia boldly crossed the threshold with the same vigour as she stalked the threshold to the otherworld. Her pale eyes were ghosted with the unknown. Cheeks hollowed by sleeplessness accented stark bones in a face that was too young for one so powerful. Dark stains marred a mud-coloured gown that brushed her bare feet. A dishevelled riot of thick auburn hair tumbled onto a black cloak carelessly swinging from bony shoulders.

Sisilia swept the councillors a gaze that both passed over them unseeing but also pierced like steel to hearts. Gooseflesh rose on Rohane's arms, her instinctive recoil in the face of the otherworld. She guessed Sisilia had sought a trance the night before, a deep probing into the Enarae. The mystery of the Enarae still clung to her like perfume.

"Such power in true Caelan blood." Sisilia spread her arms in triumph. "It is the final ingredient, a crucial ingredient. At last, I will clearly see the menace I only glimpse darkly in my visions. That threat that bears down upon us will become known. You must not deny me. You cannot."

"Do not forget, sorceress." Aine poked a finger at Sisilia. "Our warrior bloodlines remain incomplete. This man has many uses. The blood keepers must do their work."

Sisilia waved that aside with an impatient gesture. "I need his blood. All of it. It is vital. This man is immortal. He has blood to spare."

Blaire rose slowly. "You will have to be a little patient. Aine is right. The Telorian is a valuable sire, long sought by our blood keepers."

Sisilia's eyes smouldered. "Do you think me careless of the blood keepers' needs? They must do as they will with his body, but I will have his blood. You will not stop me."

She wheeled and departed, her long cape flapping.

A silence descended, taut and tense. As if seeking control, Blaire knuckled the table.

"Wretched woman," Samantha muttered. "Who does she think she is?"

"She makes a bad enemy," Sorcha counselled. "Perhaps it is best to accede to her wishes, Blaire."

"No," Blaire said bluntly. "The blood keepers have priority. They shall have this man." She half turned to Rohane. "The Telorian, we shall examine tomorrow. Tonight, explain to me about the other man. Why did we retrieve him?"

"The woman we suspect is Roaran's daughter carried this man to a ruin in the forest. He's clearly important to her. A friend, perhaps. Even a lover."

"He was badly injured," Samantha said. "Close to death."

"Roaran's daughter," Blaire muttered. "Is it possible?"

"Roaran deceived us," Samantha said. "If he has a daughter—"

"Then she belongs to us," Blaire said.

Rohane nodded. "If this man we brought from Telor is a man she values, then we can use him to draw Roaran's daughter to Quisnaf."

"She will come," Blaire said. "It is fated, after all."

GENYA

The sound of shattering glass woke her. Genya sprang from her bed. *What was that?*

Moonlight bled into the castle bedchamber through chinks in the shutters. The cold sank down into her, and she shivered as she listened hard.

A faint noise came to her—the rustle of cloth then a muffled cry and panting. It came from Alecc's room, just across the passage.

Genya tore to the door and outside into the corridor, caring little that she wore only a thin shift. Her bare feet scuffed the cool stone. She burst through Alecc's door then gasped.

He was on the bed, back to the mattress. A figure on top of him pinned him down, a knife pointed at Alecc's breast. Trying desperately to fight his attacker, Alecc pushed against the ghoul's arms to keep the blade away.

For one single moment, Genya stared, frozen with shock. Then, with a hiss, she leapt at the ghoul, knocking him off the bed and onto the floor. The ghoul landed with a thud. But before Genya could seize him, he rolled to his feet, still brandishing the knife. Moonlight glinted on the wicked edge.

Genya flung herself off the bed at Alecc's attacker. The ghoul swiped at her with the knife. The blade cut her arm, but the pain did not stop her. She grabbed the ghoul about the waist and threw him down. As he hit the ground, his breath whooshed out. At once, Genya dropped onto him, her knee to his hips, her hands about the ghoul's throat, squeezing, squeezing, squeezing.

The ghoul dropped the knife and grabbed her arms, trying to force her off. He was wheezing, struggling for air. Genya tightened her grip. The ghoul's frantic pulse fluttered beneath her fingertips. Still, she squeezed. A shocking burst of pleasure raced through her, an exhilaration, a dark satisfaction. It was as if all that had happened to her, her unspoken anger at Val, her guilt, was knotted inside, suddenly demanding violent release.

The ghoul fought her hard, twisting his body, heaving against her weight on him, kicking and squirming. At last, the strength in his thrashing subsided. His hands fell away. An ugly gasp oozed from his mouth then a choking sound. His body jerked once. Then he lay still, the pulse in his throat dying away.

Still Genya throttled him, not wanting him to be dead. Not yet.

A hand fell on his shoulder. "He's dead, Genya," Alecc said gently. "Dead."

She blinked, taking in the words. Then she drew back her hands and rose off the ghoul, startled by the strength of her anger, her need for brutal savagery. Embarrassment flooded her. She was ashamed Alecc had seen her like this: out of control, her ghoul side to the fore.

"Sorry," she muttered. "Sorry."

"You have nothing to be sorry about." Alecc sat on the edge of the bed. "You saved my life."

"Maybe," Genya said. "You were holding your own."

Alecc shook his head. "He was stronger than me."

Genya dragged her fingers through her sleep-tousled hair. Her gaze fell on shattered glass on the floor near the bed and the broken mirror on the table.

Alecc followed her gaze. "My elbow caught the glass in the struggle."

The door flung back. Nicky ran in, Cadan a step behind. They drew up sharply, staring from Alecc and Genya to the dead ghoul.

"Good gods," Nicky muttered. "What happened here? Are you both all right?"

"We're safe," Alecc said. "Thanks to Genya."

Nicky raised a brow.

"The ghoul climbed in through the window," Alecc said. "I woke to find him crouched over me, ready to stab me with a knife."

Cadan dropped to his knees and began to search the dead ghoul's pockets. He drew forth a rolled parchment. Frowning, he smoothed it flat and read.

"This is the price of treachery. Bend the knee, or the rest of you will follow the Cahirean brat to the grave." Cadan winced. "It's signed Gendrick Caelan."

Nicky made a sound of disbelief. "That snake. So now he sends ghouls after us. I'm guessing we were supposed to find that paper pinned to your dead body, Alecc."

Alecc offered a grim smile. "Gendrick must be desperate."

"He formed an alliance with Archanin. It seems that alliance survived Archanin's death," Cadan muttered.

Genya clamped her palm over her knife wound in her arm. Blood trickled between her fingers.

Nicky took a step towards her. "Genya, girl. You're hurt."

"It's nothing." She nudged the dead ghoul with her boot. "That Gendrick should send an assassin means he's scared. That's good. He knows we're coming for him."

"Not yet," Alecc said, stroking thin bristle on his chin.

Genya huffed impatiently. "Then when? Why do we wait?"

"I need you to go to Tide's End, Genya." Alecc yawned. "I've secretly sent word to my mother. She's expecting you, though I have not said who you are." He yawned again. "It's nearly dawn. Let's meet after breakfast in the great hall. I'll tell you all my plans then."

VAL ARQUES

He woke in darkness, sprawled awkwardly on cushions, with no idea how long he had slept. Val fumbled for a flint and lit the candle. Even then, he could not tell the hour.

Scooping up a jug, he gulped water, careless of how it spilled down his chin. The room was hot despite a draft from the vent. His belly rumbled. He went to the door and banged on its metal. "Rohane?"

An unfamiliar voice snapped, "Be silent."

"Where's Rohane?"

A grate in the door slid open. A woman's face appeared. "Be silent and calm. No questions."

Calm. Everyone in Quisnaf kept telling him to be calm. Irritated, Val returned to the cushions. Rohane's absence unsettled him. He had become accustomed to her presence, even to her direction. Without her, he was adrift.

Inwardly, he scoffed at his foolishness. Nothing had changed just because a stranger guarded his door. He was still locked in a tiny room. Hungry. Alone. Ignorant about his fate.

He leaned back against the cushions, head buried in his hands. At length, with nothing to do and nowhere to move, he slept again.

The door's scrape woke him. Val rose to his elbows as Rohane stepped in, carrying a lantern. She wore a dark-blue silk tunic over leather pants, her feet sandaled. Her hair was swept into a single ponytail that draped one shoulder.

But for the sword and knife in her belt, her casual appearance might suggest she was about to invite him to take a stroll with her by the river. A strange longing swept through Val. Surely he didn't really wish to wander by the river with this prickly warrior? No, it must be a yearning to be free, a yearning for Telor.

"You're awake. Good."

"Awake and very hungry." He looked for someone carrying food. Instead, there was a shape on the floor. Something small sat in the shadows at Rohane's heels.

Rohane sighed. "I'm sorry. Keeping you just a little hungry is intentional. Quickly now, get ready. It's dusk. The council expects you."

"Dusk?" Val frowned at the shape, wondering if it was a cat. Did they even have cats in Quisnaf? "You mean I've slept all night and all day?"

"Close to it."

The shape moved into the light. A fox on a lead looked balefully at him. Rohane scooped up the lead's end. "Good girl."

Val stared. "What is that?"

"A fox."

"I can see that. Why is it on a lead?"

"She's mine," Rohane said.

"A pet?"

The fox sat down at Rohane's feet and scratched at its red fur. It was a handsome creature with a white-tipped tail and black-tipped ears.

"More than that." She bent to stroke the fox then straightened and passed Val a comb.

Val's fingers strayed to his knotted hair. "You don't like the unkempt look? What about the stubble?" It gave him a slightly dishevelled, dangerous appearance. A tiny rebellion this, reminding his captors he was not tame.

"The stubble can stay. It's attractive. The ruffled hair, though, makes you look like a sweet child just woken from tender dreams. Oh, not the look you're intending?" She offered him a wide-eyed innocent look as he hastily dragged the comb through his tangled locks.

Rohane grinned. "You're shockingly easy to manipulate."

Val started to laugh until she reached for a blindfold. His spine stiffened in outrage. He muttered, "Do I have a choice?"

"Always. You could refuse. When I call more guards, you could struggle. You may even break free. Run."

"Then what?"

"I suppose we'd hunt you. Bring you back. All rather tiresome, really."

"Ha. You could send your fox after me."

"She's particular. She doesn't go after strange men."

At Rohane's gesture, Val pulled on the boots and rose. Rohane tied the blindfold about his eyes and led him outside into what he guessed was a passage. The fox padded after them, its paws soft. Smoke from wall torches and the earthy odour of wet rock prickled Val's nostrils.

"Aren't foxes very shy?" he mused.

"Yes. But she doesn't seem to be wary of you."

The passage led to another then another after that, until Rohane bid him stop.

"Greetings, Captain," a woman said. "No trouble here?"

"None."

Doors creaked open. Rohane guided him into what must be another chamber. His boots sank into thick rugs. Beeswax from candles overpowered the faintest aroma of cinnamon. His shoulder brushed a pillar's rough stone.

"This way." Rohane led him deeper into the room. From the sounds of squeaking boots and a sword rattling in a scabbard, he guessed someone followed.

Rohane bid him sit upon a tall-backed chair. Different hands grabbed him and lashed his wrists to the arms.

"What's happening?" At his powerlessness, at the constant prodding and poking, Val's unease flared. He hated that he couldn't see who was touching him and binding him.

"Hush." Rohane sounded close. "You'll be left quietly for a time. Do not be alarmed."

"I am alarmed." Instinctively, Val struggled until his wrists ached.

"This is a time permitted for reflection. You must think how you will answer questions put to you, Telorian." An undercurrent of urgency, even warning, darkened her tone. "Be still. Be calm. Be silent. Reflect on this."

"I'm still alarmed," he muttered.

Rohane walked away, the fox padding after her. The chamber emptied, footsteps fading until the door banged. A hollow silence descended.

The emptiness magnified the spit and hiss of candles. Their cloying scent choked him. The chamber, too still, too quiet, closed in about him. He twisted his hands against the ropes and rocked the chair, but it was fastened to the floor. Then he shouted at the walls, bellowing in frustration and helplessness.

For a long while, he yelled in that oppressive room, until his panic collapsed beneath exhaustion. Time was measured only in his quick breaths. When he grew thirsty, no one was there to bring him water. No one came to bandage his bleeding wrists. No moody, prickly Rohane came to laugh off his fears.

The doors thudded open. Val's head shot up.

After the quiet, the flurry of activity brought with it a cacophony of noise. Heels tapped stone. Cloth swished. Voices rumbled. Chairs being drawn out scraped on the stone floor.

"Who's there?" Val hissed. "What do you want with me?"

"Be still. Be calm. Be silent."

"Why should I? Why am I bound? Take off this cursed

blindfold." The ropes slid against his torn skin, slick with blood.

A smattering of conversations reached him, three or four different voices.

"There can be no doubt. Roaran would not make a mistake. This is the man."

"Now I've seen him, I advise caution," another voice said.

"You would punish him for his beauty?"

"No, no. I mean he's clearly a bladesman. Too powerful. The stories... Best to be careful... Perhaps reconsider who guards him?"

"Do you mean what I think you mean?"

"There is already a bond, Regenta." Val recognised Samantha's voice. "He seems to like her."

"Perhaps. Let me consider it." Someone clapped their hands. "Huntress. Free him. Let us look at our prize."

Val caught the fresh scent of Rohane's washed hair as she leaned to release the ropes.

"He should be restrained," a new voice said.

The blindfold came off in time for Val to see Persia push into the room ahead of a small group of warriors.

Persia wore a heavy sword as elegantly as she did a swirling silk cloak over a tunic that hung just above her knees. She, too, had exchanged boots for sandals. He supposed others might think her pale hair and ice-clear eyes striking, but he found her repellent.

The battale captain compressed her lips. "He caused trouble on the ship."

Papers rustled. Val tore his gaze from Persia to a raised dais before him. Five women sat behind a long table. Samantha offered him an encouraging smile. At her side sat a woman of middle years with short-cropped brown hair and a stern expression. The younger woman at her side looked less forbidding. She possessed plump cheeks and dancing eyes the colour of blackberries.

"What trouble?" she asked.

Val hardly heard her. His gaze had fallen upon the woman in

the centre. He stared with undisguised interest.

She was far from a girl, perhaps about thirty, and outrageously lovely, with the cold perfection of chiselled stone. High cheeks crafted an elegant face. Black brows framed dark-blue, almost-purple eyes. Her ashen hair fell straight and long. But there was a coldness to her beauty that did not attract him. *Unlike Rohane's warmth.*

The thought startled him. No, surely not. He wasn't even sure he always liked his grumpy escort.

Frowning, the blonde woman stared at the parchment. "Persia reports the guest set a captive free and allowed other prisoners to escape—though they were caught and punished."

She flicked through papers. "Our retrieval captain makes no mention of this in her report."

Accusing eyes fell on Rohane at Val's shoulder. She bristled. "The councillor spoke with him. The matter was dealt with. Only at the last did he cause real trouble. I expected it and dealt with it."

"I see."

Persia glared at Rohane. "He dived overboard in a bid to escape. It would not have happened if Rohane had done as I ordered and restrained him. After he freed that prisoner, I told her to put him in chains and discipline him with leather across his shoulders."

Blaire shuddered. "Oh, by Cyrah, no. After all this trouble?" Her cool gaze swept over him. It was as tangible as a caress. "Are you ready to answer to this council?"

Val hunched his shoulders. "A lord of Telor answers to no one but his king."

An angry stir snaked about the chamber. A guard stepped in to deliver a stinging slap. Val ground his teeth into a snarl. A slap demeaned a warrior the way a blow from a fist did not.

"Stop. I will not have this." Blaire stormed to her feet. "We are patient with guests." She flicked a hand to banish the guard to Persia's corner.

Once more, her gaze fell on him. There was intelligence in her eyes but little warmth. He guessed her wit cut as sharply as her cheekbones. "Will you answer to this council?"

Val would not hold his tongue. "Who is this council? Or are you all to remain nameless? Shall I address you only as councillor one or two or three?"

The plump-cheeked woman laughed merrily. Her hand fell on Samantha's. "Well, you said he had a mouth on him."

"I do not find arrogance in a man amusing," said the brown-haired councillor. She glared, her mouth pinched and her expression dour.

"What prince is not arrogant, Aine? He will learn," Samantha soothed. "After so many years, surely it's worth taking the time to win such a man gently?"

Blaire pressed her palms into the table and leaned towards Val. "Samantha is right. You will learn. Heed this first lesson now. You speak only when asked a question. And if questioned, you must answer. The word of the Quisnaf council is absolute. Remember that."

She sat down. "As to how to address this council, 'councillor' will do nicely for my companions. However, as a gesture of goodwill, I will satisfy your curiosity with our names."

"Why?" Aine sniffed. "You do not answer to a slave. Let it be."

"I answer to whom I choose."

Aine looked down, scowling. "You are Regenta, Blaire. You must do as you like."

Regenta. Val reassessed the woman. She seemed young to lead her people.

Blaire raised her voice. "I am Blaire, daughter of Bogdanza, and Regenta of Quisnaf. Samantha, you know. To my right is Aine." She swept a hand at the brown-haired woman. "Kenna." She gestured to the woman with plump cheeks. "And last, Sybil."

An older woman offered a cold stare.

"The council numbers eight. High Priestess Sorcha is at the temple of Cyrah—"

"Not his business," Aine broke in angrily. Val already disliked her.

"Be gentle, my good Aine," Samantha soothed. "He is alone, among strangers, uncertain of his fate. Imagine how you might feel. We are strong enough to be generous and show a little compassion."

"And patience," Blaire said.

"I care only that this man bends an obviously stiff neck and does as he is told," Aine muttered. "Persia has told me everything that happened on the ship. *Everything.* He must learn his place."

Val could not listen to this. "And what place is that?" He surged to his feet. "I was promised fair treatment. But I am chained and blindfolded, prodded, forced to go this way and that without explanation."

A hiss coiled about the room. Kenna whispered behind her hand to Samantha.

Aine leaned forward. "Will someone stop his mouth?"

"Stay where you are," Blaire commanded as guards rushed to do Aine's will. They drew up at her sharp gesture then retreated to the door.

Amused, Blaire raised an eyebrow at Val. "An Isles prince to the bone. Stubborn. Prideful."

Val swept her a casual bow. "I am also wilful and disobedient."

The Regenta laughed.

"Such disrespect." Sybil shook her head. "You must deal with him harshly, Blaire."

Blaire frowned with displeasure. Her glare projected her will like a thunderous wave. Despite her beauty, Val recognised the woman's strength.

"You all seem to forget we do not deal with a petulant Wardorian prince today. We do not even question a fierce Circle Kingdom mercenary. This is a man of Caelan's blood, a warrior whom our texts record won the infamous contest of swords in Wardour so many centuries ago. We sought this man because of the very qualities that seem to trouble some of you. Did you expect him to fall to his knees? I would be disappointed if he did."

Aine sneered. "There are rules. Quisnaf lives by its rules, its traditions."

At a barely audible noise, Val glanced at the shadows, his scalp prickling. Someone had entered and now watched. Their gaze fell over his skin like a spiderweb. He shivered.

"It does not break our laws to be patient," Blaire said. "After all, this council achieved what every other could not. This man represents a missing bloodline of immense potential."

Aine dropped sullen eyes. Blaire turned to Val. "You have a complaint, Telorian? That you are chained and taken this way and that—without explanation."

Val nodded. His anger subsided beneath disquiet. Someone was observing from the shadows.

"You will have explanations. But tonight, you must first answer. You have been permitted a period of reflection. Now stand straight. Speak directly. This is important. Someone is here who will judge what you say."

He peered in vain into the darkness at the back of the room.

Blaire paused. "You are called Val Arques Caelan?"

"You know I am," he snapped. "What fool game is this?"

"And you surrendered to us because…?"

"A matter of honour between Roaran Caelan and me." Val glanced again at the shadows. Gooseflesh rose along his arms.

"Look only at me. You will keep your word to Roaran?"

"Yes."

Blaire nodded at a guard. The woman came forward with a goblet and offered it to Val.

"Drink."

"I think not."

"It is wine of the goddess. For a sacred vow. Please. You have my word it will not hurt you."

Val did not trust her. He could not trust any of them. Uneasily, he glanced about at his captors. Reluctantly, he took a sip.

"I ask you now, solemnly, before the goddess, that you give your word not to attempt to escape Quisnaf or leave unless it is my wish."

"I gave my word to Roaran to surrender myself to you," Val said gruffly. "I did not give my word to obey."

Another displeased hiss passed through the chamber. Blaire held up a hand. She sat forward, her body tense, her tone urgent. "I fear you do not understand. If I do not have your oath before the goddess, I must surrender you to the blood keepers."

At those words again, Val shuddered. Whoever—whatever—they were, it sounded like he would be imprisoned if he refused to give his word. Through gritted teeth, he said, "I will not attempt to escape or leave."

Blaire released a breath. A sigh passed between the Quisnaf women in the chamber.

"You understand what we want of you?"

Val hesitated then nodded.

"Yes or no," Blaire said sternly. "We must hear an answer."

Val swallowed. He made sure his voice sounded strong. "Yes."

Blaire nodded slowly, her look dwelling on his face. "Then I shall—*we* shall consider you a guest of Quisnaf. That means we gift you with certain freedoms most men here do not enjoy. Privileges. But disobey or break the rules, and we withdraw these privileges. We will no longer consider you or treat you as a guest. You are warned. But now"—her gaze flickered—"I must ask you something else, Val Arques Caelan."

The air thickened with tension. It was there in every held breath, in the way the councillors drew straighter. Even Rohane stiffened.

"I must ask you," Blaire said, "what you know of the fate of a retrieval captain called Matilda and a warrior called Morgan."

Val swayed slightly. Dread turned over in his gut. He forced himself to meet Blaire's gaze. "What do you want to know?"

"Matilda, Morgan, and Matilda's squire. The last Regenta sent them to the Icelands to bring you here. They did not return. I can only assume they are dead. Did they reach you?"

Val nodded, not certain if he could speak. *Oh, gods, Kaell.* He must keep Kaell out of this.

"And you went with them?"

"I had no choice. They had strange bracelets…"

Blaire nodded distantly. "Unpleasant magic if abused. So the Damadars did not betray us," she murmured. "What happened after you left the Twin Cities? Tell it as you remember."

Val shuddered, remembering months chained to a rock in a dark cavern. Remembering Heath's laughter then the sound of his scream as he fell in the fire cavern. Remembering Myranthe's vicious games that had stripped Val bare.

"We started out from the city. But at once, we found Matilda's squire, his throat slit."

"Who killed him?" Persia demanded, clenching her hands. "The Damadars?"

"Matilda believed thieves followed the man from the markets. They stole horses and money."

Blaire frowned. "Matilda usually knew what she was about. And then? Be honest. If you are honest, I can be lenient."

"Without horses, we continued on foot. The journey was long, and when dusk fell, Matilda found cover in a cave." He paused. Now, whatever the cost, he must protect Kaell.

"In the night, I saw my chance to escape and took it. Matilda and Morgan came after me. We fought."

"You killed them?" Blaire's tone was grim with disbelief. "I hoped this was not true. I knew they must be dead, but I hoped it was not you."

"I killed them."

"Murderer!" Persia leapt up, her hands curled like talons. One of her companions pulled her back. But others took up the shout, howling out their anger. Rohane glared at him, her eyes dark with disgust.

"It is not the truth." A voice came from the shadows. Val shivered.

An elderly woman hobbled into the candlelight. She wore a long robe of sackcloth and carried a stick carved with sigils and swirling patterns. A hood shadowed her face.

Voices fell away into an angry silence.

"Speak, truthsayer," Blaire commanded. "You listened to his words. Tell us."

The woman shuffled to Val. The tip of her head reached only to his breast, but power rippled from her like waves. "His words are true until the last. He does intend to keep his word to Roaran. He does intend to do what we desire of him. He suspects what that is but has not quite faced it in its entirety."

"Yes, yes," Blaire prompted. "And my warriors? Did he kill them?"

"He did not," the truthsayer pronounced. "It is true about finding the dead squire. And indeed, Matilda did make camp in the caves."

She paused. Magic and danger swirled in fragrant air. Val recoiled a step.

"Then." The truthsayer jabbed a gnarled finger at Val. "Then he lies. He did not kill them, not Matilda, not Morgan. Another came in the night."

"Why lie?" Blaire spread her hands in confusion. "Why invite this council's displeasure? I was about to strip him of his rights as guest, to allow harsh treatment."

"He is protecting someone. He knows who came in the night, though I cannot say if they killed Matilda and Morgan."

"It must be someone close to him. To risk punishment for another…"

"He left them a knife," Val said. "To free themselves. He left them alive."

"Who?"

Val dropped his head. He would say no more.

Persia pressed forward. "Regenta, I will have the name from

him. I can make any man talk, no matter how stubborn."

The hooded woman whipped up a hand. Persia shuddered back, lips pressed tightly.

"You will bring him to me," the truthsayer said. "Then I will bring you the name."

"When?" Blaire snapped.

"Tomorrow." The truthsayer sighed. "I am too weary tonight. To sift truth takes too much out of me these days. Bring him tomorrow."

She turned and hobbled towards the door, thumping her stick like a third leg. When the door clunked behind her, the tension snapped. Someone laughed. Conversations broke out.

Val's shoulders tightened with dread. He would not give up Kaell. No matter if they tortured him. Kaell had fought with Morgan, but Val could not believe Kaell would have hurt either woman. It wasn't in the young man Val had raised to kill like that.

Blaire stepped off the dais. She walked to Val and grasped his jaw. "Look at me."

He lifted his head. She was as gloriously lovely as a frosty morning in the Mountains. But anger enflamed her eyes with a cold blue flame.

"I do not appreciate lies. You will not lie to me again. Do you understand?" Without waiting for an answer, she dropped his jaw and faced Rohane. "I sense a bond between you."

Rohane frowned. "Not as you think…"

"Silence, Captain. I am decided. You will take charge of this man."

Voices rippled in surprise. Women whispered to their companions.

Rohane huffed. "My part is done. I wish to return to my duties as a huntress. I am ready to retrieve my next target."

"You are relieved of that duty. Branwyn will take on your next assignment. It is more important to keep watch on him." Blaire gestured sharply. "No. Do not argue. This is my command. You will obey."

Rohane scowled at Val as though this were his fault. "As you wish."

"I am pleased you are so reasonable," Blaire said drily. "I am told you trained as a guardian. You once acted in this role before."

"I was not suited to the role, Regenta. I asked to return to my other duties."

"Nevertheless. Take him to Mairin. Then, tomorrow, the truthsayer will question him."

"Who's Mairin?" Val whispered.

"None of your business," his reluctant guardian snapped.

❧

Rohane strode ahead at a fast pace, fists clenched at her side, her sword slapping her thigh.

"Am I that bad?"

She didn't break step. "I'm not a nursemaid. I am a warrior. I fought for years in the battales to earn my rank as captain." She laughed drily. "You can hardly understand."

"Why not? I'm nothing if not a soldier. What do you think I am?"

"I know what you are. I've read the texts."

"Oh, texts." That sparked his curiosity. It hadn't occurred to him they kept "texts" about him. "Are there lots of texts?"

"It is a whole book." Rohane flapped an impatient hand. "Stories and reports collected over the centuries. Everything the Quisnaf learned. The name of your mother. Her mother. Her mother's mother. What is known of your father's family, too. I just read the bits that concerned my task—delivering you to the council."

"Did your texts say I'm stubborn?"

"Branwyn had much to say about your temperament. I think the word was *tricky*. Violent. Trouble."

Val's shoulders tightened. "I don't see why I should help someone take me prisoner."

"I was only interested in anything about how you might fight, your training as a warrior. Of course, there are gaps in our knowledge. For it seems you managed to disappear a good few centuries ago."

"It was lovely and quiet." Val gave an exaggerated sigh.

"Then the Quisnaf received word you called yourself Vraymorg and hid in the mountains."

"I hardly hid. It was more… banishment." Val laughed coldly. "I know Rozenn sent word to the Quisnaf. I always thought she liked me."

"If women who like you betray you, then you clearly have a way with women." Rohane drew up with a frown. For a moment, she peered about. "Yes, back this way. It is a while since I had cause to come here."

"Who's Mairin? What is here?" He peered about, relieved to have left the council chamber.

Rohane walked on. "We're deep in the seers' quarters. Only sorceresses or seers or whatever else unworldly lurks here. I'd watch out if I were you."

"Just so long as spiders don't lurk and I walk into their sticky webs. I hate that. Where were we before?"

"Warriors' caverns. One day, if you're good, I'll show you the chamber where the Quisnaf kept Roaran Caelan. The sorceress who taught him magic kept him close." Rohane laughed. "Close and behind a locked door. Roaran was an unwilling guest."

"That sounds like an interesting story."

"Be good, and I might know someone who can tell you more."

"What's good?"

"Whatever you're not. You might fool Blaire, but I know just how wicked you really are."

"What a low opinion you have of me."

She turned into another tunnel cut into the rock, long and sloping downwards. In places, it was braced with wood or brick pillars. Darkness loomed ahead. Rohane snatched a torch from the wall and headed into it. Val followed, grinning. She must leap recklessly into battle the same way she stalked these shadowy tunnels.

His new guardian reached a door flanked by two Quisnaf sentries. They flicked Val glances. He had become too familiar with that look: suspicion tinged with a vague sort of carnal interest as though he were a slave on the auction block.

"We're expected."

"Indeed, guardian," a sentry said.

She bristled. "Don't call me that. This is temporary."

The guards grinned and stepped aside. But before Rohane could knock, someone inside threw back the door.

Torchlight fell upon a young woman with gleaming hair the colour of soot and black, black eyes. She looked out of place among her blonde sisters. Val wondered at her heritage. A few days in this cursed place, he had become as obsessed with bloodlines as the Quisnaf.

"Ronnie." The girl ushered them inside. "Quickly, now. I do not have all night." She peered into the passage. "Where's Roxy Foxy?"

"Sleeping on my bed," Rohane said.

Val raised a brow. "Roxy Foxy?"

Rohane screwed up her face. "She's called Florentine."

"Florry Foxy," Val said, following Rohane into a large, rock-walled room. Dried herbs and roots strung in bunches from roof beams. Oddly shaped pots and vials filled shelves. The musty scent of hemlock clashed with the rose and lavender aromas of healing balms and lotions.

"You must be Mairin," he said. "From the bottles and things, you're a healer."

The dark-haired girl flicked him a curiously impersonal glance. "What is it to you?" She went to a table and considered scrolled papers. "Does he know what I am bid do?"

Rohane slid Val a look. "No."

"That's unfortunate. Will he run?"

"Oh, gods, this again?" Val huffed out a breath. "I am right here. And I'm not deaf."

"He understands our tongue. You can speak to him."

"I think not. I'm asking you. Will he run? Quickly now. I can call the guards to restrain him."

Rohane hesitated. "No. It will be all right."

"Just as well." The woman bent over scrolls, her finger following lines. "The others were chained. He should be chained."

Rohane sighed. She took a rolled parchment from her pocket and handed it to Mairin. "He's a guest."

Mairin's gaze sharpened. "Really? That is vaguely interesting." She snatched the paper, straightened it with her palm, and read. After a moment, she frowned. "Not too intrusive? Blaire cannot be serious."

"Intrusive in what way?" Val asked. He turned to Rohane. "She's going to torture me? Some guardian you are."

Mairin moved from behind the table. "Remove your shirt and lie on the bench."

"She *is* going to torture me."

Rohane whirled. "Don't be stupid. She's going to make sure you are not flawed."

"Oh, is that all?"

"It's nothing," Rohane muttered. "Take your shirt off. You can just stand there. Let's just get this done."

Panic tightened Val's throat. He tried to breathe through it, but a memory snapped of the room in the Icelands where Velleran's buyers had hidden behind a screen and viewed the "merchandise." Him. Reluctantly, he unlaced his tunic and pulled it over his head.

Rohane studied her knife. Mairin, though, swept him with another impersonal, analytical gaze. She circled, at times prodding and poking. "Good muscle tone, not only in the shoulders but the legs and torso. A warrior's build. Scars but not too disfiguring. Very well. That will do."

Rohane looked up sharply. "That's it?"

"Blaire says not intrusive."

Val scooped up his tunic. Surprised, he followed Rohane outside.

"The baths, I think," she said. "Then I'll send food to your room. You need to sleep."

DANNON

Murky dreams fell away to wakefulness. His head rested on a pillow upon a soft bed. A candle on a nearby table guttered. Dannon lit a new one, placed it in the holder, and looked about. Stone. That was the first impression. Windowless stone above him encircled him like a tomb. Panic tore through him. He snatched a slow breath. *Just a room.*

He padded to the door over a rug that was warm and soft beneath his toes. Other rugs clung to the walls, a shield against the chill and the bleakness of endless rock.

The door had no latch or knob, no way of opening it from his side. Cold fear prickled at the back of his neck. This was what he'd feared when he'd first learnt he was aboard a Quisnaf ship—that he was indeed a prisoner.

Wandering back to the bed, Dannon sank onto the edge, hands about his drawn-up knees, considering his situation. So this was Quisnaf. Except for the locked door, the room was hardly a cell. It was furnished with wooden chests, tables, and a few stools. The bed was comfortable. He had light, a jug of water, a bucket for his needs, and a bowl of water and cloth for washing.

It appeared they did not intend to treat him unkindly. True, he still wore a nightshirt, unsuitable for anyone bent on escape. *And that door...* It suggested control, that he was held subject to someone else's will.

Hearing footsteps outside, he lifted his head. A latch rose, then the door scraped inward. Samantha stepped inside, carrying a rolled parchment. A woman armed with a sword and a dagger followed her and set a tray upon a table. It held a silver jug and silver goblets. The armed woman pulled the door shut as she left.

"I'm guarded?"

Ignoring his question, Samantha waved a hand at a stool. "May I sit?"

Dannon frowned, surprised she sought his permission. "Ah, please." He pulled up a stool opposite.

"Will you have wine?"

When he nodded, she filled the goblets and passed him one.

"So, we're in Quisnaf?" Dannon laughed harshly. "I really don't remember how I got here. Poppy juice or some potion in my drink?"

Samantha winced. "We thought it might be easier."

"For me?"

"I would like to say yes, but it was also easier for us. We had other captives to concern us."

"Other captives." He thought about the words. "Then that's what I am?" Dannon squeezed his hand into a fist. "No, I can't accept that. I am grateful, truly grateful, for your care. I know I would be dead without Elena's tending. However, I only wish to return home."

"No." Samantha's tone was resolute, offering no bargaining.

He arched a brow. "No?" A slow-burning anger kindled within him. "You said the fight goes on. The ghouls must be stopped. They..." *She...* "They need me. Especially if Roaran is dead."

"No."

He clutched the edge of his nightshirt in his curled hand. "Why not?"

"You are our guest."

"*Guest.*" Dannon's fury flared up. He surged to his feet. "That's a polite word for captive. By what right do you hold me? How did I offend you? Is there some grudge you bear me? I know there are things I've done, things I'm ashamed of. Others have cause to hate me. But I do not remember wronging the Quisnaf."

"We hold no grudge against you, Cahirean."

"So I'm free to leave?"

"No."

Dannon grunted in exasperation. "What then?" he shouted. "I don't understand."

"Calm yourself," Samantha said. "I did not expect this to be easy for you. But it is senseless to do anything but accept your situation."

"I just want to know why I'm here."

She waved a hand at the stool, but Dannon did not move. Then he growled and threw himself down. With furious abandon, he drained his cup. Samantha filled it with more wine.

"Maybe we can start with who you are?"

"Maybe we could. I am what you might call an elder of Quisnaf."

"And do you have a special role?"

"I am officially titled Protector of Men."

A bitter laugh ground up his throat. "Oh, that says it all."

"Oh?" Samantha leaned forward. "How?"

"Protector sounds benevolent but is in fact patronising. A man should not need protecting. It degrades, dehumanises, says a man can't make his own decisions or be responsible for himself. Like a child."

Samantha sat back with a pleased smile. It was the sort of smile a teacher might offer a clever student. "You are sharp. I applaud you."

He thumped his glass down onto the table, fighting a useless urge to throw things about. "Like you applaud a dog taught tricks?"

"No, I'm impressed. You cut to the heart of the structure of

Quisnaf society. Well, well. If you think about your own words, it should make it easy for you to adapt."

He drove a hand through the air. "I don't want to adapt. I don't belong here. The fight waits for me in Telor. That is my purpose."

Samantha made a dismissive sound. "The fight will go on without you."

Dannon said nothing, seething silently. Why didn't she understand? He had to return. He was nothing but a warrior. Without that, what was left? A man broken by his wounds. A man without purpose. No one.

Genya. What would she think of this broken man she had so readily invited into her bed? Was she even now searching for him? Maybe once he was no longer there, she wouldn't care. Gods, he had to find a way to return to Telor. *To Genya?* He was fond of her, had found comfort in her bed. But beyond that, he wasn't sure.

Oh, how the gods played with him. Dannon gave another bitter laugh.

Samantha regarded him with raised brows. "That is indeed a strange laugh. Do tell what strange thought brought it on."

"I begin to think the gods have a certain ironic sense of humour," Dannon said.

"How so?"

"You know what I was? A slaver. And now the slaver must grapple with submission."

She sat back, smiling. "I think they call it 'poetic justice.'"

He tried again. "Why am I here?"

Samantha swilled wine, taking her time before replying. "The girl, Genya Caelan."

Dannon stilled then asked warily, "What about her?"

"Roaran's child." She tapped the scroll on her knee. "Perhaps it's easiest to show you. I'm sure that quick mind will leap to its own conclusions." She passed the scroll to him.

"What is this?"

"A contract. It is written in both Quisnaf and Telorian."

Reluctantly, Dannon unfolded the parchment. From her manner, he sensed he would not like what it said. He skipped the Quisnaf words and trailed a finger through Telorian writing. The handwriting seemed familiar. Slowly, what the words meant sank into him.

"No," he muttered. The scroll slipped from his hand to the floor. "That cannot be. He would not."

"Yet it is. Roaran always found sanctuary here." Samantha shrugged. "I suppose he felt accepted in Quisnaf, not judged. We celebrated what he was. To us, he was special, very precious."

Dannon shook his head. "Genya will not accept this. She is... well, she is not only Roaran's daughter. Another man raised her. I see him in her always. His temper, his stubbornness. But his self-assurance, too."

Samantha flashed an unexpected grin. "Oh, stubborn indeed, that one. And a wit as sharp as yours, though his mind turns more in the usual manner for a warrior. Unlike you."

Dannon sat back. The truth shivered through him. "I'm bait to draw Genya to you."

"As I said on the ship, you have value. You are loved."

"You're wrong." Slowly, he got to his feet. "Genya doesn't love me. She has strong feelings, passions, because of what she is. I'm convenient. She makes use of me."

"Do you think that poorly of yourself?"

Dannon stared. His throat knotted. Thickly, he swallowed. Compared to others of Roaran's brotherhood, he was exactly what he'd told Samantha. No one of significant birth. A Varee slaver who'd done things he could not forget or forgive. Only one thing set him apart. But he must stay silent about his mother.

"It doesn't matter. She won't come for me."

Samantha rose and brushed a hand down her gown. "The Quisnaf council thinks she will."

"The Quisnaf council?" He rubbed his eyes wearily. "So much I don't know about this place."

"I'll show you your new home. Not tonight. But soon."

She turned for the door. At her tap on its wood, a slat opened. The guard peered inside then lifted the latch.

"So what now?" Dannon gestured to the room. "I'm confined here?"

"You're not comfortable? The chests contain garments, should you like to dress. Guards will bring food. Bathe? You can do that every day if you so choose. Quisnaf has four public baths and two private ones. Tell me what you need, and I will arrange it. We may have some books in Telorian somewhere."

"My gilded prison, then."

Samantha sighed. "See it how you will." She pulled the door shut at her back.

VAL ARQUES

A fter the gloomy caves, the sight of the valley in daylight the next morning revived Val's spirits. Pausing on steps carved from rock, he let the sun strike his face and sighed with pleasure.

Rohane glanced over her shoulder impatiently. "Never seen the sun before? Is that it?"

"Not for days."

"Telorians." She tapped her head and turned away.

Val followed her down into the lush valley surrounded on both sides by towering rock broken by gaping caverns. Grass bowed in a lazy breeze carrying the perfume of honey. Bees hummed; butterflies bobbed. Amid willowy trees, wildflowers sprouted everywhere: blue forget-me-nots, borage, and violets. Jacarandas carpeted the ground with delicate flakes of purple.

Autumn, it seemed, was little different to summer in Quisnaf. Oddly content, Val exhaled deeply again. The caves might have been dark and strange, but a tranquillity clung to this fragrant valley.

Rohane took a path through the trees. Very soon, Val heard metal clashing on metal, shouts, and stamping feet. In a clearing before them, warriors wearing leather armour trained with swords, exchanging good-natured insults as they parried and weaved from daring cuts and thrusts and wild swipes. Hard-eyed instructors watched on, correcting strokes or footwork.

The scrape of iron and the smell of dust and sweat were all so familiar, his heart ached. In castle wards across the Mountains, training fields churned to dirt beneath many feet enacting the same steps in this fierce dance. What startled him, though, was the sheer number of combatants. By his reckoning, several hundred warriors covered the field.

"Is this just one battale?"

Rohane squinted. "Two, I think. Under different captains. Persia and Johanna from the badges and colours. The two battales we sent to Telor to aid Roaran."

"How many battales are there?"

"Four. And four battale captains. A battale captain has particular power in Quisnaf. We are a martial state, after all."

His gaze fell on a striking woman with a dark sweep of hair. "Who's that?"

"Persia's lieutenant, Marlisa." She grinned. "And I thought from the way you gaped like a stunned boy, it was the fair Blaire who stole your heart. Love at first sneer and all that."

"I'm fickle," Val said. "Love at first sneer, then a different love at second sneer and so on."

Rohane laughed. She led him along the field, through more trees, then up rock stairs to a ledge along the cliff face. Young women dangled their legs over the edge to watch something unfolding below. At the sight of Val and Rohane, they fell silent, their eyes following him.

"They wonder why you're not cloaked," Rohane muttered.

"Cloaked?"

Rohane only peered below, frowning. In a small clearing, two women were dragging a fair-haired man to a stake. They shoved him against it and forced his wrists into dangling shackles. The women walked off. The man tugged at the chains listlessly. Then he slouched, his head down.

"What's he done?"

Rohane's lips set tight. "Attacked someone, I'd guess. Or even killed. Maybe a guard. This is a severe punishment."

"Severe? What? He'll stand with his back to that stake all day, thirsty?"

An armed woman strode past the stake. Seeing the man, she stopped. He pressed back, terrified. She advanced. Metal glinted in her hand. She slashed at the prisoner's arm. Then she walked on.

"I don't understand."

Rohane grimaced. She strode off along the ledge, expecting him to follow.

Val caught her up. "Won't you explain?"

"You don't need to know."

"I think I do, Rohane. I need to understand everything. So I can survive."

She stopped and turned her head to consider him with her dark eyes. "Very well. But you won't like it. Every woman who passes that stake will either strike him or wound him. But that's not the danger. The danger is when the light fades."

"What happens then?"

She nibbled her bottom lip, hesitating. "This punishment is deliberately cruel and humiliating to scare others who might challenge our ways."

"I still don't…"

"He is disowned. No one protects him. That means he has no rights. Anyone can do what they like with him."

"Oh," Val said.

"They won't come until dark, those with a taste for it. If he's fortunate, someone will kill him before that. Let's not linger here. The truthsayer means to talk to you, then I am called to the council room. No doubt to receive instructions about what to do with you."

"What would you like to do with me, Rohane?" Val wriggled his brows.

"Not what you're thinking. Given a choice, spear you. Or find a bow and arrows and use you for target practice."

"You'd miss on purpose. Come on, admit it—you like me just a little bit."

"Florentine, I like. You, I'm not so sure about."

"Lucky Florentine."

<hr />

The truthsayer's chambers were within a deep cave splintered into a web of tunnels. The door was open. Rohane called out a greeting. A thumping, shuffling sound came from within. The truthsayer appeared at the door. She uncurled a gnarled finger. "Good. Come in."

Remembering the menace he'd sensed in the council chambers, Val shivered. This woman might look frail, but she was powerful. And she intended to draw a name from him.

Squaring his shoulders, he trailed inside after Rohane. He was prepared to face pain today. It held less terror than loneliness or guilt. Pain, he understood. It was an old friend.

The room brimmed with all manner of odd bottles and phials, with roots and dried pressed flowers, and medicines and lotions with rancid odours. In a hearth, a fire burned. Its smoke billowed up into a hole in the roof. Val glimpsed a cot amid the chaos, but it seemed little more than a necessary evil, an afterthought.

The truthsayer's stick thumped as she shuffled into the centre of the room, gestured at a stool resting upon matted vines. "Sit."

He shot a doubtful look at Rohane. At her nod, he sat.

"Captain, wait near the door." The woman's voice was feeble but commanding.

Rohane took up stance away from Val.

"Say nothing. Do nothing. Unless he tries to run."

"I'm not going to run," Val said firmly to convince himself.

The truthsayer chuckled. She padded away, lighting more

candles. She bent over what looked like dried insects on a table, humming.

He braced, his muscles tense. "What... What will you do to me?"

She removed the lid from a ceramic container and sniffed. "We shall discover the truth, you and I. Together."

The truth must stay hidden. He would not give up Kaell. After what he had just seen in the valley, the Quisnaf were vengeful, vicious. According to rumour, they would always track down someone they thought had wronged them.

The woman shuffled to the fire and added herbs and odd insects to a black iron pot in the flames. A rancid odour rose with the smoke. Mesmerised, Val watched, wondering what her potion would do to him. Despite his words, he wanted to flee the dark room and the strange woman.

The truthsayer hobbled towards him, her staff thumping the ground. Val imagined how that *tap, tap, tap* would terrorise others as the old witch moved through the caverns. It would be the sound of doom approaching. Judgement.

"I need your blood." She cut his forearm with a knife.

As a thin red line bled, he winced. The woman collected a few drops in the vial. Then she plucked a hair from his head. Nodding, she returned to the fire and added the hair and blood to the pot. She stirred, humming again.

Val shifted his weight uncomfortably.

"Surely a warrior knows the value of stillness," the old woman muttered.

"Surely a witch knows the value of speed. Before her prey bolts."

"Witch? Prey?" Her laugh turned into a cackle. "Is that what you think I am, boy?"

"I don't know what you are," Val admitted.

His gaze held on the pot. Steam rose off it as the woman leaned forward and sniffed. She gave a satisfied nod. Rising slowly, as though her limbs pained her, the truthsayer fetched a stone goblet and dipped it into the potion. She shuffled to Val and held out the cup. "Drink."

He recoiled. "It smells like a cesspool."

The truthsayer thrust the cup at him again. He shook his head.

She rolled the goblet in her palm, thoughtful. Then she began to chant.

Cold air licked Val's neck. A shiver rippled down his spine. Vines sprouted from the floormat, snaking about his wrists and body. With a cry of horror, he tried to rise, straining against the thick green bonds. More curled about his arms and chest then up to his neck. The vines tightened.

"I can't... breathe," he rasped.

The truthsayer waved a hand. The vines at his neck loosened. Val sucked in air, glaring. "By what right—" He broke off with an angry hiss. This was Quisnaf. He had no rights.

"Stubborn and arrogant. Just like a Telorian." She grasped his jaw. For a woman who looked frail, her fingers possessed a terrible strength. She held Val's mouth open and emptied the cup down his throat.

It tasted bitter. He spluttered but could not help swallowing the liquid.

"Rohane, fetch me the other stool."

Rohane pushed off the wall and carried a stool from the fire to the truthsayer. The old woman sat so close to Val, her breath warmed his face. She gripped his brow between her thumb and finger, her palm over his eyes.

"Sleep. Dream."

At once, a languid heaviness stole through his limbs. Every sound fell away until there was only her voice, speaking soft, comforting words. Words that lulled. Words that quietened his mind.

His body slumped. It would be so easy to let go. There was a reason he shouldn't. The thought drifted away. Shadows danced behind his eyelids. Was he sleeping? It was a strange slumber, like a lucid dream.

"We're in a cave in the Icelands," the truthsayer whispered. "With friends. Matilda and Morgan. Do you see them?"

Val shivered. "Matilda has told me to rest. I fall asleep at once."

"But then you wake?"

"I go outside. Not far. The bracelet is tight on my arm, a reminder I must not stray." He frowned. "Someone is there."

"Who?"

"He's come for me. He's so angry, so hurt. I don't know how to reach him. It's my fault."

"Does he hurt our friends? Does he hurt Matilda and Morgan?"

Val wanted to run from the dream, from the cold and the darkness. But the nightmare rolled on, unstoppable. Part of him knew it wasn't real, but he could not control where it took him.

"He leaves them a knife." His voice trembled. "So they can free themselves. He isn't really interested in them. It's me he wants to hurt."

"Who has come?" Her voice sharpened. "You must answer."

Unease niggled in the recesses of his mind. He must not answer.

"No," Val said. "I must protect him. Always I must protect him."

"To protect him, you must answer me. That is the only way to keep him safe."

"No."

"A name," the woman said. "Give me a name."

Without knowing why, Val tried to hold back the words. But her command was so compelling. The name formed in his mind. He would not say it. He must not say it.

"Give me his name."

"Kaell," he whispered. "It's Kaell."

The old woman grew quiet. Ice prickled on Val's skin. Sadness swept through him. When would he see Kaell again, if ever? They had been honest with each other for the first time, then fate had cruelly torn them apart again.

"You will sleep now," the woman said. "A long sleep, very deep. You will wake and remember nothing of what we talked of."

ROHANE

"Kaell?" Blaire looked up from the scroll on her knee. "Do we know who this is? Rohane?"

Rohane shrugged. She, Blaire, Samantha, and Persia were in the council chamber, an unlikely group bound by necessity. By duty.

"According to the texts, when this man was Lord of the Mountains, he trained a young bonded warrior of that name."

"That makes sense. Of course he'd try to protect a boy he raised," Samantha said.

Persia ground her fist into a palm. "We'll find him. The usual way. Put it about that we'll pay gold for information. We will bring this Kaell to Quisnaf to answer for what he did."

"We're not sure he did anything," Rohane cautioned. "Val said Kaell left Matilda and Morgan a knife so they could free themselves. What happened to them might have nothing to do with this bonded warrior."

"We'll have the truth out of him once he's in our grasp," Persia said.

Blaire looked at Rohane. "And how is our friend after that dream walk? The truthsayer did not hurt him?"

Rohane shook her head. "She brewed up something nasty. Val

thought he was dreaming. He doesn't realise yet it was real, that he gave up the name. Maybe he won't."

If he did, he would be furious at himself. His vulnerability, how quick he was to judge himself, surprised her. After centuries brawling against life's disappointments and sorrows, surely he had learned to ignore guilt, had developed a thick armour to protect his heart.

She had. And Rohane, though nearing thirty, was a child compared to him. Yet she shielded herself with all manner of weapons, cynicism among them. Loneliness and solitude guarded her against having to see fear in another's eyes.

"How is he settling?" Blaire asked. "Will he accept his fate? Or cause trouble?"

"Of course he'll cause trouble," Rohane said. "He is stubborn and prickly."

"What warrior is not prickly?" Samantha's eyes gleamed with amusement. "From my conversations with him on the ship, this man also has a sense of humour. He is highly educated, with a quick wit."

Rohane scoffed. "He bucks at commands, dislikes any form of restraint or discipline." Beneath it all was self-loathing and guilt. But Rohane would not share that with the other women. She would leave him his dignity at least. Besides, Rohane understood that sort of shame too well.

"Why not use bracelets to control him?" Persia asked. "This is a dangerous man."

Blaire sighed. "I would prefer he came to this willingly. The alternatives are unpleasant."

"But necessary," Persia insisted.

"And a last resort." Blaire rubbed her temples. "Every Quisnaf council has battled with this dilemma. How to achieve our goals without cruelty, force."

"You have a kind heart, Blaire," Samantha said drily. "For a Regenta."

Blaire laughed. "That is a backhanded compliment, Samantha. You mean I am not as cruel as some. That is not what my enemies say, Councillor."

Rohane rolled her palm over her pommel, thoughtful. Blaire's enemies feared her. The lovely face masked a steel will. But the Regenta, though clever, had one blind spot.

Rohane's gaze drifted to that particular chair in the chamber, the one that stayed empty each time the council met. Blaire was foolish not to recognise that the woman who should take that place upon the council resented Blaire. Hated her even.

Holding together a society like this was no small task. Despite the city's strong traditions and allegiances, tensions simmered. It was a disciplined land of law. But should anyone challenge those rules, how quickly the veneer stripped away to reveal the torrent of disquiet beneath.

"How fares the other man we retrieved?" Persia asked.

"I thought he'd die." Samantha shook her head. "A healer tended to him for many days."

"We should still keep his presence secret," Rohane said. "Especially from Val Arques. No way of knowing what their relationship was."

Samantha laughed. "Especially as our beautiful Isles lord has already freed a woman he called friend. Kate someone. No, Val Arques cannot be trusted in that regard."

"But he has recovered?" Blaire arched a brow. "This man, what is his name again?"

"Dannon," Samantha said. "He's kept under lock and key. Already demanding we release him."

Blaire leaned back. The chair rocked. "And Genya Caelan will come for him?"

"She'll come for both of them," Rohane said. "There was quite a scene when I took Val Arques prisoner. She begged him not to go."

"How is it that our seers did not know of her birth?" Blaire asked. "They would know at once that Roaran had a daughter."

"Roaran would never lie to us like that," Samantha said. "He had his faults, but he was always truthful."

A silence fell, laced with undercurrents. Rohane knew of Roaran Caelan's promise to the Quisnaf centuries ago, his solemn blood vow made in the temple of Cyrah. No seer would be foolish enough to break such a vow.

"Roaran would never lie to us," Samantha repeated. But she sounded less certain.

"He is a Telorian," Persia said darkly. "You all seem to forget that. He is a man. They are capricious and emotional. Not to be trusted."

"You'll carry a message to the blood keepers." Blaire considered Rohane solemnly. "When you go to their caverns."

Rohane shivered. "I've never met a blood keeper."

"Few have," Samantha said. "You're fortunate, Captain."

"We have a different view of fortunate," Rohane said.

⁂

Her journey took her deep into the Quisnaf caverns, down and down. She passed through three iron gates, all guarded by silent, hard-eyed women. Beyond the last, the tunnels twisted into darkness.

Rohane snatched up a new torch, shivering as cool air from the vents brushed her neck. Despite the current, a dank odour filled these passages. Nerves on edge, she stole forward. Shadows welled and shifted for no reason. Unseen eyes followed her. The only sound was the hollow echo of her steps.

No one walked these deep passages without good cause. The blood keepers were dangerous, private, and unpredictable. They dwelled in a twilight close to the otherworld, a secretive place of mystery and magic.

Don't attract their attention. That was what the other girls had whispered when Rohane was a child. The blood keepers might slit your throat to milk your blood then capture your soul and turn you into a sleepwalker who did their will. *Don't go near the ancient caverns.*

Rohane shook off her unease. The old stories were just that—stories. Most likely, the blood keepers were pathetic, sad, lonely creatures, punished with a lifetime of service deep in the earth.

Someone said her name. Rohane turned fast. A lamp flickered and smoked in a sconce. No one was there.

She groped for her sword. Steel answered all danger. Even a witch could be struck dead with a thrust through the heart. A bladeswoman need not tremble, even in the face of magic. A bladeswoman *did not* tremble. Never.

A cobweb stuck to her face. Rohane brushed it off, waving her torch at pillars of broken rock, a low roof, and a sandy floor. Onward she walked, the scuff of her boots like thunderclaps in the quiet.

The sloping tunnel curved, bringing her to yet another gate. A guard menaced her with a spear, calling out a challenge.

Just as she had at the other gates, Rohane hastily passed the guard Blaire's note. The woman read it. She narrowed her gaze suspiciously. "You are the retrieval captain, Rohane?"

Rohane cleared her throat. "I am."

The guard turned to thrust a heavy key into the gate. It swung open noiselessly as though well oiled.

Rohane passed through. Metal clanged at her back, then the key scraped. This was indeed a prison. If the keepers chose to milk her blood, there would be no point running.

Shoulders squared, she walked on. More torches blazed here at least. The air smelt fresh, and a wall of bricks broke the endless stone leading to two bronze doors twice her height.

Rohane rocked to a halt and tilted her head to peer up. The doors were etched with images of strange creatures: a two-headed wolf, a bird with drooping wings and a crown of fire, and a snarling dog with pointed teeth dripping with blood.

She shuddered, her fingers again brushing her sword hilt. Then, seizing a breath for courage, she raised a fist to hammer against bronze.

The door creaked open. A tiny, birdlike woman poked her head out. She beckoned. "Well, do not stand there gaping like a fool. Come inside."

Rohane blinked. The woman did not look like a terrifying witch. Her nut-brown hair fell onto bony shoulders. Thin brows arched above wide grey eyes. True, she wore a long robe as a witch might, but it was a soft mauve, much too cheerful for a dismal lair.

"Are you deaf? Come through, fool girl." The woman waved Rohane inside.

A little dazed, Rohane walked in. The woman grunted as she dragged the door shut. "Fool door. Fool girl," she grumbled. "Blaire sent you? Come this way."

The woman stalked off down a well-lit passage. Rohane followed at a respectful distance, wondering how her companion knew her purpose.

They reached steps that wound down through close-cut rock. The design, spiralling clockwise to impede a right-handed swordswoman, reminded Rohane of castle stairwells at Vene. The castle in the principal Venivan city, though, was really a palace rather than a dense mass of walls and towers built for defence. Venivan border fortresses were much more intimidating.

The stairs opened into an enormous chamber, its stone walls decorated with frescoes. To her surprise, sunlight streamed in through a square hole in the ceiling, suggesting the caves were closer to the surface at this point than where she had entered.

The welcome light, plus numerous candles, illuminated vines entwined about carved pillars and shadowy alcoves filled with potted orchids and low couches. And scattered throughout the deep, long alcoves were shelves that held leather-bound books. At once, Rohane wanted to rush forward and touch them. Such treasures. And so many.

"Not what you expected?" The woman raised her brows. "Thought this a den of wicked magic? Heard the nonsense the blood keepers would steal your soul?"

Rohane grinned. "Steal my soul and turn me into a mindless slave. Yes."

The woman threw back her head and laughed. "Hear that, Clo?" she called to someone unseen. "The girl thinks we're all witches down here."

A woman poked her head from an alcove, her hands full of books.

"You're..." She searched her memory. "Rohane. Well, look at you. All grown up."

Rohane knew she gaped like a fish. "You know me?"

The woman dumped the books on a table and stepped into the light. Wispy grey hair fell untethered to a slender waist. She was stick thin, and her face was all carved bone and very pale, somehow elegant. Her mauve gown swished as she swept across the room to grasp Rohane's hands. "I knew you as a child. Your mother and I are friends."

"I...I..." Rohane blinked. "Who are you?"

"Clotild. I serve the blood keepers. It is not a task that appeals to many, but it is important and most prestigious." She squeezed Rohane's hands. "You will greet your mother kindly from me? Tell her Clotild sends her best wishes."

"I...yes." Rohane wondered if Clotild ever left the caverns. The blood keepers did not. Instead, their servants brought them food, drink, and captives to examine. It was this last thing that had earned them their dark reputation. To examine...

"Come." Clotild led Rohane to a couch. "Before you venture into the deeper caverns, we'll have tea and sweet cakes. Or wine, if you prefer. I mean, you are a warrior."

"Tea would be pleasant."

"Tea, then." She nodded at the other woman. "Veena, will you?"

Rohane sat. Clotild sank into the couch opposite. She leaned forward eagerly. "The blood keepers are very excited about the Caelan warrior. You brought him here, I believe?"

"You mean Val Arques? I did."

"So." Clotild's eyes danced with mischief. "What is he like?"

"I…" What should she say?

"Rohane, be kind and tell me the gossip." Clotild pretended sternness. "I like to gossip as much as anyone else."

"Well…" Rohane smiled. Her shoulders relaxed. She recognised that she'd fallen under Clotild's charm and was more than willing to be caught. "He is Telorian. Dark-haired, dusky eyed."

"And handsome? Is he handsome?" Clotild sighed. "After all these centuries, I hoped he was handsome."

"Much too handsome, if you ask me."

Clotild slapped her thigh. "You like him." She laughed loudly. It was so well-natured, Rohane could not take offence.

A flush rose in Rohane's cheeks. Did she? True, she enjoyed sparring with Val, battling with words. Laughing with him. Something in his character, in his nature, and even in his humour appealed to her. "Not as you might think. I can admire a beautiful man as much as any woman. But he is mercurial, quick to rise up like an angry bull. Then other times, he is surprisingly gentle, with a teasing humour. He exasperates me, and I've barely known him a few weeks."

"You *do* like him."

Rohane flushed again. An image of Val laughing flashed in her mind, his lips curved upwards. For a single moment, she wondered what it might be like to kiss his mouth. "I recognise he must be disciplined. No swordsman of his reputation could be anything less, but he bucks at commands and finds offence in even a simple order to walk forward, to stop."

"A proud man, then."

"Proud. Certainly. Too proud…" A shadow crossed her mind.

Clotild grasped her hand. "What is it, child?"

Rohane rubbed her arm as she examined her thoughts. "I fear for him," she said slowly, the truth hitting her only then. "I fear he won't bend that stiff neck, and that means trouble—for him. Not for me. There's nothing that can hurt me. Not anymore." She bit her lip to hold back the words. The private thought had slid out unbidden. She glanced at Clotild.

The other woman's expression held compassion. She did not press Rohane on what she meant.

"You sound angry at him. I can understand that. But we must be patient with such a prize. Ah, these Caelan princes. The stories of Roaran suggest he was far, far worse in those early days when he was here. Truly recalcitrant, disobedient, careless of punishment. The most stubborn, difficult man."

"He was held against his will. Roaran would hardly have found that congenial."

"The sorceress charged with training him proved very clever," Clotild said. "According to her private papers, she seduced Roaran with information. When he behaved, they even permitted him to train with one of the battales. It became a game of obedience and reward. So much better to be clever, don't you think, rather than brutal?"

"It is always better to be clever."

They smiled at each other. Rohane leaned back, relaxed. She liked this woman.

"Do you know what the blood keepers called Roaran?" Clotild asked. "No? They declared him a mistake. The keepers did not plan that bloodline. Roaran's mother deliberately sought out a Caelan lord, deliberately created this new bloodline. What a terrible, terrible kafuffle. And, now, it seems, Roaran has a daughter he did not tell us about."

"If Roaran has a daughter, and she has Caelan blood, what makes Val so important?" Rohane asked. "He has no magic."

"Ah." Clotild shot to her feet. "Come with me while we wait for our tea."

She led Rohane into an alcove deep within the chamber where citrus-scented candles burned. It was cool and shadowy. Clotild pulled a heavy book from a shelf above her head. It was not dusty, and Rohane guessed Clotild had consulted it recently. The other woman turned the book sideways. It fell open upon lists of names connected by lines.

"See how the lines extend down to the bottom of the pages? They continue on the next page and then the next. So it is like an enormous chart." Clotild flicked pages. Then she paused, her finger stabbing at the paper.

"These are missing bloodlines. Possibilities. Ever since the Quisnaf learned of a male child with 'true' Caelan blood, they began to plan possible matings. How powerful, for example, to bind the Caelan bloodline with Sorganne's. It is all more complicated than that, but that is the basic idea."

"True Caelan. I read this also. Both mother and father with Caelan blood."

Clotild nodded vigorously. "Never happened before. Or since. The priests and priestesses of The Three disallow cousins to wed. How much more valuable did this child become when he proved himself a brilliant bladesman by winning that deadly contest in Wardour."

"Then he disappeared."

"For centuries." Clotild shut the book and returned it to the shelf. "I do go on. But preserving bloodlines, determining potential couplings, consumes you after a while. The blood keepers obsess about creating the perfect warrior, the perfect seer, the perfect healer, the perfect leader."

"All for the good of Quisnaf."

Clotild flexed a brow. "You are young, Rohane, to be cynical."

She was young to be many things. Alone. Bitter.

"I suppose one day you'll choose someone for me, given my blood," she mused. "Or perhaps it is better my cursed bloodline ends with me."

Clotild sank onto the couch. "I imagine it's already decided."

Veena returned with a tray holding cups of steaming tea and a plate of cakes. She set it down on the table then sprawled in a comfortable chair. "Did I miss the gossip?"

Clotild passed Rohane a ceramic cup. "The captain says the Telorian is much too handsome for his own good."

Veena snatched up a cup and drank noisily. "Roaran was handsome. I saw him once when I was a child. Everyone knew who he was. We all stared with awe."

Rohane drank her tea. "Why did he come?"

"That time, for sanctuary. Roaran was troubled, needed somewhere safe to think. That's what I heard, years later, mind you. I always wondered." She peered up mischievously through her lashes. "If there was a dalliance between Roaran and Sabin, centuries ago."

"He and Sabin were close." Clotild nodded. "But Sabin… always so proper. Or so the texts say."

Rohane drank more tea to hide her flushed cheeks.

"You've embarrassed her," Clotild said.

"Not me. It was you."

"I…" Rohane shook her head. "Sabin is one of my heroines. She's everyone's heroine. Fearless. Clever. Undaunted by the destruction of Quisnaf in the Great Fall. Sabin the Rebuilder. Quisnaf would not exist but for her determination."

"And of course, she is your ancestor. All part of that careful breeding plan."

"I can't begin to understand how complicated it all is."

"We have bred out weakness," Veena said proudly. "Our warriors are strong. Since Sabin's time, our sorceresses grow more powerful every generation. No one will dare threaten us."

From somewhere close, a man began to shout.

Rohane's head shot about. "What is that? Who?"

Veena nervously licked her lips. She and Clotild exchanged a glance. "He's awake. I'll check on him."

"Give him a sleeping draught. We're not ready for him yet."

Rohane thought about the look that passed between them. The atmosphere did not feel quite as comfortable. "Who's here?"

Clotild sipped tea. "One of the new Telorian slaves. He's caused trouble. Tried to escape on the ship. Persia gladly gave him up."

"Gave him up for what?"

Stillness settled about them. Clotild drank tea.

"Give him up for what?" Rohane repeated.

Clotild put down her cup. "I'm surprised you haven't heard stories."

"I'm often away," Rohane said. That was by choice. Quisnaf held her past, the truth of what she was. Constant assignments left her with less time to think.

"Very well. Let me put it like this. You cannot have blood magic without blood. When the high sorceress Sisilia casts strong spells, we must sacrifice to the goddess."

"I… " Rohane stammered. "I didn't realise."

"Do not worry. There is no pain, no fear. It is quick. And it is only a few. Most are kept here for different purposes. Unlike your handsome Telorian, they are not guests. Valuable men, selected carefully, who will help us create even better warriors, stronger sorceresses, wiser leaders."

"It's necessary," Rohane said firmly. "We must keep Quisnaf strong." *Whatever it takes.*

Veena returned. "The blood keepers are asking for her."

Clotild rose and dusted cake crumbs off her gown. "Well, child. Enough pleasantries. If you would take that corridor—" She gestured. "Follow it to the end."

Rohane stood. "Thank you for the tea."

"Thank you for the gossip," Clotild said, smiling.

Rohane walked into the brick-lined passage. Her newfound ease fell away. She was entering a place where few, even council members, came. Ahead, two more doors appeared, again made of bronze etched with three symbols, a chalice, a dagger, and a shape like a water droplet. The symbol for purification.

She raised her hand to knock, but the doors opened. Her belly knotted with nerves, Rohane hesitated a moment. Then she walked in. At first, she could not see anything in the gloom. Then a candle flared to life. A figure with long white hair lifted the candleholder and regarded Rohane steadily. Her skin was thin and translucent, her eyes wide and very pale.

A shiver ran through Rohane. She could not have spoken even if she'd wanted to. There was something otherworldly about this creature.

"I am Hesora," the figure said, her voice ethereal and breathy. "We've been expecting you, Rohane of the blood of kings."

Rohane swallowed. "I was told there were three blood keepers."

Hesora took a step closer. Her milky eyes bored into Rohane's. "My sisters, Nyx and Rhea, and I. We served the first sorceress of Quisnaf, Sorganne, as we serve her descendants."

Rohane could not hold back a shiver. "You have been in this place many centuries."

That steady gaze dwelled on her face. "We have our work. It is eternal." The blood keeper spread her arms. At once, hundreds of candles flared, brightening a cavern even larger than the one Rohane had just left.

She gasped. Upon every wall, even stretching over the ceiling, were names written in glowing ink linked to other names by lines. Beneath, an enormous bench dominated the room, its surface covered with parchments, inkwells, pens, and more candles. A door stood open to a vaulted room stretching back as far as Rohane could see. It contained stacked shelves, all filled with rolled-up parchments.

Other tunnels disappeared into darkness. Rohane could only imagine how deep they led into the mountains.

Without a word, the blood keeper turned and walked into the vaulted chamber. She returned with a parchment tied with string. "The names."

Rohane solemnly accepted the paper.

"There are three," Hesora said.

"Three." Rohane frowned. "Is that a lot?"

"For a man such as this, there were hundreds of possibilities," Hesora answered. "We contemplated them over many centuries, from the day of his birth. Three is not many to begin with."

"How did you determine which bloodlines should be pursued?"

"We cast spells," Hesora said. "Blood magic. We sifted the Enarae, sought the will of the goddess. In the end, we identified two strong warrior bloodlines and one speculative seer line. Though this man, Val Arques, has no magic, Caelan blood is the blood of the gods. Nyx believes magic might lie dormant in this man. It may come out in the next generation."

Rohane's head spun. This was the role of a blood keeper: assessing what procreation between different couples might produce and judging the flawed or wonderful possibilities.

Every Quisnaf woman knew to do her part and accept the will of the blood keepers. That was why Quisnaf warriors grew stronger and taller every century. As for the other... She'd once heard Blaire say that Quisnaf magic might one day rival Seithin at its peak.

"I was bid to bring this note from Blaire." She passed over a rolled parchment.

The blood keeper grabbed Rohane's hand. The skin on Hesora's hand was spidery thin, the blue veins close to the surface. "Take care, Rohane."

Startled, Rohane blinked. "Why do I need to take care?"

"A path opens up before you, but it is fraught with peril. He is not for you. The outcome of any joining between you is cloudy, suggesting danger."

Rohane laughed in embarrassment. "I know my place. I only ever wanted to be a warrior." But fate had been unkind. Retrieval captain was the best option for a cursed creature such as her.

"The blood keepers have assessed possibilities for you. Yours is a bloodline we are keen to cultivate. You must keep yourself ready.

Now go. Return to your duty, retrieval captain." Hesora dropped Rohane's hand. She took Blaire's note to the bench and dragged a candle on a silver holder closer. She seemed to have already forgotten her visitor.

Shaken, Rohane returned to the first chamber. Even though Quisnaf was a place of sorcery, Rohane had never come upon anything like Hesora before.

Looking for Clotild and Veena, she found the outer chamber empty save for one tall woman. Though the woman's back was to Rohane, Rohane knew her at once.

"Councillor," she said.

The High Sorceress Sisilia turned. Auburn hair wisped untidily about her strong, pale face. Dark-lashed eyes flashed nearly as bright as the gold pendant dripping from a chain about her neck, but they were shadowed by weariness.

"Why are you here?" Sisilia asked coldly. "This is no place for a retrieval captain."

"Blaire sent me for the names."

Sisilia stared at her, unblinking. The sorceress was single-minded, fierce in her service to the goddess and to Quisnaf. She was also a humourless woman who would not be crossed. But Rohane had no cause to fear her. A captain's position was powerful.

Veena appeared at the entrance to one of the tunnels. "Sorceress." She dipped her head. "We kept a close eye on the Varee prisoner. He is quiet now. We took his blood."

Sisilia's hard gaze shifted to Veena. "*All* his blood?"

A silence fell, creeping with disquiet.

Veena licked her lips. "All?"

"I want him drained," Sisilia said. "I need every bit of his blood for my spell. I thought you understood that."

"As you wish." Veena bowed her head then scuttled away like a mouse.

Sisilia glanced at Rohane. "Keep those names close, Captain. Show only the council. There are those who might prefer these bloodlines to remain incomplete. One in particular will stir up resentment."

Rohane remembered the symbols Blaire had discovered on the walls near the council chamber. "Do you mean the Order?"

"Quisnaf is a dangerous place. You should remember that."

Faint menace simmered within the words. Rohane frowned. "That sounds like a threat."

Sisilia shrugged. There will come a time, soon, when you will need to choose a side, Rohane. Choose wisely." She turned her back, dismissing Rohane.

Blaire's cool, lovely face masked her reaction as she read the list. But she gripped the scroll so tightly, a fragment tore off beneath her fingernails.

"Did you know?" Rohane ventured softly.

Blaire lifted ice-blue eyes. "Of course I knew." She flung the scroll onto the table. "Begin tomorrow night. But first, I want you to talk with Ianthe."

"The slave mistress?"

"She has prepared other guests. I spoke to her yesterday. She will instruct you."

Rohane bowed and retreated.

GENYA

"Come closer, child." The queen sat tall in her high-backed chair, her hands upon her swollen belly. "I must say you're nothing like your mother. A most unfortunate chin, she had."

The women with Rozenn tittered politely. They stood in a loose group behind the queen. Morning sunlight, already harsh, streamed upon floor mosaics in a long chamber in the castle of Tide's End. Arches on one side opened onto a veranda overlooking a glimmering sea.

Genya shuffled forward in an awkward gown, her head down. *Demure.* That was the word Alecc had used. *Look demure. Keep your eyes lowered. Blush.*

"Who is this wretched girl? I've never heard you speak of a cousin." A stern-faced older woman at Rozenn's elbow glowered suspiciously at Genya.

"Dameta is a *distant* cousin, Yvonne," Rozenn corrected tartly.

"Well, your *distant cousin* does not behave correctly in the presence of a queen." Yvonne jabbed a finger at a cushion at Rozenn's feet. Genya knelt clumsily, resolving to rip her ridiculous gown down the side the moment she was alone.

"Your Grace…" She pretended to stammer. "It is an honour… to serve you, Your Grace. My mother is grateful." *She of the fictional long chin.*

"Grateful and poor." Rozenn sighed. "Never mind. We shall find a place for you, cousin. And perhaps, in time, if you serve me faithfully, we shall arrange a suitable match. With an older lord."

Genya jerked her head up, only to catch the twitch of mischief on Rozenn's lips. The women laughed. *Vapid creatures.* How they would scatter if she drew a sword. But Genya was unarmed. The gown offered few places to hide weapons.

"Leave us." Rozenn clapped her hands at her women. "I should like to talk with my cousin, alone."

The women dutifully took their leave. Yvonne was the last to go. She cast Genya a disapproving glance.

The moment the hall emptied, Rozenn leaned forward. "Come with me to the shore. Do not speak until we are away from the castle."

She rose awkwardly. Genya eyed the queen's belly, guessing it was only a month or two before Rozenn's time. According to rumour, the child the queen carried wasn't Gendrick's.

Thoughtful, Genya followed Rozenn onto the balcony then down a small set of steps, past attentive guards. One started after them as if to act as escort.

Rozenn waved him back. "I am safe with my lady-in-waiting."

They crossed a garden, passing through a gate onto a path that led to the cliffs where a hot breeze stirred through feather-tipped grass. Only there, with the castle at their backs, with the murmur of the sea swelling against rocks, did Rozenn pause. She faced Genya, her expression anxious. "I don't know who you are—Alecc no doubt thought it too dangerous to name you in his message— but he writes that I can trust you. My son. He is well?"

"Alecc is well," Genya assured her. "He has called together the Mountains lords. He named himself Lord of the Mountains and rightful King of Telor."

Rozenn's eyes gleamed. "Word reached Gendrick of Alecc's

declaration. The king is displeased." She laughed harshly. "Displeased. Ha. How he ranted."

"What will he do?"

"Nothing. For now. My husband already faces rebellion in Dal-Kanu. And his spies tell him the King of Wardour has built his ships and is readying an army."

Genya frowned. "We will be invaded."

"Perhaps," Rozenn said, her expression gleeful. "When you return to him, tell Alecc to be ready. If Gendrick's forces are defending the Isles against Wardour, that will be my son's time to strike."

"Doesn't that mean we split Telorian forces and leave ourselves open to defeat?" Genya remembered Val's lessons. "Shouldn't we fear this invader?"

"We'll deal with him once Alecc is safely on the throne." The queen stared out over the waves gently rolling over rocks below, perhaps imagining that glorious victory over the husband she hated. Genya flicked sweat from her brow. After the chill of the Mountains, the Isles heat was uncomfortable, a wet coat upon her skin.

"Alecc is a dutiful son," Rozenn murmured, her hands on her swollen belly. "He shall take this land in storm, just as I swore so many years ago."

"He is… impressive," Genya conceded.

Rozenn reached beneath her skirts. She drew out a rolled parchment and flattened it against her gown. "Alecc writes that he wants me to teach you magic. Why?"

Genya shrugged. "So I may help him take down those ghoul castles that still stand in the Mountains and on the Downs. So I may help him defeat Gendrick."

Rozenn looked hard at her. "Do you have magic in your bloodlines? There is no point if you do not. I cannot just make you a witch. You must be born to it."

"I have magic," Genya said. "I am my father's daughter. I have my grandfather's blood, even though his heart was black and corrupted."

Rozenn's eyes flared in shock. She reached forward and grabbed Genya's wrist. Her nails dug into the girl's skin. "Who are you?" she hissed. "Are you of Damadar blood?"

Genya shook her head quickly. She went to speak, but Rozenn dropped Genya's arm and shrank back, her face pale.

"You're her," she breathed, her expression a mixture of fascination and fear. "Roaran's daughter. The seer king's daughter."

"I'm Genya Caelan, yes."

Rozenn shuddered. "You're trouble."

"Not to you," Genya said. "Not to Alecc."

For a long moment, Rozenn studied Genya's face. Then she nodded. "For my son's sake, I'll teach you what I know."

VAL ARQUES

V al woke in a strange chamber carved into rock. He lay on a bed, linen sheets beneath him and his head upon a pillow. Cushions spilled about him like wildflowers in a field. A thin, beautifully embroidered coverlet was drawn up to his waist. Beneath, he was clothed in a thin shift.

The room also contained a writing table, a high-backed chair, and a bucket for his physical needs. Upon the table was a bowl of fruit, a jug, a cup, a basin with water for washing, a cake of soap, and a cloth. Someone had also left three books.

He swung his legs to the floor, aware of a niggling ache in his temple. Thirsty, he poured water from the jug into the cup and drank, gathering memories.

Oh, gods. He passed a hand over his eyes and groaned. *The truthsayer.* She'd restrained him with magic. He strained to recall what had unfolded, but it eluded him.

His mind troubled, he flicked open a book. The writing was Telorian.

"Are you awake?" Rohane was outside his door.

"Just."

"I'm coming in. Make sure you're decent." A key rattled. The door swung inwards.

"What's decent?" Val asked.

"Clothed." She wore a long tunic and sandals, and her hair was caught up in a leather strap. A sword swung from a belt at her hip. "I'm easily shocked."

"You've seen me naked more than once and didn't blush."

She shook her head. "This is a strange conversation. Not at all how I thought things might go."

"Oh? Should we start again? You walk in, and you say…"

"I say, 'Does this room suit your needs?' Then you politely say, 'Yes, thank you, Rohane. You're very good to me.'"

"Should I bow gracefully as I say it?"

"Then I ask if there's anything you need. And you politely say, 'I am hungry, but I thank you for the books and the water.'"

"Do you think you might feed me?"

"Never satisfied." She sighed dramatically. "I've been with the slave mistress."

Val stilled, a little alarmed. "The slave mistress?"

"A lovely woman called Ianthe."

"Is that sarcasm? I'm assuming she has warts and carries a whip?"

"Two whips," Rohane teased.

"Carries two whips, has a sour expression, no sense of humour, and a strong view on discipline?"

"She's Blaire's half-sister."

"Oh, she sounds better already."

"She still has two whips. Anyway, it doesn't matter. You won't meet her. Not unless you run away or something."

Val threw his hands up, exasperated. "Haven't we had this discussion?"

"I'm teasing." Rohane grinned. "I know you are a man of your word. Now, shall I send for food? Wine?"

"Is it morning or night?"

"Morning. You slept most of yesterday and all last night."

"Well, not wine then. People might think I'm a lush."

"What's a lush? I doubt you care what others think."

"A lush is a drunkard. And I do care. I'm very sensitive."

"Fool." She went to the door and spoke to someone outside.

"Oh, a guard outside." Val wriggled his brows. "Someone very unpleasant must live here. Where am I, exactly?"

"You're in quarters where we hold hostages or occasional guests. The rooms are built in a circle and ringed by a passage. Beyond are warrior and guard quarters. It's a nice maze of trouble for anyone who's overly curious."

"I am suitably warned."

She laughed again. "I doubt that."

A fist rapped against the door. Rohane called, "Enter."

Mel carried a tray into the room. She plonked it on the table with an outraged look at Val. "I thought we'd done with this," Mel said. "Thought we'd be off on an adventure to another exotic place."

Rohane shrugged. "I'll sort it out. It won't be for long."

"Hmmph." Mel stalked out.

"May I?" At her nod, Val sat and fell upon the food. When he'd finished, he drank more water and watched Rohane prowl about. He was surprised at how genuinely pleased he was to see her. Her hair shone and bounced in its ponytail; the sandals and tunic showed off her long, shapely legs. Her face wasn't perfect, not like Blaire's, but it was an interesting face that he didn't seem to tire of looking at.

"So, you met with the slave mistress, whips and all, and…?"

Rohane leaned against the wall, arms folded. "Your duties begin tomorrow night. The first of three women. You'll be permitted nights to yourself, of course. But the pattern will continue."

"Oh." Alarm prickled along his spine.

Rohane's look softened. "You do understand what to do? I can explain if you wish."

Val had guessed. But it hadn't seemed real. So far, Quisnaf had been about learning the rules, biting down on his indignation at commands. Going here, going there—with Rohane.

He swallowed, nodding.

"The first time, the slave mistress says they can offer you a potion. It's meant kindly."

He shook his head. Deliberately, he turned his thoughts from tomorrow night. *Have a loose hold on the future. Think about this moment only.* "So, what happens today?"

Rohane looked relieved. Perhaps she'd thought he would weep on her shoulder or rant and throw furniture about.

"Today, I am permitted to take you outside. It's sunny."

Val peered about for his boots. They were tucked neatly beneath the bed. He sat to pull them on. "You're going to walk me about? Do I need a leash?"

"You're not funny. You know that, don't you?"

"Women tell me that all the time."

Rohane led him to a different part of the valley where paths led through woodlands or fields and blue borage and jasmine bobbed in the warm breeze. After the dark caverns, he took delight in stretching his stiff muscles, in the embrace of sunlight on his face, even the act of moving his body, of striding out.

"How do you live in the caves? It's so gloomy."

She shrugged. "I never think about it. But I suppose most warriors train outside and only sleep or eat in the caverns. It's different for seers or sorceresses; that all seems to happen deeper within." She shivered.

"I saw that. What?"

"Please learn to be less observant so I may keep my thoughts to myself." She sighed. "I visited the blood keepers yesterday. While you slept like a lazy pig."

"Charming. Do you like pigs?"

"Only lazy ones."

They laughed together. Val grasped her hand.

"These blood keepers... I suppose that was about me?"

"What an inflated head you have. Actually, it's what you said about gloomy caverns that made me think of it. The blood keepers are centuries old. Not quite human. I thought they'd be like trolls, but the one I met was ethereal." She seemed to realise he held her hand and quickly pulled hers away.

They reached a small stream. Sunlight glinted on water bubbling over rocks. Val sank down onto the grassy bank. Wind stirred through his hair. Summer's scents, golden and sweet, drifted and soothed.

Val plucked a wildflower and presented it to Rohane. "For your hair."

"Warriors don't wear flowers." She crushed it in her palm and sat beside him. "One of the guardians to the blood keepers, a charming woman called Clotild, said they might have a match for me." Rohane frowned. "I suppose I should expect it."

"What?" He stared, shocked. Then realised he did not like the thought of her with another. "Do you know..." He laughed shortly. "I don't want to share you."

Her brows rose. "What?"

"I enjoy you, Rohane. Being with you."

Her cheeks flushed. "Don't be silly."

His hand stole to her hair. With a sense of wonder, he smoothed a strand between his fingers. A stillness settled about them. She was watching him warily. Gently, he pulled her head towards him.

Rohane jerked back. "Don't," she whispered. "You can't."

Val leaned in. His lips brushed hers. Rohane stiffened. Val kissed her deeper, harder. Her tongue flicked against his. His hands slid to her waist. For a heartbeat, she melted against him. Then abruptly, she pulled away. "No, no. This can't happen."

"Rohane."

She surged to her feet and brushed grass from her tunic. "It's forbidden. If anyone saw us, I'll be whipped. You, too. No, we have to forget this ever took place."

"Whipped? That doesn't sound fair."

"Cyrah help me, what's wrong with me? I can't let myself feel anything. I must not."

"Because you're cursed? Does it mean you're cursed never to love? I know what it's like to deny your heart. It leaves you cold, barely alive. It's no way to live."

Rohane fixed a grim look upon him. "It's the only way to live."

"Who did you hurt, Rohane? Who was it?"

"Someone... Someone I cared about. Please don't ask. I can't... talk about it." She dragged her fingers through her fringe. "No, no. This is all wrong. I'm not chosen for you. Who you lie with has been carefully planned."

"I didn't like the thought of you—"

"In someone else's bed?" Rohane laughed harshly. "That's not about to happen. Not like you're about to bed three different women."

He stilled. Put like that, it sounded... well... He didn't like it.

"I'm sorry," Rohane said quietly. "That was cruel."

Val turned his head towards the stream. Soft sounds of the dying summer as it faded into autumn swirled about him. He liked summer above the other seasons. It brought back memories of carefree days in the Isles. "Not cruel. It's the truth. I need reminding."

"Well, well," a woman said.

Val squinted into bright sunlight. With a shudder of distaste, he recognised Branwyn.

Branwyn grinned at Rohane. "Ronnie. You're brave bringing him out here alone. No guards?"

"He's a guest. There's no need for guards. And address me as Rohane or Captain."

"Guest or not, I'd advise guards, *Captain*. This one's tricky. The first time I met this *guest*, he managed to pick a lock on manacles and abandon me in a dingy, grimy hut."

"You chained me up," Val said. "You groped me. I found that somewhat offensive."

Rohane arched a brow at the other woman. "Groped?"

Branwyn only laughed. "I was bored. But thanks to you, Val Arques Caelan, my failure to deliver you earned me censure and a demotion."

"How sad."

Branwyn smiled nastily. "There's that sarcastic tongue. I remember that. When news of Roaran's proposal reached us, I did hope they would send me after you, give me a second chance, given our history. Instead, they sent the wonder girl, Rohane. I always forget how well connected she is."

Val's gaze flickered to Rohane. *Well connected?* Another secret, it seemed.

Rohane bristled. "What do you want, Branwyn? I take it I have you to blame for Val taking a dive off a ship?"

Branwyn pressed a hand to her breast in mock outrage. "I'm hardly responsible for what notion he got into his head."

"You wanted him to try and escape. Why? Did you hope someone would put a bolt in him? Does your need for vengeance go that far?"

"It's a dangerous world, Rohane," Branwyn sneered. "Best watch your step." She looked at Val. "You, too, Telorian. Watch your back."

Val lay on the bed, his head on his hands, imagining what the night ahead held. He was on edge, his body tense. They could not force him to couple with a stranger. What if he simply refused to do what the blood keepers wanted?

Just as disturbing were his thoughts of Rohane, of that sweet kiss, that moment of intimacy. He liked her. But there lay the danger. He was trouble. Poisonous. His regard would bring her only misery.

A fist hammered on the door. Frowning, Val sat up. It was too early for Rohane to escort him to the baths.

The knock repeated. Someone sought permission to enter.

So he had a few rights, after all. "Enter."

A tall, blonde guardswoman pushed the door in then stepped aside. Samantha appeared.

Val shot to his feet. "Ahh..." he stammered, "this is a surprise." He fought the urge to bow. The Quisnaf had not yet broken him to their ways. His prideful streak remained.

Samantha nodded at the guard. The woman pulled the door closed behind her.

The councillor gestured at the chair. "May I?"

"Please." The usual common courtesies returned. "Will you take wine?"

"Thank you."

Val poured them both a cup. Was it late enough for wine? Drinking in daytime put him to sleep, but the Quisnaf seemed to drink either wine or ale all day long. He took his cup and sank onto the edge of the bed.

"You want to know why I'm here?" Samantha sipped wine.

"I begin to understand a councillor of Quisnaf does not visit just anyone."

She smiled. "You're not quite anyone. Besides, I told you on our journey that I would gladly continue our conversations. You are lettered, intelligent, with a somewhat-sarcastic humour I enjoy. Consider me here as a friend—for today at least."

"I could do with a friend," Val said. "This is a very strange place."

Nodding, Samantha rolled the cup between her palms. "Tonight is the first..."

Val bit his lip.

"I came to reassure you," Samantha said. "To ask if you need anything, something that will make you more comfortable, or even if I can offer advice that eases the next few hours."

"Rohane left me books."

Samantha nodded thoughtfully. "Rohane often surprises me. One is never certain what she thinks. Still waters run deep and all that."

"What is between you?"

Samantha arched a brow. "She hasn't said?"

"No."

"Then neither shall I." Samantha leaned forward, her expression solemn. "Forgive me. This is very offensive, but why not let yourself enjoy tonight? Clearly you like the company of women. Do not think of your task as punishment. You are not betraying your values if you choose to find pleasure."

"You want to make this easier for me? Why? Because you feel guilty?"

"Not guilt. This is our way. Because of the blood keepers, because of our careful breeding, Quisnaf warriors are stronger than the sisters who came before them. More magic flows through the veins of our seers and sorceresses, our mages. No, it is not guilt. But as I said, I am here as a friend. So I say this because I feel compassion."

"I don't need your compassion." Val surged to his feet. Why must she insist on talking about this? He had tried to bury his turmoil of doubt and unease deep within, refusing to look at it. Yet she wanted to paw over it.

"If you think I like this, then know I do not," he muttered. "And not just what tonight means. Everything about the voyage, just being here." That was honest. "Submission is not in my nature. Nor obedience. Every part of me bucks against agreeing to do what you want. I would prefer to unleash my rage, to shout out my defiance."

Samantha sat back. "Then do not think of this as obedience. Think of it as cooperation."

"Semantics," he growled. "I was right. You are a silver-tongued courtier."

She laughed with genuine amusement. "That description will do nicely. I've been called far worse." Samantha leaned forward. "Listen to me, proud Telorian. The Quisnaf know every possible way of breaking a man's spirit. Your pride, your strong will, neither will keep you safe. If you cannot accept your fate, you must learn to wear a mask, to pretend. Smile. Avert that prideful gaze. Cooperate. Even allow yourself to give and take pleasure. It will be easier. I promise, everything becomes easier."

"Who says I want easy?" Val stormed.

Samantha sighed. "I was afraid of that."

⁂

Burnt-orange dusk streaked the horizon, a cap to circling mountains, just as the dark twilight blue enclosed the Quisnaf valley like a glove. Fidgeting with his hands, Val walked beside Rohane through willowy trees and flowerbeds along a wide path of golden-veined white marble leading to the Temple of Cyrah.

Upon a platform at the entrance, flames leapt from braziers, their orange glow illuminating the grand façade built into walled rock. The temple beyond lay within the mountain, a majestic structure of glossy marble and dolomite. Pillars of white stone supported an arch above bronze doors surely big enough to fit an entire battale through.

Val's footsteps slowed. Half with awe, half with dread, he peered up at the ornate carvings.

"It's centuries old. The design originated in the Circle Kingdoms beyond the Ice Sea. There's a story…" Rohane broke off, staring.

Val followed the direction of her gaze.

A man ran lightly down the stairs from the temple. He moved with an arrogant assurance, his fair head held high. From his build, he looked as though he'd spent a lifetime swinging a sword. A pale-blue cloak was draped over his well-defined shoulders.

"Jenna-Dairine must be back," Rohane said softly.

"Who? And who's that man?"

"That's Riagan. Striking, isn't he?" Without further explanation, she walked on towards the temple.

Val caught her up. "All right, I'll play your game. Who's Riagan? And who's Jenna-Dairine?"

She wriggled her brows. "Wouldn't you like to know? Come on, you'll be late, and I'll be reprimanded."

At that reminder of their purpose, unease roiled in his gut. His footsteps faltered.

Rohane glanced back. "I can only imagine what you feel right now."

"Right now, I'd rather be on a battlefield about to be overwhelmed by thousands of ghouls."

"Tonight won't be so bad. Trust me."

"I'm guessing you know who the companion of my first night is?" he teased. "Won't you tell me?"

"Forbidden."

"Rohane—" Val hesitated. "Rohane... about that kiss."

"Stupid, stupid, stupid," Rohane muttered. "It's my fault. I'm responsible for what you do. I should never have allowed it."

"I don't—" Again, he paused. "I don't regret it. I should. I know it. You've made it clear how you feel—"

Rohane held up a hand. "Stop. We won't talk of this. Not ever."

They took the steps onto the platform. Armed women swung back the doors. Unlike other Quisnaf guards, they wore golden sashes and armbands. Val raised a brow at Rohane.

"Temple guards." She shrugged.

More waited inside, along with a gauntlet of priestesses lining the walls of a splendid hall. Round columns thicker than Val's arm span rose from a green marble floor to a gold-leaf ceiling. Wall mosaics portrayed swirling patterns, budding flowers, and female warriors hunting heavy-toothed beasts with spears. Except for crackling flames in braziers, the hall was silent. Moonlight through high windows mingled with lamplight. Spices like cinnamon and cloves spiked warm air.

He walked with Rohane through a central nave to a sanctum dominated by a giant statue of Cyrah. The goddess sat upon her throne with a sword resting across her lap. Even her delicately carved hand was bigger than a man.

Awestruck by the size and beauty of the statue, Val gaped. He was an intruder in this temple. Surely no male, and especially an Isles man, belonged here.

Rohane touched his arm as though to reassure him. He tried to offer her a smile. But his skin was cold with dread.

A cowled priestess approached. From the little Val could see of her face, she looked no older than thirty. Unlike her companions' scarlet robes, her gown was purple, and she wore a jewelled pendant about a delicate neck. A crown of wrought gold circled her brow.

Rohane did not bow. She gestured at Val to kneel. "This is Sorcha, high priestess of the goddess."

Reluctantly, he dipped his knee. *Think of it as cooperation, not obedience. Ah, Samantha and her smooth tongue.*

When he rose, the high priestess appraised him with an impersonal stare.

"Captain, depart. The temple guards will watch him."

Rohane shot Val a doubtful look. Then she nodded and turned away. With a curious sense of abandonment, Val listened to her steps fade.

The high priestess addressed Val. "Come with me."

Val followed her towards the statue. The priestesses came after them, their bare feet whispering over stone. Sorcha led him to a stone altar below the statue, where another cowled figure knelt. As he dropped to his knees, he glanced at her, but he could not see her face.

Sorcha bid him rest his hand, palm open, upon the altar's polished surface. She drew her knife.

Cooperate. Samantha's words returned like a strident echo.

The other priestesses pressed close. Sorcha sliced his palm. Val grunted at the pain. Blood ran from the cut. When he started to lift his hand, Sorcha shook her head and pressed his palm down onto the altar. Turning to the cowled woman, Sorcha gestured that she should rise. Then she cut the stranger's palm as she had Val's and pressed it onto the altar.

What happened next was beyond Val's understanding. A tingling began in his fingers and spread into his wrist. Slowly, it coursed up his arm. Beneath his palm, rose-tinted water oozed from the stone. It became a torrent, spilling a deeper, darker red down the sides of the altar to grooves in the floor. Startled, he watched the bloody water course towards the statue, disappearing beneath.

The high priestess spread her arms and chanted. A chill blazed down Val's back. The words weren't Quisnaf. *Seithin?* A dead tongue, but the language of magic. The language of the old gods.

A wind picked up, whistling about the hall, swirling about the statue. It omitted a single clear note, as if the stone were singing. It was low, drawn out, and very clear. Haunting.

The wind disappeared. The eerie melody died away. The water leached into the stone, leaving the altar dry. The priestess stopped her chant. She let her arms fall to her sides. Then she wrapped a cloth about Val's wound.

"This way."

The priestesses moved aside as Val trailed after Sorcha, his thoughts in turmoil. The strange ritual had unnerved him. Uneasily, he glanced back at the figure again kneeling by the altar, hands clasped together as if in prayer. She had not moved.

Sorcha led him through the pillars into a shadowed corridor. Temple guards fell in around him, an escort to a room at the far end. They pushed open the doors. Inside, robed women lit candles. Others put wine and food on a carved table. A woman came forward, offering to help him disrobe. Val shook his head.

Sorcha clapped her hands. The room emptied. Alone with Val,

she threw back her cowl, revealing shoulder-length, thick coppery hair.

"We are never unkind without good cause. Unless it is in battle, we do not intentionally cause fear or hurt—without cause." She removed a phial from her robes. "This will ease your nerves. It is not meant to insult you, only to help."

"There's no need," he replied stiffly.

"As you wish. You will wait here. Presently, Devyn will join you."

She walked out. Guards shut him in. Val sank into a chair to remove his boots. Then he studied his surroundings with interest, trying not to think about what would happen when the doors next opened. But that name played in his mind. *Devyn.*

It was a sumptuously pleasant chamber with glass windows overlooking the valley. Dark-green vines encircled two thin columns supporting the ceiling, their purple flowers releasing an overpowering perfume. The floor was tiled; the wall mosaics showed couples in lewd poses. The centrepiece was an enormous four-poster bed impossible to ignore. The headboard was dark mahogany, the covers exquisitely embroidered silk, the pillows plump.

A brisk knock sounded at the doors. Val rose, bracing. His heart skidded, its thud impossibly loud.

Guards held open the doors. The hooded woman walked through with deliberate poise. She threw back her cowl and let her gaze wander about the room. Then she glanced at him uncertainly. When the doors banged at her back, she flinched.

She was slender and very young, determined to hide her nervousness. In the face of her unease, Val's disquiet washed away. It wasn't only his feelings he had to take into account. Before him was a young woman who had also been commanded to lie with a stranger. What must she be thinking? Feeling?

He went forward to take her hands. "I'm told you're Devyn."

She blushed. Her hands shook beneath his. "Sorcha said to call you Val."

"Welcome. Would you like to sit and talk a while?" He gestured at the table. "They've brought wine, food."

Devyn considered him shyly through her lashes. "Yes, I would like to talk a little."

He led her to a chair. She sat straight-backed, fingers entwined in her lap. Val stole a look at her face as he poured wine. She was softly pretty with a sweet, upturned mouth and wide grey eyes. Hair the colour of sunlit wheat flowed freely about her shoulders. Tattooed swirls and sigils curled dramatically up her neck. The signs of the goddess.

She wore sandals and a simple gown belted at the waist. A gold necklet circled her throat and a silver bracelet her arm.

"Thank you." Devyn accepted a cup of wine and drank quickly.

He noticed another tattoo on her hand. Val tried to make sense of the marks. "You're a priestess? A healer?"

"No." Her voice was low and breathy. "I am a seer. Not as powerful as someone like Roaran Caelan or the high priestess Sisilia, but when the goddess wills it, I walk the Enarae. I glimpse what may come. Possibilities, at least. It is not a certain art."

Val frowned. He had assumed his warrior blood would be matched with the same. Clearly, he did not understand.

"Did you see me?" he teased. "In these journeys beyond the Enarae?"

Devyn shot him a frightened look. "I glimpsed you once in a dream. I did not know then who you were." Her gaze fell to the floor. A slow flush rose from her throat to her cheeks. Oh, gods, he could imagine what they'd done in her dream.

"Forgive me, Devyn, but you look very young."

"I'm nineteen. You need have no fears there."

"Fears?"

She lifted her eyes to his with resolve. "I know you're trying to be kind, to put me at ease. But I am afraid that you will think me too young, that I will leave this room shamed because you do not want me."

His heart went out to her. "I... no," he stammered. "I will not shame you."

Devyn drained her wine. With great dignity, she rose and sat on the bed. It creaked beneath her weight. Without fuss, she slipped off her sandals. "Will you...?"

Val sat beside her. When he put his hands on her shoulders, she shivered. Gently, he leaned to kiss her lips. She tasted of wine. Her hair was the fragrance of roses.

His kiss deepened. Devyn's lips parted to allow his tongue. He trailed his fingers lightly down her bare arms. Beneath his touch, gooseflesh rose. She sighed softly. Val brushed the gown from her shoulders. It fell to her hips. She wore nothing beneath. His body wakened.

Devyn drew back from his kiss. "My sisters said to do this." Tentatively she slid her fingers down his thighs and groped between his legs, growing bolder when he groaned in pleasure.

"What else did your sisters say?"

"Next, this." She fumbled at the ties to his pants. Her caress moved inside to his groin, her strokes long and slow.

She broke off, only to stand and wriggle from her gown. Val let his eyes drink in her nakedness. Heat flushed through him.

Devyn stooped to draw off his pants. Gently, she pushed him back against too many cushions and crouched over him, her knees against his thighs. Again, her hand stroked his arousal.

"This is nice," she whispered. "My sisters said if you were considerate and slow, it would be."

Val lifted his head to capture her mouth with his again, tongues entwined and flickering. His hands softly moved over bare skin, then he swept a caress down over her hips to her thighs. She shivered. When he rubbed his palm over a nipple, she moaned.

"Oh, now," she pleaded. "Now, now."

He half rose so she was in his lap, legs stretched behind his back. Carefully, he pushed inside her. She tilted her hips to take more of him. Val groaned. His body demanded rhythm, but he held himself back.

"No, do not be gentle."

He thrust deeper. Devyn gasped and trembled. She clutched the silken coverlet. Her lips eagerly sought his again.

Beneath a wave of sensation, Val thrust again and again, her body like moist silk. She cried out and dug nails into his back as she moved with him, finding the angle she liked. Then he climaxed with an explosion of pleasure, hearing Devyn whimper.

They clung to each other for a long moment, panting. Val trailed fingers gently through Devyn's hair. "I didn't hurt you?"

She smiled and made a contented sound.

"Was I too quick? I…"

Devyn silenced him with a brush of lips against his. "No, no. My fault." She considered him with wide grey eyes. "How long until we can do that again?"

⚬∾⟊∽⚬

At dusk, the ritual began again. He bathed, reluctantly submitting to servants washing him then dressing him in a simple tunic. It fell below his knees, sweeping the top of his boots. A cloak swung from one shoulder.

Rohane delivered him to the temple. She was quiet. More than once, she rebuffed his attempts to talk.

Val's thoughts strayed to Devyn. A sweet girl. He remembered her charming giggle as they had talked, covers loose about their legs, candles burning down towards dawn. She'd grown bolder as the night had aged, her hands demanding his attention, rousing his body again and again. Val realised he anticipated next week eagerly.

The encounter, the simple joy of it, might have quelled his fears about tonight—but for Rohane's obvious unease.

"You're angry at me?"

"No."

"You're worried about something. Is it… tonight?"

Rohane stopped abruptly. She turned and grabbed his shoulder. She was nearly his height and gripped him with savage strength. "Promise me... just promise me you won't invite her anger." Rohane bit her lip, frowning. "No, forget it. You'll do as you will."

She strode on quickly.

Val caught up with her. "I'm listening. If you have a warning for me, then I'll heed it."

Rohane sighed. She faced him. "Put aside that pride tonight. Please."

"I can be good."

"No, no. Not good. *Careful.*"

The temple rose before them. Val followed Rohane up the stairs. A knot of priestesses awaited him. Sorcha stepped forward. She dipped her head at Rohane. "Captain."

"I'm staying tonight." Rohane sounded determined. The two women exchanged a look.

The high priestess nodded. "You may wait in the main chamber."

Sorcha led Val to the altar. He glanced about, but there was no hooded woman kneeling. Only him.

"She is... delayed," Sorcha said uncomfortably. "She will bend her knee to the goddess later."

Apart from the woman's absence, the same ceremony unfolded, just as mysterious. Sorcha bound his hand and ushered him into the same room as the night before.

Everything felt familiar. Again, candles blazed. Again, food and wine waited on the table. And again, Sorcha drew out a phial from her clothing.

"No," he said.

"Tonight comes Madenn. Would you reconsider?" She held the phial.

He waved the offer aside. "No."

"As you wish." She backed away, and guards pulled the doors shut.

Val sat on the bed, watching the doors uneasily. Rohane was afraid for him. Why? And even Sorcha's manner was strained, odd.

He did not have long to wait. The doors burst open. Guards scurried aside. The woman who strode in still wore a steel helm and weapons belt as though she had just come from the training field.

She whipped off her helm. Released, long blonde hair flowed over her shoulders. If not for her cruel, tight mouth, her face might have been pretty, with dark brows shading blazing emerald eyes.

"Let's get this done with." She tossed her sword belt onto the bed then sprawled after it, back against the headboard, still dressed in boots, leather jerkin, and pants. There wasn't an ounce of excess weight on her, but she seemed to take up the entire bed.

Val stood stunned. Then he wanted to laugh. The sheer arrogance of this woman. He could imagine her on the battlefield, tromping on her enemies, kicking heads, slicing limbs, and laughing as blood splattered her face. Ha, she probably licked the blood off then later drank it by the cupful.

He snatched a breath. "You're Madenn. I'm—"

"I know who you are. And it's pronounced Marhden." She folded her arms. "Well, you look nicely formed. And tall. I dislike men who are smaller than me. Perhaps this won't be totally disagreeable."

Val's hands formed fists. His breaths pumped through his skull. He tried to cage his anger. "Would you like wine, Madenn?" His tone was icily polite.

Her green eyes flickered. Kaell had emerald eyes, but they never looked that lifeless.

"Oh, very well. Pour me wine."

He drained a cup quickly before he took wine to her. Gods, how to get through this. The drunker the better. In fact, insensible seemed the most pleasant option.

She drank then held out her cup for more. Val filled it. This time, Madenn rolled the cup in her palms. "Well, I have wine. I doubt it will make this any better. Come, service me."

His brows shot up in shock. Had he misinterpreted the Quisnaf word? Actually, he had. She meant something much cruder.

"Let's get this over with," Madenn said.

Val's pride reared up. "No. I don't think so."

She surged up, crowding in on him menacingly. He stood his ground. Her hand rose. The slap stung his cheek. A hot flush of anger stirred within him. But he did nothing, only glared.

"Frigid, are you?" She stared at him with contempt. "As bloodless as the rest of your race. Or maybe you're shy? Shy little boy." Madenn grasped her sword belt and buckled it about her waist. Then she filled a cup of wine and drank. It spilled down her mouth onto her throat.

"Be ready for me next time." She retrieved her helm and stalked off.

⁓∙⊷∘≀⊶∙⁓

"She didn't even take off her boots. She barely took off her sword." Val grimaced. "I suppose I'll be punished."

Rohane leaned a shoulder to his door. "She's already complained to Sorcha. Sorcha will take her complaint before the council."

"Hmm." Val rested his head on his hands, comfortable beneath the coverlet on the bed. In the distance, squalling rain fell as dusk gathered shadows in his room. A brawling wind rattled wind chimes. When Rohane had entered with a skirr of air, his candle flame had gyrated as though to wild music.

"What did you expect me to do? Just lie there and take it?" Whatever the punishment, he would not submit to Madenn.

Rohane crossed her arms. Flickering light fell softly on the strong lines of her face. "Madenn makes a bad enemy, Val. In battle, she is vicious. Unstoppable. Terrifying—to our enemies. Do you know what warriors in other battales call her? Madenn the Malicious. Not to her face. She'd strike them dead with one blow."

"Charming."

"Val, are you listening to me? She's a battale captain. She has power. You can't antagonise her."

"How can she be a captain? Aren't they your best and most respected warriors?"

"Usually."

"Well then…" He arched his brows. "What happened there?"

Rohane sighed. "It happened quickly. She was lieutenant to a captain called Trevin. Trevin was…" She smiled. "Remarkable. Then the impossible happened. Trevin was captured in battle, taken far away, beyond the Ice Sea, to the Circle Kingdoms."

"Is she alive?"

Rohane nibbled her lip. "I don't know. No one does. Part of me hopes she isn't. Can you understand that? For such a woman to be a captive…"

"I can understand that," he said.

"Madenn was elected battale captain by her warriors. They love her. But a certain type of soldier seems to be attracted to that battale. I could never join it. They are brutal. They seem to enjoy killing more than others. Consequently, they're given the most unpleasant tasks, the ones not for the squeamish."

"So that's three battale captains I know of. Persia—I don't like her, but I understand her. Madenn, well, I hate her. Joanna, I glimpsed from afar. Who's the fourth?"

Rohane sat beside him. She leaned in conspiratorially. "The most extraordinary. Perhaps the most powerful woman in Quisnaf."

"I thought that was Blaire."

"Blaire would like to think so." She rose with a sigh. "Are you going to get up? It's dusk. We should go."

"We should. Especially if you're not going to tell me about this mysterious captain of virtue and everything good." He flung off the light coverlet, rose, and padded to a table for water, careless of his nakedness.

Rohane appraised him with a long look. "You're bruised. Your cheek."

His hand flew to the mark. "Why are you looking at my face? This is an attempt to seduce you."

"Funny." She passed him a tunic.

"You could help me dress. Put your hands all over me."

"That's even funnier."

He stared at her with sudden longing. A longing for intimacy. For friendship. For comfort. For belonging. "Rohane…" His voice caught huskily.

She turned away before he could speak words she clearly didn't want to hear. "Tonight will be different, Val. And it will be better."

⁓∞✝∞⁓

They walked through quiet passages into the garden. Dark clouds banked above streaks of purple and mauve. The air simmered with warmth. The night, the garden were serene and quiet and scented of that warm, earthy fragrance from the downpour.

"We're heading for the temple?" He raised his brows. "Not the bathhouse. Is it because of who the last woman on your list is? Do you know who it is?"

"Yes."

"But you're not saying." Val sighed and began to count on his fingers.

Rohane scowled. "What are you doing?"

"Listing the things you refuse to talk about. First, you and Samantha share a bond, but you won't explain it. Second, you say you're cursed but don't say exactly how. Third, you mumble about someone called Jenna-Dairine with awe in your voice. Then there's this mysterious fourth battale captain."

She threw up a hand in surrender. "As my mother always says: 'It is best to learn from observation and consideration, rather than simply be told.'"

"In this instance, I'd rather be told. Wait. You have a mother? I imagined you arrived fully formed, carried by a bird of prey."

"You're hilarious," Rohane said.

Beneath bunched clouds, misty rain fell upon the temple steps, hardly enough to wet the stone or even dampen his hair. Guards flung back the doors. Sorcha came forward at once, guards at her back.

"Thank you, Rohane."

It was a dismissal. Rohane turned away. She did not look at Val. At that, at both her and Sorcha's tension, nervousness kicked in Val's gut.

"This way," Sorcha said.

The guards fell in about him. Val's unease kicked up a notch. Rohane had said tonight would be different.

Sorcha led him through the sanctum dominated by the majestic statue of Cyrah, past shadowy alcoves where candles burned, down cool, tiled, unfamiliar corridors. They took a corner stairwell that coiled lower, the air smoky from torches in cressets.

The steps ended at a splendid bathhouse. It was a chamber of white marble, columned like the hall, a place of shadows and soft light. Candlelight fell on carved statues of naked warriors and on gleaming floors, in parts covered with woven bamboo mats. Barefoot young women wearing only thin shifts tipped jugs of hot water into fine, pale marble baths, far different to the natural springs in the rest of Quisnaf. Steamy air breathed with the aromas of lavender, rose, and musk.

"I thought the tasks of the bathhouse fell to servants or slaves," Val said.

"In the temple, only servants of the goddess may preside." Sorcha clapped her hands. Through the steam, two young women appeared. They bowed to the high priestess then began to unfasten Val's clothing. Though surprised, he submitted, even allowing them to guide him to the bath. It was shadowy and misty, a hidden place. As he sank into the water, one woman joined him and picked up cloth and a ladle. Wordlessly, she soaped and washed his body.

Val closed his eyes. Steam fogged, hiding them from the other attendants. Slowly, his muscles relaxed, his breath sighing out as his mind quietened.

Sharp pain seared in his temple. The blow knocked him back. Strong hands gripped his throat, forcing him beneath the water. With no time to draw in a breath, he panicked, grappling at the hands holding him under. But he was unbalanced, his body weightless in the water with nothing to brace against.

In vain, he tried to twist, to thrash, to break the hold around his neck. His lungs burned. *Eighty-seven seconds.* The number flashed in his mind, a half-forgotten memory of his training with the Serravan. Eighty-seven seconds. That was how long before his body would take over and he would breathe in water. Then he was done for.

The pressure at his throat fell away. Hands yanked Val's attacker off him. Others reached for him, pulling him up. Val gasped in air.

Spluttering, coughing, he only distantly registered voices and figures milling about. Then the parts of the scene in front of him settled into place. Temple guards held a young woman, her wet hair plastered about her sullen face, her gown soaked.

"Let me go," she hissed. "You have no right."

Val's rescuers lifted him from the pool and laid him upon a bench, a rolled-up cloth beneath his head.

Sorcha bent over him. "Are you unhurt?"

Val took a moment before he answered her. He rose to his elbows, aware of a dull throb in his temple and a tremble in his limbs. "I'm all right."

Sorcha whirled on guards and bath servants. "How could this happen? In the middle of the temple." She glared at the woman held by guards. "Why did you do this? Who sent you?"

The captive smirked. It was a sick, smug grin. Then she began to chant in a strange tongue. "No," Sorcha cried. "Stop her." She lurched at the woman, just as the prisoner sagged, limp in the guards' grips. Sorcha slapped the captive, but the woman did not respond.

Bewildered, Val stared. "What just happened? What's wrong with her?"

Sorcha dragged a fist down her cheek. "It's a spell that keeps her unresponsive. So we can't question her."

"You've seen this before?"

Sorcha nodded. "There was another one. She came after the Regenta in the valley one night. Blaire fought her off. The woman was arrested, but before we could take her for interrogation, she spoke those same words."

Val frowned. "Nothing rouses them?"

"Nothing," Sorcha said. "But we will deliver her to our sorceresses to see if they can break the spell." She glanced at him. "Are you well enough to see this night through? I think it is more important now than ever."

"I've a bit of a headache." He touched fingertips to his temple, finding a lump. "And a sore throat, but I'm in tolerable shape, I think."

Sorcha snapped her fingers. A bath attendant appeared in front of Val. Gently, she drew him to his feet and dried him with a cloth.

"His hair is so very dark," she murmured to a companion.

"His eyes are even darker," the other woman said. "Quite exotic. I've never seen a Telorian before. Everyone says they're uncivilised, almost barbarians."

Sorcha clapped her hands in irritation. "He understands everything you say, silly girls. He speaks Quisnaf."

"Men do not speak Quisnaf unless they are here a good while," one scoffed. Nevertheless, they fell silent, eyeing him doubtfully.

Another young woman appeared with folded garments. She placed them on the bench beside Val. He put aside the cloth and dressed. The silken tunic was soft, the pants tight.

Nodding, the high priestess circled him slowly. "A cloak."

The first attendant fastened it to his shoulder with a jewelled clasp. Again, the high priestess studied his appearance. She reached to flick stray hair from his eyes. "That will do. Come with me."

Val held back. "Boots?"

Sorcha shook her head and made her way to the stairs. A shadow moved. Val glimpsed the outline of a raised arm. At a whir, he instinctively flinched. A knife tore past his head.

Sorcha shouted. Guards whirled. Quick steps echoed in the stairwell.

"After them," Sorcha commanded. The guards gave chase. Shocked temple servants whispered to each other.

Val tried to take in what had just happened. Two attempt within minutes of each other.

Sorcha approached him, her face grey. "You're unharmed?"

"Yes," he said shakily, shocked by the second assault. "What's going on?"

"Someone must have told about what is to happen tonight. I need to get you to safety."

"What *is* to happen tonight?" Val asked. "What makes tonight different?"

One guard returned and shook her head. "Whoever it was disappeared into the darkness. I've left my companions to search, but—" She shrugged.

"This is beyond my understanding." Sorcha hissed. "I had him brought to the temple to keep him safe. Assist me." She snapped her fingers at the guard then gestured to Val. "Come."

The temple servants bowed as she passed. Val trailed behind, unable to banish the fluttering in his gut. Who wanted him dead? And why? Why now? An assassin could have cut him down any time in the valley.

At the top of the stairs, more guards fell in around him, escorting him through the temple hall. Night had fallen, and shafted moonlight silvered the tiles. The brazier flames danced shapes on the wall. Val's skin prickled. He shot an uneasy look at the statue of Cyrah, almost certain she watched him.

A figure stood before the altar, her back to him, a hood hiding her face and hair. Sorcha bid him wait and approached the woman. They spoke quietly for a long moment. Whatever the high priestess said, the figure jolted and glanced at him. Then she hurried away.

Sorcha returned to Val and took him to the altar. Hastily, she performed the blood rite, bandaged his hand, then led him through more torch-lit tiled passages. She walked on her toes, her shoulders tensed. The guards, too, were watchful, their gazes shifting left and right. Val found himself glancing at shadows, remembering the knife that had come out of the darkness.

At ancient embossed silver-leaf doors, Sorcha stopped. Their panels depicted the goddess Cyrah as a ruler upon a throne, as a huntress, and as a warrior armed with a spear. To Val's surprise, two men flanked the entrance. They were armed with swords and wore the loose-fitting garments typical of Veniva. At the sight of the high priestess, they drew back the doors.

Sorcha marched in. Val trailed after her into a chamber with pale-blue marble walls and floors, except for a central garden of palms, ferns, and orchids directly below a large opening in the ceiling. Around the garden were divans with cushions and bright coverlets. Lattice and arches created shadowed corners with tables supporting overflowing vases of flowers or cushioned chairs beneath tapestries.

Val took another step, his bare feet soundless on the polished marble. All that broke the quiet were his own elevated breaths and the faint soothing trickle of water from a fountain in the garden. Oil burners released scents of bergamot.

Footsteps approached. A man strode through the pillars. He was about Val's height, with sun-bleached hair tied back in a thong. A short beard shadowed his chin. The man prowled with a hunter's awareness, his fingertips brushing the handle of a long-bladed knife poking from a belt slung low over his hips. A tunic embroidered with gold thread fell to his thighs.

The man stopped. His grey-blue eyes moved over Val. Then he half turned as sandalled feet slapped the floor. A woman appeared, stepping gracefully between the divans and couches. Val forgot to breathe. Everything fell into place; the guards, the elaborate preparations, even Rohane's disquiet. What didn't make sense was why someone had attacked him this night of all nights.

"They went after him." Blaire's voice trembled with anger. "In the temple. How is this possible, priestess? No one knew."

Sorcha wet her lips nervously. "Someone must have told. Someone sent two assassins. The first, we took hold of, but she used magic to put herself into a trance."

"Another one." Blaire fisted a hand. "Who is behind this? Who has this sort of magic?" She slitted her eyes. "What happened to the second assassin?"

Sorcha looked at the floor. "That one got away. I've guards searching. With your permission, Regenta, I'll find out what's happening." She bowed stiffly and backed away.

Blaire's jaw worked. Anger again flared in her eyes. "In the temple," she muttered. "This attack strikes at the heart of Quisnaf."

"Whoever is behind this is mocking you," the man said.

"They'll answer for it." Blaire's gaze again drifted to Val. She took a step closer. "You're not injured? Should I send for a healer?"

"My head aches a bit."

She lifted her arm and touched his temple with her fingertips. "Perhaps tonight should be delayed. You must be shaken."

"Who attacked me and why?"

"The Order," Blaire said. "They do not want me to carry your child."

Val arched a brow.

The man touched Blaire's arm. "I'll leave you."

"This is Brenin," Blaire said distantly. "Prince of Veniva... and my husband."

Husband. Val frowned, bewildered. That explained the Venivan guards.

Blaire offered him an appeasing smile. "You're shocked. I am sorry. It is a strange situation. But the Regenta of Quisnaf nearly always weds a prince or king of Veniva. It is the first bond between our people."

"This is awkward," Val admitted. "If you are wed, then—"

"Wed, not wed, it makes no difference to the gods. The blood keepers have decreed you and I shall couple, Val Arques. In many ways, it was inevitable. You are a warrior without equal. I am the result of centuries of careful breeding of strong warrior bloodlines. I will do my duty to Quisnaf."

Val swallowed hard and glanced at the Venivan prince. "And… surely you object?"

Brenin shrugged. "I understand these matters. A prince of Veniva must be as dutiful as a Regenta of Quisnaf. Blaire is more than my wife; she is a symbol of Quisnaf strength. Besides, we have a son, my heir. I am content. You may give her, you may give the blood keepers, and the council of Quisnaf the Caelan daughter they seek."

"I don't know what to think." Val shifted his weight. "Why does this Order not want us to lie together?"

Blaire seized his hand. "They do not wish me to have a daughter," she said. "Especially to a man descended from not only kings but also the gods."

Val frowned. "They fear what that daughter could become?"

"No," Blaire said. "They fear that once I have a Quisnaf heir, it will make my hold on power unassailable." She drew him to the couch and bid him sit. "We'll talk, Val. Then we'll see where the evening leads."

❦

Val woke in a strange bed, alone and naked beneath the sheets. Bright sunlight spilled through the temple's glass windows. Lying still, he sought to remember the night before. Memories stirred sluggishly. He knew he had kissed Blaire on a couch. But events after that blurred into a haze of wine, passion, and intimacy.

Groaning, Val rolled from the bed and searched out his discarded clothing. A dull ache throbbed behind his eyes.

"You've slept the day away."

He spun. Rohane sat in a chair, legs crossed at the knees.

"Oh."

"Hardly surprising, given what occurred last night." Rohane swooped up her weapons belt from a table. "I didn't realise temple security was so lax." An edge of anger roughened her voice.

"As you can see, their attempts to kill me were unsuccessful."

"Attempts?" She stared. "I heard about a knife. What do you mean attempts?"

Val rubbed the lump on his head. "One of the initiates tried to drown me."

"What?"

"Guards stopped her, arrested her, but she cast some sort of spell so she fell into a trance or something."

Rohane frowned. "There was another woman who did the same thing. They have her locked up, but she does not move, does not react. It's as if she's made of stone."

"Blaire says it's the Order. That they didn't want her to have another child."

"A female child," Rohane said. "A male would have no power. Now, are you decent? I'd best see if I can get you back to your chambers without anyone trying to throttle you."

"I can't defend myself here," Val muttered. "It isn't right that I have to rely on someone else to protect me. I'm a bladesman, Rohane." His hands fell to his side.

"It's the way it is, Telorian. Do not worry. What happened last night will not happen again. I can assure you of that." Her tone held grim resolution.

"No, you don't understand." Frustrated, he flung an arm wide, knocking a lantern off the table beside the bed. It clattered to the floor and rolled. "Without a blade, I'm helpless."

Rohane put the lantern back onto the table. Her gaze dwelled on his face. "I think I might understand."

"I need to bathe."

Rohane shook her head. "No. That's not what you need."

A ring of torches blazed about the training field. The night rang with the clang and shriek of steel. The familiar song of swords that hummed through the humid air comforted Val as a lullaby might a child. Moonlight glinted on helms as lines of warriors exchanged blows, their feet scuffing dirt or trampling grass, their curses and grunts rolling together.

Rohane snatched two blades from waiting servants. She led him to a corner of the field beneath spreading trees, apart from the other warriors, and tossed Val a blade. "You do remember which end to poke with?"

Val gripped the hilt and sliced the air with a satisfying swish. Anticipation coursed through him. It was like heat rising in his body on a chill night. A joyous elation. A freedom, as though his spirit soared.

"Hit me," Rohane said. "That is, if you can, Telorian."

He grinned. "And if I do?" He wouldn't. Both blades looked sharp.

"You can't. You're out of practice and not in shape." She crouched in a fighting stance, sword extended.

Val thrust lazily. Rohane didn't bother to parry. She didn't even need to step back. "A five-year-old Quisnaf girl could do better than that."

Chuckling, he jabbed deeper.

She retreated a step, still without using the blade. "That's it? How are you still alive?"

Val shrugged. "My charm?" He stabbed on the same line, but quicker, with a late disengage.

Rohane swept the blade left and right. "Still too slow, old man."

Val considered. He'd just shown her a straight hit with disengage. Now how did she think? Would she expect two disengages? Or a straight hit alone? A curious game, this. He would have to study her for a bit to understand her tactics.

He threw out his blade, ready for her parry and riposte. "Very nice," he teased.

"I'll give you nice." Rohane struck high.

Val ducked beneath swishing steel. She was on him again at once, jabbing low. He dropped his blade to knock hers aside. Rohane whipped her sword clear and circled, a lunging distance from him. "That's it? You're just going to let me attack?"

"I'm guessing your weapons masters taught the same as mine. The odds are better in attack."

She dropped the tip. "Then attack."

"Into that obvious invitation? You're deliberately too close." Still, he willingly thrust short, a feint, the blade slipping forward with each of two disengages. Rohane used a circular parry that rendered them useless. Val blocked her riposte, then unleashed a series of attacks at less than his usual speed.

She let him drive her back, ducking and weaving to evade his cuts, his slashes, his stabs. Rohane let him chase her then took over the attack when she thought he had overreached.

Val used the game to test his unused muscles, to embrace the feel of the blade as it crashed and slid against hers. He welcomed the burn in his muscles and the sweat upon his throat and chest. Almost at once, his legs and arms responded as they had been trained. Nothing was lost or forgotten.

"You're not really trying," Rohane complained. "Don't insult me. I picked up my first sword at four." Moonlight caught the flash of her teeth.

He'd held back, uncertain how skilled she was, and neither of them wore helms of even leather armour. Val quickened his pace, his mind pinpricked to the blade and the rhythm of swordplay. There was a space opening within him, deep inside, a quiet place where only he and the sword dwelled. It was a calm void, empty of emotion, even though an avalanche of sensations rushed him.

When he fell into this place, he did not lose himself. Instead, time and space became instruments of his will. He could surrender to finely tuned training that had produced a bladesman without peer. Not then, not now.

By now, his opponent's sword spoke to him as clearly as his own. Rohane's patterns had been exposed. She had tried to disguise them, but his speed, his precise, delicate bladework gave him the edge. Rohane's steps grew rushed, her blade swinging frantically as she tried to match his pace.

He grew vaguely aware of figures edging closer, that the roar and clang of swords had dulled until the only sounds were the scrape of his blade against Rohane's and their harsh breaths.

Someone called a warning to Rohane when Val tricked her with a feint. At the last instant, he held back his sword. But his skill, how close he had come to wounding her, loosened tongues. A tumult of shouts exploded as they did on any tournament field, the spectators yelling out encouragement or gasping at strokes.

Again, she missed his feint, and he could have wounded her, but again he stayed his arm. Some part of him did not want to shame her in any way, even with an inevitable defeat.

And his victory was always inevitable. The song of steel hummed deep inside him, his mind calculating every combination, every possible reaction to a stroke, before his muscles and hand flawlessly performed his will. It was more than a dance. It was breath.

No matter how he tried to check his strokes or slow his furious speed, to temper his lethal steps, she left too many openings. At last, in frustration, he trapped her blade, his hilt to her tip, circled a bind, and ripped the weapon from her hand.

As her sword flew high then clattered to earth, Rohane cried out in anger. She stood for a moment, lost in battle fever. Then she clapped his shoulder and laughed.

"That was impressive," a new voice said. Nearby, a woman leaned her back to a tree trunk, arms folded. Moonlight sheened upon golden hair and turned already-flawless skin to ivory. Her pants and tunic might have been worn by any Quisnaf warrior. But her stillness set her apart.

Unhurried, she pushed herself upright. Warriors parted as she advanced on Val and Rohane. Up close, her face was oval with strong, straight lines. Her eyes were very dark.

Her cool gaze swept over him like the caress of a blade held by a lover. "I shall have to know more of you, swordsman." The woman turned to Rohane. "He guessed your patterns. Learn from it." She began to walk away, calling over her shoulder, "And it is forbidden to train without helms. Do not let me see that sort of recklessness again, Rohane."

In her wake, the crowd slowly dispersed. Women wandered back to their discarded weapons, laughing and talking. Val stood for a moment as though those dark eyes still fell upon him. Her voice, too, pursued him. *I shall have to know more of you. A threat or a promise?*

"Who is she?" His voice sounded breathier than he intended.

Rohane stared at something unseen in the distance. "Huh." She grunted. "I didn't know the field was hers tonight."

"Come on. No more secrets. Who was that?"

"I'll tell you about her another night. How do you feel?"

He grinned. "Better. How did you know?"

She did not return his smile. Her expression was solemn. "This is who you are, Telorian. Do not forget it. Whatever else happens, do not let anyone else or anything in Quisnaf define you. Promise me."

"This is very serious talk."

"Each of us needs something that brings us back to who we are. I think for you it is the blade."

"You're right. And what is that brings you back, Rohane?"

"It's too late for me," Rohane said.

ROHANE

"They came after him in the temple." Hands fisted, Rohane stalked up and down Blaire's bedchamber. "Here, in the temple."

"Don't you think I know that?" Blaire spread her arms. "Oh, goddess, Rohane. I don't know who I can trust. Not after this."

Rohane drew up abruptly. "What do you mean?"

"How did the second assassin get away? What if the temple guards are all against me? What if the Order's influence is everywhere?"

"No." Rohane shook her head firmly. "It's a few."

"A well-placed few."

"We need to hunt them down."

Blaire slammed her cup down. Her cheeks flushed with anger. "Every step I take, every reform I implement, I meet resistance. I find defiance, both open and surreptitious. Someone is acting against me, someone on the council, and I don't know who, but when I find out—"

"Sorcha? After all, two women attacked Val in the temple."

"No, not Sorcha. She is mistress of the temple. She could choose her moment to attack and succeed."

"You know what I think," Rohane muttered. "Go slower. Pull

back on your reforms. There are rumours about what you intend to do with the battales."

"We only need three battales," Blaire said. "To keep four battales operational costs a fortune. And Quisnaf has never used all four against an attacker."

"It's not popular. There's talk—"

"I didn't set out to be popular," Blaire snapped. "I set out to do what's right for Quisnaf. We have to change to survive."

"It's very quiet." Rohane glanced towards the passage, listening for the shuffle of feet from Blaire's guards. Nothing. A pulse of alarm coursed through her, an instant before a sword scraped from a scabbard.

The door flew back. Four masked figures stormed inside. For one useless moment, all Rohane could think was, "Who would dare come after the Regenta here?"

Then chaos unleashed. Rohane whipped out her blade and knife as the four figures rushed her and Blaire, weapons drawn. Blaire snatched her sword from a table to hold off two assailants. The other two came for Rohane.

She was already moving, already inside the nearest assailant's guard. As they swiped uselessly at air, Rohane grabbed them around the waist, faintly registering the assassin's womanly shape, and threw her down. The woman hit the ground hard, her breath huffing out.

Rohane whirled, throwing up her blade to catch the second attacker's thrust. With her other hand, she stabbed with the knife. The tip drove into soft flesh. The woman clutched at her belly, shrieking in pain.

The sound was like a siren's call. A rage flamed within, wanting to take Rohane over, wanting to shut down her thoughts to everything but the thrill of fighting and the odour of blood.

No. She could not surrender to the berserker fury, that mindless butchery. Not here, where she could kill Blaire.

Leaving her opponent crumbling to her knees, Rohane spun to

go to Blaire's aid. The Regenta was holding off both assailants, her blade furiously smashing left and right. Rohane moved in from behind. As if sensing the danger, one attacker started to pivot, just as Rohane cracked her sword hilt into the woman's head. The would-be assassin dropped.

The woman on the floor had recovered her breath and came at Rohane, her sword swinging. Rohane ducked. The woman moved in again fast, blade raised. Blaire shouted something, but Rohane's sword was ripping across ribs, the knife in her other hand tearing through flesh.

A clatter of footsteps and armament came from the passage. Guards rushed inside, Persia with them.

"Regenta, are you hurt?" Persia said.

"Arrest this woman." Blaire backed up the fourth assailant against the wall, her sword to the woman's throat.

"A servant found the guard at your door dead," Persia said. "I came as quickly as I could."

Rohane sheathed her sword. Persia issued orders. Decan guards took hold of the fourth attacker.

"That one, too." Blaire pointed at the assailant Rohane had hit on the head. "She is also alive. Take them both for interrogation."

Rohane took a step closer and looked hard at her. "Are you unharmed?"

Cheeks flushed, her chest heaving, Blaire shook her head. With quick, angry steps, she went to the assailant the guards had hold of. She whipped off the woman's mask and drew in a sharp breath. She went to the next and to the remaining two, removing their disguises.

Persia hissed in shock. "Three of them are from the one battale." She lifted her eyes to Blaire's. The Regenta seemed dazed. "You must see what this means?"

"Leave us." Blaire gestured at the guards. Her voice wasn't quite steady.

The guards cleared the room of bodies and prisoners. When

they were gone, Persia confronted Blaire. "You know who's behind this. You have to admit it now."

"No," Blaire said sharply. "It means nothing. She wouldn't."

"We were so close as children, as girls," Rohane said. "The four of us. You, Blaire. Me. Trevin. Jenna-Dairine. Inseparable. I won't believe it of her."

"There's no proof it's Jenna-Dairine," Blaire said.

"What sort of proof do you want?" Persia muttered. "A knife in your breast? Her hand about the hilt?"

"You don't understand."

"Oh, I think I do," Persia said.

GENYA

"I'm tired of this." Genya thumped a jar down on the table. "Teach me *real* magic."

Rozenn arched a brow. They were in the queen's chambers, the doors locked. Moonlight bled through opaque curtains at the balcony doors. It was after midnight, and the castle was silent but for the tread of steps on the walls and the distant drift of "all's well" from the towers upon the quarter hour. The night was heavy, the air stiff with humidity. With no ripple of wind over waves, the sea's voice was only a murmur over the reefs.

"The power to heal or hurt isn't real magic?"

"Potions," Genya muttered in disgust. "Always potions. Always herbs and roots. For months and months. Spells to fling bowls about. Spells to slam doors. How is that going to help me destroy an army?"

"Patience," Rozenn said. "I've taught you a few Seithin incantations as well."

"Patience?" All of Genya's frustration balled in her belly. She swept up a glass ampule and hurled it at the wall, shattering it. The liquid contents dribbled down the stone. "There's no time." She huffed a breath. "Alecc is in danger. That's what my dreams tell me. Someone is going to betray him."

Rozenn gripped Genya's arm, her fingers biting into muscle. "Who? Who threatens my son?"

"The future is shadowy," Genya said. "I catch glimpses in my dreams. Sometimes just a feeling. I only know I need to get back to the Mountains. I can't be here learning to brew love potions or spells to give your enemy warts."

"I have hardly wasted your time or mine with love potions," Rozenn said coldly. "I have taught you how to kill with poisons so lethal, it takes only one sip. I have taught you how to make healing salves and lotions. There will come a day when you will be asked to save a life, Genya Caelan. Or even to stealthily take one."

Genya tilted her chin, facing Rozenn. "Teach me blood magic. Teach me how to destroy."

Rozenn dug her teeth into her bottom lip, one hand about her swollen belly. "Blood magic is dangerous. Its power comes from within." She pressed her hand to Genya's breast. "It drains your life force."

"I am part seer," Genya cried. "You forget that. I am my father's daughter."

Rozenn blinked, her gaze on Genya. "Yes," she murmured at last. "Yes. The seer king's daughter." She tapped a finger against her chin. "And a seer can use the power of the Enarae and perhaps leave her life force untouched. Yes."

"I've walked in dreams," Genya said eagerly. "Since childhood. I'm ready."

"No one is ever ready."

"There is no more time for potions and poisons. Teach me what you know of blood magic so I can return to Alecc." She would serve Val's son. She would seek redemption in saving him, in showing her guardian she could choose what was right, that her heart was not as dark as Val believed.

Rozenn's stare fell upon the windows opening onto a balcony, as if seeking the sea beyond. Moments passed in silence. Then she nodded to herself as if decided. "Light the candles. As I've shown you. Tonight, I will teach you a blood spell that will help you discern the future."

"And tomorrow?" Genya gathered up the candles and placed them in a ring on the floor. She knelt to light each one then sat cross-legged in their circle.

Rozenn did not answer. Slowly, she eased herself down onto the floor inside the ring of candles. "The circle of light concentrates magic. Here." She handed Genya a knife. "For blood magic, blood must be spilt—an offering. The most powerful magic, though, requires a sacrifice. Rumour has it Myranthe Damadar sacrificed not only Aric Caelan but her own brother to create death riders."

At Myranthe's name, Genya shivered. "Is she as powerful as they say?"

"She is, but she is a bitter woman these days. Still vowing vengeance on Val Arques Caelan. Summoning the dead to try and find him. She seeks only revenge."

"A worthy goal," Genya muttered.

"Be careful, Genya," Rozenn cautioned. "Vengeance puts us on a dark path. The darkness is seductive, and dark magic at first is easier, but in the end, it takes your soul." She shrugged, her palms laced across her belly. "That is where shadow sorcery comes in. Though I am not gifted enough to be a shadow sorceress."

"Is Myranthe?"

"No. Her magic draws from her life force. A shadow sorcerer creates a shadow self so that the dark forces they conjure hurt the earth, the sea, the water, and air around them and leave the sorcerer untouched."

"Who would be so selfish?"

"In the pursuit of power? I think there are those who will not care just as long as they get what they want." Rozenn frowned. "There are rumours of a powerful practitioner of such harmful magic in a kingdom far from here called Cadasha. It is said this shadow sorcerer has destroyed his land in the pursuit of knowledge and control."

"Will you teach me shadow magic?"

"No," Rozenn said. "I will not. Even if I knew how, I would not."

"I need to know everything."

"Blood magic is dangerous enough."

"It's not enough. Teach me Seithin magic. I've heard of curses that can kill. Teach me."

"You're not ready."

Genya gritted her teeth. "I have to be ready."

Again, Rozenn gave her a searching look. "Seithin magic is perilous."

"I'm not afraid."

Rozenn sighed. "Very well. Though I know only a little, I will share it with you. If you are right and Alecc is in danger, we do not have the luxury of ordinary magic. First, however, a simple blood spell. Shall we begin? Take the knife and cut your arms."

Bracing, Genya carved two thin cuts in her skin, the pain scorching down her forearms.

"Now look within at the Enarae. We shall see if blood magic enables you to see what is to come more clearly."

Genya closed her eyes. She murmured the words Archanin had long ago taught her to pierce the Enarae. With a rush, it folded about her like velvet, with a chaos of colours and images, of sweet and bitter scents, some like roses, others like decay.

"Say these words," Rozenn told her. "They will only have power if you indeed have magic within you. Say, 'Sino mihi inmeo.'"

"Sino mihi inmeo," Genya repeated, then again, louder. All at once, heat burned beneath her skin. She cried out in pain. "Will it stop?" she begged Rozenn. "Will it stop?"

Rozenn shook her head. "Control your pain."

Slowing her breathing, Genya pictured Alecc in her mind, holding tightly to him as she might grip a sword. Then a different pain, blinding pain, overtook her as her spirit wrenched from her body. Fear jagged through her. Always before, her walk through the Enarae had been gentle. This time, her soundless cry of agony was trapped deep within her.

Without warning, the pain left her, and she floated, staring down at herself upon the floor, hands folded in repose. Foreboding squeezed her heart. Desperately, she sought calm, determined that nothing, not her doubts, should stop her. Magic meant power. Power meant the ability to fight for Val's son, to be redeemed in her guardian's eyes.

The rippling sea appeared below her, cold and grey. Lights blazed in the cliff castle, gaunt like a skeleton of stone. A cobbled courtyard appeared below, then she drifted, spectre-like, into the keep and through a hushed, shadowed great hall.

Why quiet? Why empty? If Alecc was a guest here, then he should be welcomed with feasting and celebration.

Her spirit flitted through a passage. It was stone-walled and whitewashed. A boy lighting a torch flinched and shivered. He shot a look around but did not see her. Then with a whoosh, she soared high above the castle before plunging down, as shapeless and formless as a wisp of air, into the waves. She sank lower and lower to the sand and rock. Something soft and pulpy brushed against her. Genya's heart smashed against her ribcage. Chained by its ankles to coral, a body drifted in the sea's draughts.

She caught a single glimpse of a face before the Enarae snatched at her spirit, drawing her away in a swirl of scents, shadows, blazing light, and roaring wind. With a gasp, Genya came back to herself. She had collapsed on the floor in the ring of candles. Rozenn knelt beside her, gently calling her name.

Groaning, Genya pushed to an elbow. Her journey through the Enarae had stolen her strength. If only she could lie there, let her eyelids grow heavy, and sleep. Dream. Forget what she had seen. But it was too horrific, too disturbing, to keep to herself.

Shaking, she faced Rozenn. "I saw Alecc," she whispered. "I saw his body."

Rozenn shrank back, her face ashen. "Then we are running out of time. I need to teach you how to control the skies, the sea, and the wind."

"No," Genya said. "You need to teach me how to kill."

"Call up the wind," Rozenn said.

She and Genya sat within a circle of candles on the headland. Uncomfortable with her pregnancy, the queen sprawled on the grass, legs extended. The night was eerily still, heavy and black. It was as if a pall had fallen upon the castle and the land.

After midnight for the past month, they had met in Rozenn's chambers when the castle fell silent then stolen through quiet passages, past guards snared in an unnatural sleep, and onto the cliffs. Beneath the open sky, the wind a whisper, the sea rumbling over distant reefs, the queen had taught Genya blood spells. How to drive another back, to propel them through the air, to force a man or woman to their knees with a single word. How to lift and hurl a blade with magic. How to pass by an enemy unseen, to become a shadow.

But tonight, there was a shift. Genya knew it from Rozenn's urgent steps as she led them to this place hidden from the castle.

"We are near the end of our time together," Rozenn said. "I cannot risk teaching you like this any longer." She pressed her hands to her belly.

Genya looked at the queen's fingers stretched over her body. She was deeply curious who had fathered this child. "Does Gendrick suspect what we are doing?"

"No." Rozenn frowned. "He is cunning but too stupid to see what is before him."

"He does not perceive you as a threat," Genya said with sudden clarity.

Rozenn's gaze sharpened on her. "He has discounted me, yes. Dismisses me as a simple witch. Forgets the heritage of magic in my veins. He'll learn soon enough, he has underestimated me." Again, her hands stole to her belly.

"This child—" Genya stopped. She had no right to ask. But there was something secretive, almost sly, in Rozenn's look whenever she touched her belly.

Rozenn shrugged. "An encounter one night when the music played in a street far from the castle. I followed him, because of who he was, though he never learnt my name." Her eyes hazed with memory. "Gendrick knows the child is not his. My son will not live a day once he is born—if my husband gets his hands on him."

"You're sure it's a boy?"

A serenely vicious smile appeared on Rozenn's face. "I know it." She gripped Genya's arm, her nails digging into the girl's skin. "You must get the child to Yvonne. She'll know what to do. Only far from here will he be safe."

"I gave you my word." That had been Rozenn's price for teaching her magic.

Rozenn nodded slowly. "We need to begin. Tonight, you must summon a storm."

"I am not afraid," Genya said. "Teach me."

"Then hear the darkness. Listen. Command the storm to rise."

"How?"

"Be one with the night. With the elements. Be one with the waves. With the moon, the stars."

Genya breathed deeply, listening to the sounds beneath the silence. A rustle of leaves. Distant paws scurrying through bushes. A quiet whisper, little more than an eerie undertone. She shivered. Moonlight bled onto tall grass. The air was sullen and heavy.

Rozenn began to chant, ancient words she had taught Genya that had been passed down from the days of Seithin. Genya joined her, arms extended, entreating, commanding the elements.

"Arise," they shouted. "Arise, the storm." Their words rose towards the starlit sky, a lonely melody in the night. A breeze stirred the feathery tips of foxtail grass. Then the breeze began to whistle, a song like notes strained through a recorder.

A haze gathered on the horizon. Clouds banked, swift and dark. The wind gathered pace, its voice strong. The moonlight fell like a hoar frost on the surging ocean, on white-tipped waves now pounding the shore. Then it vanished with the stars beneath the thunderheads.

The tempest unleashed. Lashing rain, streaking lightning violently took over the sky and the land and the sea. Waves thundered. Within the gale, the sea bellowed.

Genya began to laugh. She rose to her feet and danced on the clifftop, her face turned to the rain and wind. It was as if she was a child again, defying the storm, shouting that it could not hurt her. That she was destined.

"Enough," Rozenn said. "It is enough. You have called the storm to us."

"No!" Genya cried. The released power flowed through her. Exhilarating. Enlivening. She took her knife from her belt and slashed her arm, wincing at the sharp pain. She had no purpose beyond what she could give to Alecc via her magic. She would help Val's son and make her guardian proud of her again. No matter the danger. No matter the cost. "Arise!" she shouted. "Arise, the storm."

The wind howled, the sky black. Sheets of lightning fell about her, illuminating the earth and sea. The castle sat like a silhouette upon the clifftops, a dark outline against the blackness.

"Arise!" Genya shouted again. On and on, the storm raged. The sea roared, and the wind hissed and howled. On and on.

"Stop." Her gown sodden, her hair wild, Rozenn grasped Genya's arm. "You have enflamed the skies with the use of blood magic. It's too dangerous. A Seithin spell was enough."

"Not to me," Genya cried. "I am the seer king's daughter. His blood is in my veins."

"But what is in your heart?" Rozenn asked.

The desire for redemption, she might have said. *Forgiveness.* "It is vengeance," Genya said truthfully. As if an accompaniment, thunder clashed.

At the thought of what was before her, a sudden weariness overtook her. She must kill every ghoul to prove her loyalty to Alecc. She must prove herself to Val. They must forget she had sided with Archanin.

"There was darkness in Roaran," Rozenn said. "And I fear it is in you, too." Yet she did not look afraid. No, there was brazen interest in her expression, speculation even. "But we have commanded the elements long enough."

Lifting her arms, she called to the squalling wind and rain. Gradually, the skies quietened. Soon, stars flickered, and the tempest blew out across the sea. The thunderheads dissipated like mist, leaving in their wake only murky skies, pattering rain, and sodden earth. An eerie quiet settled upon the now-glassy sea.

"I am not afraid of the darkness," Genya said. "Teach me more. I want to know everything."

Rozenn was watching her intently. "What *do* you fear, Genya Caelan?"

Genya considered that a moment. To never be forgiven. For Val to always look upon her with disgust. "To be no one," she blurted. "For my life to mean nothing." At once, she wished the revealing words unsaid. But Rozenn only hunched her shoulders.

"We are all of us destined when we die to be lost to time," Rozenn said sadly.

"Except my father."

"Even he, one day, will be forgotten." Rozenn stared inward then sighed. "There is only one more thing I can teach you."

Genya caught her breath in eagerness. "Tell me."

Rozenn hesitated. "I do not know if I can trust you with this magic."

"If you want Alecc safe, then you must."

Rozenn turned her head to stare out over the sea, her expression troubled.

"We have very little time," Genya said. "If there is magic that will help keep Alecc safe, then I must know it."

A shudder went through the other woman. "It is the most dangerous magic. Not even Myranthe Damadar, for all her brazen defiance of the gods, would use it. For this spell is the path to destruction. The path to death."

"Tell me."

"It is a Seithin curse. It must be used only as a last resort. And the words must never be spoken more than thrice. Do you understand?"

"I understand."

Rozenn gripped Genya's arms. Her stare searched the girl's face. "Never more than thrice."

Genya trembled and whispered, "I swear it."

Rozenn hesitated, her chest rising and falling. For a moment, she closed her eyes. Then at last, as if resolved, she said, "Draw close."

With a shiver, Genya moved nearer. Soft, cool rain misted her cheeks. She leaned towards Rozenn. The queen cupped a palm to half cover her mouth and whispered in Genya's ear.

At even the rhythm of the words, their cadence, their music, a thrill, a fierce joy coursed through Genya. She mouthed the spell silently to herself, taking it within.

"I'm not afraid," she whispered. But she was. Oh, yes, she was.

DANNON

Dannon limped at Samantha's side, his hand on her arm. Night closed in about them. A soft night, despite its harsh voices. Branches ground against each other like scraping iron. A peacock screeched. Less forbidding, a stream murmured over rocks, its lyric waters silvered by a waning moon. After the closed-in caves, Dannon thought it all impossibly beautiful.

They walked along torch-lit paths through hollows and along cliff ledges, passing groups of Quisnaf women drawn by the cool night from the cavernous halls and chambers. They sat chattering on the grass or with their legs dangling in pools, pants rolled up and boots abandoned at their sides.

As he and Samantha passed by, voices hushed. Eyes followed. Some stripped him as they swept up and down. Just as he had on every night Samantha had brought him outside, Dannon folded his arms over his body, uncomfortable, anxious to move on.

As the first stars glimmered, a rustling in bushes proved to be a girl and young man. They offered startled looks and scuttled off. Samantha sighed. "He is not cloaked. I wonder where she found him?"

"Cloaked?"

"Protected. Quisnaf women of certain status or rank may cloak a man. He belongs to them, becomes their responsibility."

"Enslaved," Dannon muttered.

Samantha laughed. "Trust you to interpret it like that. Yet the Varee are slavers, Dannon."

"Did you hear judgement in my voice? I only stated a fact."

Samantha turned to consider him seriously. "There is nothing false in you. Not ever." She walked on.

"I can only be who I am." Dannon caught her up. Except who or what was he now? He was a man who had believed in nothing but his own strength, his skill. Now he didn't even have that.

They crossed a stone bridge over a fast-running river, moonlight sheening on its ripples. The contrasts in Quisnaf struck him anew. So beautiful was this valley. The caverns were richly furnished, with thick rugs upon the stone or dirt floors. The steaming bathhouses, frequented by a people who valued cleanliness and good grooming, gleamed with marble, and the air was richly perfumed of bergamot and creamy soap.

Yet their lives and laws were harsh, especially to a man. If he should turn his head in any direction, he might glimpse a sentry, watchful within. Others in towers and forts built into the mountains watched for dangers without. Despite the shady paths, perfumed blossoms, and whispering streams, this remained a garrison city. Always at war. Always ready for war.

Pausing, he rested his hands on the bridge's wall, rough to his touch. The stone was warm from the vanished sun. "Is that why they stare at me?" he wondered aloud. "If I were cloaked, would it stop?"

Samantha stopped beside him. "It bothers you? The way women regard you here?"

Dannon winced. "I know that kind of assessing look. My slaver's gaze still shames me, so I recognise it easily in others. My mind still leaps to what others might value. I remember even the first time I met Roaran—" He gave an embarrassed shrug.

Samantha sighed. "We can all admire a beautiful thing. That's why they stare. You have a quality. I cannot quite put my finger on it."

"Even crippled?" He pressed his palms into the stone. "My right knee and ankle are next to useless. I find myself wondering what I am now. A warrior cannot survive if he is not whole. Yet I was always a better archer than swordsman, and this crippled leg surely will not affect how I loose arrows."

"Who crippled you?" Samantha asked again.

"Does it matter?"

"Maybe."

He hesitated, exhaling slowly. A fragment of his nightmares shadowed his mind. That foul room deep in the earth with its stench of blood and fear would always be with him. "A Telorian lord called Felix Hillborn."

"Why?"

"He believed I robbed him of both his brothers."

"So this man, Felix, held and tortured you. If this is the same Felix who betrayed Roaran, then he is outcast, a price upon his head."

He turned to stare at her. "Felix escaped. How?"

"That, I do not know. Battle is always chaotic. That is what drew the Quisnaf to Telor. Chaotic battle. Roaran sought our help to fight Archanin, and we came."

"He never said." Dannon frowned. Roaran had kept so much to himself. In that, Genya was like him. Or like Val Arques. Genya had once told Dannon she had quickly learned as a child that keeping secrets was necessary to survive.

"What did you get out of it? What did Roaran offer you in return?"

"Gold. And a man we'd sought for a very long while. A very valuable man."

"What man?"

A shout rang out in the valley. A man ran onto the bridge, pursued by armed women. More guards appeared at the other side to cut him off.

The man desperately peered behind then ran to Dannon. His face was wild, his hair tousled. He clutched at Dannon's arm. "Help me."

Startled, Dannon glanced down at the man's hand then at the advancing women. "What would you have me do?"

The man's gaze fell on Samantha. Then he looked back at Dannon. His expression darkened. "Oh, I see. You're one of them," he sneered. "A breeder, maybe. Pampered while other men are enslaved and murdered. You disgust me." He spat at Dannon.

His pursuers reached him. They grabbed his shoulders and marched him off. One woman delayed to salute Samantha. "Councillor. Apologies for this interruption."

Dannon wiped his face, frowning after the prisoner. The man's anger and accusation had rattled him. "It's true what he said," he said slowly. "I have given no thought to those who are captive in your city."

Samantha shrugged. "It's the way of things."

"That never made anything right." But the words held no heat. Quisnaf was nothing to do with him. He was an unwilling guest, confined to his room for many weeks now, apart from moments when he was escorted to the baths or the gardens.

Her face split into a thin smile. "Even you, Cahirean, cannot change centuries of tradition and law."

"Oh, don't worry," Dannon said. "I don't intend to try." When they were done with him, he would return to Telor and forget about this place with its matriarchal rulers and structure.

"I'm pleased to hear it." Frowning, she turned to stare over the water. "Beneath the calm, Quisnaf boils with tension. I am afraid—" She shook her head.

"Of what?"

"It's afraid of whom," she said distantly. Then she shook herself and touched his hand. "Come, we'll go through the scent garden. Then I must return you to your chambers"

"Return me to my prison, you mean." He screwed up his

mouth. "I'm as much a captive as that man they dragged off."

"You're safe. You're protected. You are comfortable. What more do you want?"

"Freedom."

"Men do not know what to do with freedom," Samantha said.

From nowhere, an arrow struck the top of the bridge just below Samantha's chest. Figures appeared in the trees.

"Quickly." Samantha grabbed his arm. "Stay down." Keeping low, she led him off the bridge into a mass of undergrowth. They ploughed through shrubs and ferns, into a thicket of bamboo. Both crouched, listening.

For a long moment, there was nothing but the eerie call of a curlew. Then a dry leaf crackled beneath a stealthy footstep. Dannon held his breath. Someone stood very close, unmoving. He glanced at Samantha. She put a finger to her lip.

For an age, nothing happened. The stillness settled about them, tense with danger. Then a woman said, "Any sign of her?"

"Nothing," another woman answered. Someone exhaled. A hand brushed through culms of bamboo close to Dannon's head. At last, whoever was there moved on.

He and Samantha stayed where they were, even after they were certain they were alone. Time passed. The second moon glided through the canopy of trees about the valley. Cautiously, they emerged from the bamboo.

"They were after you," Dannon whispered. "Why?"

"Because I am what you might call a 'Blaire loyalist.'"

"Who were they?"

Samantha glanced about uneasily, gesturing they should move towards the trees. "The Order," she said sombrely. "They wish to return Quisnaf to the old ways. But that means they must overthrow the council, overthrow Blaire."

"I couldn't protect you." Dannon huffed in dismay. "It isn't right that I couldn't protect you. Even if I had a weapon—"

Even with a weapon, what good was he?

"You could not have saved us," Samantha said. "Armed or not."

"Who am I?" Dannon cried. "I am nothing." He dropped his head, his shoulders bowed.

Samantha rested a hand on his back. "You must be still, you must be calm, and reflect upon this. I pray the goddess shows you the path forward."

"The gods are cruel and fickle," Dannon said. "Untrustworthy. Why should your goddess be any different?"

"There is a Quisnaf saying," Samantha said. "It is said that one who believes in nothing shall find only nothing."

"Perhaps there's nothing to find," Dannon said.

VAL ARQUES

Hundreds of lamps in trees sparkled about the valley. Torches in cave mouths gaping from cliffs blinked like a wall of fairy lights in the darkness. More lit the paths where groups of men and women strolled towards steps to an enormous cavern.

The atmosphere was jovial and light, but Quisnaf was a city of undercurrents, malice, plots, factions, and unspoken words. *Secrets.* Even glances held meaning Val could not unravel.

"Tonight," Rohane said, as she and Val walked together amidst the crowd. "You'll learn the answer to at least two of your questions."

"You could just tell me."

"My mother said…"

He whipped up a hand. "I know, I know… Better to learn from observation or experience, blah, blah."

"Blah, blah? I don't blah, blah. How rude."

He caught her grin in the flickering light. In the past few months, he had come to like her grin, its unexpected impudence, how it enlivened her face. Even now, Val wanted to curl his fingers in hers and sweep her knuckles to his lips. Then he wanted to nuzzle her neck and whisper, "I want to learn about you, Rohane.

Not through observation. Through experience."

But his prickly companion's smile would likely fade. She would mutter about duty, responsibility, and her role as his guardian.

Val gazed about. The crowd bristled with anticipation. Everyone was beautifully adorned, like peacocks, in long flowing pants with embroidered or brightly coloured silk tunics. Capes, another layer of silk, swirled. Torchlight glinted on rings and jewelled necklaces.

He considered a young man accompanying a woman with a scabbarded sword. His hair was brushed and clean, his clothes just as fine as his companion's. And like the other men, he walked unhindered by restraints and wore a tri-coloured cloak that draped his shoulders.

Despite the festivities and glittering lights, more guards than usual were sprinkled throughout the darkness, positioned on ridges near the caves and throughout the valley and gardens.

Val nudged Rohane. "Lots of sentries."

"They're part of the Decan Watch. Not members of the battales. Quisnaf's final line of defence in trouble. Most are older, former battale warriors, now tasked with keeping order inside the city."

"Why are they here in such numbers?"

"Nearly every fighting woman of Quisnaf will be at the feast tonight. A good time to attack, don't you think?"

He nodded, thoughtful. "So what is tonight? You said a celebration."

"It is a cloaking ceremony. Such a ceremony is always held three months after a battale returns to Quisnaf with prisoners. But Blaire has also called a court. It is unusual to hold the two together. It suggests trouble."

"Like what?"

"Who knows." Rohane frowned at a group of warriors talking quietly below wide steps. They stood just beyond the spill of torchlight, their shoulders tense, casting sideways glances at the crowd.

"Not everyone seems in the festive mood."

"No." Rohane's frown deepened. "Something's up. We'll find out soon enough."

"What's a cloaking ceremony? No, forget it. You'll just tell me your mother's words."

"You're so impatient, Telorian. There is an order to things."

She escorted him up a wide staircase onto another veranda of hewed stone. Before them, an opening gaped in the mountain face. Firelight from braziers roared at the entrance.

"The feasting hall," Rohane muttered. "Not as you would expect in a castle."

They walked into an enormous cavern hollowed from rock except for two rows of strong, vaulted columns. Arrays of candles, too numerous to count, blazed along the walls. More glowed in crevices, creating mysterious shadows.

Hundreds of trestle tables were set up beneath a raised platform. Servants milled about with carafes of wine. Guards stood at the entrances.

The hall filled quickly. Women greeted friends before finding seats. Val glimpsed Sorcha at the head of a table of scarlet-robed priestesses. At another, Persia held court. Voices echoed loudly; candles and braziers smoked with scents of beeswax and tallow. Laughter rang out, strident, shrill, or merry.

Rohane led him between tables. Voices died as they passed then picked up. He thought he heard, "Not cloaked, then who does he belong to?"

To Val's surprise, Rohane took him to a front table, where Aine and Samantha sat with two men. Samantha gestured at a bench. Val sat where bidden, on Samantha's left, with Rohane on his right. The man with Samantha swept him a curious look then bent his head to whisper to the councillor. Samantha replied softly. As though satisfied, the man nodded.

Servants brought platters of food. A girl unobtrusively filled Val's cup with wine.

"The servants are all women," Val muttered to Rohane.

"When it comes to food and drink, yes," she replied.

Val pondered that. So the Quisnaf feared their slaves would poison them.

He peered about. But for the presence of so many armed women, it might have been any feast in Tide's End or even the Mountains. The chaos of sounds—boastful shouts, boisterous voices, laughter, and clashing cups—was hardly strange to him. He watched a warrior at another table wave her arms about to illustrate a story. Her companions leaned close, listening intently. Then the story was done, and they all laughed.

At tables near the door, murmurs broke out among the seated warriors. Blaire walked in, her beautiful head held majestically. Sybil and Kenna followed a step behind.

Blaire's gaze flickered over him as she sat at the head of their table. The other councillors filled spaces opposite Val.

The noise picked up again, a hubbub of voices, boasting, and laughter. An uproar at one table drew glances then shakes of heads. Marlisa stood, shouting and waving a cup of wine. Others yelled at her good-naturedly. Then a servant pouring wine blocked Val's view.

Aine sniffed. "The girl has no manners. She is as wild as a Venivan street urchin."

"Her warriors worship her," Samantha answered. "Marlisa loves life. She is fearless, too. She does everything from fighting to loving to feasting with gusto."

"She has made something of herself," Rohane said. "From humble beginnings."

"Though she complains always that she is broke," Aine said.

They fell into a lively argument about Persia's lieutenant. Aine, it seemed, thought Persia a more suitable leader, a well-disciplined captain whom others might aspire to be like.

"With no imagination," Samantha declared. "She does not think sideways. It is always, 'This is what we have always done. This is how we always fight.'"

"What is wrong with that? She falls back on her training—harsh training, may I remind you—the training that has produced many, many good warriors and good battale captains."

The man at Samantha's side answered: "She may find herself in a situation that demands a solution exceeding her training."

Aine glared but did not admonish him for speaking. "There is nothing that exceeds a battale captain's training."

"Colm may be right." Blaire nodded at Samantha's companion. "Persia is fierce and determined, relentless even…"

"Everything a good battale captain is," said Aine peevishly.

"But imagine if she combined that determination with Jenna-Dairine's imagination. An unbeatable combination, surely."

"As you say, Regenta." Samantha nodded.

The mysterious Jenna-Dairine again. Val nudged Rohane. She spilled her wine onto her lap. "Thank you very much, you clumsy fool."

"Me?" He offered a look of wide-eyed innocence.

"Keep your elbows to yourself."

A clang rang out, then again as a man swung a hammer at an enormous, polished gong. As the echo died away, Blaire rose. She took the stairs to the platform and sat upon a high-backed chair. Aine and Kenna followed, taking their places beside her.

Blaire clapped her hands. Guards Val now recognised as members of the Decan Watch forced men restrained by wrist irons up onto the platform. Barefoot, bare-chested, they glared at their captors. Yet they did not appear poorly treated. Their hair looked washed, their garments clean.

Excited voices rose about the hall. A tall woman with untidy fair hair and a lined face stepped forward.

"Who is that?" Val whispered to Rohane.

"Clotild. She serves the blood keepers. I met her only recently."

"Quisnaf thanks Persia and Marlisa for returning so many captives to the caverns," Clotild shouted.

A cheer broke out. Women stamped their feet and drank more wine.

"To Marlisa," yelled a drunken woman at Marlisa's table.

"To Persia," another challenged.

Voices roared until Clotild raised a hand. "This victory is awarded to both our valiant battale captain and her lieutenant. As such, they selected a slave each." She nodded.

Guards pulled two well-muscled men forward.

"Persia, do you intend to cloak this man?" Clotild waved a hand at the nearest. "Or offer him to your sisters."

Persia pushed her chair back and rose. "I offer him."

Cheers broke out. A handful of warriors pressed towards the platform. One shook a bag in Persia's direction. "Four pieces of gold."

The man edged back, his expression wary. Val's gut turned over in pity. Captivity shamed a warrior. To then be bought and sold like a slave must cut with humiliation.

"Five pieces," a second woman countered.

Rohane whistled softly. "That is a lot. But Persia has a good eye. She would choose one of their leaders if such a man fell into our hands. Do you know him?"

"No. Who is he?"

"He's been reticent, but the other Varee captives defer to him. The bidding will go high, I think. Persia will be wealthier than she already is. And she is considerably wealthy."

"Seven pieces of gold," the first warrior shouted to enthusiastic, drunken cheers.

Val could not hide his surprise. "The money goes to her?"

Rohane nodded. "The battales elect who is awarded the victory after a battle. Sometimes it is a single warrior who performed some great feat. This time, it is Persia and Marlisa. That means they may choose and then sell or keep a captive. The rest, unless bought tonight, will be taken to the slave markets in Vene."

"Ten pieces of gold."

Rohane shook her head. "It is too much."

The first woman sneered. "You do not have it."

The other warrior jangled a pocket. "I have it."

"Ah, fool. No man is worth that." The first scoffed in disgust and turned away.

The remaining bidder grinned.

A voice rang out from the back of the cavern. "Twelve pieces."

A murmur coiled about the chamber as a woman moved between the tables. Candlelight generously softened the strong lines of a determined face framed by tumbling auburn hair. The braziers' fires reflected in her gleaming eyes. She wore a swirling cloak of red velvet embroidered with gold. A knife with a carved grip poked carelessly from her belt.

The woman walked to the platform, uncaring of the eyes that followed her. She thrust a bag at Clotild. "I assume no one will offer more?"

Clotild bowed low. "I trust not, sorceress."

Sorceress? Val's neck prickled. An aura of mystery and magic veiled this woman, just as it had Myranthe Damadar when she had tormented and manipulated him as a prisoner in the Icelands.

Clotild glanced at Persia. The battale captain nodded.

"Sisilia, daughter of Maude," Rohane whispered in answer to his unspoken question. "Try not to catch her eye."

Amused, he nudged her again. "She frightens you?"

"Oaf. You nearly wore my wine this time. Yes, she does. And she should frighten you."

"You'll protect me." He grinned.

"Keep bumping my elbow, and I'll sell you to her," Rohane grumbled.

His smile lingered. Then he looked back to the platform. Guards dragged the bought man down the stairs to his new mistress. Seen closer, he was younger than Val had expected— perhaps twenty-two or twenty-three, tall and menacingly built with powerful shoulders.

Sisilia swept him an appraising look. "Take him to the temple. Restrain him within."

"She did not cloak him." Rohane's face shadowed. "That's not good."

"Cloak? Clotild used that term."

"You'll understand in a moment."

His escort dragged the protesting man through the doors. Sisilia followed, her face impassive.

Guards forced the second captive forward. Dark-haired, dark-eyed, he looked every bit Telorian. Though his expression was wary, he showed no fear, only defiance.

Clotild looked to Marlisa. "Will you cloak him?"

Marlisa rose. "I would like to—"

A surprised mutter broke out, and Blaire tensed. She turned her head sharply towards the battale lieutenant. Samantha sat up straighter.

"I heard him singing in the slave quarters. I thought his voice sad and lovely. If I could, I would cloak such a singular man—" Marlisa grinned. "But I will not cloak him. I offer this man, who is not only a warrior but a singer. My time is… spoken for."

Salacious laughter rose up from her companions. The woman closest slapped Marlisa's back and said something that drew a grin.

"Very well." Clotild swept a hand at the captive.

"Two pieces of gold for the sweet, sweet singer," said a warrior at a nearby table.

"Ah, do not make that mistake," Marlisa said, winking at the bidder. "He fought fiercely. We only took him because he fell wounded."

"I would not know what to do with a wounded singer," a woman muttered.

"Not wounded there, fool," called someone from the back of the hall. "Three pieces of gold."

"Four."

"Ridiculous." The second bidder shook her head.

The singer seemed to at last understand what was taking place. He glanced in alarm from one bidder to the next.

At a gesture from Clotild, the first bidder approached the man. She carried a cloak in her arms. Gracefully, she swung the cloak about the man's shoulders and fastened its cords. Spectators broke into a rowdy cheer.

The woman bid the guards bring the captive to her table. As she tossed a jangling bag to Marlisa, her companions cleared a seat. The woman bid the man sit at her side, smiling as her Quisnaf friends poured him wine.

Rohane released a breath. "That's as well."

Val frowned. "What just happened?"

"Ailene cloaked him. That means he not only belongs to her but is under her protection."

"Is that important?"

Rohane nodded. "No one can touch him or trouble him unless he gives good cause. Otherwise, they will answer to Ailene and to a Quisnaf court."

"Like the court that is to be held later tonight?"

"Exactly."

Val glanced about the room, taking in the different cloaks. Councillors wore cloaks of a single colour; others wore cloaks of tri-colours in different patterns.

Clotild brought forward more of the captives. Val listened to her describing each one's attributes in a way that suggested extensive questioning before the auction. Women bid for and cloaked two more men. Guards led the others away then returned with another group of captives. The ritual unfolded again.

"What happens to the others?" Val asked. "The ones not cloaked."

"They'll fetch good prices in Vene," Rohane said. "Most look strong."

Guards escorted the last group of men away. Voices and laughter picked up. The Quisnaf fell back to drinking, eating, and gossiping. But Blaire remained seated on the platform, her councillors with her.

The gong clanged again. Heads rose. Blaire stood. "I proclaim a session of the Quisnaf Court of Dispute. An outrage has occurred."

Whispers and mutters rose to a crescendo. Women exchanged startled glances. The entrance doors thudded open. A woman strode through, her head held high, her lips set grimly. A harsh wind seemed to blow in after her. Fires leapt higher. Candle flames flattened then stiffened to attention again. The hall seemed colder, darker, full of menacing, twitching shadows.

Val recognised the warrior from the training field, the one who had admonished Rohane. A shiver took off down his spine. Cold fury shrouded this woman. It burned brightly from her dark eyes, as if fires smouldered within, harnessed, but ready to blaze at a wrong word or glance.

She moved between tables and pillars, her eyes upon the Regenta and two councillors. A silence descended in her wake, as though she scythed noise with every determined step. Reaching the cleared space before the platform, she bowed low and gracefully, her pale-blue silken cloak rustling against the floor.

The doors banged shut. The wind died. The silence lengthened. Rohane gripped her wine cup with white knuckles. Every head turned to watch.

"Jenna-Dairine, daughter of Kathryn," Blaire raised her voice. "You bring a complaint before the council."

Jenna-Dairine. Val remembered Rohane's sigh of awe at the name and that curious look she had given the fair-haired young warrior who'd walked so proudly down the temple stairs.

Deeply curious, Val sat straighter, his eyes locked on this woman.

"I do, Regenta." Her voice was as deep as he remembered from the training field. "I lay before you a most serious matter and ask that you allow me justice."

"Isn't it the court's place?" Samantha raised an eyebrow.

Another, someone weaker, might well have wilted beneath the

look that fell on the councillor. "The injury is personal. Justice will be mine."

"Tell the council what happened," Blaire said. "You have told me, but they must hear the words from you."

"An affront to both the goddess and to me," Jenna-Dairine said in a softly menacing voice. "Last night, cowards struck down and killed my consort."

Shocked voices erupted.

"My lieutenant found his body in one of the deeper caverns, in a little-used storeroom. His throat was cut. But not only that—" Jenna-Dairine paused as if to summon courage to say the next words. "But not only that. He was... interfered with."

"An outrage," a woman shouted. "Who did it?"

"Silence," said Blaire. "This is a court, not a tavern."

"My lieutenants investigated. Two witnesses glimpsed three women dragging a man towards the caves. They knew one of them."

"*Your* lieutenants investigated." Aine huffed with ire. "You take liberties, Captain. You should have brought this before the court and let the court assign an investigator."

Captain. Then Jenna-Dairine was the mysterious fourth battale captain. Rohane was right; some of his questions had been answered tonight.

"There was no time," Jenna-Dairine snapped, glaring at Aine.

The councillor did not recoil. Val knew a moment of admiration for the sharp-tongued woman.

"The trail could not go cold. Once we had a name, we took and questioned the first. She gave up her accomplices. Three are to blame. Three cowards did this, and I want justice."

More horrified murmurs ran through the hall. Blaire shot to her feet. "You took it upon yourself to torture a sister to give up alleged accomplices? With what proof?"

Jenna-Dairine's hands fisted at her side. "He was my consort," she cried, her voice breaking with grief. "For ten years."

A sympathetic silence closed in again. Rohane's eyes were wide, her eyelids wet. Val reached for her hand in her lap and entwined his fingers in hers.

"I demand the judgement of the goddess," Jenna-Dairine said. "I demand trial by combat."

"You would fight all three, one by one?" Blaire frowned.

"I will fight all three at once," Jenna-Dairine said. "If they are innocent, then the goddess will spare them."

No one spoke. It was as if a terrible fury edged with sorrow welled in Jenna-Dairine, leaching out into every corner. Then Blaire sighed. "Bring them in. I assume you hold these three you suspect."

Jenna-Dairine turned and gestured. Again, the doors thumped back. Armed warriors marched three women in.

"I know them," Rohane muttered to Val. "The tall, scowling creature is Dana. Jenna-Dairine threw her out of her battale for cowardice. That one knows how to hold a grudge."

Val glanced at a woman with short blonde hair, her small mouth lifted in a sneer.

"The second is Cinna, a sneaky little tell-tale. Just the sort to fall in with Dana. She is a Decan guard. The third, also. Keenat. Always discontented, that one, envious to the bone."

"Louisa." Blaire's voice rang out. "Stand and speak to this."

A chair scraped back. A woman lumbered to her feet. She looked slightly unsteady, but her speech was unbroken. "I cannot speak to it. It shames me that two members of the Decan Watch should be accused of murder."

"Not only murder," Jenna-Dairine muttered.

Rohane put her lips close to Val's ear. "Louisa commands the Decan Watch. It is telling that she does not defend the two accused."

"We did not do it," Dana muttered. "It is lies. All of it, lies."

One of the warriors holding her slapped her face hard.

"Enough of that," Blaire commanded. "Do you all deny it? Must we bring forward witnesses?"

"The goddess shall be mine," Jenna-Dairine hissed. "She will guide my sword. She will deliver justice. I shall be her instrument."

"You crazy bitch," Dana screamed. She tried to throw herself at the battale captain, only to be held back. "Who does she think she is? Always preening it over everyone else. And what is she? Nothing better than a bitch who spreads her legs for a man. For a slave. That's what he was. A slave who didn't know his place."

At these words, an uncomfortable silence charged with tension began building like a storm. As if sensing the growing anger, Dana dropped her head, muttering, "Crazy bitch has no proof."

"She is a battale captain." Persia rose and stabbed a finger at the woman. "You will address her properly."

"I've done nothing. Yet she drags me here like I'm a slave with no rights. I'm Quisnaf."

"It was your idea," Cinna whimpered. "We didn't want to do it. She made us." She fell to her knees and clutched Jenna-Dairine's leg. "Please. Don't kill me. I didn't touch him. It was her. Dana."

Jenna-Dairine's face twisted with disgust. She kicked Cinna off. Fronting Blaire, she said, "Do you hear? They accuse each other. Do not deny me justice, Regenta."

"Fight," Persia shouted.

Others took up the call. "Fight, fight, fight."

Women stamped the floor.

To Val's surprise, Rohane shot to her feet and shook her fist at the accused women, screaming, "Justice. Let her have justice."

The gong clanged. Blaire yelled for quiet. When it came, she said, "I've heard enough. Give them swords. Let the goddess decide."

Guards found blades and handed them to the three women.

Jenna-Dairine sank to her knees. Eyes closed, she mouthed words Val couldn't hear, but he assumed it was an invocation to the gods. Then she rose slowly and faced the three women. Dana had her lips close to Keenat's ear. The other woman nodded, her smile sly.

Jenna-Dairine ripped a long blade free. Cinna at once drew back. She turned and tried to flee. The guards grabbed her and shoved her forward.

Dana swirled her blade, testing its weight. "You stupid cow," she muttered. "You think you can face three of us at once? The goddess will have blood, all right. Yours."

She leapt at Jenna-Dairine. Roaring out her hatred, Keenat attacked also. Jenna-Dairine swept aside Dana's thrust, whirling to catch Keenat's rushed stroke. The two defendants jumped back. They exchanged a look then attacked again in unison. The battale captain shouted in rage, again blocking both swords with screeching quicksilver metal.

Sword extended, she backed up slightly. Dana circled, seeking an opening. She nodded at Keenat. The second woman came at Jenna-Dairine, cutting low at her opponent's legs. Jenna-Dairine jumped. Dana hacked high. Jenna-Dairine swept her sword up, knocking death aside. Again she took a stance, eyeing both her opponents chillingly. With cries of hatred, they rushed her. Blades sparked with a clatter of steel.

Val sprang up, shouting, "Separate them. Don't let them attack in tandem." But the words drowned in the din. Everywhere, warriors had surged to their feet, shaking fists, yelling, and edging closer.

Jenna-Dairine moved with cat-like balance, with a predator's deceptive cunning, her blade cutting and swiping. Her parries were crisp, her thrusts dangerous and deep. The other two were skilled and fought desperately, jabbing or hacking, hewing savagely. Soon, their breaths ran ragged. Sweat pooled beneath the combatants' boots, leaving the stone treacherous.

"Cinna, you little cow," Dana shouted at the third woman cowering near the platform. "Get in here. Put her down, or she'll put you down."

Hesitant, Cinna took a step nearer. She raised her sword.

"Get around behind her," Dana instructed. Then she threw herself forward, screaming out her loathing. Jenna-Dairine blocked head-high slashing steel. Again, blue sparks scattered in the air.

Rohane rushed to the edge of a crowd building around the combatants. Val clambered up with others onto a table so he could see.

Three opponents ringed Jenna-Dairine. Even Cinna found the courage to poke at her with shallow jabs. Jenna-Dairine stepped into one, binding Cinna's sword in a bid to rip it from her hands. Sensing the danger, the other woman pulled her weapon clear.

Keenat stabbed at the captain's throat. It was deep and swift. For a heartbeat, Val thought the stroke got through. Jenna-Dairine's blade rose late, but it rose fast. She used a strange perpendicular parry better suited to a lighter, thinner weapon. But it knocked Keenat's stroke aside. In riposte, Jenna-Dairine thrust once. The blade slid between ribs. Keenat staggered, her sword clattering to the floor as she clutched at her breast. She dropped.

Howling with rage, Dana flew at Jenna-Dairine, hailing blows. Jab, hack, slice, cut. Before the onslaught, Jenna-Dairine backed up. Then she leapt into an attack with a recklessness that reminded Val of Kaell. Dana had no time to retreat. When she rushed a parry, Jenna-Dairine took control of Dana's tip with the stronger, thicker part of her blade, forcing the other woman's weapon down.

Dana tried to wrench her sword clear. She cursed her opponent, her furious eyes swivelling for Cinna. "What are you waiting for? Attack her."

As if frozen with fear, Cinna did nothing. Jenna-Dairine's hand fell to her belt. Val glimpsed glittering steel. Then the battale captain drove her knife up beneath Dana's ribs. Not just once but again and again, stabbing with a cold ferocity.

Dana reeled, open-mouthed. The sword spilled from her hand. She collapsed to her knees, trying to speak. Blood trickled from her soundless lips. At last, she toppled to the floor.

Val felt no sympathy. The woman had condemned herself with her own words.

Cinna backed up. She hit the ring of spectators. They shoved her forward, hissing with displeasure.

Jenna-Dairine turned. Blood stained her garments. With her blazing eyes, the sword dripping like a beast's fangs, she might have been a demon that the gods or a vengeful sorceress raised from the Enarae.

"Lift your weapon." Her voice was cold and merciless.

Cinna retreated. Again, spectators pushed her towards Jenna-Dairine.

"Lift your weapon. Face me."

"I didn't touch him. I swear. It was Dana. Keenat. They made me."

"He wasn't armed," Jenna-Dairine said. "He was under my protection. You could have found me, told me. I would have kept you safe from them."

Cinna dropped the sword at her feet. "Please," she sobbed. "I'm unarmed too."

With one swift movement, Jenna-Dairine grabbed the woman and pulled her against her. The knife flashed. A thin line of red appeared on Cinna's neck. She gurgled a sound, her eyes stretched with shock. Then the battale captain dropped her.

For a long moment, Jenna-Dairine stared at the body. Then she hurled the knife away, threw back her head, and howled, one long cry that held all her grief and fury.

A terrible hush cloaked the hall. Every spectator was still, stunned and pitying. Jenna-Dairine stepped over the body, wiped her sword and knife on Dana's tunic, slid the blades into their sheaths, and walked to the door. Women soundlessly cleared a path for her, following her with their eyes. The silence held until the doors opened and shut.

Male servants cleared away the bodies and wiped the floor, then the court continued. Two women brought a squabble over a slave before the council, seeking judgement on ownership.

"She owes me twenty silver coins for a fine cloak," said one, whom Rohane whispered was a trader. "The debt is now six months old."

"Do you dispute the debt?" Blaire asked.

The other woman, a warrior who served in Persia's battale, sullenly glared. "Not the debt. But we agreed on fifteen silver coins initially. The price went up."

"It is not uncommon," the tradeswoman said. "I bought silk in Veniva and paid more than expected. I warned Meghan it might be as much as twenty-five coins."

"Did she warn you?"

Meghan glanced at Persia before answering. The battale captain wore a hard frown. "She said it was possible."

Blaire flicked a hand. "Give her the slave—as payment."

Two women came forward to argue over land. Val yawned, bored. "I need air."

Rohane seemed to follow the debate with great interest. "Strictly speaking, I'm supposed to accompany you whenever you leave your room. So don't go far."

He walked to the doors, drawing stares and whispers. From one table, Branwyn watched him with a vicious grin. She raised her glass in a salute.

At the entrance, guards blocked him. "You're not cloaked," one said. "Who do you belong to?"

"I'm a guest. I'm under Rohane's protection."

They blinked in surprise. "He did come in with her," the second guard said.

"She said I may go outside for air. Told me not to go far." Val almost choked on the submissive words.

"Do not then. Stay within the gardens."

They opened the doors, and Val walked through. When they shut at his back, he sighed with relief. Alone at night without his grumpy chaperone. A curious rush of freedom coursed through him. If he wished, he could even escape. *Except...* His gaze fell on a Decan guard on a ledge. The Quisnaf, as Rohane had reminded him, liked nothing better than a hunt.

The night breathed softly. He moved along a veranda outside the cavern, stopping at a balustrade overlooking the valley. Between shadows, etched trees and bushes framed the sky. Torches gauntleted winding paths. The aroma of blossoms rose from a garden. After the heady, smoky caverns, a breeze pleasantly cooled his skin.

"She loosened the leash then?"

Val started. He traced the voice to a woman sitting half in darkness on the wall, legs drawn up and hands circling her knees. A weapons belt lay carelessly on the balustrade beside her.

Val considered her sword. It was barely a lunge away. What if he took that blade and escaped this valley and its caves, its rules and strange behaviours and morals? He could flee from the humiliation of obedience and submission.

"She?" He edged closer.

The woman turned her head. Dark eyes moved over him.

"You're Jenna-Dairine." He recognised the warrior from the cavern. "I'm sorry. I did not mean to intrude—"

"Intrude on what? My grief?" She sighed. "In truth, I would not mind company. Otherwise, my thoughts dwell in darkness."

Val pressed his palms into the stone balustrade. "I'm—"

She broke in with a raspy laugh. "I know who you are, Val Arques. The caverns are awash with talk of you. And where is the moody Ronnie?"

"Inside."

"She let you wander alone? She does not fear you'll use the distraction of tonight's feast to escape?"

"No. I gave her my word I would not."

Jenna-Dairine gave him another long look. She nodded. "And your word is… not empty." She turned back to consider the valley.

Val drew in a breath. "It would be a good night to run. No moons. Your sword left where I could scoop it up."

Jenna-Dairine laughed. It was as deep as her voice. The

rumbling laugh sent a shiver across his scalp.

"The moons will rise later. It will, in fact, be a bright night for a hunt—if you want to give us some sport. From what I've heard of you, you may well reach the gates."

"I'm hurt. Only the gates? Such a low opinion of my craftiness."

"Not at all," she said in that husky tone. "The gates are a good four miles from these gardens. On another night, without Decan guards every few paces, I might worry. Or at least, Rohane should. I have no need to take on her troubles as well as my own."

Val knew the Quisnaf city spread deep into the mountains, but he had not realised it stretched so far along the valley. Then he thought about her other words. *Her own troubles.*

"I am sorry for it," he said softly. "About your consort, Riagan. I glimpsed him only once, but he seemed quite singular."

"You're the first one tonight brave enough to speak his name to me." Jenna-Dairine did not look at him. "My lieutenants are close by somewhere in the darkness, watching to make certain I don't do anything foolish like fling myself from this wall. They wish to console me, but they are warriors, uncomfortable at the sight of my grief. I am their captain. I do not show weakness. Especially about a man."

"Even Quisnaf captains are human."

She turned her head. "Are they? Our enemies think we are demons."

"Outrageous. Someone as sweet as Madenn should be insulted."

Jenna-Dairine laughed with genuine amusement. "Riagan was sarcastic, too. I think his sharp wit was what attracted me first."

"What was he like? Besides sarcastic."

"He was stubborn. Well, we both are. We fought often. But then our reconciliations were heated, too." She chuckled fondly. "He could be sweet, very gentle. Surprisingly forgiving. I remember many times when I raged about an imagined slight, and he calmed me with sense. He was so—" Her voice broke.

"I don't know if it gets better," Val said. "The sorrow. But somehow, it becomes part of you, then it fades to a sadness that sits within rather than an ache that tears at you like claws in your soul."

Jenna-Dairine said nothing. Her gaze fell upon the valley. "I am afraid, I think."

"Of what?"

"Afraid that I loved too deeply, that his death leaves only a pit deep inside me, where my spirit can only shrivel and die. I am afraid I will not love again, not like this." She paused. Her dark eyes dwelled on him. "Do you think we love more than once, Val Arques?"

"Yes. It is never the same, but that is not to say it is not as good or as rich or deep or blessed or pure, even. Just different."

"I hope you are right."

"You did not wish for the bond of children with Riagan?"

Her laugh this time was bitter. "And invite a knife between my ribs?"

"I don't understand."

"How long do you think Blaire would let me live if I announced I was with child? And especially if I carried Riagan's child?"

Bewildered, he spread his hands. "I still don't understand."

She tilted her head, thinking. "No, I suppose you have no reason to know my business. Riagan was a prince of the Circle Kingdoms, beyond the Ice Sea. The blood keepers might consider it an interesting combination of bloodlines, his and mine. But Blaire has forbidden me to have children. Unless I seek out the lowest of the low, a mate of no importance."

Val frowned. "She forbade you to have children?"

"She fears me, Val Arques."

"Why?"

Jenna-Dairine rumbled a laugh. "You must be the only one in Quisnaf who does not know. But then, I suppose Ronnie is not one for gossip. I like that about her." She paused. "I am Kathryn's daughter."

He thought rapidly, pulling bits of information together. "The last Regenta."

"That is so." Jenna-Dairine hugged her knees tighter. "I was away fighting the Gidani when my mother died. Blaire and I were her most likely successors. But I was not here. Blaire was. By the time I returned, the matter was decided, and Blaire was Regenta."

"You said Blaire fears you... Does she have cause?"

"Blaire knows if discontent festers in Quisnaf, if a growing number of our sisters fault her leadership, then the focus of that discontent would be me, Kathryn's daughter. But what Blaire does not or cannot understand is that I do not want to be Regenta. That's the truth of it. She does not see that I do not crave power or its benefits as she does. I do not want what she has. She has no cause to fear me, if only she could see that."

The words thrummed through him. There was a warmth to her, a charisma. This was a woman who would not only be liked but admired. *Loved.* Surely, *that* was what Blaire feared.

"I understand why she fears you. I've known you a few minutes, but I sense your charm," he said, surprised at both the truth and his candid words. "How must it be for those who fight with you, for friends who've known you for years?"

She grasped his hand and kissed his fingers. Where her lips fell, his skin burned. "May the goddess bless you. No one but Riagan ever spoke so boldly, so truthfully, to me."

At another brush of lips against his skin, he shivered, aware of the power in her touch.

"Your mother," he said slowly. "She was a warrior?"

Jenna-Dairine laughed. "A sorceress. Let me show you. No, don't be afraid." She leaned and touched fingertips to his chin. Her lips brushed his. A shudder of longing ran through him. It was like a fire, warming but dangerous, deliciously seductive.

She let him go. Her voice was sad. "That's all it takes. I could enslave you. But I won't. Just as I never once used magic on Riagan. Though..." She ran her hand down his arm. "A moment ago, I said

I did not want anything of Blaire's. It's not quite true."

"I'm not hers."

"You share her bed."

Footsteps tapped stone. Rohane appeared.

"Ronnie." Jenna-Dairine swung her legs down. "Come to collect something precious?"

"Precious?" Rohane sniffed. "His head is big enough already without compliments from you. This one is prideful and stiff necked."

Jenna-Dairine laughed. "Maybe. But he was just kind to me when others did not know how." She touched Rohane's cheek. "I should like to fight him. Bring him to me. Sometime."

Val followed Rohane back into the feasting cavern. A boy stood on the platform, singing. Warriors, servants, and councillors sat forward, absorbed. Even Rohane stopped to listen, her expression rapt.

The singer must have been about fourteen, with light-brown hair and soft down on his chin. He had a beautiful voice, lyrical but strong and perfectly controlled.

As the boy started another song, Rohane shook herself as if throwing off a trance. She crooked a brow at Val. "How was the moonlight?"

"Glowing." He nodded towards the platform. "Who is he?"

"Shh. Later."

Val closed his eyes. The boy's pure voice and the haunting melody sank into him until he was lost to a ménage of memory and longing. The song took him back to the Isles, to the feasting hall where Val sat beside his father, a little drunk. A young singer had performed, just like this, and Val had longed to hold on to his voice, to capture it, to hear it again and again. But he knew the singer would leave the Isles the next day and take to the road to entertain the next lord who could afford a gold coin to hear him.

Now, as he listened to another boy with a tone as glorious and beautiful, a sense of loss and sadness swept through him. When the song ended, that voice would become a memory—somehow never quite tangible, never quite reachable, never quite remembered as it was.

Applause broke out. The boy bowed his head, acknowledging the cheering audience. Solemnly, he walked off the platform. Drums broke out. A musician joined in on a stringed instrument of some sort.

"Who is he?"

Rohane's gaze was lost, hazy. He wondered what she was thinking about, where the music took her. Perhaps she remembered a lover or perhaps a time when she had been happy.

"Persia's son, Aidan." At his arched brow, Rohane grinned. "Persia has a son and a daughter. The girl wants only to be a warrior. The boy—well, you see for yourself."

"But—" Val frowned. "What is his place here?"

"At the moment, he is a child, afforded rights much like you. He remains Persia's responsibility. But when he turns seventeen, Persia must make a decision. To let him leave or choose a bonding."

"All right, I'm lost. What is that?"

"Quisnaf women may offer to cloak him. If Persia receives many offers, she will choose between them."

The drums thumped with joyous music. The tables emptied. Women surged up to join a wild dance at the front of the cavern. They linked arms and circled in a tangle of kicking legs, shouting to others to join. Some still managed to hold onto wine goblets.

"What about what Aidan wants?"

She turned to face him. "Do I hear disapproval? Tell me, Telorian. At what age did you wed? Did you choose your bride?"

"I was eighteen, and no," Val admitted. "My father determined who I wed."

She shrugged, the gesture ending the argument.

"Yet." Val was not ready to let it go. "If I had objected to my bride, I think my father might have listened." He had not objected, though. Val had loved her since childhood.

Rohane waved a dismissive hand. "Listened, and then delivered a firm speech about duty and position and alliances and all that."

He was saved from replying when a woman grabbed Rohane's arm and swept her up into the dance. Smiling, Val watched her as she, too, was lost to the music, the rhythm, the movement, shouting, and hooting. Her passion leaked from beneath that cynical, cool, caustic exterior.

Someone settled onto the bench beside him. Branwyn did not look at him. She watched the dancers. "Do you know," she said. "Before it happened, Rohane was the most spirited, the wildest of us all."

"Before what happened?"

"Oh, dear. You mean the wonder girl hasn't shared? Maybe she doesn't trust you."

"What do you want, Branwyn? To whisper to me about my fate again? Use magic to compel me into escaping in the hope I'm punished? What?"

Branwyn only offered a knowing smile and rose.

⁂

"What does it mean if Jenna-Dairine wants to fight me?" Val asked as Rohane led him back to his room through shadowed passages. His spirits were high, not only because of the wine and good food but those moments of companionship in the garden with Jenna-Dairine.

Rohane glanced at him then scowled. "She wants to bed you. Curse your precious blood and that handsome face. Though, if the blood keepers did not have plans for you, she might cloak you. You'd be safe, then, Telorian."

"Safe... like Riagan?"

"You think anyone will dare lift a hand against someone of hers? After that display in the cavern?"

"You're right. But what does fighting me have to do with bedding?"

"She only ever beds someone she respects as a warrior. She fought Riagan. He nicked her arm with his sword. That made him her equal."

"She is…" He shrugged.

"Extraordinary?"

"Something like that."

Rohane stopped to stare at him. "You… liked her?"

"Jealous?" He punched Rohane's arm.

"Don't be stupid. And you punch like a man. I'll show you how it's done sometime."

Val laughed. "You're wrong about Jenna-Dairine. She doesn't attract me. Nor does Blaire, for that matter, despite her beauty." It was Rohane who drew him, Rohane whom he missed when she was called away to other duties. Rohane who made him laugh.

But it could never be. She'd made that clear. And he must not come to care for her, to keep her safe. *I destroy. I hurt.* The insidious voice was always with him.

"Jenna-Dairine told me Blaire is jealous of her, that if she should have had Riagan's child, the Regenta would kill her."

"And Riagan and the child. That's what would worry Jenna-Dairine. I don't think she ever fears for herself. She is Kathryn's daughter to the core."

"The sorceress."

Rohane stopped to stare at him. "My, my. You learnt a lot tonight."

"I'm making my way down the list you so cruelly left me. One." He counted on his fingers. "I know who the mysterious Jenna-Dairine is. Two. I know she's the fourth battale captain. Three. I know all about cloaking and such, though that wasn't on my list." He paused and slid her a sideways glance. "I still don't know about you."

"I'm an unsheathed sword. Nothing hidden." She walked on.

Val picked up his pace to catch up. "Someone will tell me. Gossip seems a big part of life in Quisnaf."

They passed a dark passage leading deeper into the mountain, its entrance marked by two marble statues of archers. A guard at a door snapped a salute at Rohane.

The door opened. Clotild emerged and drew up in surprise. "Rohane."

"Clotild."

Clotild's gaze shifted to Val. "And this is?" Her voice sounded breathy. "This is he?" She took two firm steps and grasped Val's arm to pull him into the light. He was so taken aback, he did not resist. Clotild peered at his face, even reaching to touch his hair.

Val recoiled. "I don't know about Quisnaf, but it's considered rude in Telor to put your hands all over a stranger."

Clotild tittered a laugh, unconcerned by his admonishment. "Oh, Rohane. You did not say enough. He is beautiful."

"What am I? An ornament on your shelves to be admired?" Val asked.

Clotild patted Rohane's arm. "You must bring him. I'll speak to Blaire."

Once the woman had walked off deeper into the tunnels, Val asked, "What was that about? Bring me where?"

"Don't worry your beautiful head with it, Val," Rohane teased. "I'm sure Jenna-Dairine will protect you from the touchy, groping Clotild."

"Ha, ha." He glanced at the door and guard. "What's down there? Who needs guarding?"

Rohane's expression shuttered. She turned to walk on. "Never you mind."

"No, really. Who is it?"

She stopped abruptly. "Promise me you'll never go down there," she said. "You must never try to find out who's in that room. Promise me now."

"Tell me why."

"Listen, you fool. You do not need to know what goes on down there." Her face was determined and fierce.

Val shrugged. "If it means that much to you, Rohane. Then yes, I won't go there."

Her shoulders dropped. "Good."

GENYA

A way from the clifftops, away from the seduction of magic and power, the rhythms of the king's court at Tide's End sank into her. She took her meals with the queen and her ladies in Rozenn's chambers except on those occasions when Gendrick entertained visiting ambassadors, lords and ladies, even kings and queens.

Then servants cleaned and scrubbed the great hall, threw back shutters to let in the fading sun, unfolded the trestle tables, and covered them with fine linen cloth. When dusk deepened and stars gleamed faintly through shifting clouds, servants lit hundreds of candles in tall holders that scratched the polished floor, from swinging chandeliers, and from candelabras in wall crevices. The coming night would be gentle, the breeze rippling over the hushed, darkling sea soft and scented of frangipani. A few late sails might dance in the bay beneath a fat moon.

Though she was the daughter of a king, the splendour of the feasts left her awestruck. The music from pipes and drums always carried to every corner of the castle in fragments as thin as dewy spiderwebs until she drew near the hall.

On other occasions, always in the evening when it was cooler, Gendrick received petitioners. Occasionally, a lord who had fought with the long-dead king Cathmor, certain they had done their penance, would ask to be returned to favour. Sometimes, Gendrick retreated to his rooms to meet with his sheriffs or spies with reports from the Mountains.

One evening, Genya arrived at the great hall in a rush from the queen's chambers, where she had been practising with poisons. With his nobles assembled, Gendrick held session. Upon the wall at the king's back were symbols of The Three, though Rozenn had told Genya another mural had once depicted Rainer and Roaran.

A last petitioner made his way through the tables towards the king, his back to Genya. From his fine garments and the soft leather of his boots, she guessed he was wellborn. A lord then. Perhaps seeking a grant of land or the king's approval to tax travellers.

Others parted to let the newcomer through, their palms rising to their mouths, their eyes wide with astonishment. A murmur ran through the Isles noblemen and women in the hall. Some whispered to their neighbours or nodded grimly.

Wondering who it was who caused such consternation, Genya stole quietly along the back of the room and slipped into place beside Yvonne.

"Where were you?" The older woman licked her lips. Silvery light from the first moon caught the gleam in Yvonne's eyes. "There's high drama."

"Who is it?"

"That he should come here. That the king should receive him." Yvonne shook her head.

"Who?"

"Felix Hillborn. The traitor."

A shudder of alarm tore through Genya. She glanced at the door, wondering how she could sneak out again. If Felix saw her, he would reveal her identity to the king.

"I seek compensation." Felix's voice was too familiar. It took Genya back at once to the great hall at Vraymorg, to a night when the wind wheezed through stonework and candlelight flickered upon the giant wheel where Archanin intended to execute her father.

Squeezing her eyes shut, she banished the memory. When she opened them, Felix stood unbowed and far from penitent. "I have lost everything. My position, my lands. I demand you help me reclaim the Mountains or compensate me for my losses."

Gendrick sat back on a chair beside his queen upon the dais. He tapped his fingers on the chair arm. "Don't be ridiculous. *You* lost your lands. *You* let Vraymorg fall."

"A Quisnaf raiding party—"

Gendrick held up a hand. "I've heard your excuses. You were taken by surprise. You were overwhelmed by greater numbers. But the fact remains, you fled. You did not stay and fight for your castle."

"With what men?" Felix muttered. "With what arms?" He sneered. "You should be grateful to me. I rid you of that claimant to your throne, Roaran Caelan."

"Then where is his body?" Gendrick flicked a wrist irritably. "No, you have failed me. Because of you, the Mountains are in the hands of that bastard Alecc." He did not look at Rozenn seated beside him. She was pale, her expression carefully blank. "Now, as well as the Wardorians who are preparing a fleet to attack, I have an enemy at my back."

Boos and hisses broke out. The nobles, servants, and soldiers all ranked against the walls gestured their contempt. Genya jeered silently, taking pleasure in their condemnation of Felix. The man was a snake. For years, he had fought beside Dannon, all the while planning how he would torture and kill him. *Oh, goddess, Dannon. Where is he?*

Felix slitted his eyes, his lips compressed in a tight line. "Then you will not help me reclaim my birthright?"

"Birthright?" Gendrick scoffed. "For centuries, Vraymorg belonged to the man we now know as Val Arques Caelan and his ancestors, dating back to the time of Queen Devarsi."

"And I tell you, it was the same man. For centuries."

"This nonsense again. Where is he then? Come, come. You insist Roaran Caelan is dead but cannot produce his body. Now you insist the former Lord of Vraymorg is not dead, but neither can you produce him."

"I am telling the truth. Roaran's brotherhood was a brotherhood of the dead."

Scoffing laughter and more whispers broke out. Yet Genya knew it was to cover fear. Too many stories had reached Tide's End about the warriors who had fought with Roaran—infamous warriors from centuries ago, like Cadan Tiernan and Gethin Maelstrom.

Gendrick gestured for silence. "Tell me why I should help you," the king said. "You refused to heed my envoys—indeed, you imprisoned them. You refused to open your gates to Archanin, my ally."

"I had to pretend I was on the Brotherhood's side. To draw them in. Then I did open my gates to Archanin," Felix muttered. "And as a reward, I lost the Mountains."

"Your incompetence cost *me* the Mountains. No." Gendrick shook his head. "There shall be no talk of compensation. Be grateful I let you keep your head."

"But what shall I do?" Felix spluttered. "I cannot raise an army without funds."

You can die. Genya hid a grin.

Gendrick's smile was twisted and nasty. "You shall stay here, where you can cause me no further trouble. Enjoy the life of a nobleman in my court. Drink, eat, fornicate. I care not. Though, if I enter a room, you will leave it. I have no interest in seeing your pathetic face again."

For a moment, Felix stood flabbergasted, his mouth open slightly. Then he bowed. "Your Grace." The words were forced out through his clenched teeth. Abruptly, he whirled and started back towards the doors.

Genya dropped her head and edged back. Felix started to walk past, then he paused. He looked right at her, frowning. Her breath stalled. *No, no, no.*

"You," Felix hissed. At the disbelief in his tone, Genya lifted her eyes. He pointed a shaking finger. "You—you…" He raised his voice, the tone hot and triumphant. "What is the daughter of Roaran Caelan doing in your hall, Your Grace?"

Gendrick shot to his feet. Rozenn bit her lip. Startled murmurs spread. Genya's glance flickered left and right, looking for a way out.

"What?" Gendrick cried, his startled gaze swinging to her. "Roaran Caelan's daughter?" For a moment, his shock held him. Then he started down the steps from the dais, gesturing wildly at his guards. "Arrest her. Bring her to me."

Guards closed in fast. Genya backed away. A wall came up behind her. More guards ran from the doors. She shifted this way and that, seeking a way through them.

Then Rozenn screamed. She fell to her knees, clutching her belly. Heads turned towards her. "It's coming," she whimpered. "The baby."

Chaos erupted. Servants and the queen's ladies rushed to help Rozenn. At once, Genya ran at the guards between her and the veranda. She dodged a thrust spear, grasped the end, and wrestled it from the man's grip. Then she swung hard, catching the guard across the back with the shaft. He gasped in pain and staggered against a companion.

Genya weaved past and shoved through startled onlookers towards the moonlight. Hands grappled at her, grabbing her clothes. She pulled free and burst out the doors onto the wide, long veranda jutting over the ocean. Beneath the castle, the sea was full, the waves white tipped as they pounded the rocks.

Footsteps thudded behind. A knot of guards came for her, herding her towards the balcony balustrade. With no choice, she vaulted it onto the thin strip of grass on the edge of the clifftop. In desperation, she began to climb down towards the water, slipping on rubble, her boots sending tiny pebbles flying into the treacherous rocks below. Sharp edges cut her hands and shins, her wet palms unable to keep a grip on smooth stone.

Losing her footing, Genya plunged a few feet onto a sandy ledge. She lay winded, hearing seagulls caw overhead and shouts from the castle. The smell of seaweed and brine filled her nostrils. Unsteadily, she forced herself up and began the descent again. The rocks were wet and slippery with moss. Often, she fell, bruising her knees, skinning her legs.

The air parted near her ear. A crossbow bolt zipped past and into the sea. Another nicked her arm. Blood seeped from the wound. Genya ducked behind a rock. She glanced up. A line of bowmen ranked the cliff, arrows nocked. Several loosed bolts. They flew about her, smashing into the boulder where she hid. *Goddess. What to do?* The sea was still metres below, rough and turbulent. Whitecaps swirled where it swelled and stormed.

With a desperate glance at the waves, she rose to a crouch. "Arise, fog!" she shouted, the rock her only protection. Any minute now, her pursuers would climb down after her. "Bring me fog." She snatched up a sharp stone and drove it deep into the wound on her arm. Stabbing pain shot through her shoulder. She was dizzy with it, sick. Teeth clenched to hold in her scream, she twisted the stone. More blood oozed. She twisted until blood streamed down her arm onto the rocks at her feet.

"Fog. Fog shall cover the land. *Ego mandatum elementa.*" She shouted the words, screamed them again and again. And still, the bolts flew, scattering about her. Footfalls clattered on the cliff. Any minute, they would overwhelm her.

A black cloud bowled overhead, blotting out the moon and stars. As it descended, taking over the land, its moist, clammy tendrils brushed her skin. The sea stilled to a glassy haze. The fog rolled towards the castle, as silent and heavy as a shroud. It shifted as if alive, predatory as if scouring the land for prey.

As if far, far away, cries of fear and shouts of dismay drifted from the castle above. Genya exhaled in relief. But she was not yet out of danger.

Unable to see more than a hand's breadth in front of her, she carefully wound her way towards the sea then jumped into the churning water. Down she plunged into the spray and foam. Her leg grazed a hidden rock. Her hip hit another. More pain struck her. Her arms and thigh stung.

She surfaced into eerie pale light, with the mist like a velvet blanket upon the water. After a quick glance to get her bearings, she struck out with powerful strokes towards the headland, left of the castle of Tide's End.

Coming ashore below caves, Genya scrambled up the rock face onto the grassy cliffs and stole back to the castle. Every part of her ached, her bruised body sore, her wounds smarting. The fog lingered. Within its wisping fingers, torchlight bobbed. Shouts carried as guards searched the rocks and water.

"Anything?"

Genya dropped into the grass, holding her breath. A shape moved through the fog. A spear poked at grass only a whisker from her. She dared not breathe.

"Nothing." The figure moved on. "Maybe she drowned. The currents are strong in the bay."

Waiting until they were well past, Genya followed the clifftop to the castle walls then clambered over more rocks. A string of lights spread out below. Within the mist, she glimpsed more figures, but they were heading away.

Exhausted by her use of magic, she sank behind bushes and rested, even dozed for a short time. When she woke, clouds still covered the moon as if the remnants of her spell lingered.

Soundless, on soft feet, Genya edged towards a familiar balcony and climbed over the balustrade. Her dripping clothes left puddles as she crept into the room. The queen lay resting in her bed, her newborn infant in her arms. At Rozenn's startled cry, Genya put a finger to her lips. "It's only me."

Rozenn sat up in bed. "I thought you would be away from here by now."

"I gave you my word."

Rozenn held the baby tightly to her breast. "My husband will send someone any minute," she whispered. "It was a quick labour, quicker than I deserve." Her eyes hazed with memory. "Given what I did to make sure this child was conceived. What I took from him, the man who fathered this boy."

Genya was deeply curious about the baby's father. But both she and the child were in danger. "Gendrick is coming to kill him?"

"The physician is reporting to my husband." She shuddered. "If it had been a girl, perhaps Gendrick might have let her live, but a boy..." A shadow crossed her face. "Especially this child. If Gendrick knew, if he only knew..."

"Give him to me, Your Grace."

"You'll get him to Yvonne?"

"As promised."

"She'll be at the docks at midnight. There's a ship. They've come for him, from far across the Ice Sea."

Genya approached the bed. Rozenn touched a fair curl on the baby's forehead. "My son, my lovely son."

Footsteps rang in the corridor. Genya quickly crossed the room and locked the door. She went to Rozenn again. "Someone's coming."

Rozenn kissed the baby's downy cheek. "Goodbye, my son. Live well in the Circle Kingdoms until the day you return to reclaim what is rightfully yours."

At these strange words, Genya frowned. She wanted to ask Rozenn what that meant, but a fist thumped the door. *No time.* The only way out was the way she had come. She held out her arms for the child. "I'll get him to Yvonne tonight. Is there a message—for Yvonne?"

"Tell her." Rozenn thumbed hair from the baby's eyes. "Tell her that my son is to be called Decallion."

ROHANE

S isilia swept past guards and into Blaire's rooms. The hem of her purple gown was wet, her auburn hair tousled. Though fatigue shadowed her eyes, they burned with furious intent.

"Out!" She glared at Rohane. "I must speak with the Regenta."

"Rohane." Blaire dismissed the guards with a gesture. "Stay."

"She is not a councillor. This is nothing to do with a *captain*."

"Rohane is here at my request. To discuss the Blessing. The festival is only days away. With the recent attacks, I'm concerned about security."

"The Telorian," Sisilia said abruptly.

"If it's about Val, I am his guardian," Rohane said. "I have a right to know anything that concerns him." Wearily, she passed a hand over her eyes. After last night's feast, she had slept poorly.

The sorceress scowled as if deciding whether to argue.

"What do you want?" Blaire asked coldly.

Unperturbed, Sisilia considered her. "I sought a vision. To understand the danger that's coming. I was only partly successful. That's why I'm here. I want his blood. Give it to me."

"Whose blood?"

Sisilia stabbed a jewelled finger at Blaire. "Do not be disingenuous. It does not suit you. I want the Caelan man brought to me. I need his blood, a lot of it."

Blaire shrugged. "I promised you a little. Once he performs his duties."

"I must have all his blood now. You will give him to me."

"I will not."

Their furious gazes locked. Rohane bristled. How dare Sisilia so callously demand Val's blood? The blood keepers had defined his purpose in Quisnaf. It was not for others to question. No, Sisilia was too single-minded. She served the goddess with a frenzied passion that was dangerous.

"I have powerful spells to weave," Sisilia snapped. "Spells that will keep us safe. It is too quiet—you said as much yourself."

"I did. It is."

"Your instincts are good. Someone is plotting against us. A powerful ruler. I feel it. I must uncover who it is, what they are about. I need the Telorian's blood for these spells. The blood of the gods."

"You've woven spells without Caelan blood before," Rohane said. "If he were not here—"

"But he is," Sisilia broke in. "He can perform these other... tasks"—she spat the word with distaste—"from the keepers' caverns, where I have access to his body."

"Blaire, you cannot." Indignant, Rohane shot to her feet. "He is a guest. You cannot condemn him to the deep caverns."

"Nor will I." Blaire faced the sorceress. "Again, I offer to compromise with you, Sisilia. You may take some of his blood now. But you may not imprison him below."

"It is not enough," Sisilia seethed through gritted teeth. "I need more. I need him."

Rohane huffed a breath angrily. "You would drain him?"

"He would recover." The sorceress brushed the concern off with a sharp gesture. "I've heard the stories. I know he does not die. Think what that means. An endless supply of Caelan blood. Give him to me."

"No."

Sisilia's face twisted with fury. "I know what you did, Blaire." Her voice was low and hard. "I know you tampered with the blood keepers' list."

"What?" Rohane spun on Blaire in surprise. "What's she saying?"

"You're interfering with Cyrah's plans," Sisilia said. "That is a perfect combination of bloodlines, and you stopped it."

"I did no such thing."

"I will expose you," Sisilia said.

"Do your worst. I will deny it."

"And you deny me this man?"

"Yes."

Sisilia drove her hand through the air angrily. "You leave me no choice. I will take matters into my own hands, Blaire. Very soon, you will surrender him. I will ensure that if you do not, you break every law in Quisnaf." With a swish of her cloak and a haughty sniff, she swept from the room.

Rohane stared at Blaire in disbelief. A silence gathered about them. Blaire did not look at her, but two spots of red flared on her throat.

"It's not what you think," she muttered at last.

"You did, didn't you," Rohane said. "You removed *her* name from the blood keepers' list." She shook her head, shocked. "It's petty, Blaire. Small-minded."

Blaire's lips compressed to a thin line. "This is about protecting Quisnaf. It's not personal."

"I don't accept that," Rohane said.

"Then you're not thinking," Blaire hissed. "What do you think would happen if Jenna-Dairine bore his child? If there is not a clear succession, Quisnaf will be torn apart."

"You don't know that." Rohane's hands fisted at her side. "Who's to say that this child is not destined to lead Quisnaf?"

"I'm saving Quisnaf," Blaire said. "You don't see what's

happening, Rohane. You're never here."

"I'm beginning to see a lot of things very clearly," Rohane said. "And I don't like it."

VAL ARQUES

R ohane took Val to the walled walk above the arch at the valley's entrance. Quisnaf women gathered on the walk. They pressed against the rock balustrade, peering down across a dusty plain stretching towards a red desert where traders' caravans and carts rattled towards the arch into the valley. The traders brought jewellery, silk, swords, and jewel-hilted daggers, leatherware, singing birds in cages, and exotic fruit—goods destined for the markets at the Blessing.

As many eyes fell on other visitors, young men in noisy, boastful groups or alone on horseback, attended by a servant. One bold man, with the blond hair and well-cut beard of a Venivan, bowed to the women on the arch, flashing them a brazen grin. Some of the younger girls tittered and flushed. When he passed from sight, they fell into a knot to whisper excitedly. "That one, that one," Val heard. Then a teasing voice said, "That's what you said about the handsome Wardorian."

He turned with a smile to Rohane. "I've heard whispers about the Blessing but never dared hope they were true. So it's really just a great big orgy."

"Trust an Isles lord to simplify everything." As though exasperated, Rohane sighed. "It is a fertility rite. Any coupling during the Blessing honours the goddess."

"So there will be coupling." He wriggled his brows wickedly. "A lot of coupling."

"There shall be no coupling for you beyond your usual duties. So just stay at my side. There are some events we may attend safely. The markets. A contest of weapons—now *that* you'll enjoy."

"I'd enjoy the coupling more."

"Fool. Shall I take you to the markets, fool?"

They descended the stairs to the valley. One green meadow had been transformed into a field of commerce. Everywhere, flags fluttered from tents. Merchants erected stalls or displayed wares in the backs of carts. All the while, more joined them so that all about was a bustle of activity. Quisnaf citizens and guests wandered freely. Val noticed a couple of warriors pretend to look at goods, their gazes surreptitiously sliding to young men.

"When does the coupling start?"

Rohane put down a leather purse to consider him. "You really are just an overgrown boy."

He raised his palms. "You've found me out."

She huffed. Her hands moved to a belt, her long fingers caressing the leather. Val remembered how soft her lips had been when he'd kissed her and how she had melted against him just for one moment. With a shudder of fear, he winced. He must keep Rohane at a distance. He was dangerous, too dangerous, to let anyone love him or care for him. Nothing good came to those who did. Only trouble. Only death. It was well that he was away from Kaell.

Rohane asked the merchant the price. Upon hearing his answer, she shrugged and moved away. "Too much."

"I'd buy it for you, but I have no money." He had nothing to call his own, except maybe his boots and an arm bracelet.

"And that wouldn't set tongues wagging at all."

"Do you care?"

Rohane stopped in her tracks, turned back, and frowned. "You don't seem to realise that if either of us steps out of line, we'll feel the whip on our backs." She walked on quickly.

Val strode to catch up. "Where's my sword, by the way? I was just thinking of how little I own. Nothing except these dusty boots. I haven't seen the tunic and pants I first wore on board for a while, so I suppose they're gone, too. So… just my boots."

Rohane sighed. "Your sword is in my quarters. If anyone, like Blaire, for example, specifically asked about it, I would answer truthfully, but no one has. So I said nothing."

"I feel naked without it. You carry a Seithin steel blade yourself."

"A gift from my father. When I came of age." She whipped up a hand. "No, do not ask. I don't intend to talk about him."

⁂

Rohane took Val to bathe early then left him in his room to dress. She promised to return at dusk to escort him to the feast then to watch the archery and sword competitions.

"No coupling?" Again, he wriggled his brows suggestively.

"Only coupling you'll see is two opponents batter each other with swords."

"You spoil all my fun." But despite his words, he eagerly looked forward to tonight. Quisnaf hummed with excitement. It snaked through the caves in the whispers of groups of warriors or scribes or even in the faster pace of footsteps as though everyone had somewhere to be. Strangers were everywhere—men in exotic cloaks and tunics with all manner of odd headwear. They carried weapons freely, but the Decan Watch was out in great number.

The feast of the Blessing, too, was a splendid ritual in Quisnaf, he had learned. It was held outdoors, with hundreds of tables filling the valley. Servants brought exactly three thousand dishes. Cooks, bakers, butchers had prepared for weeks. A bonfire blazed, not for warmth but light. Warriors sprang up and danced to the music of recorders, lutes, and flutes. Drums thumped, summoning everyone to celebrate Cyrah's blessings.

Cyrah had two faces: warrior queen and mother. Tonight, every act of passion served her. A child conceived at the Blessing was considered especially fortunate. For two nights and two days, men were welcome to enter Quisnaf freely, to walk without restraint.

And they came willingly, knowing that as smoke swirled from the bonfire, as music played, and wine and beer flowed, a blonde, tall Quisnaf warrior may well grab their hand and lead them into the bushes or back to their rooms. Or even to the temple itself. "A festival of abandon," Rohane had called it. Val thought it an apt description.

He dressed carefully in clothes left for him. By whom? He knew servants scuttled in and out of his room when he was absent, emptying chamber pots, taking away discarded clothes for washing, changing sheets, and fluffing pillows. They were like ghosts, the servants of Quisnaf. Men mainly, but some women, too. He didn't quite understand the distinction.

Tonight, he wore black pants and a dark-blue silk tunic. He wondered if Rohane had chosen the colour; she had muttered once that he should always wear black or dark blue because it set off his hair and eyes. He deftly fastened a swirling cloak with a silver broach at the shoulder. It fell to his hip. Without the weight of a sword, his body was unbalanced. Too light. He wondered if he would ever grow accustomed to it.

Someone knocked. Val whirled. Rohane had returned quicker than he'd expected. He crossed to the door and threw up the bar. When he pushed it open, no one stood there.

"Rohane?" Val took a step outside and peered about. It was darker than it should have been.

The torches in the corridor were dead. A warning prickle stole up his spine. At a whisper of noise, perhaps cloth brushing stone, he half turned, his hand groping for the nonexistent blade. Then hands grasped his head. A cloth clamped over his mouth. Dizziness swamped him. Then he fell into darkness.

ROHANE

Rohane hummed as she walked through the passages in the warrior quarters, her spirit light. Rarely did she want to burst into song, but the Blessing was her favourite time of year.

As a child, she had loved the bright colours of the merchants' tents, the exotic garments of guests, and the swirl and bustle. Merry voices, laughter, and the atmosphere of celebration awoke something inside her akin to delight. Later, as a young woman, she had embraced the sensual undercurrents to the celebrations, their hint of danger and mystery tingling her skin with anticipation.

The first time she had sought out pleasure at the Blessing, she had been like any other young warrior; not yet part of a battale but serving an officer in preparation. Every potential bladeswoman did the same—tending to that officer's horse, mending clothes, cleaning weapons, running useless errands. *And keeping secrets.*

Because of her position, Rohane had ended up with the plum post of servant to a captain. Persia. In other roles, she tended to rebellion, but she had served Persia well because Rohane aspired only to be a warrior. There was nothing better, more worthy or honourable in Quisnaf, unless you craved power and wanted to be a councillor. Rohane did not.

She hardly remembered her first battle. In a tumult of iron, blood, and broken bodies, she had swung her sword about wildly, unsure if any blows landed. Her battle sister Nessa had grabbed her arm, shouting, "He's dead, Rohane. Dead. No need to keep hitting him."

A Gidani warrior lay bloodied at Rohane's feet, his body pummelled and dismembered. Rohane had blinked and stared. Surely, she had not done that.

That same year, she'd learnt about the abandon of the Blessing. Not that she had intended to experience the pleasures of the flesh. No, she'd sought only the comfort of friendship at the feast.

Rohane remembered leaping into the warrior dance about the fire, her hands on Nessa's waist, laughing. The leaping flames, the drums, and Nessa's giggle had all been as intoxicating as the wine.

Nessa nudged her. "Those two. They keep watching us. What do you think?"

"I can't see."

"Next time around," Nessa said.

Their names were Manfred and Gerald, two young Venivans. Nessa had grabbed Manfred's arm and pulled him into the dance. When the circle next swirled past, Gerald stood and beckoned to Rohane. Cheeks aflame with excitement, she let him draw her away. He was blond and sturdy, with clear, bright eyes and a wide smile. Pleasing to her eye.

She sank onto the grass beside him. They drank wine and talked, mostly nonsense. Then they drank more wine. When he kissed her, it seemed part of the dance, part of the heady atmosphere of the Blessing. They did not bother to retreat behind trees or find a lonely spot for privacy. Openly, hidden only by smoke and moon-speckled darkness, men and women coupled all about them, their limbs entwined. The drums still beat, the flutes still played, but moans, whispers, giggles, and sighs all provided a raunchy accompaniment. She and Gerald made love beneath the stars, half clothed. Rohane had her boots on at least, though his tunic was ripped.

Now, as she walked these passages, she banished the memory to the back of her mind. For it had nothing to do with who she was. The girl that night had been a different Rohane. A wide-eyed young woman who wanted to be a warrior. A young woman who had laughed with her battle sister and dreamt of honour.

Yet the past lingered, niggled, and Rohane paused in the passage. What she wouldn't give to be that sixteen-year-old girl again. But that was impossible. That Rohane was an illusion, her true nature yet to be revealed. Her curse yet to show itself.

Maybe her musings were because of him. The Telorian. Maybe it was that stolen kiss by the river—an innocent kiss in its way. Perhaps that kiss reminded her of a different Rohane, a Rohane he might well love. A Rohane who might well love him. And there it was again—useless imaginings. It would not happen. It must not happen.

Sombrely, she turned into the passage leading to Val's chamber. It was in total darkness. A chill tore down her spine. Quickly, she backtracked to snatch a brand from a sconce and returned, waving the light.

Val's door stood open. Rohane rushed in, calling his name. The room was empty. Alarm roiled in her gut. Retreating outside, she swung the torch high to the walls, to the door then to the floor. A dark stain wet the stone. Rohane dropped to her knees. She touched a finger to it. *Blood.*

A sick lurch of panic kicked inside her. Had someone attacked him? Taken him? Why?

She pushed to her feet then ran towards the cavern entrance. She must find him. Save him. It was her duty.

Around a corner, Rohane crashed into a figure. They both plunged down. Rohane was the first to stagger up, holding her head. She groaned.

"What's the hurry?" The other woman rose.

Rohane scooped up the dropped torch and shone it on the newcomer. "Oh, by Cyrah. Jenna-Dairine. I'm sorry. I didn't see you."

"That's obvious. But why the rush?" She peered at Rohane's face. "You look terrible."

Rohane's bottom lip trembled. "He's gone. There's blood."

"What's happened?" Jenna-Dairine grasped her arm.

"Someone put the torches out." The words came at a rush. "His door was open. And—" Her voice quavered. "And there's blood on the ground. Oh, goddess, I have to find him. I have to. What if someone hurt him? He's my responsibility."

"You're sure about the blood?"

Rohane nodded. "I know blood when I see it."

Jenna-Dairine gave a cynical laugh. "Of course you do. So where do we look? Who might wish him ill?"

"I don't expect you… I mean, you have to fight tonight."

"Hours until then. I'm here now, so let me help. Who wishes him ill?"

Rohane shook her head. "There's no one… Hmm, maybe Branwyn. He said she had groped him in a hut somewhere."

"What?"

"She told him to watch his back."

Jenna-Dairine rubbed her chin, frowning. "What if it's not her? What if it's just some resentful, cowardly pack like Dana and her friends, wanting a taste of what they can't have? It's more common than you know, Rohane."

Rohane's heart skidded against her ribs. "I hope you're wrong. But if it's someone like that, who knows where they'll take him."

"It's a good night for it," Jenna-Dairine muttered. "Strangers everywhere. Commotion, distraction. Drink. Women taking a man off into the darkness, no one would think twice."

Rohane braced the wall with her hand. Val might be powerful, his body strong, but he was unarmed. His protection in Quisnaf was her sword and her wits. She'd failed him.

"Start asking about." Jenna-Dairine turned for the entrance. "I'll do the same. You can't just spirit a man away from these caverns. Someone saw them. They just don't realise what they saw."

⁎

Rohane tapped her fingers on her belt as she waited for Jenna-Dairine at the temple steps. Raucous songs, laughter, shouts, and whispers filled the night. From the bushes, a woman giggled. Bristling with impatience, Rohane edged away.

"Rohane." Jenna-Dairine emerged from the shadows.

"No one heard anything." Rohane's body was tight with disappointment and fear.

"I have something," Jenna-Dairine said. "I found a Decan guard who offered to help a group of women with an insensible man. She thought the man drunk, or at least that's what the women said. They went into the storerooms." Jenna-Dairine's calm manner was deceptive. She was angry, her mouth pressed in a line. "That's where those cowards took Riagan. They knew they wouldn't be disturbed there."

"But you exposed that place. No one would dare go there now."

"That's exactly why someone very clever would do just that."

Rohane started towards the path to the caves. Jenna-Dairine ran after her and grabbed her shoulder, spinning her back. "Take a breath. Just one. I know how furious you are. Just the thought of that place…" She broke off, her face hard.

"Don't try to stop me, Jenna-Dairine. If they've hurt him, they'll pay."

"I don't want to stop you. But we have to be clever. It's just you and me, Rohane. Who knows how many of them there are?"

Rohane laughed bitterly. "Don't you know who I am, Captain? I'm cursed. Everyone says so. Even alone, I'm going to make them bleed."

She strode on. But not before she glimpsed Jenna-Dairine shudder.

VAL ARQUES

Val came to his senses blindfolded, gagged, and lying on something hard. A stale, musky smell prickled his nose. Thick rope secured his hands above his head. His head throbbed. He shut his eyes, trying to retreat from the pain.

Footsteps approached. Raised voices closed on him. Val stilled, knowing he must not alert whoever was there to his wakefulness. Not until he knew where he was and who held him.

Desperately, he searched his memory. Someone had hit him hard enough to knock him out. They'd brought him to a strange room and bound him.

"Just so long as the blindfold stays on, there's no danger," a woman said.

"We're only supposed to take him. She said to wait for instructions."

"It's just a little fun," the first woman said. "To pass the time."

"Safer to kill him when we're done then," the second growled.

"Are you witless? And have Rohane hunt us down? Or Blaire? He shares the ice queen's bed, too—don't forget. No, this way is safe. He'll be too ashamed to say anything."

"Is he awake?" The third voice sounded younger. "Who goes first?"

The first laughed nastily. "We can all enjoy this one together. But I want him kicking. It's not fun if he doesn't fight me."

Footsteps tapped stone. A shadow fell over him. A hand nudged him.

"Still out. The longer we're here, the more chance we'll be found. Douse him."

More muffled steps padded over the floor. Then cold water hit his face. Val spluttered through the gag. Fingers grabbed his jaw. "Awake? Good. Now listen. I'll remove the gag, but if you try to scream or make a sound, it goes straight back on. Nod to show you agree."

Val nodded. When the gag came out, he coughed. "Where am I? What do you want with me?"

"You're somewhere no one will look for you." The first woman laughed coolly. "We just want a little fun, that's all. No one needs to get hurt."

Cloth swished. At the sound of something shattering, Val jolted.

"Clumsy fool," the first woman said. "Why don't you smash another one so the guards know where to come?"

"There are jars everywhere," the second complained.

"Let's have a look." A blade slid free of a sheath. Whoever bent over him cut open his tunic and pulled it off, leaving Val naked from the waist up.

"I want to put my hands all over him," the second woman said. "Just like *she* does."

"You can do what you want with him. They can't stop you."

"I like his mouth," the youngest whispered.

"Then kiss him."

A finger touched Val's lips hesitantly. Disgusted, he wrenched his head aside. Whatever he lay on shifted beneath him. They'd thrown him down on sacks of grain.

Someone stooped over him. A ménage of scents swirled—rose mainly, but with a hint of sandalwood. Lips touched his. He clamped his mouth shut, squirming against the sacks, and hissed, "Do not touch me."

"Why don't you lie back and enjoy it."

"Why are you doing this? Isn't this the Blessing? There are hundreds of men outside."

"Because you're forbidden," the second woman said. "Because we're not good enough for the likes of you. Only those of a few precious bloodlines are deemed worthy to lie with you."

"That's no reason—" He broke off at a slap.

"Quiet." Fingers circled his nipples. The caress moved over his breast.

"Why shouldn't we enjoy what they have?" the second voice snapped. "That haughty cow, Blaire. How we'll laugh to know we took the man she enjoys in her bed. We'll take whoever we want. We won't be told who we can't touch."

A buckle loosened. A weapons belt plonked to the floor. The fingers on his breast trailed to his groin. Val bucked, wrenching hard at the ropes on his wrists. A knee pressed into his hip, pinning him against the sacks. Fingers entwined his hair. "He's so pretty. I wish we could keep him."

A door thumped against a wall. The women gasped. "Quick, the light." Candle flames died. One of his captors shoved cloth in his mouth. Cold metal pressed to his throat. "Silent, or I'll carve you up."

Footsteps approached, slow and careful. They stopped.

A voice called, "I know you're here. Release him, and I might be merciful."

Val's heart leapt with relief and shame. *Rohane. No.* He did not want her to find him like this—helpless, needing rescue like a child.

"You can't hide in the dark. I smell you." A light flickered. Rohane drew in a startled breath. "Ursula, what do you think you're doing?"

The first of Val's captors laughed. Steel moved away from his throat. Cloth brushed his thigh as someone rose. "Well, look who found their way back here. Want to join us, Rohane? What about you, Jenna-Dairine?"

A sword scraped free, and Jenna-Dairine said, "I want you to back away from him."

"We invited him back," Ursula said. "He was up for it. It's the Blessing after all."

"Up for it?" Jenna-Dairine scoffed. "Ropes, blindfold, and a gag?"

"Second thoughts when it got a bit rough. Typical of a man. Believe me, he said yes. He was all too willing to begin with."

"Let's ask him, shall we?" Rohane said. "Once we've freed him. Now fall to your knees and put your hands behind your heads."

"You think you're going to take us before a court? Think again."

"Ursula," the youngest whimpered. "What do we do?"

"Keep your nerve," Ursula snapped. "We won't face a court. Rohane doesn't want that."

"Ursula." The second woman sounded panicked. "We can't fight our way out of here. Not against Jenna-Dairine and the crazy one together."

Steel tickled Val's jaw again. "I'll cut his throat," Ursula hissed. "I swear I will. Now back away. We're going to walk out of here."

"You can leave… if you get past me," Rohane said.

"Rohane, no," Jenna-Dairine protested.

"I want you to go, Jenna-Dairine."

"I think not."

"Go." Rohane's voice sounded strange. Distant. "This is my fight. They took a man under my protection. You know what I'm about to do."

A silence closed in around her words, then a sword slid back into a scabbard.

"Very well." Footsteps retreated to the door. It fell shut.

"Come on," Rohane taunted. "Three against one. This is easy. Take me out and get away."

Val's heart battered his ribcage. Fear for her lanced him. They would kill her.

"Ursula." The youngest one's voice shook. "What do we do?"

"What are you waiting for?" Rohane mocked. "Afraid?"

"Of you?" Ursula scoffed. "I think not. I don't believe the stories."

"Come at me and find out."

"You'd like that, wouldn't you?"

"Come at me," Rohane hissed. "Coward."

Ursula screamed with fury. Val heard rushing steps, then steel thundered against steel. His breath cut off. *Rohane, no, no, no.* He could not listen to her die. Frantically, he tore at the ropes about his wrists, careless of the blood streaming down his arms.

A tumult of crashing, howling, shrieking metal, yells, curses, and furious steps beat at his ears. A woman howled in pain. A young voice cried, "No, no. Please."

Steel whirred through air. Then came a drawn-out scream that was more bestial than human. Hairs rose along Val's arms. Again, he couldn't breathe. A thick, awful hush gathered about him. Then, within the quiet, he heard breaths rasp in and out, in and out.

The blindfold was ripped off. Rohane stooped over him, untying the gag. Blood splattered her face and hair. More stained her clothes.

"Rohane. Oh, by The Three. I heard… I thought…"

"I'm not hurt. But you. Did they—" She bit her lip, trembling.

"Are you all right? You look shaken."

A shadow flitted behind her eyes. "It's nothing." Rohane freed his hands. "Curse them. Why take you?"

Val sat up. At once, he wished he hadn't. His head ached. His cramped arms and hands prickled uncomfortably as blood flowed. He shot a look about. They'd dumped him on two sacks. Jars and more sacks were scattered about the chamber. Grain spilled from one onto a woman's legs, her body hidden behind Rohane.

Then his breath caught in his throat. Spliced limbs, heads, and torsos in pools of dark blood littered the ground. More blood splattered the jars, sacks, and walls, as it might in a slaughterhouse.

He tore his gaze away from the carnage. "They said they wanted what was denied to them. That they deserved what Blaire and the others had. That it wasn't fair."

Rohane grimaced. "That sort of resentment is more common than the council realises. It's dangerous." She helped him up. The remains of his ripped tunic fell away. Aware Rohane watched, Val's cheeks flushed.

"It's all right," she said gently. "You're safe. You were always safe, just so long as you stayed still."

Val dropped his head, hiding from her gaze. Shame swept through him. He was a bladesman, a lord of Telor. He did not want her to see him like this—his tunic in tatters, rope marks about his wrists.

"Here."

Val looked up. Rohane unfastened her cloak and placed it around his shoulders.

"If anyone sees him wearing your colours, there will be talk," Jenna-Dairine called from the doorway. She leaned against the frame, her legs crossed at the ankles, fingers clasped about her sword pommel. A faint breeze from outside ruffled her hair. She tossed Val a grin. "You're alive at least. Unmolested, I hope."

For a moment, he couldn't speak. Then he muttered, "I feel grubby." *Grubby and ashamed.*

Jenna-Dairine did not reply. She was staring about, frowning.

Rohane's hands fell to her sides. She wore a hard, defiant look.

Jenna-Dairine's stare rose to Rohane. "It's true then."

"I didn't try to stop. I didn't want to. But the rage is more concentrated now. I can control it." Rohane's voice was dead, empty. Her face was a stranger's, withdrawn and distant.

Val knew what that shut-down expression meant, what it hid. Pity for her flooded him. Badly did he want to fold her in his arms and comfort her. But even then, that insidious whisper returned. He was dangerous. Anyone he loved, anyone who loved him, got hurt. He could not risk hurting Rohane. *Keep her at a distance. Keep her safe.*

"I could have stopped you," Jenna-Dairine said. "But the truth is I didn't want to. I walked away because I knew. I knew, and I wanted it as much as you." She kicked a sack. "This is where Riagan died."

"Goddess," Rohane whispered. "That they should choose here."

Jenna-Dairine nudged a ragged arm with her boot. "We'll hide the bodies deep in the caverns."

"Ursula is a Decan guard. There will be questions if she disappears. The other two I don't know, but surely they, too, will be missed."

"Missed. Searched for. But not found. However, just in case, all three of us must be very conspicuous for the rest of tonight." Jenna-Dairine shrugged. "For me, that's easy."

"Oh, by Cyrah," Rohane clamped her hand to her mouth. "You must defend your title."

"And Quisnaf honour. But the games don't start until the second moon rises. You both must attend. Create a stir, do something that draws the eye. Make sure everyone looks at you and remembers you were there."

"He always creates a stir," Rohane said distantly. "Just his presence."

Val's gaze drifted unwillingly to the butchery, the blood. That drawn-out scream echoed in his skull, the terror in that voice unnerving. He glanced at Rohane, worried by the haunted look in her eyes. He wanted to help her, to protect her. Whatever dreadful horror had unfolded in this storeroom, he guessed it was part of why she described herself as cursed.

But she was safer an arm's length from him. Rohane. Genya. Kaell. All safer away from him, from the destruction of his love.

"Rohane, take back your cloak," Jenna-Dairine said. "You need to hide the blood on your garments. Val will take my cloak. He's bloody, too."

"And you don't think that will cause a stir? Everyone knows your colours."

"Keep the hood up to hide your face," Jenna-Dairine instructed Val. "Then both of you, clean up, dress, and attend the contest of weapons. Then do something outrageous that everyone will notice."

⁂

Rohane grabbed new garments from their rooms then smuggled Val into one of the bathhouses. Not that anyone paid them any attention. In the shadows on the edge of the pools, men and women coupled, their limbs entwined. Through steam rising off the baths, Val glimpsed bare skin and heard moans and soft whispers.

The atmosphere of desire and abandon in the bathhouse was hardly different to the rest of Quisnaf. Even as they walked through the valley, sounds of pleasure had come from the darkness.

He and Rohane slipped off their clothing and slid into the water. In the torchlight, Rohane's skin glistened. She ducked her head beneath the surface, scrubbed her body with a cloth, then almost at once climbed out with a flash of buttocks. By the time he had washed, she was half dressed.

"Quickly now."

At her abrupt tone and the bitter twist of her lips, he could stay silent no longer. "What happened back there? I heard—" He shuddered.

She said nothing, only set her mouth stubbornly. There would be no answers, at least tonight.

Thoughtful, he threw on fresh garments then sat on a bench to draw on his boots. Rohane shifted her weight. "Hurry up. What are you? A princess?"

"I'm ready."

She turned for the door. Val trod after her, glimpsing a man's pale, muscular bare shoulders. A young woman, her back to the wall, writhed and moaned against him.

Val was far from prudish, but the Blessing shocked him vaguely. There was something undisciplined about the unbridled passion, and something about shallow sex without emotional intimacy left him cold. Many times, he had sought the comfort of a lover, but it was never without tenderness, without warmth.

Surprised by his disquiet, he followed Rohane into the torch-lit passage outside the bathhouse. She strode ahead with a resolved briskness, as though anger fired her every step.

In the valley, the night air was cool and soft. Moonlight was ivory on leaves. Val and Rohane passed figures dancing about a fire in a pit, its sparks shooting into the air. More men and women sat at tables, eating, drinking, and laughing. Even as Val watched, a woman led a man behind bushes. Others, more brazen or drunker, kissed and caressed each other about the fire. A half-naked man pulled a woman onto his lap, her tunic hitched high.

Val wondered if Rohane had ever danced about the fire or succumbed to the allure of pleasure at the Blessing. He remembered the night he had found her drinking alone on a ship's deck. "I'm no better," she'd said. "I singled out a man for later."

Yet it was hard to imagine the Rohane he had come to know, the woman so in control, surrendering to the abandon of the Blessing, that chaos of lust, wine, and flesh.

By the time they reached the marble path through the valley to the temple, a jubilant crowd moved with them towards tall bronze doors that stood open. As if in a dream, Val followed Rohane into an enormous cavern beside the temple where rings of benches sloped down about a natural amphitheatre of rock. The large, high-roofed grotto was square and lit by braziers, both at the back of the stands and at the edges of a pitted, sandy arena.

An audience already filled the benches, watching archers shoot at distant targets in the pit. Excited voices mingled with bursts of nervous laughter as more spectators spilled through the doors and found seats. The sultry air smelt of smoke and perfumed bodies, which were adorned in rich blue, green, and red silk gowns or tunics that, for a celebration, replaced sombre every-day garments. Here, at least, everyone was clothed, and though Val glimpsed occasional caresses or kisses, it was discreet. The amphitheatre was alive with anticipation. Although the onlookers applauded archers' efforts, Val sensed everyone was waiting for something else.

A heavily guarded raised platform was set against a wall of stone, where a tunnel led into shadows streaked with torchlight. Upon the platform, seated in cushioned chairs, a few Quisnaf council members watched the entertainment. At their centre, beside Samantha, sat Blaire. She looked impossibly beautiful, her perfect face serene, her pale hair loosened and falling about a long gown. Only a weapons belt holding a jewelled knife belied the impression of soft femininity.

Rohane led Val to seats just in front of the pavilion. Curious eyes followed him. Brows twitched with speculation.

"It's your hair," Rohane whispered. "No one is as dark, not here."

Blaire looked their way. Rohane nodded a greeting.

Close to their seats, Val glimpsed Persia with a young man cloaked in the battale captain's colours. Marlisa laughed with a group of young warriors swigging from wineskins. A few sat with men, whispering and smiling, their hands brushing thighs.

Involuntarily, Val swivelled sharply, sensing someone else watching him. From the back of the amphitheatre, Sisilia stared openly.

"What?" he mouthed.

She did not smile. Her expression did not change.

With a shiver, he turned back.

Applause burst out. In the arena, an archer bowed. She was young, with a sweep of tight-curled brown hair cut to her shoulders. Samantha stepped down from the platform and presented the girl with a silver cup. The archers left through the tunnel at the back of the pit.

Then the atmosphere changed, as though bridled excitement had built to a climax. Everyone waited. A hush fell. Shouts erupted. From the tunnel, Jenna-Dairine strode forth. She wore a steel helm and carried more steel at her hip, but besides loose pants, she wore little else beneath a thin cloak. Her scanty garments bared her belly, shoulders, and arms. Her feet were bare.

The crowd surged to their feet, crying out her name. Jenna-Dairine slipped off her cloak and raised a fist to the mob. The spectators roared approval. She walked to the platform, sweeping Blaire a bow.

The Regenta nodded, her face a mask. A herald stepped forward. Heads turned. The crowd returned to their seats, but many leaned forward, eager. Voices died away.

"Our most beloved captain again defends her crown." The herald's voice carried. "Four years without defeat. Who will beat her? Will someone here tonight at least stay the distance?" The herald peered slowly about the amphitheatre.

"How long do you have to survive?" Val asked Rohane.

"Seven minutes."

He shrugged. "That doesn't sound long."

"Against Jenna-Dairine, it's a lifetime."

"Most of you know the rules," the herald explained. "But for anyone at the Blessing for the first time... a Blessing virgin, shall we say—"

A smattering of salacious laughter broke out, along with a few claps.

"Anyone may challenge our champion. If you draw blood, you win one hundred pieces of gold. If you remain unbeaten after seven minutes, you win fifty pieces. But—" The herald flung up a hand. "Beware. Cyrah demands blood. Either our champion or at least one challenger will die tonight."

A low rumble of voices rose then fell into an expectant silence.

Val shook his head. "This sounds dangerous. Why does she do it?"

"Jenna-Dairine defeated the previous champion," Rohane said. "She is honour-bound to accept all challenges at the time of the Blessing."

"Who is brave enough?" The herald turned slowly, as if seeking out opponents in every corner. "Is there a warrior here tonight who might stay the distance with our champion? Do not be shy. Our champion must meet all challengers."

The silence thickened. Spectators looked at each other. A few young men nudged their companions. Then a man called, "I challenge the Quisnaf champion."

Heads whipped about. Some in the crowd stood to see who had spoken.

The man stepped into the pit. He wore a short tunic over tights, perhaps even a codpiece, that left little to the imagination.

"Your name?" the herald demanded.

The man leaned towards her, speaking quietly. The herald nodded then shouted, "Mordant of Adorean is the first warrior to stand tall tonight."

Sorcha appeared and beckoned Jenna-Dairine and Mordant to her. Both knelt. The High Priestess dropped her hands onto their heads. She began a prayer, her words ancient Quisnaf.

"She invokes Cyrah." Rohane interpreted for Val. "She seeks the goddess's blessing and offers Cyrah the gift of blood."

The combatants rose. The Adorean removed his tunic and dropped it into the sand. He followed Jenna-Dairine to the centre of the arena.

"Why is he bare-chested?"

"So any scratch or wound will show," Rohane said. "That's why Jenna-Dairine is wearing so little."

The priestess and herald left the pit. A girl adorned in a headdress of flowers brought out an enormous sand timer in glass. Etches in its sides marked minutes. She raised a hand. The crowd collectively drew in a breath. Everyone waited. Fascinated, Val sat forward.

Jenna-Dairine freed her sword. She saluted her opponent then kissed the metal. Mordant whipped out a blade and also saluted. The girl turned the sand timer. A sigh hummed around the amphitheatre.

The two fighters circled. The Adorean lunged, an obvious testing stroke. Jenna-Dairine hardly bothered to step away. Mordant lashed deeper. This time, she parried. It was nothing more than a swipe, furiously quick like flashing sunlight.

Her opponent yelled and leapt in with a flurry of cuts and slashes. The battale captain answered, her sword a blur, her riposte forcing him to bound away. Recovering, Mordant attacked again, driving the Quisnaf captain back, but Val sensed Jenna-Dairine was assessing her opponent's speed and looking for patterns.

The sand ticked down to one minute. The Adorean shot it a glance then uncoiled a series of vicious attacks, high then low strokes, deep thrusts then short jabs. Jenna-Dairine responded with clean, quick parries. The low thrusts to her legs, she answered with that strange defence Val had glimpsed before—just a rapid sideways swish of steel. Yet she turned the sword so the outside edge caught Mordant's blade then slid it slightly to strengthen the parry. He nodded approval.

"Two minutes," the girl with the timer shouted. Quisnaf women in the crowd surged up, shouting encouragement for Jenna-Dairine. Some of the men yelled to Mordant as if male honour was at stake.

Thrust, parry, stab, cut. Mordant hunted for openings, only to be repelled again and again. Jenna-Dairine hardly attacked. But her every stroke, her every step, matched or exceeded his for speed.

The air grew sticky and hot. Tension closed in like claustrophobic walls. Shouts rolled together with a riotous stamping of feet, cries or murmurs of dismay as Mordant's blows edged close to drawing blood. When a late parry held out a lunge or clever disengage, spectators groaned, disappointed.

"Three minutes."

Mordant flicked a confident grin at the timekeeper. He redoubled his attack as though sure he must wound his opponent soon. But then, Jenna-Dairine broke her pattern of defence, doubling her speed to take over an attack. The Adorean found himself on the back foot, his sword desperately swiping away her thrusts.

The Quisnaf in the crowd not already on their feet shot up, fists pumping air, yelling. Jenna-Dairine pressed home her momentum with deep thrusts, sometimes with feints, sometimes not. Her opponent fended them off deftly. He was quick enough, but Val defied anyone not to get lost in that tangle of steel.

He sensed the moment—just a heartbeat, no more—when Mordant's parry crashed late onto what turned out to be a feint. Jenna-Dairine's blade slid past. Hardly a killing blow. But dramatic. Blood pooled just beneath Mordant's collarbone. He staggered, gasping in pain.

Jenna-Dairine knocked his sword from his hand and thrust her blade to his throat.

The herald appeared in the pit. "Blood is drawn."

For a long moment, Mordant did not move. Then he laughed. "I am glad I am not your offering tonight to your strange goddess."

Jenna-Dairine stepped back, her sword arm falling to her side. "You fought well. The goddess would have been pleased with your blood. See a healer."

He touched his hand to his brow and retreated to cheers and claps.

"Nearly five minutes," Rohane muttered. "She's off to a slow start."

The herald stalked the pit's perimeter. "Who else is brave enough to try to win gold? You?" She stabbed a finger at a young man, who shook his head. "You?" Another laughed and held up his hands to gesture no.

"I will." The new challenger was young and blond. As he lurched drunkenly into the arena, his companions roared in delight. They, too, looked sloppy with drink.

"I don't have a sword." The challenger grinned apologetically as he threw off his tunic.

"Choose one." The herald waved a hand at a table holding a variety of weapons.

The man crossed the arena, swaying only slightly, and swished a few swords about. He settled on one and returned to give the herald his name. "Baldin of Wardour."

He and Jenna-Dairine knelt before Sorcha as the priestess again invoked the goddess. The timekeeper stood ready to flip the sand. The combatants rose, drew their weapons, took guard, and saluted.

Baldin attacked at once with a burst of jabs and thrusts, his footwork balanced. The Wardorian was not nearly as drunk as he'd pretended, Val realised. But then a battle of swords was also a battle of deception and wills. A game, albeit a deadly one.

In response to Baldin's attacks, Jenna-Dairine again chose defence, letting him chase her around the arena. Just when he sensed an opening, she changed the pace and rhythm to exchange a series of deadly blows with her opponent.

"Two minutes," the timekeeper yelled.

Jenna-Dairine frowned. She took Baldin's next assault high up on her blade, locking his weapon. When she wrenched hers away, the momentum forced him back a step. She sprang, nicking his thigh with her sword. Baldin clapped a palm to the wound. It must have been deeper than Val realised, for he collapsed to one knee.

"Blood is drawn," the herald cried.

The Wardorian's friends rushed to the injured man's aid. After a minute or two of heated discussion, they hoisted him up and bore him from the amphitheatre.

"Do your healers fix up foolish young men?" Val asked Rohane.

"At the Blessing, that's all they do."

Another man challenged Jenna-Dairine almost at once and was

quickly despatched without two minutes. Then a fourth and a fifth.

The sixth, a sly creature who attacked with twin blades, survived four minutes. When Jenna-Dairine wounded him in the side, he stayed down. But the instant she turned her back, he leapt up and came at her, weapon in hand. A shocked gasp ran around the amphitheatre. Before anyone shouted a warning, Jenna-Dairine whirled, unsurprised, as though anticipating his deception. Her sword impaled the rushing man, his raised blade too slow to crash down.

She wrenched her sword out. The man collapsed in fast-pooling blood. He gurgled a terrible sound. Slowly, his fingers fell away from his weapon.

Cyrah had her blood offering.

Challengers turned reluctant after that. But the herald goaded two more young men, emboldened by drink, to take their chance. Jenna-Dairine wounded both in less than a minute.

Again, the herald stalked around the edge of the pit, taunting and cajoling. Singled out, men shook their heads.

Val lumbered to his feet. "I'll fight," he shouted.

VAL ARQUES

"I'll fight." His challenge hung in the air. In the sudden hush, eyes swung his way. Then, as if released, an excited murmur ran through the cavernous amphitheatre. Samantha bent to whisper to Blaire. The Regenta sat straight-backed, her hands gripping the chair arms.

Rohane grabbed Val's arm, hissing, "Sit down, fool. You can't."

"Why not? Jenna-Dairine said to do something everyone would notice."

"Not bleed."

Val clasped his hand dramatically to his breast. "Such lack of faith. What if I promise to keep well away from her nasty blade?"

"Fool," Rohane snapped, her gaze upon Jenna-Dairine. The Quisnaf champion had taken a small pot from a pocket inside her cloak and was rubbing an ointment on her blade. "You don't understand... her sword."

He frowned. "What about her sword?"

"The champion's sword—" Rohane wet her lips. Her brows drew down. "It was forged in a witch's fire, on a three-moon night. If any blade can hurt you, it's this one."

"But not kill. Besides, she's not going to get anywhere near me."

"Val." Rohane's fingers dug into his arm. "Jenna-Dairine was just smearing something on the blade. It's likely Mord's Breath. Anyone else, it would kill. But you—if she wounds you, you'll writhe in agony for years."

The herald stammered a few disconnected words, clearly bewildered. Whispers spread as the crowd sensed the unease among the councillors. More faces turned to stare.

Jenna-Dairine found a waterskin. She drank heavily, paying little attention to what unfolded. But Val thought he glimpsed a pleased smile curve her lips.

"Why would she do that?" he muttered. "Mord's Breath is vicious."

"It's about the stakes," Rohane said. "And the contest. Jenna-Dairine believes each opponent must have something to lose. She'll know she can't kill you with steel—she's too powerful and well connected not to have heard the truth about you. And without risk, you won't fight to the extent of your ability—or so she believes."

Val's belly clenched with unease. Mord's Breath indeed raised the danger. But he would not withdraw his challenge.

Shrugging off Rohane's hand, he pushed through the mob towards the pit. Spectators cleared a path for him. Some called out; others reached to touch him.

"He looks Telorian," a man muttered. "See how black his hair is."

When he reached the pit, Blaire rose. She beckoned him to the platform.

The herald recovered her composure. "Well, well. Quite a commotion. I shall interpret for our visitors. You may wonder why we pause. A matter of law. The challenge comes from a man of Quisnaf, under the protection of the council. Whether such a challenge is accepted is a question for our beloved Regenta."

More mutters broke out. The crowd shifted in their seats, curious. Some stood for a better view.

Val walked to the platform and dropped to one knee.

Blaire waved him to his feet. In a harsh whisper, she hissed,

"What do you think you're doing?"

"My sword arm rusts from disuse. I'm itching to swing a blade about."

"It is not a game, Val Arques," Samantha said. "For all the nonsense that fool herald carries on with, Cyrah demands blood."

He laughed harshly. "And has had blood tonight, I think."

The herald approached the platform. "Regenta, shall I disallow this challenge?"

"No." Blaire's voice was tight and hard. "Let this nonsense proceed. Perhaps Jenna-Dairine will teach him a lesson in humility at least."

"One can only hope." Samantha sighed.

"Choose a weapon." Blaire swept a hand at the table.

Val picked up a sword.

"Wait." Rohane jumped down from the stands and advanced. "Here, fool. Take my blade." She put the hilt of her Seithin blade in his hand.

"It is permitted?"

The herald nodded.

"Just don't take a wound," Rohane snapped. "No, don't put your hand to your breast again and look outraged. Just... be careful. To Jenna-Dairine, this is about the contest. About Quisnaf pride. She won't hold back because she likes you."

Grinning, Val swished the blade to test its weight. The hilt was smaller than a sword of his, as though adapted for Rohane. However, it was responsive and well weighted.

The herald spoke with Samantha then returned to the pit's centre. "The challenger is Val Arques," she shouted. "He fights for Quisnaf. The Regenta has generously allowed this contest."

Cheers and clapping erupted.

"Your tunic." The herald held out her arms.

Val drew the garment over his head and passed it to her. More whispers stirred through the crowd. *Telorian.* The word passed from spectator to spectator.

"Look at the size of him."

"A bladesman, surely."

Quisnaf warriors in the crowd began to yell encouragement to Jenna-Dairine. Some of the rowdier, drunker men shouted Val's name.

Sorcha called Val and Jenna-Dairine to her. They knelt. As the priestess chanted over them, the battale captain glanced sideways at Val. "I like your spirit."

"You said to create a stir."

She laughed. "This is more than a stir. This is an outrage. You know you'll answer for it."

Val shrugged. "The crowd hopes you'll be the one I answer to."

"Oh, I think there's as many shouting for you. They're excited about seeing a Telorian fight, especially a man who is clearly a warrior." She flicked him an appreciative look. "We rarely see Telorians here. You're quite exotic."

The priestess finished her prayers. Both combatants rose and took their positions in the pit's sandy centre, weapons ready. The timekeeper flipped the sand.

Jenna-Dairine grinned with anticipation. "I shall enjoy forcing your surrender. Show me what you've got. Attack me. Come on."

"You prefer your opponents to attack. I've watched you. So, no. I think I'll hold back."

Still grinning, Jenna-Dairine cut viciously at his head. Val ducked. She hacked at his legs. He jumped. "It seems you seek to both behead and dismember me."

"Oh, one of those," she murmured, lunging.

He parried. "One of what?"

"One of those who babble as they fight."

"Not at all. I was being polite. I'll stop now."

She bore down at him with swinging steel. Val weaved from another brutal slash. He barely had time to recover before Jenna-Dairine again swung at his head as if to cleave it from his shoulders. That wasn't polite. He wasn't wearing a helm.

She cut, hacked, stabbed, and hewed, her blade hissing through the air. Beneath her onslaught, he retreated. There was a calmness about her, a detachment he recognised from fighting too many warriors in too many battles.

Val held out every blow, waiting for just a split second of hesitation, the slightest break in her rhythm. When it came, he attacked in a storm of metal. His strokes were quick, deceptive, but controlled. He had no wish to lose himself in battle fever and hurt her.

Jenna-Dairine answered with deft parries and fast footwork. Soon, both were sweating, the hot air ringing with thundering steel. They rained hefty blows or sneaky coiled jabs, looking for a way to rend skin and spill blood. Looking for deception, for weakness.

"Four minutes," the timekeeper called.

It could have been four heartbeats. It was as if he and Jenna-Dairine had been encased in a cocoon where time had paused, a place empty of everything but the contest, the sound of clanging blades, and the two combatants. The world beyond the pit had faded away.

Jenna-Dairine's blade cut about him. Swish, swish, swish. Val held out each stroke then fell back as she thrust and thrust again, driving him towards the platform. His back hit its wood. He was hemmed in.

Surprised triumph flared in Jenna-Dairine's eyes. She stabbed. Val dived sideways. The sword crashed into wood. With an angry cry, Jenna-Dairine yanked her sword out and whirled, seeking him anew. Val half rose. Abandoning his blade, he threw himself at her, grappling at her legs and knocking her down. Jenna-Dairine sprawled in the sand.

Val retrieved his sword, letting her reel to her feet before he attacked. She blocked his swing. But the momentum was his. Mercilessly, he drove her towards the pit's centre with battering blows. Jenna-Dairine answered every stroke with a flawless technique, though her cheeks flushed with exertion. Sweat matted her blonde hair.

Sweat, too, ran down Val's breast and from his brow into his eyes. The sword hilt grew damp beneath his fingers, harder to control. But his hand, his body, and his muscles worked instinctively. His feet moved as they should, without conscious thought, knowing the steps of this dance, no matter how wild, how uncontrolled, or how violent it became.

"Six minutes."

Onlookers gasped. They pressed close to the pit's walls, screaming, chanting, cheering, and cajoling. Val had just one minute to survive. No, one minute to hold back his arm. One minute to avoid hurting her.

Jenna-Dairine yelled in frustration. She ducked beneath his cutting blade and dived at his legs, her arms circling his shins. Val plunged down with a grunt. He groped for his lost sword. Jenna-Dairine was quickly on her feet, seeking to spear him with iron. Val's fingers closed on the hilt. His sword lifted. Steel clanged on steel. Just.

Again, she tried to impale him. Val rolled sideways then to his feet. Jenna-Dairine ripped her sword from the sand and jabbed at his belly. He crashed his weapon down, trapping hers beneath. She struggled to tear it free, huffing at the effort.

Val could wound her now. He could jerk his hilt up into her chin, slice her arm or even her thigh. He didn't want to. But nor did he want to lose.

"Six minutes and thirty seconds."

Anger leapt like a fire into her eyes. She kicked at his shin, wrenched her blade clear, and lashed with reckless abandon. Sparks flew into the air from his parry.

"You can't beat me," Jenna-Dairine hissed. "All I have to do is touch you."

She whipped off a glove and reached for him. Val jumped back. Jenna-Dairine came after him. Her blade flashed. Val swept away a deadly slash at his neck. With her other hand, she snatched at his arm. A fingertip wisped over his skin. *Not enough.*

"Seven minutes."

The crowd roared approval, erupting with a cacophony of shouting, clapping, and screaming. Some chanted his name, spilling into the pit towards the combatants. Quisnaf spectators sank into their seats, groaning.

Jenna-Dairine froze. Her eyes widened with shock as she stared at him. Wary, Val crouched, his sword levelled.

Still, Jenna-Dairine stared as though entranced. Then she grasped her sword hilt with two hands, and with a cry of rage, she drove the tip into the sand. Turning, she stalked to the tunnel. Passing Val, she murmured, "One day, I'll have to kill you. Either that or bed you."

Then the surging mob swept him up. A man shook his hand. Others patted his back. Everyone spoke at once, offering congratulations. Val hardly heard them. He forced his way through the crowd to Rohane.

She waited near the entrance to the pit, arms folded. "Blaire wants you."

Val turned. The Regenta beckoned him to the platform. Cheering spectators cleared a path. He approached the platform and knelt before Blaire again. The noise fell away. Every eye swivelled to watch what unfolded.

"Nicely fought," Blaire said in a ringing voice. "The council of Quisnaf congratulates you. Especially as you represent us. Although you did not defeat our champion Jenna-Dairine, you did survive seven minutes without our champion taking blood."

"Do I get the gold?" Val winked with mischief.

Blaire's cool eyes flickered over him. "Oh, you'll get your reward."

Val laughed. A euphoria filled him, just as it had that night Rohane had taken him to the training field. He was aware of his power, the strength in his body, the life in him. *The danger.* It had never occurred to Val before that he valued being dangerous.

That he could protect himself with steel, he'd taken for granted. But in Quisnaf, unable to carry a sword, he was all too aware of his powerlessness. To fight, to win, reminded him of who he was. *What* he was. A bladesman.

Blaire clapped her hands. "I think after that, we need the thrill of the melee." She lowered her voice. "Rohane, attend me."

ROHANE

As the chaos of the melee began, Rohane bid Val wait then took the empty seat beside Blaire. It was always empty at the Blessing, an invitation to whoever might want the Regenta of Quisnaf's ear. And Rohane knew they always came—a steady stream of eager merchants, of foolish young lords, even princes. They offered. They bargained. They threatened. They grovelled. Blaire had once told her that she could not count the number of trade agreements reached in this cavern, against the background of shattering, screeching steel and shouting voices that kept negotiations secret.

This was where the real struggle for power, for advantage or allies took place at the Blessing, camouflaged by the fighting in the pit.

Restlessly, still unsettled by Val's abduction, Rohane waited to hear what Blaire wanted. But almost at once, a guard appeared, whispering a message. Blaire sighed. She beckoned a man wearing long silken robes to her. "My queen," he said, kissing Blaire's knuckles with his rubbery lips. "Is it possible you grow more beautiful?"

"Why not praise her for her wit or wisdom?" Rohane grumbled. "It belittles an intelligent woman to acknowledge only her beauty."

The man waved a wrinkled hand. "My apologies. No insult was intended."

"None is taken," Blaire said with a warning glance at Rohane.

Huffing, Rohane crossed her arms.

"What may I do for you, Ambassador Odo?" Blaire said. "You are in good health? And how is your prince?"

Odo flicked a hand. "Forever plotting and watching his back as any Wardorian prince must."

"As any ruler must," Blaire corrected.

He patted her arm. "Ah, but your people love you."

Rohane considered the ambassador with distaste. He wore too much perfume; his silver-grey hair was oiled, his manner sly and manipulative.

"And is there something I can do to help ease your prince's concerns?" Blaire asked.

The Wardorian ambassador wet already-moist lips. "A remarkable fight, Regenta. Jenna-Dairine, wonderful as always. Such a warrior. I am filled with admiration. So skilled. So clever."

Rohane's gut knotted. She guessed where this roundabout talk headed. Odo would not be the last. Before the night was out, a few others representing wealthy, rapacious lords with certain appetites would find their way to this seat.

"And to think," Odo mused. "That the swordsman who finally avoided her blade should be a Telorian. Quite lovely, so exotic with that dark hair and those dusky eyes."

"No," Blaire said.

Odo pouted as if wounded. "Dear Regenta, you do not know what I am about to ask."

"The answer is still no."

"My lord will want him," Odo said. "When he hears. He will insist."

Blaire shrugged.

"One thousand pieces of gold. No? Then name your price."

Rohane started. That was an incredible offer.

"My answer stands. No."

"He is not cloaked. Others noted it, too. Then he can be bought."

"He is a guest in Quisnaf," Rohane said. "Under our protection."

Silken cloth swished as Odo leaned closer. At a whiff of his sickly sweet perfume, Rohane wrinkled her nose. "For what purpose? No, let me guess. He is a breeder."

"Crude, but yes."

"Because he is beautiful?"

"No, because he is a warrior," Blaire snapped. "I value our friendship, Odo, but this man is not for sale. You must be content with that."

He sat back. "Oh, I am content, Regenta. I am content only with your company. But I cannot speak for my lord."

"That sounds vaguely threatening." Rohane surged to her feet, groping for the knife in her belt. "Do you dare threaten the Regenta of Quisnaf?"

Odo threw up his palms hastily. "Never, my dear. But even Quisnaf needs friends. In these troubled times."

"Quisnaf has friends," Blaire said quietly.

"Your alliance with Veniva?" He rubbed his chin. "Is it wise to trust only in that?"

"It is an alliance that has stood the test of time. It is centuries old. Besides, rumour has it Wardour sets its sights on Telor. There is talk of ships—"

"Trading vessels," Odo said, peeling back his lips to reveal that oily smile. He shrugged. "We are a peaceful people, Regenta."

"By your measure, so are we," Blaire said.

When Odo departed, Rohane fidgeted with her hands on her lap. It had been a long night. She needed to return Val safely to his room. "What did you want to see me about?"

Blaire leaned closer. She drew out a rolled parchment from beneath her cloak. "Here. Read this. I've only just received the draft. Tell me what you think."

Rohane took the paper. She unfolded it and read, frowning.

Alarm tore through her. The more she read, the deeper her consternation grew. It was too much too soon.

"You can't do this," she muttered.

Blaire pressed her lips together firmly. "I must."

"It goes against ancient Quisnaf tradition." She seized a breath. "This is reckless. Foolhardy. It will provide fodder for the Order to act, to declare you are unfit to rule Quisnaf."

"It's the right thing to do," Blaire said solemnly. She grabbed Rohane's arm. "Quisnaf must advance, change. If we are to prosper, we need to be bold."

Rohane shook her head. "This is more than bold. It's an attack on everything Quisnaf stands for."

"I thought you might understand, Rohane. I thought you might share my vision for a fairer society, where the laws apply equally to women and men. Remember when we were children, the plans we had? A new Quisnaf. Odo, unfortunately, is right. We can't rely on our alliance with Veniva for ever. We need more warriors. Yet we banish or enslave men born in Quisnaf. It is a waste."

"And yet you talk of reducing the battales from four to three."

Blaire sighed. "There is too much competition between the battales. Too much division. Three larger battales with three captains will serve us better."

"Perhaps, and I understand your desire to give equal rights to any man born in Quisnaf. But you must move slowly, cautiously. Plant the seed of the idea. Let it take root. Act now, and most will oppose you. There will be anger, outrage. Revolt even."

"As it is, it's only a proposal. Not yet the law."

"Who drew up this law, Blaire? Is it someone you can trust? Or will rumours leak out even if you don't proceed with this madness?"

"Only you and Samantha have seen this. And Sorcha. She drew it up."

"Reluctantly, no doubt." Rohane stared at Blaire's face. The Regenta did not look at her, only watched the melee in the arena. "Promise me you'll think it through."

Blaire sighed. "I'll think it through."

"You've already decided, haven't you?" Rohane dragged her fingers through her hair. "If you want to bring on insurrection, this will do it."

"I trust the women of Quisnaf, Rohane," Blaire said. "They are for the most part fair-minded. They'll understand. They'll accept this."

"No," Rohane said. "They won't."

VAL ARQUES

Silent, lost in thought, Rohane escorted Val to his rooms. In the torchlight-streaked darkness, their footsteps echoed as though the caverns were abandoned, a world apart from the noise and bustle and dangerous sensuality of the Blessing.

Exhilarated by the fight, Val wasn't ready to retreat to this quiet world. He wanted to lose himself again—perhaps dance about the fire, drink from a wineskin, laugh at nonsense or nothing at all. Then he might fall down in the grass and listen to an owl's far-away hoot or just the wind's song through branches. With Rohane. Only then would the night hold magic for him.

His elation fell away. That could not be. Besides, the Quisnaf blood keepers had decreed Rohane was not for him.

"Here's your chance," Val said.

"Hmm?"

"We're alone. Time for you to berate me. Call me names. Fool. Witless. Reckless. That sort of thing."

Rohane bit her lip. By torchlight, her face was all lines, planes, and shadows. Why he hadn't found her immediately pretty, he couldn't imagine now. She was lovely in a way other more perfect faces could never be.

"No name-calling? I got off lightly."

Rohane stopped abruptly. She turned. "Enough nonsense, Val. I've had enough."

"I enjoy teasing you."

Her hands fisted at her side. Irritably, she stamped her foot. "I was afraid for you," she blurted. "Do you understand? They might have hurt you, those cowards who abducted you. Then you do something only a man who cares little if he lives or dies would do."

"You thought Jenna-Dairine would carve me up? I'm touched."

"Oh, you fool. You fool. Always joking."

"Hmm." He sobered. "What is this really about, Rohane?"

She threw him a searching look. "Didn't you see the danger? Jenna-Dairine poisoned her blade. And before. They might have—" She stopped, covering her eyes with her palm.

"Rohane—" Val reached a hand to her cheek.

She jerked away from him, turned, and walked on.

"And again, you raise your shields," Val muttered, striding to keep up. "You begin to open up to me. You let me think you care. Then you close me out. You shroud your thoughts. You hide your feelings. Why won't you let me know you? Why won't you let me see your pain?"

"We all of us have shields," she muttered.

"You've seen me when mine are down," Val said. "What's happened to me here, that's left me bare before you. You've seen my wounds, every one. I'm not ashamed that you did, Rohane. But don't pretend you care if you don't." The words tumbled out, unbidden. They surprised even him. What did he want her to say? What did he want from her?

Again she drew up sharply, her shoulders up. Slowly, she turned. "I don't care. Is that what you want to hear? My duty is to keep you safe. That's all. Nothing more. If I was worried about you getting hurt, it's because I would have failed in my duty. That's all."

"That's all," Val muttered.

With a huff, Rohane walked on, saying nothing until they reached his room. "I forgot to ask." Her voice was guarded. "Are you hurt? Should I send for a healer?"

He shook his head.

"Well then, slam the bolt in place once I've left. After that display, every drunken woman will seek you out. Gods, as if this wasn't bad enough. Now word will spread of this handsome Telorian warrior, undefeated by Jenna-Dairine. Some foul Venivan already offered gold for you. So listen up. Do not open the door to anyone but me."

"Rohane—" He took a step closer.

"Good night, Val."

Again, he raised a hand to her cheek. She slapped it away with a growl.

For a long moment, they looked at each other, Rohane with anger, Val heavyhearted with regret, a gulf of misunderstanding between them. Then Val sighed. "Good night then."

He walked into his chamber. She closed the door at her back. He listened for her footsteps, but there was nothing. It was as if she stood there, silent, not moving away.

Val pressed his palm to the door. It was his imagination, surely, but he was almost sure he could feel the warmth of her hand through the iron, as if a strange intimacy bound them in that moment.

"Rohane," he whispered, his lips close to the door.

It swung open. Rohane stood on the threshold. Her eyes were strange and terrible and beautiful.

"You want to know my pain?" she said. "Do you really?"

"Yes," Val said.

They stared at each other. A silence fell and lengthened.

"Yes," he said again.

"The storeroom, what I did—" Rohane looked down. "I lose control. I can kill without feeling anything. I'm a monster. Is that what you wanted to hear? Is that laying myself bare for you? You should be afraid of me, Val. Just like everyone else."

"You're not a monster."

"I killed my battle sister," Rohane blurted. "I killed Nessa."

Val stilled, cold with shock.

"I went mad." Rohane's face shadowed, her expression dazed and lost. "Just like I did just now in that storeroom. I'm a berserker. Like my father. We lose control. We kill and kill, whoever is near. We cannot be stopped."

"Rohane—"

She lifted her eyes to his. There was such pain in them. Anguish. "I killed Nessa. She was too close to me in battle, or she tried to hold me or stop me or something. But I couldn't stop. I didn't even know I'd done it until she lay dead at my feet, until others overwhelmed me. I remember the looks of horror on their faces. Their fear."

"You loved her."

Rohane choked off a sob. Her breath was ragged. "I loved her. I'd rather cut out my own heart than hurt Nessa."

"I understand," Val said. "More than you'll ever know." He closed his eyes briefly, remembering the blood rage that had taken him over in the Icelands, how he had killed indiscriminately, how he had butchered and slaughtered.

"No one can understand." Rohane's tears fell freely now, quietly. They streamed down her cheeks onto her chin. She did not wipe them away. "No one wants me in a battale. How could they? I might kill twenty of our enemy, but I'd kill friends, too. No one wants to be my new battle sister. They don't trust me. That means I'm no one, an outcast who isn't cast out. A ghost of sorts. No warrior in Quisnaf is alone. Not like I am. Everyone has a sister they trust with their life, whom they would give their blood to save. Everyone is part of something. But not me."

"Oh, Rohane." His heart ached for her. Not with pity but with compassion. If only he could save her the hurt, tell her she need not be alone.

"I've learnt to fight it, Val. I've learnt to calm the rage, to fight without unleashing what's inside me. But I have my father's foul,

foul blood. The curse is always with me."

"Not a curse," Val said. "A burden." He touched her arm. She flinched. He thought she might pull away, but she did not.

"Rohane," he whispered, pulling her to his breast. She was at first stiff in his arms, then she sighed and collapsed against him. Her tears wet his tunic.

"I won't leave you, Rohane," he murmured into her hair. "You don't have to be alone. I'd fight back-to-back with you. By your side. I wouldn't fear you."

Gulping a sob, she trembled. Val bent his head and brushed her lips with his. Rohane jerked away. Her palm rose as if to slap his cheek, her eyes raging. For a long moment, she stared at him. Then she grasped his face between her hands and kissed him hard.

The door stood open at their backs, forgotten.

VAL ARQUES

They undressed each other slowly, smiling at the wonder of seeing, touching, feeling. As if they had been caught up in a spell, the world beyond the chamber had faded away. The silence of the caverns, the shadows rent by candlelight, the softest breeze—only he and Rohane knew these things. Only they knew each other, like lovers reunited after a long, sorrowful parting.

Her hair was loose, billowing and soft on his skin. In awe, he touched a strand as if he had never touched anything like it before. She pushed him back onto the bed and crouched over him, her lips on his belly then his thighs.

Their lovemaking was tender, their bodies moving together to a rhythm that belonged only to them, a rhythm that belonged to this moment, to this place. Time became breaths; the candlelit darkness contained them, just them. There was nothing beyond.

His mouth, his fingers explored every part of her. He stroked her skin. He traced the shape of her lips. He caressed every bit of her with wonder. She would consume him. He gave her that power, surrendered to it. Longed for it.

How shallow, how empty every other coupling seemed in that moment. Though there had been desire, though he had been fond of many other lovers, there had not been understanding. No belonging. No bond of knowing someone's mind and heart.

For he knew Rohane. He knew how her forehead wrinkled when she puzzled out a problem. How she bit her lip when she didn't want to answer. How her face softened when she laughed. He knew how fierce and strong she could be or playful and teasing beneath that prickly shield.

When at last he drew her onto his lap and buried himself deep inside her, he wanted to stay that way forever—aware only of her, of the perfume of her skin, her hair, her curves and textures.

Gently, they rocked together, their bodies joined. Her eyes, dark and strange as though fires from the corridor's torches glittered within, did not move from his face.

"Rohane," he whispered, her name a sensual caress. "Rohane."

As pleasure flamed through him, building towards that sweet release, he pulled her down deeper, deeper so that he could no longer tell what flesh was just his or theirs together. Rohane cried out, her hands gripping his back. Val shuddered as he lost control. He never wanted to be in control again.

GENYA

From the path through the forest, Genya glanced up at Alecc standing with Kaell upon the castle's wall walk, a forlorn figure, his shoulders hunched with regret. Alecc had longed to go with the Mountains warriors, but his council ruled the young king must not risk his life raiding ghoul strongholds.

No, only she was expendable. The guilty always were. And Alecc was neither guilty nor able to be sacrificed. Yet in that need for the thrill of battle and danger, they were alike. The anticipation of fighting excited them both like nothing else—not desire, victory, or power. When she imagined steel scraping against an opponent's blade, watching that growing fear in their eyes, her heart jolted with elation, with a fierce, savage joy.

Even now, the prospect of danger enlivened her senses. The dawn flitting behind the dense trees with its chorus of pink and grey seemed impossibly beautiful. The scent of every wild rose, every lily, prickled her nostrils. A rough, dry leaf crumbling in her fingertips surprised her as if she had never touched its like before.

"Apparently, this ghoul pretender calls himself the King of the River." Cadan grinned at her. "These ghouls take themselves very seriously."

Genya shrugged. "Dharam is no pretender. A ghoul lord and very powerful."

He curved well-shaped lips into a bitter smile. "Lord, not a lord. Who cares? Just another ghoul to kill."

Just another ghoul to kill. She had lost count already of how many hundreds they had slaughtered. Three ghoul strongholds, they had raided. Three strongholds, they had destroyed, butchering every ghoul within. Still, there were more. Always more.

Genya dragged a hand over her hilt, the sword's weight at her hip comforting. She glanced at Cadan. He trudged at her side, watchful, his dark eyes flickering to the undergrowth. A small force of grim-faced warriors surrounded them. The wary, hard men of the Mountains wore steel as easily as they might a cape. Ghoul blood smeared their brows as part of her spell to mask them. They must enter the castle of the self-titled King of the River unseen. Since the fall of three other ghoul castles, Dharam would be on his guard.

Her eyes fell upon one man's broad shoulders and back. Beneath a helm, his hair was dark brown. *Dannon.* It could almost be Dannon striding ahead, a bow slapping his back.

A familiar ache swelled in her breast, catching in her throat. Dare she hope this ghoul lord held Dannon? Perhaps she would find him a prisoner in some dank, dark dungeon. Alive.

And when she did not? Searching through fallen castles for prisoners, she'd lived this circle of hope and gut-churning despair again and again, unable to admit he was not there.

But then... where?

At dusk, the thunder of a waterfall drowned the forest's creaks and murmurs. When a river came into sight, Genya called a halt. The warriors gladly sank down, looking for soft patches of grass or heaped leaves beneath towering trunks that might make a good bed.

With a weary sigh, Genya rested her back against a trunk. She did not remember falling asleep until a hand shook her. Her fingers groped for her knife before she recognised Cadan crouched beside her. "Nearly dawn," he said. "Time to kill."

Her belly rumbling, she nibbled stale bread from her pocket. They did not carry packs or tents. Comfort was not important. Stealth and speed were. There would be time enough to fill grumbling bellies or rest in warm beds when they returned to Vraymorg.

The Mountains warriors made little sound as they roused, shivering. None crept to the river to splash cold water over their faces. They could not risk rubbing off her bloody sigils. Men grouped, checking weapons. Cadan gestured through the trees. An orchestra of soft rose and magenta rimmed a misty horizon as they followed the river. Upstream, a castle's towers reached like gaunt sticks into the iron sky. Its ancient square keep squatted on an island across a guarded bridge.

The River Castle looked less forbidding than Vraymorg, but Genya remembered stories of dungeons deep below the hall that could be filled with water to drown prisoners. Involuntarily, she shivered. A supernatural menace, an unseen vicious force lingered behind those walls, as if their approach awoke a malignant presence.

The bridge was down. With a quick nod to her companions, Genya led the way across, confident her magic would keep them hidden. Just so long as no one brushed against a guard or made a sharp sound, they would walk straight in and take their enemy by surprise. That was how three ghoul strongholds had fallen. The fourth would be the same.

They crept beneath the raised portcullis and past yawning guards. From the wall, a sentry called to one of the guards. He laughed and replied.

A ghoul stiffened as they stole by, his eyes searching the shadows in the gatehouse passage. Genya muttered a calming spell. The ghoul shrugged and resumed polishing his knife.

The gatehouse opened into a closed ward circled by stone walls. A sliver of warning ran cold down her back. If her magic failed, this courtyard could prove a killing field to a retreating enemy.

But her magic would not fail. She was the sorceress who roused the storm, who commanded the skies. Shrugging off her fears, she crept past a well towards the squat keep. A servant girl drew water at the well, her eyes down.

Genya wondered how many poor men and women had been captured when the ghouls, only months ago, stormed this castle, killing its lord and host of warriors.

Like so many villagers across the Downs and Mountains. So many she had to save. It was as if Dannon's mantle, his determination to fight on, even against great odds, had become her mission in his absence.

A sentry at the keep's entrance stamped his feet against the cold. Genya stalked closer. He stilled, frowning. His hand snatched at his blade. Genya fisted her knife. With a quick glance at the courtyard and the ghoul sentries on the wall, she circled behind him, clamping an arm about his neck. Her blade rent his throat. Blood gagged his scream. More spurted through her fingers. Cadan ran up to help carry the body inside the keep.

They found themselves in a bare, stone-walled entrance chamber. Passages led off into darkness. A stairwell wound its way up a tower.

"They're still slumbering." Cadan grinned viciously. "We'll kill them in their beds."

The aroma of baking bread carried through a window. Genya sniffed then stiffened, unsettled by an overpowering odour. Blood. A deep hunger awakened in her. Desperately, she squeezed her eyes shut, concentrating on her breaths as Val had taught her.

The other warriors stole inside, as lithe and soft-footed as dancers. Cadan pointed at the ceiling. Genya drew her sword and started up the stairs, Cadan a step behind. Stealthily, the other warriors followed.

They reached a landing and an iron-studded door. It stood partly open. Surprised, Genya paused. Then she shouldered into the chamber. Her companions spilled after her.

At the far end of a large wood-panelled room, Dharam sat on cushions on a tall-backed, ornate chair. A man with a long, sorrowful face and drooping eyes stood at his side. At the sight of his scarlet robes, unease niggled at her. Those robes meant something, something she needed to remember.

Dharam turned his head towards the door. He stared right at her—and smiled.

Panic lanced Genya's breast. He could see her. Her magic had failed.

"We're visible," Genya hissed at Cadan. "They can see us. They pretended not to."

Dharam clapped his hands. Armed ghouls poured through a door at the far end, ranks of them, ready to overwhelm the Mountains warriors.

Genya backed up, shouting, "It's a trap. Get to the gates then to the forest."

For a heartbeat, her companions hesitated, torn between her command and standing their ground to fight. "Get away." Genya shoved a man behind her. He started through the door. Others whirled to follow. Their footsteps clattered down the stairs.

Cadan caught her eye. His smile was grim and resolute. "We'll just clean up here first. Ready?"

"I was ready in the womb," Genya said.

With fierce shouts, the two of them plunged towards the ghouls. Genya swept three off their feet with a slashing stroke that carved through bone. They collapsed in a pile of blood and shards, screaming. She hacked at another, her blade shattering a ribcage. A savage euphoria blazed through her. Exhilarated, she chopped and cleaved, her every stroke reaping death.

At her side, Cadan slaughtered ghouls with vicious hacks, slashes, and cuts, shouting in triumph every time he killed. But still more poured into the chamber, lines of them thick about their targets.

"Too many," she yelled to Cadan. He glanced at the door, almost stumbling over a broken, crimson-washed body at his feet. A ghoul struck at him from behind. Cadan twisted and half blocked the blow. Steel slashed his arm. With a cry of rage and pain, he hacked off the ghoul's head.

Genya grabbed his shoulder and yanked him away. Ghouls pursued, bellowing in anger. More closed in ahead. She swung the blade like a scythe, cutting down four at once, clearing the thinnest passage for retreat.

They backed up to the entrance then turned and ran, pausing only to pull the heavy door closed. As it inched towards them, hands scrabbled through the gap. Cadan hacked them off. Ghouls screamed, recoiling. Her body braced, drawing on every ounce of her ghoul-strength, Genya heaved at the door. It thumped shut. Howling ghouls beat their fists against its metal.

Cadan flashed his lop-sided grin. "That won't hold them for long."

"Long enough."

They ran down the stairs, only to hit a swarm of ghouls charging up. With the advantage of the higher steps, Genya slashed and slashed again. Ghouls reeled away, falling in bloody heaps. Beneath her breath, she spat magic. More dropped, bewildered at the invisible force hurling them through the air. In the narrow space, Cadan jabbed. A ghoul shrieked. Cadan stamped on the body for leverage to rip out his sword.

Genya stepped over dying or wounded ghouls into the entrance chamber then stormed into the ward towards the gatehouse. Early sunlight, achingly bright, glinted on a bell in a tower. At the sight of Mountains warriors struggling to lift an iron grille in the gatehouse, her breath stalled.

The grille cut off their escape. They were trapped in the ward. Any moment now, ghouls would pour out of the keep.

She and Cadan reached the others. Panicked faces brightened. "Genya. Thank the gods."

At once, Genya tried to heave the gate up. It did not budge. *No, no, no.* With wild desperation, she put her shoulder into it. It was no good. Was there a spell to raise iron? There had to be. *Just think. Quickly think.*

"Genya." His mouth tight, his eyes troubled, Cadan grasped her shoulder, his arm extended. She whirled to look where he pointed. Terror chilled her. Ghoul archers ran around the walls, taking position. They raised bows, arrows nocked... and waited.

Why wait? The Mountains warriors were trapped in the killing field, with no cover and no way forward or back. Bitterness, frustrated anger, and fear tore through her. "What are you waiting for?" she shouted. "What?"

The archers stayed silent, their gazes on a door to the wall walk. It swung open. Dharam strolled from the tower onto the wall. He leaned his elbows on the stone balustrade and sneeringly called down, "Surrender or die."

"Then we'll die," a Mountains warrior shouted.

Dharam raised a hand. An archer loosened a shot. The arrow plunged into the Mountains warrior's chest. He sank to his knees, his fingers clasped to the bloody wound.

"How can you see us?" Genya shouted in dismay, incredulous that her magic had failed. "My spell should hide us."

Dharam waved his hand carelessly. It was an elegant gesture. Unhurried. "We all have our sorcerers and magicians."

The man with the long face. The scarlet robes. A sorcerer. Someone powerful enough to overturn her spell. Someone who even knew they were coming.

"Oh, don't look so surprised, child," Dharam taunted. "You thought news wouldn't reach me of how the other three ghoul castles fell? That I wouldn't take precautions?" He turned to his archers. "I want as many as possible taken alive. If they don't surrender, wound them. We'll feast well for the next month."

"No!" Genya screamed. The sound was torn from her. All her fury, her fear for her companions, burst out in that scream. Darkness rushed her with a shuddering, throbbing rage. Blood pounded hot through her veins, quickening her every sense.

She took her knife and slashed her arms until blood streamed from her elbow to her wrists. With an act of will, she let the darkness close about her, taking her over. It blazed through her trembling body like a storm, wild and terrifying and wonderful. And at its black heart, a wickedly dangerous, unstoppable power pulsed. The magic of Seithin. The magic of Archanin.

Say it. The voice was a whisper in her head. *Say it. Release us.*

Her hand shot out. Forbidden words tumbled from her lips. A force surged through her like fire. It burst from her fingertips with a howling, wrenching shriek, an otherworldly snarl of horror. White light flashed, rippling through the air in waves, striking every ghoul with the intensity of fissures of lightning, ripping them apart.

Then the darkness closed again, taking Genya down, down, into an exhausted slumber.

A bird circled a tower. Lying in the dirt, Genya watched its languid flight. No sound came to her, not even the bird's caws. It was as if she was cocooned where she had fallen, wrapped in silent, peaceful solitude.

A shape blocked the sunlight. Cadan peered down at her, his handsome face tight and troubled. Genya rose to one elbow. Dizziness washed through her. She coughed blood onto her palm.

"Careful. You've been unconscious for an hour."

"I was?" She peered about a castle ward, trying to remember. The march from the Mountains. The River Castle. A trap. Dharam's taunts. Overwhelming fear. *Fury.*

Then she had heard a whisper, a seductive call to release

violence, to release something malignant and dangerous. Rozenn's words echoed in Genya's mind. *It must only be used as a last resort. And only used thrice.*

"What…" she stammered. "What happened?"

"Can you stand?"

At her nod, Cadan helped her rise but did not let go of her arm. Genya shot an uneasy look about. A group of Mountains warriors was securing the portcullis. Others sat on the steps to the wall. Some glanced at her then quickly looked away.

"We were trapped…" Genya passed a hand over her brow. Her skin was hot and damp. Cadan pressed a waterskin into her hands. She drank heavily and wiped her mouth on the back of her hand. "I was angry…"

"They're all dead, Genya."

Her heart bolted against her ribs. "What?"

"Every ghoul in this place. Dead."

Dead? She blinked, not understanding. Slowly, the words sank into her. A fierce joy blazed through her. The spell. How powerful was she to kill like that?

Cadan squeezed her shoulder. "You saved us." He offered a hesitant grin, but she sensed he was wary of her. "Whatever magic that was, it terrified me."

"What… What did you see?"

He considered with a frown. "Light leached away as though a cloud fell about this castle. Your face was dark and terrible. You shouted words in a language I'd never heard. Then light and fire shot out of you, from your hands." He shuddered. "The ghouls made no sound. They just fell down dead. What was that magic?"

Magic Rozenn had warned her to use only as a last resort. Yet Genya could think only upon the sensation of power, the elation, the euphoria that had engulfed her when she had spoken the Seithin curse.

Powerful magic, yes. Dangerous, yes.

Magic she longed to use again.

VAL ARQUES

"**Y**ou held back." Rohane lay in his arms, naked and warm, her smile soft. It was the third night she had come to his chambers, the third night they had lost themselves in desire.

"Just now?" he teased. "What more would you take from me?"

She nuzzled his neck. "Fool. You lovely fool. I mean the other night when you fought Jenna-Dairine."

"You're thinking about that? With me naked beside you?"

"If I think of you naked, I'll fall upon you and ravage you again."

"Please think of me naked."

"Don't you need to recover your strength? And when you do, get up and shut the door. I left it open again."

"In your haste to ravage me."

"I've become careless in my old age. Now, about that fight. I've been thinking about it. Your control was as I expected. Even when she surprised you, your speed and technique held her out. But you had moments. You could have struck, drawn blood at least. You didn't."

Val tapped her nose with his finger. "Observant Rohane."

"Why?"

He sighed. "I know too much about pride, Rohane. It's one of my weaknesses. I didn't want to lose. I'm not that noble. But I didn't want to diminish her. She's proud, too."

"She won't thank you if she finds out you held back, Val."

His laugh held a touch of bitterness. "As it is, I think I must watch my back."

Rohane rose on one elbow to consider him. The blanket fell away from a bare breast. His desire prickled anew. For one moment, all he wanted to do was run his hands down her naked body, to rouse her again and again.

"I knew she said something as she stomped off. Tell me, or I'll tickle you to death."

"I'm not ticklish. You'll have to torture me. In fact, please torture me."

"Fool. What did she say?"

"That one day she'd have to—"

From the doorway, someone gasped.

"Mel!" Rohane leapt from the bed and rushed to the door, forgetting her nakedness. "Oh, goddess, Mel. It's not what it seems."

"It's exactly what is seems." The girl's voice blazed with anger. "Everyone warned me I was witless to serve you. But you were a retrieval captain, and I wanted adventure. I wanted to see strange places, other lands. Only what happened? We are called back here, and I end up stuck in Quisnaf, not even serving a battale captain."

"Mel, listen, I can explain—"

"Shut up!" Mel screamed. "You're bedding him. Against every rule. I thought you were different, but you're as bad as the rest. You disgust me."

"Mel, stop."

The girl's footsteps hastened away.

Rohane stumbled inside, her face stricken with shock. She shut the door and leaned her back to it.

Val rose quickly. He went to her and led her back to the bed. Her skin was cold.

"We didn't shut the door," Rohane muttered. "Why didn't we shut the door? What's wrong with me? We'll be whipped. It's my job to keep you safe. How does this keep you safe?"

He enfolded her in his arms. "Maybe she won't say anything. She's fond of you."

Rohane pulled away. "Get dressed. They'll come for us." She stooped to snatch up her clothes. Her face was strange, her expression shut down and distant.

"Whatever happens, it happens," Val said. "I'm not sorry about this, Rohane."

She stilled, her hand upon her tunic. In a small voice, she said, "I'm not sorry either, Val. I should be, but I'm not."

⸎

Decan guards led by their commander arrived within the hour, hammering their fists against the door.

Rohane let them in at once. "I know why you're here," she said. "I will, of course, comply."

Louisa pushed past her into the room. Hard eyes passed over Val. "He's to stay. Give me the key."

Rohane handed it over.

The Decan watch commander nodded. "You're to come. You must answer to the council over an accusation of improper conduct."

"I understand."

Guards fell in about her as Rohane stepped into the passage. She did not look at Val. Then Louisa slammed the door shut and turned the key.

Afraid for Rohane, Val spent a sleepless night. Quisnaf law was a mystery. What punishment awaited them both? Was this considered a serious offence or a minor matter? He did not fear for himself. But he would do anything to save Rohane pain or shame.

When dawn's grey light crept into the chamber, he rose and dressed. The insidious whisper would not be silenced. Others got hurt around him. He was dangerous. He had to keep those he cared about at a distance. Did he need further proof? First Kaell, now Rohane. No matter how much it hurt, he had to let her be free of him.

Sometime later, the key rattled, and the door crashed back against the wall. Louisa glared at him. "Val Arques Caelan."

Val nodded and stood.

"You'll come with us."

He walked out. Guards fell in about him, but no one bound him. He was glad of that, at least. Chains, restraints not only rekindled his shame and dread at what had befallen him at the hands of a sorcerer centuries ago but reminded him of his powerlessness in Quisnaf.

A dreary quiet clung to the passages. A bleary-eyed warrior moved aside to let them pass. A man sleeping off a hangover huddled against a wall. The commander nudged him with her foot. When he groaned, she shrugged and moved on.

The unfamiliar route brought them to wide, tall wooden doors. Val's escort took him through into a rock-walled chamber filled with rows of benches before a table. On a bench nearest the table, Rohane sat stiff-backed. The guards dumped Val beside her. She did not look at him. Badly did he want to reach for her hand to reassure her.

Two councillors appeared through a second door and sat at the table beside High Priestess Sorcha.

Kenna carried scrolls and leather-bound books to the table then took the central chair. She cleared her throat. "For the benefit of our guest, I shall introduce myself."

"I remember who you are, Councillor," Val said.

Guards rushed to silence him, but Kenna threw up a hand. "Speak only if I ask you a question. Do you understand? You may speak to answer."

Val bristled at the command. "I understand."

"For your benefit, let me explain that I administer our laws,

Cyrah's laws, as handed down by the goddess. Temple law and secular law are two separate codes, but in this instance, they overlap. A complaint has been made, and I am here to apply our laws. That is all. You may answer that you understand."

"I understand."

"Captain?"

"I understand." Rohane's voice sounded brittle.

A *thump, thump, thump* carried from the passage. Heads turned towards the door as the truthsayer entered. Val took advantage of the distraction and grabbed Rohane's hand. "Are you all right? Did they mistreat you?"

"I spent a sleepless night in a cold cell," she replied in a low voice. "Not so comfortable as your bed."

"Silence." Kenna snapped. "Part them."

A guard moved in to pull Val away from Rohane.

The truthsayer's stick struck the ground as she sank onto a bench on the room's edge.

"We are grateful." Kenna inclined her head.

The old woman waved a hand. "Be quick about this, Kenna. I am on my way to Veniva."

The councillor nodded then faced Rohane. "I will be direct. A witness swears she found you in bed with this man. She declares what she saw is unambiguous. Is this the truth? You are a captain. If you deny it, we will accept there is doubt and examine the witness."

Rohane glanced at the truthsayer. "No. It is the truth."

The other councillors muttered. Guards exchanged looks.

Val waited to be asked the same question. But Kenna spoke only to Rohane. "Do you know the law, Captain? Do you understand relations between you and this man are forbidden? How many times did this happen?"

"Thrice," Rohane answered. "Apart from a kiss one day in the valley."

Kenna looked to the truthsayer.

"It is so." The woman flapped a disinterested hand.

"Very well." Kenna sniffed. "We understand this happens. You are not the first guardian—indeed, nor the first retrieval captain—to succumb to temptation in this way."

"Especially during the Blessing," Sorcha said.

The door creaked again. Blaire entered quietly and stood observing.

Kenna frowned at her. Blaire offered an almost imperceptible nod. The councillor shuffled papers. "What Sorcha says is true. Temptation is always a danger at such a time. However, the law is clear. You will be taken from this place, both of you, to receive twenty lashes each."

"No." Val shot to his feet. "This is my doing. I seduced her. She… resisted. Only I deserve punishing."

"Sit down, you fool," Rohane hissed.

"I will not. Let me take Rohane's punishment as well as my own."

"This is irregular," Kenna muttered.

"You cannot let him do that." Rohane leaned forward, her hands clasped tightly. "I am to blame. This man is under my protection. The power was mine."

"I ask the council to consider my request," Val said. "Let me bear her punishment, too."

"No, no, no," Rohane muttered.

Again Kenna exchanged a glance with Blaire. The Regenta nodded.

"Very well then." Kenna stood. "The council permits this. Guards, take him to a place of public…" She looked to Blaire, who shook her head. "No, I correct that. Take him to the whipping post within the temple so that the slave mistress may administer forty lashes. No more, no less. Then you will take him to the healers so they may tend his back. From that place, return him to his room." Her stony gaze passed to Val. "While your back heals, you will contemplate your mistake. Pain is never our goal. It is only a means to bring you to realise your error."

"He cannot do this," Rohane started. "You cannot."

Scowling, Kenna whipped up a hand. "Silence. It is decided. You, Captain, will return to your rooms, where you also will reflect upon your misconduct. This court will at a later time consider whether to leave you as guardian or whether to appoint another."

ROHANE

Rohane strode along shadowy corridors then out into bright daylight. The valley's blaze of colour was muted beneath clouds as though it, too, breathed with relief after an excess of life and lust. Merchants packed goods into wagons and dismantled tents. Amidst the bustle, young men tried to sleep off hangovers. A blackened fire's thin smoke wisped into the trees.

She walked through the quiet, verdant gardens to the temple and stood staring up at its marble façade. A hush clung to the air as though everyone still slept after the excesses of the Blessing.

Inside, behind a heavy iron-studded door, guards would take Val to a wooden post with straps for a prisoner's hands. She shivered, remembering times she had felt the lash across her back. Once for falling asleep on sentry duty. Once for talking back to Persia.

This time, Val would take her punishment upon himself. Rohane shifted her weight, aware of a press of fear in her breast. He had breached her heart, she who was determined to let no one in who could hurt her. She hadn't sought to care. Caring left her vulnerable, open to the pain she had endured when Nessa died. Rohane never wanted to feel like that again.

Her mind in turmoil, her thoughts awhirl, she started to turn away. A shout came from inside the temple. Raised voices picked up. Fear lanced her gut.

Val.

Rohane took the stairs at a run. She burst into the nave. A group of temple guards bustled about the slave mistress and interrogator Malgaria. "He's gone," she said, her face blank with shock. "Gone. Just now. A guard's dead."

Sorcha appeared at a rush. She pushed through onlookers to confront the slave mistress. "Who's gone? What's happened here?"

"The Telorian," Malgaria muttered.

"No," Rohane cried. "What do you mean 'gone'?"

Malgaria turned to look at her. "The door's open, and there's no sign of him. And there's a dead guard in the passage. He's run."

"That can't be right," Rohane spluttered. "Val wouldn't."

"How else do you explain a dead guard?" Sorcha asked. "Sound the alarm. Gather some warriors, Rohane. Hunt him down and bring him back."

"Val wouldn't." But doubt turned Rohane's stomach.

"He offered to take your punishment so he could run," Sorcha said. "He's as devious as any other man."

"I don't believe that." Nausea pushed up into Rohane's throat. Had he deceived her? Could he? After she had let down her guard for the first time since Nessa died.

"Maybe you don't know him as well as you think," Sorcha said.

VAL ARQUES

A fierce sun beat upon his face. Hard ground bruised his hip. Val snapped his eyes open. Wisping cloud hung in a glaringly blue sky. Dizzily, his skull aflame, he rose to one elbow. A flat, empty desert of red earth and wind-brawled stunted trees stretched about him. A two-edged sword lay beside him. Quickly, he gathered his memories. The whipping post. A blow. Then nothing.

Bewildered, he touched a bump on the back of his head. The guard who had taken him to the whipping post had hit him then brought him here, leaving him the clothes on his back, his boots, and a sword. *Why? And why here?*

Dust clouded on the horizon. Val squinted. Hooves drummed the earth. *Horses.*

Hairs rose on his arms. The Quisnaf controlled only the city of caves. The nomadic Gidani claimed the desert lands about the valley. According to reputation, they were bloodthirsty and violent. If he was in Gidani territory, he was in trouble.

Snatching up the sword, he rose. Nausea nearly took him to his knees. Val closed his eyes until the sickness passed. Then he peered about, seeking cover. A crop of rocks was closest. His best chance was to hide and see who approached before he revealed himself.

Vision blurring, Val staggered forward. Hoofbeats now thundered like a storm. Dust rolled towards him in an enormous red wave.

He began to run. If he could be certain it was the Quisnaf, he would stop and surrender. Explain. But it might be anyone. Even Venivan slavers. Maybe he wasn't even near Quisnaf.

A shout rang out. In panic, Val glanced over his shoulder. They'd seen him. With no chance to outrun them, he turned, sword levelled, feet parted in battle stance.

Through swirling dust, sunlight glinted on metal. The closest riders reached him. They were women. Reassured, Val let the sword droop. *Quisnaf.*

"Thank the gods," he called. It took all his strength to stay on his feet. "How did you find me?"

Armed warriors ringed him. At their hard expressions, unease curdled in his gut. "Oh, you can't think that," he muttered. "You can't think I fled."

The main body of riders closed in. At a command, they halted. Recognising Rohane's voice, Val sighed in relief. "Rohane."

She slid from the saddle, a bow slung over her shoulder. Her blade rattled in her hip scabbard. "Drop the sword. Get on your knees."

At her cold tone, Val's breath caught in his throat. Did she, too, think he'd tried to escape? "Rohane, listen. I didn't run. I just woke up out here. Right now."

"With a sword? The sword you stole from the guard you killed?"

"What?" he stammered, lost. "Killed?"

"Your trail was easy to pick up. How far did you think you'd get?"

"Captain," another rider said. "How do you want to do this?"

"If he doesn't fall to his knees in the next minute, put a bolt in him. Somewhere—it doesn't matter. Thighs, buttocks, shoulder."

"Rohane." Val gaped in shock. Her face was a stranger's, remote and angry.

The other warrior drew back her bowstring. Val swirled. His

sword flew up. It was instinctive, no act of will. The arrow twanged off its steel. Women gasped.

Calmly, Rohane twisted her bow about and nodded. The other archer fired. Val knocked the arrow away just as Rohane loosed a shot. He was fast enough to deflect it with the blade, but it grazed flesh above his knee.

Gasping with pain, Val clasped a hand to the wound as his leg buckled. Blood streamed through his fingers.

"Unless you put the blade down, the next is aimed at your other knee. Then a shoulder." Rohane's voice was hard. She gestured at some of the warriors to dismount.

Val rocked his head in disbelief. "You shot me. I would have surrendered. I just need you to know, to understand—"

"Understand what? That you killed a guard and ran? That you broke your word? Not only to me but the council. And why? For no better reason than to avoid the whip?"

"No, no. This isn't right. Someone hit me. I woke up here."

"Drop your weapon. Put your hands behind your head."

Not a grain of sympathy softened her expression. Val did not want to yield until she accepted the truth. Desperately, he glanced about. Not only was he ill and wounded, there was nowhere to run. With a frustrated cry, he flung down the sword.

At once, women grabbed his wrists and lashed them together behind his back. All the while, Rohane watched. Unmoved. Cold.

"Bind his wound. Then put him on a horse. The council wants him back immediately."

"Rohane," he pleaded, trying to reach her. "Listen to me. I didn't run—"

"Gag him." Rohane turned away.

Twice, he retched: once into the gag and once after dizzily tumbling from the horse and crashing onto the stony track.

Groaning, he lay still as faces peered down at him. Hands lifted him and removed the gag so he could drink water. Quarrelling voices faded in and out.

"Get him back on the horse," Rohane snapped. "Tie him so he can't fall off."

"He's ill."

"It's not far."

The nightmarish journey rolled on and on. Val's belly churned, the thump in his head and the pain in his thigh blurring into misery. Against the slow clop of horses, slumped over his mount, he drifted between blackness and dismal wakefulness.

At last, they untied him and pulled him off the horse. Women again bound his wrists and took his arms to lead him forward. Though night curtained at his back, he recognised the Quisnaf valley where the darkness was alive with the sounds of water trickling over rocks, paws scampering in bushes, and the hum of beetles.

The noises faded. Stone surrounded him, its chill rolling like fog through tunnels. In disbelief, Val kept his eyes upon Rohane's stiff back as she strode ahead. She did not look at him.

Is this what you think of me? he wanted to shout. *That I am the sort of man who could do that?* Her mistrust, her disappointment, cut through him. He valued her. That gave her the power to hurt him.

Exhausted, his hands bound, caged by their close-pressed bodies, he walked where bidden. If his steps faltered, a sword poked the small of his back, or a woman barked, "Move."

The passages all looked the same, but they wound lower. Flames from wall torches barely licked at the gloom. When they reached steps spiralling down into the murk, dread squeezed Val's heart. They were not taking him before the council, where he could try to convince them of the truth. They took him to a prison.

Panicked, he bucked. Hands groped for his shoulders, forcing him on. Sounds from above fell away. In the airless stairwell, his every ragged exhalation and inhalation was magnified.

At an iron door at the bottom, his captors paused. An argument broke out.

"He's ill," one woman said. "He needs a healer."

"He killed a guard. His comfort is not a consideration." Rohane's tone was icy. "Not until he goes before the council tomorrow."

Val's heart plunged to his gut. Rohane indeed believed the worst of him. Sunken in despair, he no longer resisted as his captors dragged him into a cell. The light from a single torch was enough to show dark stains marring the rock floor. It was little more than a hole, dank, dim, and fetid.

At the sight of shackles struck into the roof, Val's panic kicked again. He pulled up hard, struggling against their holds. His guards' grips tightened. Some cursed him, yanking his arms up and shackling his wrists. Two dodged kicks to hold his legs until iron fastened his ankles to the floor. Another shoved a fresh gag in his mouth.

They stepped back. Val yanked at the chains. Iron clanked and rattled but held tight.

"Save your strength." One guard offered a sour smile. "It'll be a long night." She turned for the door. The others followed.

Rohane was the last to leave. Her dark eyes dwelled for a moment on his face. Val rolled his eyes and tried to get words out. *Listen to me. How can you think I killed a guard and ran? I wouldn't do that to you. Not to you.*

But she turned away. The *tap, tap, tap* of her footsteps across the room then up the stairs grew ever softer. Until there was only silence.

In the long empty hours of night, Val thought through what had happened. Someone had hit him and left him in the desert to make it appear as if he had run. Someone wanted him punished, hurt, or shamed. Who hated him enough to go to all this trouble? Elle? Or did he have other enemies? Rohane had said Quisnaf was a divided city with all manner of undercurrents. He might be a pawn in someone's scheming.

Dully, he wondered what lay ahead. Torture? Imprisonment? They thought he'd killed one of their own. When they took him before the council, he must make them listen, hear the truth.

By the time he heard footsteps, his shoulders and arms had cramped. A headache still pounded behind his eyes. The gag had bruised his mouth. A four-strong escort appeared. Two freed his hands and legs then tied his wrists.

Val tried to ask for water through the gag.

A guard menaced him with a sword. "No trouble from you today, or you'll be sorry. Nod if you understand."

Val nodded. He did not intend to resist. He must confront the council, to convince them someone had set him up.

At a shove, he stumbled up the stairs, swaying with dizziness and exhaustion. Hands held his shoulders, forcing him onwards. At every step, the wound in his thigh throbbed.

They took him through gloomy passages to the same judgement chamber where he and Rohane had been forced to answer for their so-called crime. His guards dumped him on a bench before the table then backed away.

Val sagged. Decan Watch guards took up positions at the doors. A handful of councillors entered. Blaire found a seat at the bench, her lips set firmly. Stern-faced, Samantha followed. Then sour Aine. And last, the sorceress Sisilia. Her dark, cold eyes settled upon him. It was a long, long look, full of sly triumph.

The councillors sat. Blaire considered him. She sighed. "Why the gag?"

A guardswoman stepped forward. "Regenta, the huntress ordered it. She said she did not wish to hear his lies."

Blaire tapped her fingers on the table. "Do you mean to tell me you left him like that all night?" Her voice held an undercurrent of anger. "Remove the gag. Give him something to drink, at least."

Two guards rushed to do her bidding. Hot and light-headed, Val breathed with relief as the gag came off. A woman brought a cup and held it to his lips. Gratefully, he drank.

Blaire watched with a tight frown. "He doesn't look well. Did a healer attend him?"

"The captain said there was no need."

"And what did Rohane bid you do with him?"

The guard swallowed. "We shackled him for the night. Below."

They'd left him there, sick and despondent. Alone. Of every quality, every characteristic that had drawn him to Rohane, even her temper, he had never counted her cruel.

Blaire was on her feet, saying something. Val tried to focus, but dizziness and nausea flooded him. His body slid to the ground. Disorientated, he was hardly aware of the hands that lifted him.

"This man is far from well," Blaire said, tight-lipped. "Take him to the infirmary. This matter must wait. Return him here, in good health, in three days."

Val barely took in her words before he passed out into welcome blackness.

GENYA

In the great hall at Vraymorg, Alecc sat regally upon a cushioned chair, the nobles of the Mountains loosely gathered about him. Chin on his hand, he listened silently to Cadan's story then looked at her. The men and women with him all turned their heads to stare, their eyes wide with awe and suspicion.

Genya's blood pounded in her ears. Still, she was judged. Condemned. An outsider. Unforgiven. No matter what she did, she could not find a place here.

"She saved us," Cadan repeated. "Every one of us would be dead or a prisoner…"

Alecc nodded slowly. "What is this magic, Genya? Did my mother teach you such a curse? Can you use it again?"

Genya had to be careful what she said. If she said it was Seithin magic, they, all of them, would hear only one word: *Seithin.* Then they would think of Archanin. They would remember how she had betrayed the brotherhood.

"Magic Rozenn taught me, yes," she muttered. "Dangerous magic. She said I could speak those words only thrice. Never more."

"Thrice." Alecc stroked his beard. "Then twice more."

"Hold on there." Nicky pushed forward. "I know what you're

thinking, but you can't use Genya for that."

"For what?" Genya asked.

Alecc sighed. "Word has reached us from across the gorge. Ghouls are building a fortress the size of which we've never seen."

"What?" Genya's breath caught. "How far away?"

"Half a day's march. If they succeed, they can harry us then retreat to hide behind their walls. No one will be safe. Every villager will be at risk. They'll raid the Mountains at will, and we will be powerless to stop them."

"Nevertheless, you can't sacrifice Genya." Nicky's voice was tight.

"I'm all right," Genya said. "Tell me what you need me to do."

"You can't let her do this." Nicky fisted his hands. "Magic powerful enough to kill like that drains the life of the one casting the spell. Even Roaran only once risked using a killing curse."

"I want to," Genya insisted. Warmth blazed through her. She was more powerful than her father. Unafraid to use deadly magic.

Cadan touched her arm. "You didn't see your face when you slashed your arms. It was frightening, altered, as though magic cloaked you in darkness. It wasn't you, Genya. Your eyes blazed with fire. And your voice. It was low, deep. The language was so strange, hairs lifted at the back of my neck."

Nicky nibbled his bottom lip. "I've seen Roaran like that. Lost to me. And a dangerous undercurrent in the air that draws a shiver."

"It hardly hurt me." It was only half a lie. Genya had recovered her strength after a day or two. And Rozenn had said the curse could be used thrice. As long as Genya did not use it more than that, she could kill ghouls. Stop this fortress ever being built.

She could show them all she was to be trusted. That she was on their side.

She would show Val.

Seeking solitude, Genya ran into the forest beyond Vraymorg's formidable walls. With her every step, she was incandescent with glee, with jubilation. She needed to understand this new power in her. Whenever she thought of the curse, of that moment she had spoken forbidden words, elation ripped through her. The spell gave her such control, such command over life and death.

But there was anger, too. New, dark, and ugly. It festered deep within, like a sore. Little things irritated her, as if she were always on edge, always ready to erupt to violence.

If Val were there, she would have told him about the anger. But he had abandoned her.

So be it. She wouldn't let him wound her anymore. The rapacious strength in her, how triumph had hummed through her body when she'd spoken the Seithin incantation, shielded her from pain. Magic was enough. It had to be enough.

Deep within the trees where sunlight barely reached, the forest hushed. Birdsong died away. No wind stirred branches or rattled through dead leaves. No paws softly crushed grass or indented moss. With hesitant fingers, Genya traced the scabs forming over the long welts where she had cut herself.

Rozenn was right. Such power was seductive. Darkly wonderful. Her anger allowed her to reach for it, to use it… or did the darkness feed on her anger?

Restless, she prowled farther into the trees. Her body yearned for something. The release of the flesh? She knew her blood stirred too readily when she looked at a desirable man. But no. It was a different kind of hunger—a hunger not satisfied by meat or wine or pleasure. The ghoul part of her demanded to be satisfied. She must find a beast to slay, or the gnawing in her gut, the taste in her mouth would torment and torment her.

She stopped, sniffing. *That scent. What is that scent? Blood.* With a strangled groan, Genya plunged through undergrowth, following the delicious aroma. *Blood.* All at once, she could think of nothing else. *Blood. So hungry.*

The trees fell away. Her boots sank into soft earth on a riverbank. Before her, a man sat on a rock, his legs dangling in the water. He held a fishing pole.

Her heartbeat pounded in her temples. Moving as if in a dream, Genya stole forward, hardly aware of her surroundings. There was only the intoxicating scent of blood coursing through the man's veins.

She licked her lips, anticipating the taste of him. Her mouth filled with saliva. A heady, overwhelming, hot surge of desire coursed through her. The aroma of his blood called to the beast within her, a fearful beast she denied. Contained. But now the beast raged, released by the blood magic.

With a carnal roar, Genya leapt on the man. He had time only to throw up his hands before her teeth ripped open his throat. Blood coursed down her throat as she drank and drank. Ah, how he tasted. Like fine wine, when she had only ever feasted on rancid brews before. How could she drink the blood of beasts when men and women tasted like this? Oh, gods, it was headier than making love—though part of her sought that, too, as though blood awakened her appetite for all pleasures.

Leaves crackled beneath footfall. Kaell pushed aside a branch. His gaze swept along the riverbank. "Genya? Are you there? Alecc wants you—" He stopped, his eyes upon the dead man.

Unrepentant, Genya peeled back her lips in a bloody grin.

Kaell said nothing, his face frozen in shock. Then, as though snapped free of his trance, he spun away and stalked off.

DANNON

The fever struck unexpectedly. Headache, shivery, his bones aching, he took to his bed and curled up, unable to lift an arm. Drifting in an out of heavy dreams, he thought he heard whispering, that hands took hold of him and hoisted him. Beyond his half-closed eyelids, torchlight flickered.

With no sense of how much time had passed, he woke in a bed in a long, shady room, beside other beds, beside other men. Someone coughed. Another moaned. Soft shoes squeaked on tiled floors. Bowls rattled on a tray.

His skin damp and irritated, his hair wet and matted, Dannon could only groan.

A woman leaned over him. She wore a light-blue robe.

"Elena?"

The woman smiled and spoke words he could not understand.

He must have looked blank, for she repeated in stumbling Telorian, "She's not here at this hour. I'm to take care of you."

The woman supported his head so he could drink.

Dannon drained a cup of water then lay back. "What's wrong with me?" he whispered as she pressed a cold cloth to his forehead.

"You're in the infirmary with an autumn fever. It strikes many at this time of year."

Dannon let his drooping eyelids close. Often, he suffered with winter ailments—coughs, sweats, and fevers. Too many nights, a Varee healer had sat by his bedside with cool cloths and hot wine laced with strange herbs when his chest grew tight.

"The infirmary," Dannon muttered. Rarely did he go anywhere except into the valley with Samantha to stretch his muscles. Otherwise, the Quisnaf confined him to his room. Oh, he had books and paper for writing. Time to think. Too much time to think. To ponder how he might escape or at least be gifted with greater freedom.

"Must I stay in my room?" he'd asked Samantha more than once on their evening strolls.

"It's to protect you," she always answered. "You're valuable to us. We need to keep you safe."

Because of Genya. He was bait to lure her to Quisnaf. He had worked that out, at least. Still, being unable to protect himself rankled him. He balked at depending upon others to feed him, clothe him, and free him for those nighttime walks.

"Just sleep," the woman in the infirmary encouraged. "Nothing to do here. Nothing to worry about except getting well."

She didn't need to ask. Obediently, Dannon fell into comforting slumber.

GENYA

Genya washed in the river then took off after Kaell. Fear of what he might say to others, not remorse, drove her quick steps. She followed his scent to the castle walls. "Kaell."

He stopped upon the path and turned. By the river, his face had been blank with shock. Now his lips were compressed with anger, his eyes dark with accusation.

"You killed him. By Khir, what have you done?"

Fury swept through her. He of all people should understand her appetites. These same temptations had surely been his, too. Of course he had surrendered to them. He could not be stronger willed than she.

"Oh, gods." Kaell dragged taut fingers through his hair. "It's murder. No, wait." He looked hopefully at her. "Did that man attack you? Were you defending yourself?"

"No," Genya said.

His face shadowed with alarm.

She grabbed his arm. "Surely you know about the hunger. I couldn't control it. It took me over. I had to kill him. Don't you see?"

Kaell shuddered. "You have to fight it, Genya. We're not like them—ghouls. We're not beasts."

"I don't know what I am." Genya let his arm go.

His face softened. He took one step towards her then hesitated. "I understand how overwhelming the aroma of blood is, how heady. But no matter the temptation, you and I have to control our appetites. Let me help you."

She curled up a lip. "I don't want *your* help."

"Genya—"

Genya laughed coldly. "I'm not sorry. If you're so weak to deny your nature, then you'll never understand. I've never felt so powerful, so strong. Nothing can touch me."

Kaell blinked slowly. His lips parted as though he were in pain. "I heard about the spell," he said quietly. "Cadan said it saved everyone, but maybe it did this to you. Awoke the ghoul part of you. Changed you. This magic is dangerous. You can't do that sort of spellcraft again. Not if it leads you to kill afterwards."

"What do you know?" she jeered. "Do you know who I am? I'm only beginning to uncover all I'm capable of."

Kaell shook his head. "This isn't the way, Genya. Listen." He touched her shoulder. "I understand. I've fought the darkness, the hunger. You have to keep fighting, Genya. You can't let your appetites take you over, not again."

She brushed off his hand. "Why not?"

"Because we have no right to murder simply to satisfy our desire."

Genya tilted her chin and stared him right in the eyes. She wanted to shock him, to taunt him. "I liked it."

Kaell stilled in horror. For a moment, he could not speak, then he muttered, "Oh, gods, what do I do? If Roaran were here... Nicky. He has to know. Yes, Nicky. You'll listen to him."

"No!" she screamed. She lurched at him, her hand raised to hit him.

He stood his ground. "Genya, you need help to stop this."

No. Nicky could not learn what she'd done. She could not bear to be diminished in his eyes. Not when Val already thought so poorly of her. Forcing back the anger, she sought words to appease Kaell. Lies.

"Please." Desperately, she fell to her knees. "Please. This was the first time I've killed. I swear it. It won't happen again."

His face hardened. "I wasn't born yesterday."

"It was the spell. Like you said. I didn't recognise the danger of using such a curse. I only knew every warrior with me was about to die or be taken prisoner by ghouls. My fear for them overwhelmed me. I had to do something."

Kaell fidgeted with his belt. "I want to trust you…"

Genya swiped at a tear. "We've never been close. I wish we were, you and I."

"I…" Kaell looked confused. Then he flushed guiltily. "My fault," he muttered. "I wasn't ready. I woke up and learned what Roaran had done. I thought my lord—" He shook his head. "I was angry. But I know none of it is your fault."

"Can we… Dare we start again?" She looked up at him hopefully.

For a long moment, Kaell's gaze dwelled on her face. Then he smiled, touching a tear on her cheek with a fingertip. "I'd like that. But this—" He gestured towards the river. "The killing has to stop."

"Will you help me?"

Alone, Genya slid her back down against a tree trunk. A vicious laugh bubbled up inside her. How easily he'd believed her lies.

Will you help me? A flutter of eyelids, her tearful gaze holding his, and he'd believed she wanted to end the division between them. *What a fool.*

She didn't need help. She was powerful. A sorceress. With one spell, she had struck down every ghoul in that cursed castle. And the spell had cost her little. Instead, it allowed her to embrace what she was. Without the spell, she would not have dared drink human blood.

Even if she could turn back, she didn't want to. Her body thrummed with power, quivered with invincibility. It no longer matter what Val thought, what anyone thought. They couldn't touch her now. Her skill, her magic shielded her against hurt.

Everyone had lied to her about spellcraft. Val. Rozenn. Even Nicky. Neither Seithin magic nor blood magic should be feared. That was nonsense put about by sorcerers, sorceresses—*seers*—too afraid to unlock the forbidding power that lay dormant within. She would embrace that power. She would do what it took to save Telor.

For a sorceress with ghoul blood, the daughter of a great seer, no magic was dangerous. She could control it. Oh, yes, it might be perilous to others, but she would not shrink away from using blood magic. Not after she'd tasted its mystery.

Genya rolled her tongue about her mouth. The taste of blood fired up her taste buds. *Delicious.* No wonder ghouls hunted men and women. At that thought, a flicker of unease shifted in her mind. No, she was not like them. She would kill only those who deserved to die. The blood of the wicked, surely, tasted best.

VAL ARQUES

Someone was sponging his body with wet cloth. Puzzled, Val opened his eyes. A woman bending over him smiled. "Hush, hush. Do not be alarmed. I'm Elena, a healer."

Val tried to understand where he was. He lay on a narrow cot, naked beneath a sheet drawn up to his hips. The bed was against a wall in a shadowy alcove lit by a lantern swinging from a roof beam. Between arched pillars, a wispy white curtain closed in the small space around his bed.

"Where am I?" he croaked, lifting his head.

"You're in the infirmary," Elena said. "You've slept two days. How's your head?"

"Not so bad." The thump had retreated to a dull ache behind his eyes.

"And your vision?" Elena waved a finger close to his face.

"It seems steady enough."

"Good." She smiled again. It was a peaceful smile. And she had kind almond-brown eyes that dwelled without judgement. Her lashes dipped towards very pale skin as though she never saw the sun. Strands of brown hair escaped a long, loose knot plaited with ribbon.

Elena resumed washing his body, dipping her cloth into a bowl resting on the bed. Val lay back without alarm.

"There," Elena pronounced. "You'll feel more comfortable now." She pulled the sheet up to his waist. "Not too hot?"

Val shook his head.

"I've cleaned and bandaged your thigh, but if you're in pain, I can give you a little more poppy juice."

"No, though I'm hungry."

"I am pleased. I'll fetch you something to eat. It's the middle of the night, but I'll manage. If you feel strong enough to stand, there's a chamber pot in the corner. But if you need my help, please just ask."

"The middle of the night?" He frowned. "I've lost all sense of time. What day is it?"

"Just after midnight on Thursday. They brought you to me two days ago. I treated your wounds and gave you something to ease the pain." She shrugged. "Thankfully, you slept. Dreamt, perhaps."

He laughed. "My dreams, I think, are all that I truly own here."

"Then you are rich, indeed." Elena rose and brushed her hand down her long blue gown, which was belted at the waist by a golden cord. With another reassuring smile, she turned and pushed through the curtain.

Still a little faint, Val sat on the cot's edge. Rising, he stretched and tested putting his weight on his injured leg. Not too painful. Rohane's arrow hadn't reached the bone.

Rohane. At the thought of her, an awful, sinking sadness gathered in his belly. How warm, how lovely, how tender she had been those nights they had lain together. Now she didn't trust him.

After using the pot, Val limped to the curtain and drew it aside.

Upon rows of cots in a long room, men slept. A young woman moved between the beds, bending at times to touch a brow or adjust covers and pillows. The dim room was cool and split by stone columns. The walls were rock and the floor tiled.

The door must be at the far end. Val wondered if it was guarded. For a moment, he did truly consider escaping. *To where?* Frowning, he retreated to the bed and sat with his back to the wall, his arms about his drawn-up bare knees. This was a temporary reprieve. Very soon, they would take him before a judicial council for judgement.

Elena returned, a bag slung over a shoulder. She carried a bowl and spoon. "Here. It's soup." She closed the curtain again.

While he ate, she took a shirt and pants from the bag, shook them out, and laid them on the bed. "I had your clothes washed. When they come, you'll feel better wearing clean garments. And there's this." She put a simple shift on the bed. "We undressed you to tend your injuries. But this is suitable for sleeping."

"When will they… When will they come?" Even to his ears, Val's voice sounded thin.

Elena's eyes held sympathy. "Blaire sends someone every few hours to ask after you. I shall be able to put them off for a little while but…" She shrugged.

"Who comes?" His heart drummed. *Rohane. Let it be Rohane.*

"Only Blaire's servant."

"No one else?"

"I am sorry." She sounded sincere. "Is there anything I can get you? There's spring water for drinking in that jug by the bed. I'll bring warm water before you face the council. So you can wash. I am forbidden to give you a knife, though, for shaving."

"I'm grateful."

Elena nodded and walked away.

"Thank you," Val said.

She paused to look back. "For what?"

"For—" He sought the right words. "For treating me like a man. For being kind."

Elena looked astonished. "What a strange thing to say. What else can I be?"

"Indifferent. Harsh." He shrugged.

A serene smile spread across her face. "I believe in a kind god," she said. "Not Cyrah. Another. I can do no else than follow his word."

DANNON

He thought it might be night. Not because the room was dark; every chamber in the city seemed dark to him. But a slumbering quiet cloaked the long room.

His body beneath a thin linen shift no longer ached, shook, or sweated. He wasn't terribly sleepy, only lethargic and content to stare at the roof and listen to sounds drift in and out. A man's snore droned. Ceiling chimes stirred by a breeze jingled. Careful steps scuffed stone as healers trod between two rows of beds.

Dannon propped the pillow against the wall and drew himself straighter. A blond man slept in a cot beside him, his wrist shackled to the iron frame. Unease prickled down Dannon's spine. Though Dannon wasn't restrained, he wasn't free to leave either.

Idly, he watched a blue-robed woman pause beside a man tossing in a nearby bed. She stooped, her fingers touching his throat as if checking his pulse. With a shake of her head, she roused the man so he could drink from a cup.

Another woman approached the first. Dannon heard her mutter something about a "Telorian." The women moved away. When their footsteps faded, Dannon considered the room. It contained twelve beds in two rows, though only four men besides him lay in them. At the far end, steps carved into stone led to a

VAL ARQUES

At dusk the next day, a woman arrived. She was tall and stalk-thin, with her grey hair sternly pulled back in a bun. Unannounced, she pushed through the curtain and pulled up a stool.

"Who are you?" Val sat up in bed.

"I am Aldith. Your defender," the woman said.

Val frowned. "Defender?"

The woman tapped her fingers on her thigh. "Men are rarely permitted to address the Quisnaf court. I shall speak for you."

"Hmm." Val huffed in irritation. "That hardly sounds fair. These accusations are false. I must be able to defend myself."

"You must leave that to me. Now—" She leaned forward. "I have been apprised of what occurred. If you are sensible, you will throw yourself upon the court's mercy. They may be lenient if you admit your mistakes."

"You think I'm guilty?" Val swung his legs to the floor, his hands curled as fists. "I tell you, I didn't kill anyone. Nor did I run."

Aldith brushed a thread off her tunic. "The retrieval captain's testimony is damning. You were found in the desert with a sword. When Quisnaf riders approached, you fled."

"It seems you've already made up your mind. What sort of

defender are you if you're not even prepared to listen to what I have to say?"

Mouth pinched, the woman frowned at him. Then she waved a hand disinterestedly. "Very well, tell me what you say occurred."

"A guard hit me," Val said. "I woke in the desert, the sword beside me. Someone set me up to make it look as though I killed a guard and ran."

Aldith lifted her brows. "Do you have any proof?"

Angrily, Val kicked the bedpost. "I have a head wound—"

"Which the captain says happened when you fell from your horse."

"Ahhhh." He cried in frustration. "It didn't happen like that."

"They have a witness," Aldith said. "To the killing."

Val stilled. "What? Who?"

Aldith spread her arms. "I am not in possession of a name."

"Whoever it is, they're lying."

"Why? Does someone wish you ill?"

He heaved a breath. "I don't know."

Aldith stood. "They'll come for you in a few hours. Be ready."

"That's it?" Val huffed out a breath.

"For now," Aldith said.

Elena brought warm water, soap, and cloth. "The truth is always best," she said as he washed. "The council will be merciful if you tell the truth."

"I didn't run. Nor did I hurt anyone."

She shook her head and took away the bowl and cloth. Val dressed quickly, wondering about her previous words. *I believe in a kind god.* Not Cyrah, like the rest of her sisters. *Strange.*

Soon afterwards, guards arrived to escort him from the infirmary, through a myriad of passages to the now-familiar council room. A knot of Decan Watch guards, warriors, and scribes parted to make way for Val and his escort. Angry glances fell like hammer strikes.

They brought him before the bench, where Aine already sat in judgement, Blaire and Samantha at her side. Jenna-Dairine watched from near the door. Sisilia stood a little apart, her esurient stare fixed upon him. Nowhere did he see Rohane.

Aldith appeared and gestured at the chair before the bench. Val's escort shoved him into it. Behind him, women found places on benches, murmuring to each other. Then a guard stamped a spear against the floor and called for silence.

Aine cleared her throat. "We trust he is recovered?"

Aldith glanced at Val. "He is."

"Very well." Aine scribbled on parchment. "The accusation is thus: That in attempting to flee, this man not only broke his promise to the Quisnaf council and the temple but is also guilty of killing a guard, one of our own."

Hisses broke out. Furious faces turned his way.

Blaire leaned forward. "This is a bit of a mess, wouldn't you say, Val Arques? You may answer me if you choose."

Val laughed bitterly. "A mess, yes, but not of my doing."

"Oh?" She arched a finely shaped brow then addressed Aldith. "He denies the accusations?"

Aldith dipped her head. "He does. He says someone hit him. Then he woke in the desert, the sword beside him, just before riders approached."

Blaire stabbed a finger. "He killed a guard. He was found with her sword."

"I woke to find the sword beside me." Val shifted in the chair.

"Silence," Aine snapped. "Defender, instruct him not to speak unless the council asks him a direct question."

Aldith turned to frown. "Do you understand, Telorian? You must address the council through me."

"Then tell them I kept my vow to the council not to leave. Someone dumped me in that desert."

Aldith repeated his words.

Aine folded her arms. "No one would bother to kill a Quisnaf woman just to set this man up. The simplest explanation is usually the correct one." She turned to address her fellow councillors. "He ran to avoid the whip. He seized his chance when left with only one guard."

"I did not." Val rose from the chair, only to have guards move in to push him back down. "My words are true. Why doesn't anyone listen?"

"Settle down," Aldith said.

"No," Blaire said. "Let him answer."

"It's most irregular—" Aldith started.

"Let him answer." Blaire faced Val. "If your story is true, why didn't you surrender when our riders appeared? Instead, Rohane had to put an arrow in you to force you to return."

Oh, gods, he knew how it looked. "I didn't know what I was doing. I was sick, dazed. I just wanted her to listen, just listen. And I didn't know the riders were Quisnaf, not at first. It could have been anyone."

"This is nonsense." Aine threw out her bejewelled hands. "Call the witness."

"Very well," Blaire said.

A guard went to the door and addressed someone outside. A woman entered.

Val's breath cut. In dismay, he watched Branwyn walk to the centre of the room before the bench.

"Will you tell the council what you have previously revealed to me?" Aine asked.

Branwyn nodded. With a vicious glance at Val, she said, "I was in the tunnels. I heard a noise like a cry of pain. I went to investigate and saw him"—she pointed at Val—"bending over a guard lying on the ground."

More mutters broke out. Women whispered to their companions.

"And then?" Aine asked.

"Then he saw me. Quickly, he picked up the guard's discarded sword and ran. I went at once to the guard to see if she was hurt." Branwyn dropped her head. "She was dead. A sword wound to the gut."

This time, women hissed in disgust and anger. Aine held up a hand for silence.

"This is not right." Val again stormed to his feet. "This witness hates me. She's lying to punish me, for some twisted notion that I'm responsible for her demotion or something."

Again, guards shoved him back in his seat. One held his shoulders. Aldith turned, frowning. "What's this you say?"

"She warned me to watch my back." Val dragged a hand through his hair. "Oh, gods, I see it now. Someone went to a lot of trouble—the guard, the sword."

"Is this true?" Aldith asked Branwyn.

Branwyn shrugged smugly. "As if I'd make up a story like this to get at him." She scoffed. "He's not worth the effort."

"The law is clear," Aine said, her eyes slitted. "A woman's word must always be accepted over the word of a man. You know that, Aldith."

"Yes, but—" Aldith started.

"Rohane does say he was violently ill on the journey back," Blaire interceded. "Dizzy. Before he fell off the horse. That is consistent with an earlier head wound."

Aine sneered. "And consistent with extreme thirst. He took a sword but no water. Again, a simple explanation. And even you, Regenta, cannot overlook the fact that a woman of Quisnaf is dead by his hand."

"No." Val shook his head. "I demand you bring the truthsayer. She'll know that I'm not lying."

"The truthsayer is in Veniva. It may be weeks before she returns."

Dread cut through him like a blade of ice. Val slumped in the chair. He didn't know how to convince them. Even Rohane believed him guilty.

"So what do we do with him?" Samantha's tone held regret.

For the first time, Sisilia spoke. "The Protector of Men asks a question. Why stay silent, Regenta? The law is clear. You will strip him of his rights as a guest. Then you will surrender him to the temple."

"Surrender him to you? You mean Sisilia." Blaire glared at the sorceress.

"He is here as a sire, so he becomes the responsibility of the blood keepers. You have no choice. You must obey the law. Your duty is laid out."

When Blaire did not answer, Val glanced up. The Regenta's face was taut, as if she were reining in anger.

"If I learn you had anything to do with this," Blaire muttered. "Then—"

Sisilia took a menacing step forward. "Do you dare accuse me? With what proof?"

Blaire pressed her palms into the table. "Be very careful, Sisilia. I know the temple is a law unto itself, but you cannot hide behind that and do as you wish."

The sorceress laughed. Val's spine crept with coldness. This woman was not afraid, certainly not of the Quisnaf council. "I would offer the same advice, Blaire. Do your duty. Surrender this man. Or does the law not apply because you share his bed?"

Blaire started to rise, only to carefully sit again. "You go too far, Sisilia."

"Blaire understands the law," Samantha said coldly. "She upholds it in every instance."

Sisilia flicked a wrist. "Well then."

Blaire sat perfectly still. But for the rise and fall of her chest, she might have been carved in stone. Faces turned to her, expectant. Even Val stared, the breath lost in his lungs.

"I will uphold the law," Blaire said, her tone icy. "But I want you all to remember what is behind that law."

"And what is behind the law, Regenta?" Sisilia jeered. "Tell us all. We all love to be lectured."

Blaire fixed a cold look on her. "Of every law enacted to keep Quisnaf strong, this is always the most troubling. Even the first council, those women who established Quisnaf—who established our plan to produce the best warriors, the best seers, the cleverest leaders—too, struggled with this."

"If you mean holding a man against his will?" Aine shrugged. "Forcing him to comply. It is as it always has been. In this case, can you have any qualms? He killed a woman of Quisnaf."

Against his will. The words beat with foreboding in Val's skull.

"Hear what the Regenta says." Jenna-Dairine pushed forward. "We, as women, understand how important it is that our bodies are never made use of. Yet if we are to achieve our aims, this terrible thing is what we are required to do to men."

"A necessary thing, surely, Battale Captain." Samantha gestured with open palms. "The first Quisnaf council recognised it was so. That is why that council also established rules to minimise pain and fear."

"They also decreed that surrendering a man to the keepers, robbing him of choice, of his will, should be a last resort," Jenna-Dairine said. "That any other compromise must be first sought. We seem to forget that. So I ask—" She looked slowly about the room. "Is there not another way? Is there a compromise?"

Val's heart skipped with hope. But after one look at the resentful faces, his hope died.

Sisilia glowered. "You have no right to speak in this place. You are not a councillor. Oh, no, you refuse to take your place in the chamber. It is beneath you, it seems. What do you, *Captain*, know of the law?"

"I understand our laws," Jenna-Dairine said quietly. "I also understand the spirit of that law."

"What nonsense is this? Next, you will suggest a man should be treated equally before our law. Equally to a woman?" Sisilia laughed harshly.

Others murmured or shook their heads.

"The law is clear," Aine proclaimed ponderously. "We do not compromise. We do not forgive when a man strikes down one of our own. We punish."

Stares openly fell on Blaire. Val dropped his head. She would surrender him to the blood keepers.

Blaire rose. "The law is clear." She looked to Val with eyes empty of emotion. "Val Arques Caelan, you broke your word to this council. But worse, in attempting to escape, you killed a Quisnaf guard. I have no choice but to declare you no longer a guest. You no longer have any rights. From this moment, you will become the blood keepers' responsibility."

"It's not enough," Sisilia snapped. "You know what I want. I must have his blood to keep Quisnaf safe. You know I must. Say it."

"Very well." Blaire released a slow breath. She looked hard at him. "I specifically rule that not only your body but your blood belongs to the keepers. They shall ensure you sire children as commanded by the goddess and do otherwise with you as they must."

Disbelief and fear kicked in his gut. Surging up, Val shouted, "No. You can't do this. It's not right. I didn't break my word. I did not kill the guard. Why don't you believe me?"

Decan Watch guards swooped on him. They took hold of his arms.

Blaire's scowl passed to Sisilia. "Take what blood you need, Sisilia, for your spells. I only ask you are mindful of how serious it is to make use of another's body, to strip them of every right. I only ask that you try to be… kind."

The sorceress offered a low, mocking bow. "I am pleased you've proved reasonable. Anything else would be… dangerous, shall I say." She turned to the guards and clicked her fingers. "Bring him."

GENYA

Her every step enlivened, her senses heightened, she stalked about the castle, restless with a need she could not name. Others greeted her cautiously. A Mountains warrior, bolder than his companions, flirted with a smiling, "You look beautiful today, my lady." She grunted a response. Men and women all seemed so mundane. So tedious. Below her.

Again and again, her mind turned to the moment she had sunk her teeth into the fisherman's neck. Such strength had flowed through her. Such life. She needed to hold on to that invincibility. That power was protection against pain. Against rejection.

A commotion broke out in the ward. Onlookers circled two men exchanging blows. At every punch, the spectators jeered or shouted encouragement. Clothes torn, faces bruised, the grappling combatants swung their fists, kicked, and shoved. Moving in fast, Genya grabbed one by the shoulders, trying to break them apart.

"Get off, you interfering witch," he snarled.

Genya's anger, quietly simmering since the forest, unleashed like molten fire through her veins. Growling, she leapt at the man, knocking him down into the dust.

Flat on his back, he snarled, "Stupid cow," and kicked at her. A boot smacked her belly.

Genya grunted, the air whooshing from her lungs. In that instant when she doubled over, fighting for breath, the man surged up. With a furious roar, he ran at her. Sunlight glinted on a slashing knife.

Genya twisted. The blade swished past her side. With a hiss of rage, she grabbed the man's arm and swung him away as easily as she might flick a whip.

He hurtled like a rock, sprawling at the feet of astonished onlookers. Recovering to his knees, he groped about for the dropped knife. Just as his fingers closed about the hilt, Genya sprang at him, throwing an arm around his throat. As he choked for air, she stamped on his hand, her heel grinding into the soft bones. With a strangled yelp, the man dropped the knife. She kicked it away and squeezed harder. Her target punched and slapped at her, thrashing his body in a frenzy. Blood coursed from his wounded hand. The scent of it hit her with a storm of desire.

"Genya!" Someone tried to pull her off. She growled and bucked them aside. "Genya, stop. Stop right now. You're killing him."

The words slowly penetrated the fog. She grew aware of a shocked silence and Cadan peeling her arm away. With a cry, she dropped the man. He collapsed, spluttering for breath, fingers clutching at his bruised throat.

Cadan was breathing hard, his dark eyes shuttered. "By The Three, girl. What's up with you? Ever since we took that castle—"

Irritated, Genya snatched long breaths. The odour of blood lingered in her nostrils. Goddess, how she desired that blood. Her gaze fell on a vein throbbing in Cadan's neck. She licked her lips, wanting to tear the clothes from him, throw him back onto soft cushions, and plunder his mouth. To taste him. To breathe in the scent of him. To feel his weight on her, pressing skin against skin. And once he was deep inside her, his body trembling towards release, only then would she put her teeth to that vein.

The image was too vivid. She squeezed her eyes shut, forcing it away.

"Genya," Cadan's fingers dug into her arm. Beneath his touch, her skin burned. "Genya, are you all right?"

She seized more slow breaths, battling for control, then threw him a curt nod. The crowd had thickened. As well as guards summoned by Cadan, she recognised a few warriors she had fought beside. One grinned and shook his head, but it was an admiring rather than an admonishing shake.

The injured man knelt in the dirt, the mark from her arm bruising his neck. "Witch nearly killed me."

Cadan turned on him. A mask she recognised came down—the controlled, confident captain. "There's no fighting in the keep. Who started this?"

The other combatant stabbed a finger. "He did."

"Both of you can spend a night in the cells." Cadan turned to a guard. "Have a physician attend them." At his gesture, guards grabbed the two offenders.

"Here, she was ganna killed me," the wounded man protested. "What about her? Or don't the rules apply to the half-ghoul witch?"

"Lock that one up for three nights," Cadan said.

The man clamped his lips shut and shot Genya a hateful glare.

Cadan turned to Genya. "Alecc wants you."

"What for?"

"There's trouble."

They walked together to the keep. A whisper broke out behind them. Genya didn't care. That was one thing she had learned from Val. It didn't matter what most people thought of you. It only mattered what those you trusted thought. Those you loved.

Like Val. She dug her teeth into her bottom lip. In her mind, she could see that look on his face when he had stared at her seated beside Archanin. Not anger. Anger she might accept. But hurt. A deep disappointment as though she had ripped the heart from his chest and held it, bloody, pounding, in her hands.

Men had died, and Val blamed her. But she had saved her

companions in that ghoul castle. She had saved Dannon. She had hid him. Kept him safe... *Safe.* Someone had him. When she found out who, they would suffer.

Alecc and Nicky were stooped over a map spread out on a table in the hall. It seemed the young king was always looking at maps, hearing reports, and discussing tactics with Nicky or Cadan. Sometimes even talking alone with Kaell.

Cadan dropped artfully to one knee. Alecc waved him up, his gaze shifting to her. Chin tilted haughtily, Genya did not bow. He might be her king, but she was Roaran's daughter. And a sorceress bowed to no one.

"You sent for me."

Alecc came forward and touched her cheek. "You've been fighting?"

"I stepped in to break up a fight."

At her side, Cadan stiffened but said nothing.

"We can't have fighting in the castle." Alecc whirled on Cadan. "Who was it?"

"That brute Anthony and one of the bakers. I don't know what it was about. They're locked up as an example."

Alecc nodded. He waved them towards the table.

Nicky cast Genya a look. "You all right, girl?"

She nodded. But her throat tightened. The odour of the brute's blood still lingered. Her every sense was enflamed, as though she might explode. She was too aware of Cadan's heavy shoulders, the bulk of him. How he might feel beneath her.

"Cadan said there's trouble?"

Alecc bit his lip. "The fortress is nearly done. They're using slave workers and bringing rock from a quarry we never knew about."

"You can see the walls from our towers," Genya said. She also liked to wander sometimes across the gorge and spy on the ghouls, but she wouldn't tell them that. "The fortress is on a flat-topped hill. That gives them control of not only the gorge but the lands for miles around." She shrugged. "We'll put a stop to their plans."

"Not so simple," Nicky said.

"Of course it's simple," she snapped. "We go in at dawn. Kill them all. Or at least the ghouls. Free the slaves. Burn anything we can find."

A silence held. Alecc exchanged a look with Nicky. What did they know that she didn't? A burst of resentment flushed through her. She needed to be informed of every part of Alecc's plans at every stage.

Alecc sighed. "I only wish we could. But this site is heavily guarded."

"How heavily?"

"Our scouts count up to one thousand ghoul warriors."

Genya's belly lurched. That was an army. It was one thing to slip silently into a ghoul castle with a handful of men and the advantage of surprise. But to face down an army took another army.

"We don't have enough warriors."

"No." Alecc watched her with a strange look. "That thing you did... at that ghoul castle."

Genya should have shuddered. Deep regret and fear should have trembled through her. *You ask too much,* she should have said. *You don't know what that magic does to me.*

She did not. Instead, that memory of power, of absolute control, thrilled her blood.

"The Seithin curse," she said.

Alecc hesitated. "I would not ask... I know it's a risk..."

"No. It's not." Gladly would she do that magic again. Gladly would she seek that exhilarating authority, that heady rage. It was wonderful, dangerous, and exciting.

"Are you sure, girl?" Nicky came forward and clasped her hands.

She looked him in the eye, letting him see she was not afraid. "It doesn't hurt me, Nicky. Not like it might another."

"Cadan says you passed out. The other time."

At his look of concern, her heart softened. "I woke in no pain, not weakened or diminished. I can do this. I want to."

"There's something else," Alecc said. Again, he and Nicky exchanged a glance.

Genya frowned impatiently. "What?"

Alecc dragged his tongue over his lips. "It's unexpected. A messenger from Gendrick."

"That toad," Genya muttered.

"There's danger, Gendrick says. He asks for our help."

"It'll be a trap."

"Maybe not," Alecc said.

Genya shifted her weight. "So what's this so-called danger? Let's hear it. Let's hear Gendrick's feeble attempt to deceive us."

"The Wardorians. Their fleet is ready. That's what the false king's spies tell him. Telor is soon to be invaded. Gendrick says the Isles alone can't fight Wardour. All of Telor must rally. That means not only the Falls, the Plains, Dal-Kanu, but the Mountains."

"There was talk of a fleet," Genya mused. "When I was in Tide's End with the queen."

Alecc spread his arms. "But first, our other problem. The ghoul fortress. We can hardly march south and leave ghouls to take over the Mountains."

Genya leaned over the map. "So, my king, what do you have in mind?"

VAL ARQUES

Afraid and outraged by the injustice, Val struggled hard, breaking free of the guards. With no clear plan, he ran for the door.

"Grab him," Sisilia shouted. "What are you waiting for? Take him." Alarm laced her voice, as though he were a prize she'd fought for.

Just as he reached the door, guards swooped in, seizing his arms and shoulders. Val thrashed. More guards fell on him, trying to force him into the passage. Desperately, he clawed the walls, skidded his heels against the stone floor, and lashed out with his fists. Women grunted in pain, cursing as he landed blows.

Other members of the Decan Watch rushed to help. Bodies pressed against him until they overwhelmed him, forcing him to his knees then facedown on the floor.

"Stop this nonsense," Sisilia shouted. "Find rope. Chains. Anything."

Hands squashed his face against stone. A knee pressed into his back. Val yelled in helpless anger, "I didn't run. Don't do this. You can't do this."

A woman brought rope. His captors lashed Val's wrists together, pulled him up, and dragged him forward.

"You can't do this," Val shouted, bucking and twisting. "It isn't right."

"My patience is at an end." The Decan Watch commander, Louisa, thrust her face close to his. "Stop this, or I'll knock you out with my sword hilt, and we'll carry you." She waved a blade. Her angry breaths warmed his cheeks. "Do you understand?"

Raging with fury and indignation, he wanted to strike out, but it was pointless. Nor did he wish to be carried like a sack of grain. Closing his eyes, Val fought for control. Reluctantly, he nodded.

"Good." Louisa rocked back. "Bring him."

His escort pulled him into the passage. Relieved voices and uneasy laughter rose at his back. At a shove, Val stumbled, his belly roiling with dread.

The caverns opened into the valley. The guards took him through gardens dripping with blossom along the Marble Way to the temple stairs. Val's steps faltered. Rohane had told him about the blood keepers' chambers deep within.

"Walk or be carried."

His pride reared up. *Face this. Do not show fear.* It could hardly be worse than the breaking stone in the Icelands or the tower room where Myranthe had tormented him with his miserable past. He had withstood that. He would survive this, too. He must.

Decan guards surrendered him to temple enforcers, hard-faced women who dragged him through the sanctum past a towering Cyrah. The statue's eyes glittered with secret knowledge. The goddess's gaze mocked him as if she knew this would always be his fate. Shaded corridors speckled with sunlight and scented of incense and myrtle branched ahead. When they trod down a twisting corner stairwell, even the temple seemed far away, as though the guards were taking him into a remote world where few willingly tread. The only sounds were his captors' breaths and their echoing footsteps.

Another passage ended in yet more stairs leading to narrow tunnels lit by torches in sconces, the floors and ceiling naked rock.

The enforcers unlocked an iron grate. His escort pushed him through.

"Where are we?"

"Shut up."

Another iron gate stretched from ceiling to floor. Its lock was enormous, as though it took a giant key. When a temple enforcer opened it, Val shuddered. Every instinct shouted, turn and run. *Fight.*

They passed through two more gates then descended yet another staircase winding through rock that ended in a spacious chamber. Val caught his breath in astonishment. Beneath a high ceiling, it was filled with potted palms and ferns, streaming sunlight, comfortable chairs and couches, and shaded alcoves.

Clotild emerged from an inner passage. At the sight of Val's roped wrists, she frowned. "Is that necessary?"

"He fought," a guard said. "He's more reasonable now."

"We were expecting this one," Clotild said calmly. "Bring him."

Val glanced over his shoulder. He had nowhere to go. No escape. His breaths shortened. His head swam. His knees collapsed. Fear closed in on him.

Guards hauled him up. Clotild frowned. "Oh, you poor man. It will be all right." She strode quickly into the alcoves and returned with a waterskin. "Drink. This will calm you."

The skin held wine. It tasted rough, but it warmed Val's limbs.

"Better?" She smiled.

He managed a nod.

Clotild took the skin and led them down a short corridor and through a door. The cramped room held only a mattress on an iron frame, a stool, bucket, and a small table with a jug of water and cup upon it. Val reeled back. The whitewashed walls were too like his tower cell in the Icelands.

Impatient guards again grabbed his shoulders, forcing him inside and dumping him on the cot. Two held him down, their knees on his chest as he tried to thrash beneath them. Others strapped his wrists and ankles, fastening him to the bed.

As they backed away, Val writhed against the straps. "You can't do this," he shouted. "You can't. Let me go." Beneath his violent jerks, the bed creaked.

"You'll have your hands full, Clotild," a guard smirked.

The enforcers stomped from the room. Clotild shook her head at Val, her look sympathetic. "Sisilia will talk to you soon. Try to be calm."

"Don't leave me here like this," Val yelled. "Stop. This is wrong."

But she only closed the door and left him to darkness and to his useless struggle.

ROHANE

Shoulders stiff, hands fisted, Blaire stalked about the council chamber. "That scheming, double-dealing, wretched woman," she hissed.

Surprised, Rohane glanced at Samantha. "Do you mean Sisilia? You think she's behind this?"

Blaire broke off her pacing. "What if she set him up? Would she go so far as to kill a guard just to get her own way?"

Samantha laughed coldly. "Sisilia is the most ruthless woman I've ever met. She would bring down the mountains if it served her purpose."

"I should have guessed she'd do something like this," Blaire muttered.

"Why?" Rohane asked.

Blaire sighed. "Sisilia demanded I give her Val Arques."

"Demand?" Samantha huffed in annoyance. "The nerve of the woman."

"Demanded I surrender him so that she may use his blood for her spells. She insists an attack is coming, from across the Ice Sea, that she must see clearly. I told her she could have a little—in time. A compromise, I thought."

"What are you saying?" Rohane asked. "That he didn't try to flee? But a guard is dead."

Blaire dragged her fingers through her hair. "Something feels wrong about all of this."

"His story can't be true," Rohane said. "It's all too impossible."

"Yet Sisilia is relentless, remorseless, and entirely obsessive about her duty," Blaire said. "I don't know how far she'd go."

"All this?" Samantha shook her head angrily. "For a little blood?"

"Sisilia wants *all* his blood. She knows even if he is killed, this man will recover." Blaire scowled. "Sisilia believes only what she does is vital. She does Cyrah's will, so no one can stand in her way. She must have what she wants, and she must have it now."

Rohane was shaking her head. "No. I don't believe it. Even she would not go so far as to kill a Quisnaf woman."

"Rohane, dear, don't you think it's all a little too convenient?" Samantha asked.

"Or it's all a little too simple. He ran. He didn't care about who he hurt." Rohane whirled on Blaire. "Why am I here?" She did not want to think about Val Arques or what would happen to him now.

"You summoned me, Blaire? I'm expected in the temple. Twenty strokes because a man escaped on my watch."

"It is the law," Samantha said.

Quick steps came from the passage. The door flung open. Jenna-Dairine shoved past guards and stomped in. She glared at Blaire. "I knew you were jealous of me, but this is beyond decency."

Blaire dismissed the guards with a gesture. "What are you talking about?"

"The blood keepers." Jenna-Dairine drove a hand through the air. "The list. Did you think I'd never find out?"

Rohane glanced at Blaire. The Regenta's face had paled. "Rohane, Samantha, leave us," she said.

"Stay," Jenna-Dairine said coldly. "Listen and hear what our oh-so-perfect Regenta has done."

"Who told you?" Blaire was very still, her hands clenched at her side.

"Sisilia. She thought I knew. She thought it was something we had discussed." Jenna-Dairine scoffed. "Discussed. You and I."

"Sisilia." Blaire spat the name in disgust. "Is it she who acts against me? Is she behind the so-called Order?"

"Sisilia is too single-minded to plot revolution."

"Is it you?" Blaire's voice was very quiet, her gaze upon Jenna-Dairine.

"I don't want your throne," Jenna-Dairine shouted. "Why can't you see that?"

"Then take your place on the council." Blaire still spoke in that quiet tone. "Again and again, your seat is empty, a symbol of discontent, of division. Show we are united. For the sake of Quisnaf."

"For the sake of Quisnaf." Jenna-Dairine repeated the words as if in disbelief. "Don't play that game with me, Blaire. I know you, remember. *Know* you."

Blaire thrust her hands to her hips. "I was acting to keep Quisnaf strong."

"Is that right?"

"You can't have this man's child. You know why. The line of succession must be understood. My daughter will succeed me. I will not suffer a rival."

"The line of succession?" Jenna-Dairine curled her top lip. "Were you thinking that when you took my throne?"

"I'm better suited to rule than you, Jenna-Dairine. You were always destined to be a warrior."

"We were friends, Blaire," Jenna-Dairine said. "Since childhood. Maybe I didn't want the throne. Maybe I would have surrendered it to you. But we'll never know now, will we?"

"Jenna-Dairine. Jen—"

Jenna-Dairine threw up a hand, spun on her heel, and strode from the room. The door banged shut at her back.

Rohane glanced at Blaire. The other woman had clutched the edge of the table. Her face was tight with shock.

"You went against the blood keepers' edict. That will not end well."

"I'm protecting Quisnaf." Blaire shuddered, her stare falling in the darkness along the edge of the room. "Everything I do is always for the sake of Quisnaf."

"For the sake of Quisnaf, you must reconcile with her," Rohane said quietly. She ran her fingers through her fringe. With all that had happened with Val Arques, she was so very tired. Tired of thinking. Of hurting. "Why am I here? I'm expected in the corrections chamber. I am to be whipped, remember."

Blaire turned slowly to face her. Her faraway gaze sharpened on Rohane's face. "Forgive my distraction. I have an assignment for you."

"Oh?" A spark of interest flared in her. Such a task offered an escape from the turmoil of her thoughts. "Where?"

"Telor."

"I have no desire to see Telor again," Rohane muttered.

"And yet you must. With so much at risk, there's no one else I can trust but someone of your birth. My friend. My husband's sister. The daughter of my closest ally. I can trust only Samantha's daughter."

⸎

Rohane gripped the ropes dangling from the ceiling. Gooseflesh rose along her naked back. Pain hardly bothered her. Waiting, anticipating; that was the worst.

"Who stands for the temple?" The Regenta's chief interrogator, Malgaria, was a petite woman of middle years with a cloud of white hair. Behind her back, folk in Quisnaf called her Mad Mal. She relished the nickname, grinning when she overheard it. Despite her size, or because of it, this was a woman who liked to be feared.

"I do." With a quick look at Samantha, Persia stepped forward. Given Rohane's rank, only a battale captain or a councillor might act as accuser. "I accuse Rohane, daughter of Samantha."

"Then I shall record the offences and the tribunal's judgement.

Rohane, daughter of Samantha. You shall receive twenty strokes because a man escaped on your watch. On the earlier charge of unlawful carnal relations, our gracious Regenta has commuted the sentence because your co-accused had agreed to take that upon himself."

"The Telorian could still receive those lashes," Persia muttered.

Malgaria whirled on her with a stabbing finger. "He is in the care of the blood keepers. Their purpose ascends ours. We shall not see him again."

Not see him again. The words were like knife cuts in Rohane's flesh. Quickly, she thrust them aside. *Duty.* That was all she had left. In the end, she'd been foolish to think there could be anything else. Certainly not love.

Glancing about the dank stone chamber, she shivered. It had only one purpose. Punishment. At least she was not to be shamed publicly; only Persia, Mad Mal, and Samantha would witness this dispensation of justice.

"Do you wish to dispute the charge, Captain?"

"Just get on with it," Rohane snapped.

"Very well."

Malgaria stepped closer. Leather swished through air. The lash fell hard. Rohane breathed through the pain. *One.*

Leather cracked against her naked back. More burning pain erupted. *Two.*

At the sixth and seventh, she jerked, teeth gritted, her back aflame. Agony washed away all thought, everything but that river of fire blazing from her shoulder to hip.

Eight. Rohane slumped. By sheer will, she pulled herself back up via the ropes. Her hands clutched at the coarse, knotted cord as though clinging to life itself.

Nine. Wheezing, she dangled from the ropes, her knees jelly. Again, she forced herself to stand. She could bear this.

Ten. Her bloodied body shuddered and twitched. A scream caught in her throat.

"That's enough." Samantha said.

The strokes stopped.

Rohane gripped the rope, breathing hard. "That wasn't twenty." She turned to glare at her mother. "Do you think me weak? I can take this."

"I know you can," Samantha said. "However, Blaire commuted the sentence to twelve lashes. For my sake. Not yours."

Malgaria gave a curiously cheerful laugh. "And instructed if I should deliver fewer, she would overlook it."

"How dare she? How dare any of you? I can take it," Rohane insisted angrily. "I don't want your kindness."

"Rohane." Samantha shook her head sadly. "Always so proud. Please. Accept our goodwill."

"I don't want to be treated differently just because of who I am." She had only ever wanted to belong, to be accepted as a warrior of Quisnaf, not a privileged daughter of a councillor.

The interrogator shrugged. "Accept Blaire's kindness, girl. If anyone asks, I delivered twenty lashes. No one shall hear differently. Believe me, your back is shredded as it is."

"Rohane." Samantha reached for her arm, her face full of compassion.

Rohane shrugged off her mother's hand. She groped for her tunic and shoved it down over her burning, broken skin, gasping at the pain.

"See the healers, Rohane," Persia said. "They have balms to soothe your back."

"Maybe."

"No need to endure unnecessary pain. Bite down on that pride, Captain."

"What if I want the pain?"

Their eyes rounded in surprise. Samantha's lips compressed with disappointment and a strange sorrow, as though Rohane's misery was somehow her mother's failure.

Rohane wanted to embrace the pain like a lover. It was true, constant. It wiped every thought from her mind, leaving only her and the pain. It washed away thoughts of Val Arques Caelan.

A surge of fury heated her body. *How could he?* He had run and left her to face the consequences of his betrayal. After she had given him her body. Her will.

Her hope. That hurt most of all. She'd let him kindle a tiny flame—the possibility that she might be happy. That she might be loved.

"Cyrah," Rohane whispered. "You know about love. You loved Khir. Why did you let me love? Why did you let me hope? Why dangle happiness only to snatch it away with lies and betrayal?" *Oh, graceless goddess. Cruel goddess.*

"I'll see the healer." Rohane snatched up her cloak and headed to the door.

VAL ARQUES

He raged at the walls, shouting his defiance and anger, thrashing at the buckles until his wrists and ankles bled. At last, he lay back, exhausted and panting. The silence settled about him, endless, cold, and miserable. A pall upon his spirit.

Rohane. Oh, gods, how he had hurt her. Again, he had brought only misery to someone he cared about.

A bolt lifted. Val stilled, his furious gaze levelled like a sword at the door. Sisilia stepped in, her dark eyes gleaming with satisfaction.

Val hissed. "Are you behind this? I've done nothing to deserve it. You can't just throw me in here and bind me."

She placed a lantern on the table and considered him with a predatory smile. "Oh, but I can. You broke the law. Further, you are a murderer, without rights."

Val stiffened. "I didn't kill the guard. Why doesn't anyone listen to the truth?"

Sisilia stooped over him. With cool fingers, she touched his brow. Growling, he whipped his head sideways.

"Dear boy," she muttered. "So precious. What lovely blood you have." Her eyes held a fanatical glitter. "I shall take care of you."

"No." Val tugged at a strap.

"So angry. It does no good, you know. We must release this anger." Sisilia's condescending tone irritated like an itch he couldn't reach. "I want you to struggle. I want you to scream. Yell, kick, flail. Get it out. This is the time, the only time. I'll even leave you the light. You'll feel better if you let it all out."

Her fingers trailed down his cheek and jaw. "We'll talk more when you're calm and accept your situation. Don't forget what I said. Do not hold back. Scream. Shout." She shrugged. "No one can hear you here."

⁓⁓⁓

He bellowed. He yelled. He writhed and convulsed like a mad man. It brought no relief, only accented his helplessness and guilt. Finally, his body tormented by thirst and hunger just as dark imaginings tormented his mind, he fell into an exhausted sleep.

A sound woke him. Though the lantern had burned out, light pooled beneath the door. Clotild swung open the door and stepped inside, carrying a candle and a tray that held food and a bowl of water with cloth. She placed them on the table beside a linen garment.

"Water," Val moaned.

"Of course." Clotild filled a cup and held it to his lips. "More?"

Val nodded, his throat parched.

"It's your own fault. All that shouting," she scolded. But a warm smile stole any sting from the words.

Val considered her with a frown. Though she seemed kinder than Sisilia, she wasn't his friend. No, far from that. His gaoler.

"All this blood. Tsch, tsch." After wetting the cloth, she dabbed at his ripped wrists. "Such a racket. It's very quiet here normally. You probably woke the ghosts."

"Ghosts?"

Clotild slid a cheerful look about. "Not in this room. But yes." She bobbed her head up and down. "Oh, yes, restless spirits."

"Wonderful. This gets better and better."

"Sarcasm. Lovely." She smiled with genuine warmth as she dabbed at a welt on his ankle. "I thought you might be sarcastic."

"Please tell me what you intend to do to me. Must I be tied down?"

Clotild sighed. "It's hard at first. I know. But it won't be forever."

Val groaned in despair. "How long?"

"We try never to punish with pain, only curtail freedoms that may be won back through good behaviour."

Val wet his dry lips. "What... What does that mean?"

"Tonight, you'll be given a sleeping potion." Clotild clicked her tongue against her teeth. "Such a lovely long sleep. No pain. No fear. It's not our way to be cruel, Val Arques—may I call you Val Arques?"

His throat tightened. "What happens to me while I sleep?"

"Sisilia wants your blood. She works away in her lair close by, summoning spirits, creating all manner of potions, seeking visions so that she may protect Quisnaf."

Such lovely blood... Precious. He shuddered.

"Oh, I've frightened you. I am sorry. I do not want you to be uneasy." Clotild leaned over him to unbuckle a wrist. "Now, Val Arques. Swear you'll cause no further trouble, and I'll free you until the candle burns down. There's a bucket. Water for washing." She pointed. "Food. Make the most of the time. But the instant I return, you must drink the first draught of the potion prepared for you."

He growled through gritted teeth. "So that's how you intend to restrain me. Keep me insensible. Why bother? I might escape this room but not this dreadful place." Again, he shuddered. "Those gates, the guards. This is a prison, I know."

She considered him sorrowfully. "Unless you give your word, I cannot release you."

"Apparently, I broke my word. That's why I'm here."

"I can only judge on my experience, and we have no history yet, you and me. So I shall trust your word. If you give it."

"I give it," he muttered. "Reluctantly." Val did not want to drink whatever the potion was, but he was desperate to eat and move about, to stretch his tight muscles.

Clotild freed his other hand. At once, Val sat up and untied his ankles.

Nodding, she rose and started towards the door. Hand on the latch, she turned back. "Oh, and if you would please remove your clothes by the time I return."

"What?" he stammered in disbelief.

She didn't quite look at him. "I am sorry. But you may not own anything here, not even the garments you wear. The blood keepers will clothe you. You are now our responsibility."

Her words cut with humiliation.

"You will find clean garments on the table," Clotild said gently.

When she left, a bolt thudded into place behind the door.

Val fell upon a bowl of stew and bread. He drank more water and used the bucket. Then he threw off his tunic, boots, and pants and washed as best he could.

The candle burned to a stub. Any minute, she would return. Val fingered the new garment. It was a simple shift, clean and white, the material grainy like coarse linen.

He hesitated. If he were to resist, the guards would strip him by force. No point clinging to his pride. Not here. With a helpless sigh, he dressed, bristling against submission.

Clotild returned. A temple guard trailed in her wake, watchful, naked steel in her hand. Clotild put a cup on the table. "I believe you gave me your word."

Val ground his teeth in frustration. "Why must I be kept asleep? There's no need. I can't escape. I understand that."

"Please. Drink the potion then lie down."

Seething, Val snatched up the cup and drained it. Then he sat on the edge of the bed.

"Thank you," Clotild said softly. "You may not believe me, but I understand how hard this is. Especially for a warrior." She bit her lip. The gesture reminded him of Rohane. The sorrow he had resisted lumped within. Where was she? Did she know what had happened to him? Did she even care? Maybe Rohane thought he deserved it.

Already drowsy, he stretched out on his back on the bed and closed his eyes. Muted steps moved towards the door. When it banged shut, the sound echoed throughout the passages. Then came silence. Only silence.

⁓⥁⁓

"I warned you." Samantha sat upon the stool by the bed. "Obey the rules. That's all that's asked, Val."

Sleepily, he murmured incoherently, hardly able to form words. He could not understand how much time had passed since they had brought him to this room. Always, he drifted from dreams to a drowsy wakefulness then back to dreams.

"You proud fool." Her sigh was drawn out. "The moment I saw you, I was afraid for you. I suspected with the way you look, so beautiful, and with your Caelan blood, that you are fated to be held, to belong to someone." She shook her head sadly. "Others will always seek to use you for their purposes. It is your fate to be hunted, wanted, desired."

The words struck a faint chord. Surely Myranthe had said something similar.

"Perhaps this is where you belong," Samantha said. "At least you are safe. No one can hurt you here or keep you captive for reasons of desire or power."

Val rocked his head on the pillow. No, he wanted to tell her that wasn't right. He could stay safe, but he needed to be free.

"Do you remember the Blessing, how you foolishly took on Jenna-Dairine before hundreds of shouting spectators? You don't know what forces you unleashed that night. A beautiful, young Telorian in Quisnaf? A bladesman? What a prize. And clearly, if in Quisnaf and not cloaked, then for sale. Blaire rebuffed a number of offers for you that night. Even so, I suspect someone will seek you, try to take you from us. It's inevitable."

"Then free me," Val croaked, uncertain he spoke aloud. He could defend himself. Nothing was inevitable. And yet, after so many centuries when he had stayed hidden, too many people now knew his name—and his secret.

Samantha sighed. She pushed back the stool and rose. *Don't go,* he tried to whisper. *Do not leave me like this. We are friends, aren't we?* But sleep was taking him over again.

"I'm sorry, Val," the councillor said. "Really, I am. But at least we can keep you safe."

Her footsteps rang on stone. The door opened and shut. A whisper of voices came to him then an echo of heels, fast fading. Then came nothing but darkness and stillness. Hopelessness.

ROHANE

R ohane smoothed a palm down her formal dark-blue tunic, the linen rough beneath her fingers. Even her silk undergarments prickled against her scarring, greasy back. The heelers applied salve each day, though a week had passed since she had faced the whip. Thank the goddess no wound had enflamed.

A new cloak swung from her shoulder. Her sword, the sword Val had used to fight Jenna-Dairine, poked from a scabbard tied to her weapons belt.

"This way." Clotild touched Rohane's arm. "You don't have to do this, Rohane."

"I must. I won't return for at least two months."

Clotild sighed. "I hear you're bound for Telor. Again."

"Blaire graciously has given me an important task." Because Rohane belonged to one of Quisnaf's oldest families. Because she was a councillor's daughter. Always, she had sought to make her own way. But today, she didn't care. She just wanted to be far from Quisnaf.

"I must hunt down the man who killed Matilda and Morgan." *And deliver a message to Roaran Caelan's daughter.* But she could not share that with Clotild. Only the council knew.

"May the goddess be good and the winds fair." Clotild reached a door, drew back the bolt, and pushed it open. Her pulse wild, Rohane walked in.

Val lay on the bed, his tousled dark hair streaming about his face, his eyes closed. She was glad of that. If he looked at her, she didn't know if she could stand it. Too much roiled within: a flurry of guilt, of anger, of confusion.

"Will he know I'm here?"

Clotild clasped her hands at her breast. "No, child. For the most part, he knows only dreams."

Rohane swallowed hard. "And that's… it? That's his life now?" Why did that twist like a dagger in her gut? She should be glad they'd punished him.

"Only for now," Clotild said gently. "They wake him up so he can eat. Take him to the baths. Sometimes they walk him around a bit. He's not really aware of it."

"For how long?"

"When the potion infuses his every pore, his every sinew, the sorceress will reduce the dosage so that he is able to function, though he will remain very calm."

Rohane approached the bed. Val wore a shift that stole up to his hips in sleep. Tenderly, she pulled a blanket over him. Her gaze stopped on the long gashes in his arms. "What did you do to him?" she whispered.

"Sisilia wants blood." Clotild patted Rohane's shoulder. "He doesn't feel anything, child. There's no pain."

Rohane could not speak. A surge of emotions swirled within her. She could not separate them. Nor did she want to face them. Whirling, she walked from the room and strode towards her duty.

VAL ARQUES

"Rohane," he muttered. A whisper of her fragrance danced in his nostrils. Desperately, he tried to lift his arm. But his limbs did not obey.

Dreams, lovely and wonderful, snatched him away. Rohane sat with him in the grass in the Quisnaf valley. A stream trickled over rocks. Branches creaked softly in a gentle breeze dense with the fragrance of honey. The sun warmed his scalp. Just as comforting were her fingers on his face, her dark eyes large and forgiving. "Val."

He wept. "You think so little of me, you believe I'd hurt you, leave you to be punished because of me."

"Val. If you say you didn't run, then I believe you."

He sobbed harder. Rohane pulled him to her breast, her fingers tangling in his hair. "It's all right. I'm here. I didn't doubt you."

"I thought we were friends. I thought we trusted each other."

"Is that all we are, Val?"

Sunlight faded to gloaming dusk. A hand brushed his cheek. A different hand. Cold and indifferent. "Time to rouse."

"No. Don't leave me," he pleaded. *Rohane. Where is Rohane?* With desperate longing, he tried to reach for her, to stay in the dream. But that insistent hand dragged him to wakefulness. Sleep dazed, he blinked, not recognising Sisilia at once. "What… where?" he stammered. What was this place? Why was he here?

"Dear boy." Sisilia bent over him. "Dear boy, no need to fear. I'll take care of you. But I need you alert for a little while. We haven't given you the potion today. For this spell, I can't have your blood tainted."

"My blood?" Still, Val didn't understand. The dream wavered. Rohane was real. Sisilia was not. She was the dream. If only he could push that dream away and wake in that place where he sat with Rohane.

"The guards will take you to the baths now. Then they'll bring you to me."

"No," Val said. Desperately, he reached deep for clarity.

"No?" Her laugh was brittle. "You have no choice, dear boy."

"You don't understand." He shook his head to clear it. "I want—" The thought drifted away.

"What do you want?" She peered at him disinterestedly. "What is it?"

Val gathered his scattered thoughts. He had something to say to her. Something she had to understand. He ran a tongue over his dry lips. He croaked, "I want to make a bargain with you."

Sisilia's brows arched. "A bargain. With me?"

Val nodded. He forced himself to hold her gaze so she could see his sincerity, that he intended no deception.

Sisilia spread her arms. "You are a prisoner of the temple, a man without rights. What could you possibly offer me?"

"My co-operation."

Her eyes flared. "I have that. You are contained. I have access to you. Dear boy, what more do I need?"

"I won't fight you. I'll willingly go where you want. When you need my blood, I won't resist. Do what you desire with my body."

Sisilia tapped a finger on her chin. "It has appeal. But you spoke of a bargain? What do you want from me?"

"I don't wish to drink your potion. I want to have a clear mind."

"No. Impossible."

"I'm not asking to be set free. Imprison me as you will. But don't force your sleeping potion on me. I don't want to spend my life lost in dreams."

She touched his brow. Val forced himself not to recoil at her caress. "But the dreams are not so bad, surely. Over centuries, those who serve the blood keepers sought a way to contain our captives without pain, without despair. The answer was a lovely potion."

"Isn't this cell enough?"

"You mean we should lock you in alone with your doubts, your fears, your troubled thoughts?"

Val stared at her, frowning. "You mean you think you're being kind?"

"We are. Long ago, Quisnaf councils tussled with the morality of restraining any man and making use of his body. This is considered the most benevolent way. You've known nothing but sweet dreams for many days. I would spare you the struggle, the fear."

He rocked his head. In endless dreams, he lost himself. "Isn't my co-operation worth anything? I just need to know, to feel."

Sisilia leaned forward. "You'll willingly do what I want? Tomorrow night, when I come for you, you'll go with me? You'll let me open your veins?"

"Yes."

She straightened. "Indeed, I would prefer you calm tomorrow night. I do not want anger or fear to stir your blood. And your blood must be pure. I cannot use the potion."

"I will do as you wish. I only ask that you don't force me back into dreams where I don't know who I am."

Her gaze turned inward. For a long moment, she said nothing. Then she nodded.

"Very well. We have a bargain. You shall no longer be forced to drink a sleeping draught each day. I shall even let you roam the blood keepers' caverns at will. But should you try to leave or break our bargain in any way… well, you have been warned."

"Thank you."

Sisilia nodded. Her eyes were feverishly bright. Again, she bent over him, her hand on his cheek. "Tell me, what is it you dread? Why resist our gift of dreams?"

"I don't like the lack of control," Val admitted.

Sisilia studied him. "Curious. Most would prefer to avoid struggle. I thank you for your honesty. In return, I shall offer you a further gift."

"What?"

"I shall suggest that the women come. Tonight. You shall be permitted to feel, to give and take pleasure, if you choose."

"They… they have not been here?" Val frowned. Fragments of awareness had drifted through his dreams. Devyn's tears. Blaire's regretful sigh.

"Oh, they have. The work of the keepers is vital. You are vital. But for tonight, I offer you awareness, unlike those hazy other nights."

Val swallowed. "And tomorrow?"

"I'll send for you at dusk. Perform your duty tonight then rest well." Sisilia smiled condescendingly. With nimble fingers, she freed his wrists. "Clotild shall take care of you. I must purify myself before the gods, prepare for the ritual." Her reptilian smile flashed again. "I'll see you soon, sweet boy."

ROHANE

The skin of her father's hand was as dry as parchment. He was older, his fair hair streaked with grey, the lines of worry and strain etched in a once-striking face. A sword stroke long ago had almost crippled him. Yet he walked unbowed as though through an act of will.

Never would he appear diminished before others, despite the pain of old wounds, despite his troubles. Nor would Veniva's enemies make the mistake of thinking the realm's ageing king weak. Cassian of Veniva remained formidable. But when he died? What then?

Brenin would be king. Rohane held few illusions about her brother. Brenin's cruel streak would serve him well—as a ruler. She even respected him as a swordsman and warrior. But he surrendered too readily to needs of the flesh. It was ill disciplined. And a warrior must be disciplined above all things.

Rohane coughed a laugh. And she dared judge?

Cassian squeezed her hand. "A bag of gold for your thoughts, child?"

She sighed. "It's nothing."

They strolled together through the Venivan palace gardens. It was a wild, wonderful place, a riot of colour and fragrance. The perfume of frangipani spilled from pink flowers scattered among the bluebells and borage. When she brushed a hand through lavender bushes, they released their pleasing scent. Usually, Rohane loved this place. But her thoughts mired in sorrow and disappointment, robbing her of simple pleasures.

The paths wound through garden beds tended by sun-browned gardeners. Willowy trees dipped. Tall trunks crowded one another, their branches rattling like rusted iron in a soft breeze. In the distance, she glimpsed the conical tip of the abandoned tower.

It was haunted, as every ruin should be. The tower had been a place of childish mischief for her and Brenin, well away from adult eyes, where they pretended to fight vicious foes or dared each other to climb the stairs to the top chamber, where the door creaked and the wind roared through broken stonework.

"I had it partially repaired," Cassian said, seeing where her stare fell.

"What a pity. I like ruins. I hope you didn't rouse the spirits."

"The structure is sturdy. And the tower's remote location makes it perfect for any manner of uses."

"Secret liaisons?"

"Wicked child. I thought it would make a suitable prison. For valuable hostages or those I capture in battle and hold for ransom." Cassian walked through a leafy arch and sank down upon a garden seat. Rohane followed.

"Talk to me, daughter," Cassian said as she sat beside him. "Do you know how good it is to see you? You are too rarely in Veniva. Oh, I know, I know..." He whipped up a hand with a disarming smile. "You are a captain. You are dutiful. But it warms your father's old heart to have you beside him."

"Old, you?" she teased.

He sighed. "Even I age, Rohane. I worry about what will happen when I die. Brenin is..." He made a disapproving sound. "Stubborn. Ruthless."

"Some might find those good qualities for a king."

"If you were here to guide him, Rohane, I should feel comforted. You could offer sage advice when he veered from the right path."

"He does not listen to me."

Cassian sighed. They sat in companionable silence for a moment. The warm, fragrant air and beating sun reminded her of sitting with Val on the riverbank. Of a kiss. So curiously innocent. Rohane had felt like a girl again, not a warrior burdened by her curse.

"Blaire is wondering what has become of the truthsayer, by the way. She sent her to you, and she has failed to return."

"Ah," her father said.

"What does 'ah' mean?"

He grimaced. "The truthsayer has taken to her bed. She has the best care, but she is gravely ill. I was about to send a messenger to Blaire."

"The poor woman," Rohane muttered. "Will she recover?"

Cassian shrugged. "She is very old. It is in the hands of the gods." He paused to look at her. "Where is Blaire sending you?"

"Telor."

"Again?"

Rohane shrugged. "I'm taking Blaire's greetings to this would-be king in the Mountains. But really, I have another task. I am forbidden to speak of it."

"Then speak of what is in your heart." He shifted slightly to see her face. "I know there is something. Sadness clings to you. Oh, there is always sadness in your heart, ever since that day your battle sister died. But this is a different sort of sorrow."

Rohane smiled fondly. "You are too clever."

Again he squeezed her hand. "As a girl, you always confided in me. Told me about your childhood dreams of battle and honour, your dreams, too, of love. I remember how you blushed when we spoke of the first Blessing you were old enough to attend."

"One should not talk of such things to your father."

"And now? What is this pain in your eyes?"

For a moment, she said nothing, only listened to the wind through the trees, to a faint chime from a string of bells tied to a branch. A distant rumble of voices and laughter drifted from two labourers turning soil in a flower bed. She considered them vaguely, wondering if they were free born or slaves taken in battle. "There is a man. There *was* a man."

"I thought there might be. His name?" Cassian asked quietly.

"His name is Val Arques. He is Telorian. A warrior. I retrieved him after that battle where Archanin died. He has old Isles blood. The blood keepers have plans…"

Cassian waited, silent. He never pushed her, always understood she had her own pace to things, even to words.

"He is… important—to the blood keepers. I was appointed guardian." She gave a brittle laugh. "I spent every day with him. Things… happened."

"You loved him. Did he love you?"

"I thought he did. But he tried to run. I had to hunt him down, bring him back." The now-familiar anger kicked inside. She fisted a hand. "Why would he do that to me? He cannot love me, not when he would betray me like that."

In the quiet between them, the wind chimes tinkled. The sound always reminded Rohane of summer, of slow days absent of worry or cares about the future. There were times in this garden when she had lost herself to dreams and imaginings. Times when she wasn't the daughter of a king or a warrior of Quisnaf. Times when she forgot she was cursed.

"It is hard for a warrior to accept restraint," Cassian said at last. "If I were him, I would run too."

She curled her fingers around the edge of the seat. "He broke his word." Val's betrayal was personal, even though what was between them had not been stated.

"And you're angry at him."

"I hate him. I think I do. Because… because…" She tried to unravel the swirl of disappointment and anger.

"Because you loved him." Cassian smiled. He brushed hair from her face. "My darling daughter. She who always guards her heart. What manner of man is this who should break through your shields?"

"I dared hope," Rohane admitted. "He made me feel for the first time that life might be good. That the future might not be bleak."

Cassian's hand stilled on her cheek. He arched his brows.

"I gave him my hope," Rohane said. "And he, he ripped that apart."

"Maybe you're looking for reasons to be mad at him. So that you don't have to deal with loving him."

Rohane frowned. "Don't be ridiculous." But a tiny niggle of doubt stirred.

"Your anger seems out of proportion. You have not known him very long. No, I think you want to hate him, that it's easier. So that you can again retreat into your loneliness, where it's safe."

"I didn't make him run," Rohane muttered.

"And when he fled, you brought him back. Now he is suffering for his rebellion. And you feel guilty."

"No!" Rohane shot to her feet. "No. I do not. He deserves everything he gets. I am only too glad Blaire is sending me to Telor. I want to be far away from Quisnaf, far from him."

Far from her thoughts. But she couldn't escape them, no matter how she tried. Nor could she escape dreams—those shallow, disturbing fragments that came to her near dawn. Val tormented her then. Sometimes she dreamt of that first night in his bed, and her body stirred and shifted as though beneath his caressing hands. But worse, far worse, were the nightmares where she stood over him as he lay insensible, tied down, and helpless. Unseeing. Unknowing.

No. Rohane would not feel guilty. What befell him, he had brought on himself. With his deception. In time, she would forget him. Her purpose was to serve Quisnaf. That was enough.

"I do not need love," she muttered, as much to herself as to her father. "I've lived without it, and I can do it again." Val's faithlessness just proved what she had always feared—opening her heart only opened her to hurt.

Cassian's gaze rested on her face.

"What?" she challenged.

He only smiled a strange, knowing smile. "Nothing."

GENYA

Beneath a darkening sky, Genya raised her bloody arms. Terrible words shrieked out of her as though spoken by someone else. Her blood dripped into the earth. Power scorched through her body, from her body, visibly rippling through the air towards the ghouls and their half-built keep.

The curse struck in murderous, thunderous waves. Ghouls fell in lines—first the guards on the curtain wall then those in the barely visible ward. Some tried to run as though sensing the ring of death rolling towards them. Then they, too, fell dead.

As the spell tore from her, light and fire shot from her fingertips. Genya staggered, momentarily weak, but she did not pass out this time. Instead, as she shouted the words once more, magic flowed through her like a blazing river, empowering and enlivening.

"Wait," she said to Cadan at her side. "Wait."

The curse surged like an enraged storm tide smashing again and again against a cliff. Black clouds billowed above, a cap upon the dark ribbons of power undulating over the castle. Cries of fear and agony rang out from within.

Slowly, the clouds lightened to mist and drifted away. Genya sniffed the metallic currents, tasting the spell and taking the last of the darkness within. There was coldness in her now, a pleasurable chill seeping into her bones. Exhilarated and drunk with power, with that seductive mystery of witchcraft, she shivered with awe and wonder. It was as if she had become one with the goddess, more than human.

Cadan bristled with impatience. He was a true warrior. Not content that his enemy should die, instead desperate to be at the heart of the killing.

"It's safe."

He flashed her a fierce glance and bellowed to the warriors loosely bunched behind them. With a roar, they flung themselves upon the castle. A few wounded or dazed ghouls at the edge of her killing wave struggled to their feet to meet the men.

Swords clashed. The air thickened with clanging steel, screams, and the scent of fear and death. The fight was short-lived. Almost at once, the ghoul line broke. They turned tail and ran. The whooping Mountains men chased them down. Genya listened to the cries of ghouls struck dead as they fled. Elation burned through her.

The men wandered back. They began to survey the carnage in the castle.

"Gods, they've built even more than we thought," Cadan muttered, his gaze raking the keep and the almost-intact curtain wall.

Genya nodded distantly. If a few towers, a gate and perhaps a barbican were added to this castle, it could be held.

She climbed through the unfinished wall, beneath the shadow of the circular keep. A black-winged bird cawed as it circled then roosted in the keep's roof. When it burst into song, the pure melody prickled her skin. She trailed a hand through feathery knee-high grass, plucked a wildflower, and held it to her nose.

Touch, smell, and every sense was alive in her. If she shut her eyes, the wind rippling through grass and the crackle of leaves sounded like music. To brush her fingers over the keep's cool stone was immensely pleasurable. Everything was different: every scent sweeter; every noise deeper and layered; and every colour brighter, sharper. At the same time, she was apart from her surroundings, her body as light as air. Nothing could touch her. Nothing could harm her. Oh, how she wanted to hold on to this power, this wondrous detachment.

Alecc's warriors moved about her, gathering the dead into a pile, offering food and water to weary, dirty slaves they had found chained in a camp beyond the castle. Cadan stalked among them, ordering men to gather branches. They would burn and salt this site so that no one, ghoul or human, could use it again.

"And yet, we could hold this castle," Genya muttered. "It could be useful."

"Alecc says it must burn," Cadan replied.

Genya shrugged and turned away. The scent of blood drew her into a ward. There, at the heart of the spell's darkness, ghouls without obvious wounds lay lifeless.

As she passed by, men glanced uneasily at her before their gazes slid away. She didn't care. No one spoke to her. If Genya drew too close, warriors shivered or made signs with their fingers. Pleased by their fear, she laughed. They should tremble, for she was so much more than human. She was pure power. Why, she wondered, would Roaran resist this? This wondrous euphoria, the remnants of magic coursing through her body, shielded her from pain. It was like life and spirit bursting in every vein. Sensation upon sensation.

In a cloud of elation, she wandered through the rings of faded magic. Its lingering power passed through her, strong at the centre and slowly fading as she moved to the edges.

Here, death was different. Falling stone had smashed heads or broken bones. Swords had gutted or slashed flesh. The blood of many, many ghouls seeped into the Mountains soil.

A wounded ghoul crawled to the curtain wall. Resting his back to the stone, he clasped his hands over a gaping belly wound. Blood oozed through his fingers. Genya breathed in that intoxicating scent. A hunger burned in her, stronger than desire. *Need.*

She did not try to hold herself back. She could not, even if she wanted to. Teeth bared, she fell upon the wounded ghoul. Terrified, he cried out until she bit into his neck, silencing him. He jerked once, choking a sound. Genya drank until she drained him. Then she began to laugh and laugh.

VAL ARQUES

Val swung his legs to the ground and stood shakily. The open door beckoned. He wandered out. The dim, cool chamber was filled with potted plants, couches, and tables. Sunlight flickered through a hole in the ceiling. Scents of beeswax and lavender stirred.

Clotild appeared with a disarming smile. She swept a hand at a table. "Sisilia explained about your agreement. There's food. Then amble about at will. If you want company, I'll stay. If you don't, I'll leave you."

Val didn't know what he wanted. Still half in a daze, he drifted to the table and picked up an apple. When he bit into it, it was sweet.

"What day is it?" He tried to pull his scrambled wits together. "Is it day or night?"

Clotild plonked into a low chair beside him. "It is late afternoon. We've cared for you for two weeks."

Weeks? Bewildered, he shook his head. Surely, he'd lost barely a day or two in dreams.

Clotild poured wine into a goblet then pressed it into his hands. "You must be thirsty."

Val took the goblet and sipped as he resumed wandering,

enjoying the luxurious sensation of moving freely. Slowly, tension unwound from his shoulders. Yet a haze clung to him, as though his conversation with Sisilia had been unreal. "What's wrong with me? My mind is dull."

"Merely the potion's lingering effects. You'll feel better soon."

He fell to pacing. "I thought I heard Devyn sobbing. She was here. Blaire, too." Other faint memories niggled. The comfort of warm water and gentle hands in the temple baths. The touch of velvet skin beneath his fingers. Devyn's hands running through his hair. The taste of her lips. Blaire undressing him, whispering, "I'm sorry."

Val groaned. How much of that was true? How much had he imagined or dreamt? Desperately, he gulped wine.

"I hope you recognise how fortunate you are," Clotild said. "Sisilia is very pleased with herself."

Val rocked to a halt. "That she agreed surprises you?"

"Sisilia never stoops to bargains, no matter how pitiful the pleas. But then, your surrender must suit her. Do you understand what she wants from you? Of course, she's taken your blood a few times already."

Val touched a cut on his arm. He'd half thought he inflicted these gashes himself when he struggled. "This is her?"

Clotild nodded.

"But..." He fought to understand. "My blood wasn't clean when she did this."

"No." Clotild leaned forward, conspiratorially. "But she used only a few drops for minor castings. Tomorrow, she intends a dangerous spell. Something important."

"Val!"

He turned. Devyn clattered down the stairs, her moist eyes round. She flew at once to him. "Oh, Val. You're awake. Thank the goddess."

Val's arms closed about her. Her warm, lovely body pressed against him. Desire roared like a fire through his veins. He glanced suspiciously at the wine glass. Then he glared at Clotild. "What did you give me?"

She didn't answer, but her face flushed guiltily.

With a cry of annoyance, he hurled the goblet away. It smashed on the wall, the dregs of wine dribbling down stone. Even now, they manipulated him.

"Sisilia says it is her gift to you. It enhances pleasure. You don't like it?"

Val didn't like to surrender his will, even to something that enflamed his senses.

Devyn clutched his arm. "Please don't fight it. Black Velvet hurts if you fight it. I don't want to see you hurt."

He took her face in his hands. The rancour blew out of him. "Devyn. Sweet Devyn."

She trembled. "It was so awful seeing you like that, in that room. You didn't know me, not really. But I had to... I had to."

He kissed her lips. "I don't blame you. You serve the goddess."

"We both do, Val."

No, he wanted to shout. The goddess wanted too much from him; obedience, yes, but she sought to conquer his will. A stab of resentment speared him. In the name of their goddess, the Quisnaf took his blood and his strength, twisted his desire for their purposes, and scrambled his mind with potions.

Clotild rose. "Your room is that way." She pointed. "Devyn is right. Do not fight. Take your pleasure with one another. It is a gift from the goddess."

When Devyn left him, Val did not bother to rise. He dangled his foot over the bed, turning his ankle this way and that, the brush of the sheet against his bare skin pleasant. Val huffed. *Curse Black Velvet. Curse the Quisnaf and their confounded potions.*

Though he and Devyn had satisfied the goddess twice, he was

still half aroused. Desperately, he needed sensation, either fingers smoothing his hair or the taste of wine upon his tongue. Anything.

The candle guttered and died. He shifted on the bed, wondering what Sisilia intended tomorrow. More than once, she'd taken his blood already, so what was different this time?

Unless she intended to take a lot…

A shudder ripped along his spine. The darkness closed in about him. Val lay back, wondering at the sunlight streaming through the roof in the outside room. Yet they had brought him deep within the earth to this chamber. *The ground above must be lower at this point. A valley perhaps.*

At last, despite his niggling anxiety, he slept. Rohane waited in his dreams. She stood in a sandy pit like the one where he'd fought Jenna-Dairine. Moonlight glinted off her blood-stained blade. Slowly, she turned to face him.

"This is your fault," she said and thrust at him.

The sword pierced his chest, between his ribs. Val dropped to his knees, bleeding. He felt no pain, only shock.

"I despise you." Rohane put the sword's edge to his neck.

"No!" Val screamed. But no sound came out.

Her sword whipped back… and swung.

GENYA

She sought Cadan in the keep. A guard pointed above, and she trod up a stairwell to the top chamber, its roof unfinished.

Cadan did not hear her. Genya paused in the doorway and watched him prowl. He moved with the grace of a cat, but there was nothing feline in that beautifully proportioned swordsman's body. Beneath a tight tunic, muscles bulged in his back and shoulders, accented by tension.

His expression was unguarded. When he tilted his head to the sky, she recognised the remote look of someone caught by the past. Strange to think he had lived his life so many centuries ago. Cadan didn't talk about that other time. She wondered why.

"There's blood on your chin." He had turned to stare at her.

"I must have brushed against something."

Cadan edged closer and grasped her jaw, his touch cool and pleasurable. "You're not hurt?"

She shook her head. "What are you doing by yourself up here?"

He dropped his hand and wandered back to a gaping hole in the wall. Perhaps the ghouls had intended a window there. "It reminds me of somewhere. Of someone…" He shrugged. "Never mind. I suppose I thought I'd have a good look before we bring this cursed keep down."

"It reminds me of somewhere. Of someone..." A lover? She slid a gaze down his elegant body, again imagining pressing her lips to his damp skin and trailing her fingers over his hips and thighs.

Genya screwed her eyes shut. What was wrong with her? Every time in his presence now, all she could think about was clawing his clothes off. From that first spell, that first delicious taste of Seithin blood magic, her need for sensation had heightened, her appetites enflamed. For blood, sex... and violence.

She began to laugh.

"Genya, what's wrong?"

"Nothing's wrong." She laughed harder.

"That curse. Did it hurt you? Are you all right?"

At his concern, so genuine, guilt warmed her face. Her thoughts about Cadan were far from pure. Yet she professed to love Dannon. She *did* love Dannon. She ached for him, worried about him. But Dannon was... not there. And desire burned through her blood.

"Nothing's wrong." She leaned in and touched Cadan's cheek. Surely his skin heated beneath her fingers. Cadan did not recoil, but a wary frown altered his face.

"I just need—" She pressed her lips to his, nibbling. His mouth tasted impossibly good.

He did not kiss her back. Very gently, he pushed her away. "Genya, I can't do that to Dannon. Not if there's a chance he's alive."

"He's not here." She shoved him against the wall. With his palms flat against its stone, he watched her warily. Genya moved very close. With one hand, she grabbed his wrist and pinned it above his head.

"Someone will see us." He was breathing fast.

"I'll hear them." With hungry desperation, she began to plunder his mouth. The touch of his skin, his scent, the taste of his lips spun her head.

Cadan wrenched his hands free and tried to force her off. "We can't do this."

"I'll stop if that's what you want." Groaning in pleasure, she licked his neck, her body pressing and rubbing against his. Fiercely, she kissed him, her tongue lashing rather than exploring his mouth. "Is that what you want?"

He struggled briefly then moaned, his arousal thickening. She longed to slide her hand between his thighs, along the length of him. Instead, she slipped her fingers between laces onto his breast, her caress feather-soft. Beneath her lips, his resistant mouth softened. He moved up and down against her, stoking his erection, his heartbeat so fast, it fluttered.

When his hands fell about her waist, holding her against him, she teasingly slipped from his grasp, dropped to her knees, and began to unlace her shirt with trembling fingers.

Cadan sank beside her, taking over the task. He tossed away her shirt. A gentle breeze lifted gooseflesh on Genya's naked skin. His trailing fingers drew a rush of lust. Bending his head, he teased her nipples with his teeth. With a shudder of pleasure, Genya's head shot back.

His wet lips kissed her breasts and belly, his caress gliding like silk across damp skin.

Hot desire burned through her. Moaning, she raked his clothes with her nails, ripping his tunic from his bared torso, her hands roaming over his muscular chest. "I want you naked."

In answer, he gripped her hips and lowered her onto her back, her head upon the remnants of his garments. As he crouched over her, Genya wriggled out of her breeches and spread her legs, enjoying the delicious sensation of lying unclothed for his eyes.

With deliberate slowness, Cadan's gaze wandered down her body then returned to her face. When their eyes locked, the hungry desire in his fired up her hunger and lust. Growling, she pulled his head down until she could seize his mouth again. Own it. His pulse ran wild, but no wilder than hers as she ran her palms greedily down his chest to his hips and onto his groin.

"What do you want me to do?" she whispered.

"That," he moaned.

His belt unbuckled easily enough. Genya slipped her fingers into his pants. He was well erect, but beneath her touch, he grew harder and harder yet. She flickered her tongue in his mouth, her thrusts matching the rhythm of her hand.

Her every sense narrowed to that delicious sensation of wet lips on moist skin, his searching tongue, nipping teeth, that wonderful masculine scent, and Cadan's velvet touch roaming all over her naked body.

She ached to take him deep within, to fall on him completely with beast-like passion. Instead, she edged his pants down over his hips and stoked his arousal with long, twisting strokes. Cadan stifled a groan. His breath was hot in her mouth, his flesh warm.

"More," Genya begged between kisses. "More of you."

Hands on her hips, he entered her, shallow at first, then deeper and deeper, his body pressed against hers. Genya's back bruised against the hard floor, but she didn't care. The ecstasy of his driving thrusts, of his weight on her, pulsed sensation after sensation through her. Colours burst in her head. Her skin grew fevered.

Genya threw her head back and screamed in ecstasy. There came a moment of release, then her flesh clamoured for more, her arousal building. When she cried out a second time, Cadan gasped, his body trembling then jerking.

His dark eyes sought hers. She could not read his expression. Then he laughed and collapsed against her, still breathing hard.

Genya lay still beneath him, breathing in the scent of passion and cooling sweat. His head rested on her shoulder. His thick black hair was soft against her cheek, his throat stretched and bared. A blue vein throbbed in his neck. She licked it. He was still deep in her, their bodies joined. His heart, his pounding blood, was part of her. Her hunger, part of him.

Genya remembered the flavour of the ghoul's blood. Cadan's blood would be the flavour of lust, deliciously wonderful. She would only take a little, just a mouthful. Her tongue slid over his bare flesh to the vein, then she nipped at him with her teeth. Grunting, he shifted slightly.

She sank her teeth in. She didn't want to hurt him, but oh, how she needed to taste him. Warm blood wet her lips, metallic on her tongue, the texture delicious in her mouth. She wanted more.

"Ouch," Cadan turned his head sharply. "Good gods, Genya. Did you bite me?"

Sighing deeply, she licked her lip, savouring his blood. "You taste like nothing else. Of pure pleasure."

He stiffened. Then he pushed himself away from her and rose. "You want to drink me?" Incredulous, he stared down at her. "Just how much ghoul is there in you?"

"I just wanted more of you in me. All of you."

A flash of disgust shaded his long-lashed eyes. Then his expression shuttered. Without looking at her, he yanked up his pants and groped for his ripped tunic. Every movement was precise, deliberately controlled, as though he gave himself time to think.

Genya sat up and watched him. "Don't pretend you didn't enjoy this."

For a moment, she thought he would ignore her. Then he dragged his fingers through his tousled hair. "I'm not pretending anything. I try to be very self-observant, to never lie to myself."

"Cadan…"

"No, Genya. Just leave it be. I don't know what to make of this. Or you." He found his cloak and flung it about his shoulders, clasping it tightly. "Don't follow me at once. There are enough whispers behind my back as it is."

He didn't look at her as he stalked out.

Alone, Genya drew her knees to her chest. A trickle of air caressed her back. Beneath the odour of death and blood, the perfume of jasmine and of river reeds prickled her nostrils. Sitting naked in a tower, a warm shiver down her body, she was wild and free.

She wondered how she could make this feeling last and last. She wondered how she could forever bask in the glow of magic. Safe from hurt, from pain, from others' disappointment and judgement. But mostly, she wondered when she could use the Seithin curse again.

⁂

The journey back was hardly silent. Men stirred up after fighting and victory joked or exchanged stories. Their gestures were loud, their voices louder. Except for Cadan. He said very little. And nothing to her.

Genya laughed off his ill ease. What intrigued her more was her own reaction to him. He was beautiful, but when she stared at his body, she found him pleasing without it arousing any real emotion in her. Perhaps this was what it was like to view lovers as nothing more than conquests, to chase a desired lover then lose interest once the target surrendered. She shrugged, not really caring.

Across the gorge, a rider met them. It was one of Alecc's courtiers, a young, brown-haired Cahirean with a downy beard on his jaw. A number of Cahireans had been drawn to their cause, resentful of Gendrick's reign over their country.

The courtier spoke quietly with Cadan then rode ahead to return to Vraymorg. Genya pushed her horse forward. "What's that about?"

Cadan didn't look at her. "Messenger arrived at the castle. Alecc wanted to warn us. A woman from Quisnaf."

A tingle of excitement coursed down Genya's back. *Quisnaf.* With a message from her guardian? Did he beg her forgiveness for treating her poorly?

"Maybe a message from Val. Or about Val."

Cadan frowned. "Don't count on it."

Genya pursed her lips, disappointed he would try to deflate her hope.

He must have seen her look of dejection, for he sighed. "Maybe. It's just I don't trust the Quisnaf. I'll never understand what happened between Roaran and Val to make Val surrender himself like that. He must have known what would happen to him."

That festering sore of bitterness itched. Words poured out of her, words she instantly regretted. "He wanted to get away from me. He couldn't even look at me. I disappointed him. Because of Roaran. Because of the Brotherhood. I think… I think he hates me, and I can't bear it. *I can't bear it.*"

Cadan's hands tightened on the reins. He slid her a sideways pitying glance then stared straight ahead. "I'm sorry."

Genya's anger unfurled. At herself for her words. At him for hearing them. She had revealed pain too close to her heart, and she didn't want him to see it. To see her wounds.

"I don't want your sympathy," she snapped.

His shoulders stiffened. In a cold voice, he said, "What *do* you want from me?"

"Nothing, Cadan." She wanted to hurt him, to prick him. "You're very beautiful, and I desired your body. But now I've had you, and you don't interest me anymore. So there's nothing I want from you."

Cadan made no reply. But for all his control, the muscles tensed in his jaw.

She did not feel sorry that she'd wounded him. In fact, Genya felt nothing at all.

ROHANE

In the antechamber to the great hall at Vraymorg, Rohane impatiently tapped her fingers on her belt. She didn't want to be here. The castle was a bleak place of stone and shadows, alien and unwelcoming. The caverns of Quisnaf might have been rock walled, but torches always blazed with warm light. Here, a single lamp glowed, and the gloom defeated even that.

She shrank into her cloak. The autumn cold nipped at the back of her neck. It misted off the cold floor, snapping at her legs through her leather boots and pants. Rohane stamped her feet. How did anyone survive in these cursed Mountains when winter set in? How had Val Arques survived in this terrible place, year after year? Century after century? No, she would not think of him—even here, in what had been his home.

The doors to the hall swung open. An elegant warrior with very dark hair and eyes appeared. He beckoned. "The king will see you now."

Rohane followed him into the hall, half distracted by the graceful way the warrior moved, head held high. His every step was confident and balanced. A long cloak flowed at his back, and he wore a sword at his waist.

The hall was practical rather than ornate. A huge fire roared in a hearth, and a few tapestries and carpets clung to stone walls to fend off the cold. Even so, it was like the rest of this miserable castle. Every wall, every tower was gaunt and dismal. Every cold, silent room of stone felt repellent.

Their boots scraped over the slabbed floor. The rhythm of Rohane's steps matched her heartbeats, a little too fast. She reined in her anxiety. Baiting a trap was just her duty. No worse than any other assignment.

Ahead, a loose group of warriors and robed figures gathered about a young man seated upon a chair padded with red velvet. Among their number was a tall, slender-muscled girl. She might have been Quisnaf with her leather pants, calf-length boots, and pale hair. Her cloak was fur lined, and a long-bladed sword dangled at her hip from a weapons belt that also contained two jewel-hilted knives.

The girl turned to stare. As her eyes flickered over Rohane, they glittered with suspicion but also interest. Though the girl held herself very still, Rohane sensed a restless energy, an underlying menace that was tightly controlled but ready to be unleashed.

Her heart drummed. Surely this must be Genya Caelan. *Roaran's daughter.* Rohane must find an opportunity to speak with her alone... then prepare her trap. A multilayered trap. The first veneer was obvious so that Genya recognised the deception and did not look deeper.

Though she was Roaran's child... That meant she was likely clever. Dangerous.

Instinctively, Rohane grasped an amulet about her neck, a gift from the Quisnaf seers to protect her against whatever magic this rather striking young woman might possess.

Other heads turned as the dark-headed warrior led her forward towards the young man seated among his warriors and courtiers. At the sight of him, Rohane shuddered. He looked too like Val to be anyone other than Alecc Caelan.

Her escort bowed. "Your Grace. The Quisnaf messenger."

The young man leaned forward. A keen stare raked her.

Rohane dipped her head. "Your Grace."

A ripple of amusement tore through the young king. "Pay up, Cadan."

Rohane's escort grinned. "How'd you know she wouldn't kneel, Alecc?" He drew a small bag from within his cloak and jiggled it on his palm for a moment before tossing it to the dark-haired young man.

At their banter, Rohane lifted an eyebrow. Not quite the reception she'd expected. She fixed a hard stare upon the man who must be Alecc Caelan. Shivering, she drew her cloak tighter.

Alecc chuckled. "The sight of me doesn't usually draw a shudder from young women."

An older man patted his shoulder. "Not when you're clothed anyway."

"I… Your Grace," Rohane blurted. "Forgive me, but you're so like your father."

The young man stiffened. His companions stilled also. Genya's stare smouldered.

"You've seen my father?" Alecc asked slowly, as if controlling his emotion. A good ruler revealed little. Rohane had learnt that from watching not only her father but also the ice-cool Blaire.

"I have."

Alecc passed his tongue over his lips. "He is… well?"

Rohane chose her words carefully. "He is in good health."

"And unharmed?" the girl snapped. Her voice was low and compelling. A sorceress's voice.

Again, Rohane touched her amulet. "He is safe."

Alecc waved a hand at the girl. "May I present Genya Caelan."

Another shiver tore through Rohane. Roaran's daughter, indeed. She seized a breath. "I am Rohane, daughter of Samantha, representative of the council of Quisnaf."

"I remember you." The man at Alecc's side stabbed a finger. "You're the one who came for him. They called you 'captain.'"

Rohane quickly searched her memory for what she remembered of that night. Too much. Savaged limbs. Blood. The stench of death. Fear in Persia's eyes. Willingly, Rohane had lost control that night so that she might reap ghouls, that her sword might harvest death and more death. At what cost? What did it cost her to surrender to the darkness within?

Then later, at the castle, the girl she now knew to be Genya Caelan had run after Val, begging him not to go, her cheeks wet.

"It *was* you." Genya turned the words into an accusation. "You look different without steel covering your head and your hair loose, but Nicky's right."

Rohane braced. "My task was to retrieve a man promised to the Quisnaf by the seer."

"And what is your task now?" Nicky demanded.

Rohane returned his stare calmly. "I am an ambassador of goodwill, if you like. The Quisnaf council sends their best wishes to His Grace Alecc Caelan. I am to convey the Regenta's personal regard. Blaire offers friendship."

"Does her friendship include her support?" Nicky growled.

Rohane gave a meaningless shrug.

A woman with short-cropped black hair entered the hall in time to hear Nicky's last remark. "I think that says it all, Alecc," she said with a laugh. "The Quisnaf will see which way it goes before taking a side."

That laugh. Rohane squeezed her eyes shut as a fragment of memory returned. Once more, she was on deck, drinking as moonlight sparkled on waves, watching Val with a stranger. "That was you," she whirled on the newcomer. "He freed you. You swam away."

The woman raised an eyebrow. "Val told you?"

"I was on deck. I did not stop him—or you."

The stranger touched a hand to her brow. "I'm grateful. I hope Val didn't suffer for it."

Rohane shook her head. "I said nothing." No need to explain

the rest. Val had been forgiven that indiscretion, at least.

"What's this about, Ka… Kate?" Genya scowled at the woman.

Kate grinned. "Oh, the night I went after Val and found myself chained in the hold of a Quisnaf ship."

"They had no right." Nicky's face darkened.

"No harm done. My skull ached from a crack over the head, and I had a bit of a midnight swim."

"But they grabbed you, for no good reason."

"She crept into the Quisnaf camp," Rohane muttered, stung to anger. "What would you do with a stranger you found sneaking about this castle?"

"Likely throw them into a dark cell." Nicky's gaze swept over her, assessing. Given his curling dark hair and dark eyes, he was another Isles man. And from his poise and watchfulness, he, too, was a warrior. Rohane nodded inwardly, approving of who this young would-be king chose to trust.

"So you are a retrieval captain," Nicky said. "I think that's the term I heard. And an ambassador of goodwill?"

"My role is only to serve Quisnaf and the Quisnaf council. Blaire bid me bring her good wishes. She said Roaran Caelan was always a friend to Quisnaf. She hopes our good relations continue."

"I hope so, too." Alecc nodded slowly. "May I ask you a question, Rohane of Quisnaf?"

"Of course, Your Grace."

His dark eyes dwelt on her face. "Rohane is an unusual name. Are you by chance the Rohane who is daughter to the king of Veniva?"

Rohane's cheeks heated. "I am, Your Grace," she muttered reluctantly. She disliked taking advantage of her position. Even in Quisnaf, she pretended she was Rohane, Captain, and not Rohane, daughter of the councillor. Princess of Veniva.

"And daughter of a Quisnaf councillor?"

"You found me out, Your Grace."

Several dark Telorian eyes swung her way, reassessing. Half

Venivan. What did that make her? Half suspicious?

"That's why she didn't bend the knee," Cadan said. "You knew who she was, Alecc, and knew she wouldn't." He held out his hand. "I think I'll have my money back."

Rohane looked from one to the other. "You had a wager? About me?"

Alecc rose and extended an arm. His smile was warm. "Will you walk with me, Rohane? The wind has died, I think. The gardens are spectacular in autumn."

VAL ARQUES

T ormented by dreams, Val spent a restless night. At last he gave up on sleep, lit a fresh candle, and dressed. But the long stretch of day, or what he guessed was day, passed too slowly. He paced, drank from the water jug, lay on the bed thinking, and paced again.

No one came. No one brought food or a word of comfort. Nothing. The candle burned down. When the door at last glided open, he was on edge, impatient for Sisilia's dreadful ceremony to be done with.

Clotild stepped into the room. She gripped a lamp in a tarnished holder tightly as though to stop her hands shaking. "It's time." Upon the bed, she placed a pale folded garment. "Sisilia asks that you wear this."

She turned her back as he undressed and threw on the long smock. When she looked again, she nodded. "Come."

Barefoot, a shiver in him, Val followed her outside into the empty passage. "No guards?"

"I would guess it is a test of sorts," Clotild said. "To see what you do."

"Hmm." He would do nothing but keep his bargain with Sisilia.

Clotild did not take the stairs but led him along another

corridor leading further underground. The air was heavy and smelt vaguely of smoke. Sparse torches glowed from wall brackets, their flames a flicker in the darkness. His bare feet made no sound, but Clotild's heels scuffed stone. Their *tap, tap, tap* beat in his head with foreboding.

"Where are we going?"

"To the temple."

The passage twisted higher. Yet the darkness deepened, as if Val's gloomy thoughts cast a pall on his surroundings. At the top of a stairwell, an ornately carved door barred their way. Patterned sigils carved into the wood were protection, he guessed, against spells.

Clotild knocked.

At once, a woman opened the door. Except for her eyes and lips, a golden mask hid her face. Her feet were bare. Her pale hair flowed onto her priestess's robes. "This is him?"

Clotild nodded.

"Did he fast?"

"I gave him nothing to eat."

The priestess beckoned Val forward. Clotild turned to him. "I can go no further. For your sake, remember your bargain with the sorceress. Sisilia will not be crossed."

Val hunched his shoulders as he trudged past. "I'll remember."

The rock-walled chamber had to be below the altar, for two enormous carved sandals belonging to the statue of Cyrah from the temple nave above dominated the space.

Uneasily, he peered about. Forbidding shadows darkened the stark room. Despite blazing candles and a fire roaring in a hearth, it was cheerless. In the close, expectant atmosphere, a pottage of fragrances simmered. Burnt wood, spices, and lilac perfume all filled his nostrils.

Sisilia stood facing the base of the statue in the centre of a circle marked by deep grooves cut into the tiled floor. A robed, masked priestess knelt at Sisilia's feet. Other women, also wearing long

THE SWORD AND ITS WOMAN

gowns, lifted their heads to stare at him. Each wore a different mask: a cat's head, an owl, the face of a hawk, and other mythical beasts Val could not name.

His steps faltered. Despite his resolve to appear unafraid, dread cut through him. What happened now? How would she take his blood?

Sisilia turned. Her auburn hair fell lank about a hollow-eyed face. She wore her customary gown, but it was ripped and stained. Her feet, too, were bare. "Welcome. You are here of your own will?"

"I am."

She nodded and brushed her hand against chains dangling from the roof. "For that reason, I will not string you up and drain you like a beast. Prepare him."

Masked priestesses took his arms, their touch gentle but insistent. As they tore off his long garment and pressed him to his knees inside the circle, Val did not resist. The heat from the fire struck his naked body like a furnace. Sweat broke out on his chest. With growing alarm, he watched a priestess wearing a snake mask remove an iron pot from the flames. Whatever bubbled inside stank like rotten vegetables.

The other priestesses surrounded him and Sisilia. They dropped their robes and stood naked. The sorceress slid off her gown. Her body was firm like a young woman's but too slender, almost bony. Water droplets gleamed on her back.

The women began a low chant. The snake-masked woman tipped some of the contents of the pot into a goblet. She waited a moment until it cooled then brought it to Sisilia. The sorceress sipped.

The incantation grew louder and wilder. Sisilia passed the cup to Val. He took a mouthful. It was so foul, he nearly spat it out. Gagging, he managed to swallow the liquid.

"Bring me the knife."

A priestess sprang up. Reverently, she carried a gilt-handled blade to Sisilia. The sorceress held the knife close to her face. Firelight gleamed off its metal.

"Let us begin. Take him." She waved a hand.

Again, priestesses came for Val, urging him to stand then positioning him with his back to one of the statue's legs. One thrust his wrists into manacles struck waist high in the stone.

Val tugged at the fetters, angry he was restrained even after bargaining with Sisilia. Yet he had to see this through, or the sorceress would again keep him drugged.

Sisilia fisted the knife and walked to him. Her eyes were strange—not dazed like a sleepwalker's but bright and dead like a jewel. She mouthed words beneath her breath. At her back, the priestesses chanted. Their excited chorus rose in pitch.

The knife lifted. Sisilia slashed. Val winced as the blade gashed his wrist. The wound burned. Blood streamed down his inner arm to the floor and trickled into grooves surrounding the statue. Mesmerised, he watched it flow as if pulled by an invisible force.

Coldly, Sisilia gashed his other wrist. More blood flowed into another groove. The priestesses shrieked. Light flickered eerily on their inhuman masks. Coldness burned through Val's skin to his spine.

"My blood will clot."

Sisilia shook her head. Her empty eyes passed over him but did not really see him. She touched his gashed wrists, her lips moving in a soundless incantation. Heat rushed through his body. It roared from his chest into his shoulders and up his arms towards his hands. His heart drummed, pulsing blood to his wrists until it spurted from the gashes, torrenting down his arms and into the grooves. The current surged along its stone river in two directions, merging together in a red stream around the statue's legs.

Sisilia dipped fingers in his wounds. She painted a symbol on her brow then whirled and returned to the circle's centre. The priestesses trembled with awe. Sisilia spread her arms and shouted strange, powerful words that might have been Seithin. Her spell rang out above the priestesses' chaotic cries, her commands like fire.

Val could not look away. He knew no pain, only a torpor spreading through his body. His legs were heavy, his arms limp, his lips cracked and dry. No sound came from his tight throat. But all the while, blood poured from his rent wrists, flooding the grooves circling the statue. Within seconds, he sagged, weak and dizzy.

The chanting reached fever pitch. Sisilia's face was terrible. Her eyes smouldered with flames leaping within. For an instant, he glimpsed something shift beneath her cheekbones, as though another woman's face thrust through.

Cyrah. Val shuddered. But he could not hold on to the thought and what it meant. All warmth had left his body. Coldness then death embraced him.

⁂

His heavy limbs pinned him to a bed. Snatches of voices reached him, with fragments of words.

"It's been two days," Blaire said.

"He's sleeping, but he is alive," Clotild answered.

"Keep this close. The fewer who know who he is, what he is…"

Sweat broke out on Val's brow. More whispers came to him as though from far away. Shapes flitted. Darkness replaced light.

"You must hang on, Val." Jenna-Dairine's voice pierced the veil where others had failed. "I have a plan. When you're well, I'll cloak you."

He groaned and tried to speak, but no words came out.

"It will free you from Sisilia, at least," Jenna-Dairine said. "I will protect you. It will be better, you'll see. You'll be safe."

Val shifted on the bed. Maybe Jenna-Dairine wasn't really there. She was like Rohane, a figment snatched from his yearning, offering false hope. Because Rohane was gone. Because Rohane despised him.

No, Jenna-Dairine wasn't there. Val gave up the struggle and slept.

⁓❦⁓

He woke upon his bed in the stark chamber in the blood keepers' caverns. When he groaned, figures turned his way. Cool hands touched his brow and cheek then moved over his body.

"Val." Blaire leaned over him. "You're back with us."

"How do you feel?" Elena wore her healer's blue gown.

"Well enough," he croaked. "Hungry."

Blaire laughed in relief. "Can you sit up?"

Val rose weakly onto his elbows, staring down at the shift covering his nakedness. A memory nagged at him—his life being drained away in that awful chamber beneath the temple. "I died," he muttered. "She took all my blood. Every ounce."

"All that matters is that you're well," Blaire said.

Val looked past her at the open door. *Rohane.* Still, she did not come. Still, she cursed him.

"I'd not have believed it if I hadn't seen it," Elena muttered. "To be dead one moment, then alive again. So strange."

"And a close secret," Blaire warned.

The healer nodded. "Do you need me, Regenta? I would return to the infirmary. An autumn fever has a number of sisters coughing and ill."

Blaire waved a hand. "Go. But remember—not a word."

Elena bowed and departed. When the door closed, Blaire sat on the bed. "Two days." She teasingly slapped his shoulder. "Elena was about to pronounce you really dead. Couldn't you return to life a little quicker?"

Val tried to smile. He couldn't stop shaking.

"Your skin is icy." Blaire frowned with concern.

"It's always like that. It passes."

She nodded then gestured to a table. "There's food. Then stay warm. Clotild left a bell beside the bed. Ring if you need anything." She rose. "We'll talk tomorrow."

Val swung his shaky legs to the floor. "I had a strange dream. Jenna-Dairine was here."

A muscle moved in Blaire's jaw. She said nothing.

"She told me to hang on, not surrender to despair. Said she had a plan. Was it a dream? Do you mean to leave me here? Forever? I swear I did not do what I'm accused of."

Blaire's gaze drifted to the shadows. "I need to talk to Jenna-Dairine. I need her on my side. We must be reconciled. For the sake of Quisnaf."

Her eyes shifted back to his face. For a moment, she frowned at him, as if considering. Then she hastened to the door and put an ear to it before returning to his side. "Just be patient a little longer. There's danger."

He frowned. "For me?"

"For Quisnaf," Blaire said.

⁘

A young priestess with bright-blue eyes hovered in the doorway, wringing her hands nervously. "You're to bathe." Her voice quavered. "Please come with me."

"Gladly."

As he took a step closer, she shrank back. "You won't give me trouble, will you? I mean, you're so… big. They didn't say you were so big."

"No, lass. No trouble." He glanced at an armed woman outside. "The guards will keep me in line."

She passed her tongue over her lips. "I… suppose."

The guard fell in behind him, her gaze dispassionate. Clearly to join the Decan Watch, a woman must learn to wipe all expression from her face. They were nearly always mute. Tall, bulky, and emotionless.

By now, Val knew the route to the temple baths. In one tunnel, they passed a boy whistling as he replaced torches on the stairs. Val didn't know the tune, but it cheered him. It was so ordinary. Ordinary was so different to his life since he had surrendered to Rohane.

A figure appeared in the passage ahead, a hood covering her head. Without a word, she placed a candle on the floor and scattered silver dust in the flames. Smoke billowed. It rolled through the tunnel towards Val and his escort.

The guard and priestess coughed violently. Val covered his mouth and nose with his sleeve. But already, the sickly-sweet smoke was in his nose, in his throat, thick and choking.

The women collapsed to their knees then to the ground. Drowsiness struck Val. He staggered, a hand braced to the wall.

The figure in the tunnel ran towards him. Through dissipating smoke, he recognised Persia's lieutenant, Marlisa. "Drink this." She passed him a small vial. When he hesitated, she said quickly, "I'm here as a friend."

Coughing, spluttering, Val searched her earnest face then did as she bid. The liquid within the vial tasted like honey.

"Come quickly."

The cloying scent still filled his nostrils. He shook his head to clear it. "To where?"

"Don't waste time arguing. Blaire has a plan."

"I don't feel right."

"It's the smoke. What you drank will keep you awake."

She gestured for him to follow her. Thoughts slow and disjointed, Val lurched past the sleeping guard and priestess lying where they had fallen.

"Quickly." Marlisa took him back towards the blood keepers' caverns, but instead of descending the stairs, she snatched a torch from the wall and turned the other way into darkness.

Val stumbled after her. "What's down here?"

"A way out."

"Are you taking me to Blaire?"

For a second, she hesitated. "Yes, to Blaire. But we have no time to waste."

Footsteps echoed ahead. Puzzled, Val stopped. Marlisa waved the torch. Her raised shoulders relaxed. "Thank goodness," she said to someone unseen. "Where were you? He's asking questions. I think he's going to give me trouble."

The words took a moment to sink in. *Trouble?*

A man stepped from the darkness. Val didn't know him. With a prickling of alarm, he whirled to run. Something heavy crashed down upon his head. Then came blackness.

GENYA

Genya dug her elbows into the windowsill, watching Alecc and the Quisnaf captain stroll through willowy trees, their rusted leaves shed in piles in the castle grounds. Each evening since Rohane's arrival, they had walked together, talking quietly. Genya always sat at her window, staring after them and wondering what they discussed.

"I remember her," she muttered in a tight voice to Kaell. "She looked stern and frightening beneath that helm of steel."

"I didn't pay particular attention to her," Kaell said. "Too much else was happening that night."

"Without the helm, with her hair loose like that, she looks younger somehow," Genya mused. "Vulnerable."

"She is very sad."

Genya threw him a doubtful look. "What? What makes you say that?"

Eyes fixed upon the couple in the garden, Kaell smiled. "Her manner. As if her heart is breaking, as if she's barely hold on to herself. She aches with sorrow, I think."

Genya straightened. "I suppose that makes the brooding, sorrowful Rohane fascinating."

"Jealous?" Kaell teased.

"No," Genya protested. "Why should I be jealous of some Quisnaf woman?" She dropped her hands to her hips and regarded him with a scowl. "Why are you here, anyhow? You're always following me around."

"Not true. I've been gone for days. I'm surprised you didn't miss me." His eyes lingered on her face hopefully.

"Maybe a bit," Genya lied. "I'm grateful you've kept searching for Dannon. Was there any word. A whisper even?"

"Nothing." Kaell's expression darkened. "It's as if Dannon vanished into the mist."

A silence fell between them. Genya's stomach twisted. She refused to believe Dannon was dead. But no one in the Mountains had seen him since the battle. Even in Tide's End, she had heard nothing about any Varee prisoners.

"What do you think they're talking about?" Kaell mused.

Genya leaned forward on her elbows. Cold air scented of wood smoke from numerous cook fires in the ward iced her cheeks. Alecc and Rohane strolled arm-in-arm, heads bent close. Dull light faded towards a rosy dusk.

"He'll ask her about Val, won't he? She was evasive before."

"She said Val was well."

"She paused. Just for half a heartbeat. There was a shadow in her eyes."

Kaell shook his head. "You imagined it."

"No, there was something. Every time his name was mentioned."

"Maybe Val broke her heart."

Genya frowned, surprised he had made that connection. Though, just how well did this Rohane know her guardian? From the whispers, Genya knew Val's bed in Quisnaf would not be empty. Oh, Goddess, there would be children. More rivals for his affection.

No, she refused to care about him. Caring left her vulnerable. She had cared about Dannon, and that had left her heart in tatters.

She had cared about Val, about what he thought of her. It had weakened her. She could see that now. For a moment, a shiver of longing ran through her body, a desire for the release, the freedom, and the elation of blood magic. For its protection against pain.

"Genya, if you want to know how he fares, maybe you should..." Kaell winced. "Maybe a spell..."

Genya pressed her hands into the stone sill. "I can't trace Val. I've tried. And Quisnaf seems hidden behind some veil of magic." She grunted in irritation. "Even blood magic is useless."

Kaell turned slightly to look at her. "About blood magic—"

"What about it?"

"Be careful who you talk to about practising Seithin spells. Everyone in these Mountains fears you already."

"What do I care? Is it my goal to be liked?" She no longer cared what anyone thought of her. She cared only about magic, the exhilaration, and the euphoria of power it gave her. With magic, she was invincible, untouchable.

"About blood magic—" He paused. "It changes you. So I've heard. Its use is dangerous."

Genya scoffed. Not to her. She was in control.

Kaell turned back to watch Alecc with the Quisnaf woman. "Maybe Alecc will propose. She's not exactly pretty, but there's something striking about her. And it would be a worthwhile match. The king of Veniva's one and only daughter. Gendrick would quake in his boots when he heard."

Genya scoffed. "Don't be silly. Alecc? Wed?"

"He should wed. And soon. Gendrick Caelan has no heir. If Alecc were to have a son—" He shrugged.

"Bah. He's a child."

"He's a king, Genya."

VAL ARQUES

A rattle woke him. At first, he glimpsed only the starry sky and a wedged moon, its shimmer upon a barren desert of red dirt and spindly shrubs. His head rested on wood. He was in a cart.

A man sat upon the cart's bench, his back to Val. A second man beside Val offered a lopsided smile as if sharing a joke. "Back with us?"

Val grunted. He tried to rise, only to realise rope bound his wrists.

"Let me help." The man pulled him into a sitting position. Dizzy, head aching, Val groaned.

"Here." His captor held a waterskin to his lips.

Val drank then lifted his strapped hands to wipe his mouth on a sleeve. "Where am I?"

The man grinned. "In a cart."

Val hissed a breath. "Where are you taking me?"

The grin widened. "Somewhere you get to by cart. Do you want more water?"

"I want answers. Who are you? Did you hit me?"

"Marlisa seemed to think you were about to run off. I couldn't have that. If it makes you feel better, I broke my back dragging you out of those caves."

"Dragged me out of those caves... to where?"

The man shook a finger. "Let's stop with the questions and sit back and enjoy the ride. Nice night for a ride."

Val huffed in irritation. With narrowed eyes, he assessed his companion, seeking clues to who he was. The stranger wore a coarse tunic, dark in the moonlight, over pants, with a cloak that might be worn by anyone in Telor, Wardour, or Veniva.

"Oh, a careful inspection that," the man said. "What do you see?"

"Nothing."

"No, really. Tell me what my appearance has revealed."

"Your clothes could be from anywhere. You speak Quisnaf with no obvious accent. So you are a puzzle. Even more puzzling is why you were with Marlisa."

"A puzzle. I like that."

Val grimaced and twisted his wrists to loosen the ropes.

"Don't bother." Amused, the man watched him. "Tied those ropes myself. Ask my friend here about any knots I tie." He turned to the cart driver. "What do you say, friend?"

The cart driver didn't look about. "His knots don't come loose."

"There, you see? So let's be calm and professional about this. You've been out cold for a while, so not long to go. In fact, we're getting close." He whipped a cloth out from beneath his cloak.

Val backed up against the side of the cart. "No, don't do that."

The man smiled lazily. Without warning, he struck Val in the face with a fist. The blow dazed him just long enough for the stranger to blindfold his eyes.

"You'll pay for that," Val muttered.

"Probably not. Now why don't you rest? Your head must ache."

Stubbornly, Val wanted to pretend the man was wrong. But his skull hurt. Groaning, he rested his head on his arms then fell into an uneasy slumber until the cart rocked to a halt. The two men lifted him out and set him roughly on his feet.

Wet grass brushed his shins. When the blindfold came off,

darkness pooled in a vast empty sky as though the moons had slinked away while he slept.

"Lovely night for a walk," the man from the cart said. "So how about you walk."

At a shove, Val lurched forward. He was in a garden, a place of willowy trees bowed by blossom, of garden beds where wild roses twisted. Passionflowers, their blue lost to the night, chaotically spilled onto paths.

A cylindrical shape loomed ahead, etched against the darkness. A tower. Dread cut through Val. What was this place? A prison? Who had him brought here and why? It wasn't Blaire—he'd guessed that at least.

A hand poked the small of his back. "Onward and upward, friend." The stranger gestured at the tower.

"I really don't like you," Val said. "And you're not funny."

"That's not what my friends say."

"Oh, you have friends?"

"Tonight, I'm *your* friend," the man said. "I'm going to take good care of you until you're nice and safe."

The door to the tower stood open. Stairs wound upwards. Torchlight flickered from cressets. A thick rope looped from brackets on the walls to prevent falls on the narrow, steep steps. The air was stale and thick.

The man from the cart nudged Val up. The driver trudged behind. From the look Val caught of him, he seemed a dour, sullen sort, the opposite of his companion.

The stairs ended at a landing. Val's steps faltered.

"Walk on, friend." The man began to whistle.

Val tried to pick the tune. That might tell him where he was. But it was a sailor's ditty, sung on any ship from the Isles to the Ice Sea.

Outside a metal door, the driver gripped Val's arm as though expecting him to bolt. His companion lifted a bar and poked keys at a lock. Hinges shrieked.

With that too-familiar grin, the man swept a hand. "If you don't mind, friend."

Val paused, assessing whether he could run. Body shivery with shock, his head aching, he barely had the strength to fight. Reluctantly, he stumbled inside. The man brushed past to light a lamp. He turned back and whipped out a knife. Instinctively, Val recoiled a step.

"Steady. If you promise to behave, I'll cut you free. Nod if you agree."

At Val's nod, the man freed his hands with one slash. Val brushed the rope off and rubbed his sore wrists.

The two men turned to leave.

"Wait," Val cried. "What is this all about? Where is this place? Why am I here?"

Neither looked back. Neither answered him. The door shut. A key turned. The bar fell into place.

Bewildered, Val listened to their footsteps fade. He had no clue who they were, where he was, or why he had been abducted.

GENYA

Oblivious to the wind that chilled her ears and nose, Genya stalked the gardens below the castle wall until she reached a covered walkway. Early moonlight pierced gloaming dusk, silvering the paved path. Ivy clung to carved columns of stone.

On any other night, she might have found it peaceful. But tonight, her thoughts tangled in a mix of fear and frustration. Trouble lay ahead. Despite her warnings, Alecc was resolved to go to Gendrick Caelan's aid to save Telor. The Wardorian fleet was about to set sail.

How she longed to use magic, to unfurl a spell at the garden. Magic banished all doubt, banished her unease. It wasn't that she *needed* it. No, she could stop her spellcasting whenever she liked. For now, though, blood magic was a release. A shield. Necessary.

"He's alive," a woman said quietly.

Genya whipped out her sword as she spun. "Who's there? Show yourself."

A scrape of sound, no more, came to her. A careful footstep. Hooded and cloaked, the Quisnaf woman appeared. Moonlight glinted on a knife at her hip. "I thought we should talk."

Genya glared. "In the garden, at night? You hid on the chance I wandered by?"

"Not at all. I followed you."

Genya blinked, shocked anyone could get close to her without her knowing. Her ghoul senses picked up every sound, even a distant solitary paw turning a dry leaf. Angry at her carelessness, she shoved her blade into its scabbard. "I'm impressed."

Rohane shrugged. "You were distracted. And in Quisnaf, I am deemed a huntress."

"And my guardian was your prey."

Rohane raised an eyebrow. "Guardian. Is that how you think of him?"

"Why did you say to me, 'He's alive'? I would hope Val is alive. If you've done something to him, then you will know my fury."

Rohane threw up a hand. "He is well. Val is valued by my people, Genya. They are responsible for him now, and they take that responsibility seriously."

"And are you responsible for him? You say his name like you know him, like you have a right to call him just Val. Anyone else would say Val Arques."

Rohane turned away. The night cast shadows upon her face.

"Kaell says your heart is broken," Genya blurted. "Is it Val? Is it something to do with him?"

"Kaell?" Rohane spun to face her. "Is this Kaell here?"

At her slip, Genya flushed guiltily. "Why?" This woman called herself a huntress. Did she even now stalk new prey?

"Val talked of a Kaell."

Genya's breath snagged in sudden hope. "Did he—did Val talk about me?"

Face half hidden by her hood, Rohane's expression was unreadable. She shook her head. "No, Genya Caelan. But you can be reunited with him. When you come to Quisnaf."

Genya's shoulders fell. Of course he hadn't thought of her. Only of Kaell. "Why would I come to Quisnaf?" she muttered. Unless Val had told Rohane to ask her to come. "Did he…" She almost choked on the words, on the need in them, the hunger for Val's regard. "Did my guardian ask for me? Is that why you're really here? He wants to see me?" Her heart leapt. He had forgiven her. He still loved her.

Rohane tilted her chin. "No."

The single word stuck Genya like a blow. She drew a shuddering breath.

"That's not why I'm here," Rohane said. "That's not why I followed you for a chance to talk to you alone."

"But you said, 'He's alive.'"

"I meant another."

The night closed in about them. An owl hooted. A distant stream trickled over pebbles in a riverbed. Genya's pulse took off. Did she dare believe Rohane meant Dannon?

"Who?" she whispered.

Rohane licked lips dried by the cold air. "We found a man after the battle—"

"What man?"

"A wounded man. We did not know who he was, why he was there in that ruin."

"Ruin?" Genya's heartbeat thumped in her temples. "Oh, gods, you have him. Dannon."

A silence fell. Rohane watched Genya's face too intently, as though she must understand and weigh her reaction. "That's what he says his name is."

Stunned, Genya could not speak. Then a flurry of words spilled out. "I looked everywhere. I thought Gendrick had him or that the Varee imprisoned and tortured him." Tears of relief wet her eyes "Please. Tell me he's well."

"He nearly died. Our healers tended to him for weeks."

"Your healers? Then—" Genya frowned. "Then Dannon's in Quisnaf?" A ménage of emotions struck her. Relief that he lived, that she had found him. But dismay that he was in Quisnaf, far away. Like Val.

"But now you'll let him go. You'll let him come back to me."

When Rohane did not reply, a ripple of anger tore through Genya. "Is he a prisoner? Is that why you don't answer me? No. That's not right. You can't just find a man and imprison him."

"Quisnaf is a dangerous place for a man."

Genya stared at Rohane in disbelief, in bewilderment. Why wait in the darkness to tell her this privately? She nibbled her lip, puzzling it out.

"You're holding him deliberately," she said slowly, the truth sinking into her. "Somehow you learnt I care for this man. You want something of me."

Rohane shrugged. "I am instructed only to tell you we have him."

"That's it?" Genya fisted her hands. "There must be more." She grabbed Rohane's sleeve. "What else? What is the rest of the message? How do I get him back?"

Rohane's cool gaze settled on Genya's face. In that shadowy, moon-speckled light, it struck Genya that the other woman had a quality that wasn't apparent at once. An ethereal, mysterious aloofness. No, a sadness, just as Kaell had said. Genya had never realised until then how sorrow drew and intrigued just as much as joy.

"I was told if you asked, only if you asked specifically, to reply that if you want him back, then the Quisnaf council would like to meet you."

"Meet?" Genya echoed.

Rohane spread her arms in a gesture of conciliation. "It is nothing more than an invitation to talk. Then to be reunited with a loved one."

Or a loved two. The Quisnaf held two men she cared about.

"It's a trap. Are the Quisnaf my enemy? Are you my enemy?" She stared into Rohane's eyes. "Are you, Rohane, daughter of Quisnaf?"

The other woman did not look away. "No, I am not your enemy, Genya Caelan. I am only a retrieval captain, tasked to bring a message of goodwill to Alecc Caelan and an invitation from the council to you."

"If only I could trust you," Genya muttered.

"Trust must always be earned," Rohane said.

"And tested," Genya said.

"There's something else," Rohane said.

Genya waited silently.

As if uncertain what to say, Rohane peered into the night. "About this Kaell—"

"What about him?"

Rohane faced her. "I am instructed to tell you that if you should somehow bring him to Quisnaf, the council might be predisposed to return the Cahirean to you."

"Predisposed," Genya spluttered. "Do all Quisnaf speak in such a roundabout manner?"

"I think my words are clear enough," Rohane said.

"And still, I say it's a trap," Genya muttered. Yet with sudden resolve, she knew what she must do. Even if Val refused to see her. Even if Dannon blamed her for leaving him alone in that ruin. Even if they both despised her, she must walk into the Quisnaf trap.

"Listen closely," she said. "I have a message for your council."

VAL ARQUES

Daylight bled through gaps in shutters. Hot, Val kicked off a thin coverlet. Through the sludge of sleep, his thoughts stirred, shifted, and assembled into some sort of sense. Someone had grabbed him last night—Marlisa and another man. The man and his dour companion had brought him to a tower. Somewhere.

Resting his head on his cradled hands, Val considered his surroundings. Last night, the lamp had barely pierced the gloom.

The room was circular, with many windows shuttered against the dawn heat. Pillows covered the large bed he lay upon. Chests, chairs, tables, and a divan filled the space. Rugs covered a wooden floor. A garderobe jutted off the main chamber. His captors, it seemed, wanted him to be comfortable. Whether he should be relieved or alarmed by that, he wasn't sure.

Rising, Val padded to the door and gave it a tug. It hardly even rattled. He shoved. It didn't budge. He strode to the windows and flung back the shutters. Sunlight flooded the chamber, every remnant of night gone. He'd slept deeply, as though his fears and the thumping ache in his head had knocked him into oblivion.

He leaned out. The tower stood in a clearing surrounded by leafy trees. The only sounds were the chirrup of birds, dry leaves crackling in a ghosting breeze, and a distant hum of the sea over rocks.

Footsteps sounded in the stairwell. Val whirled in time to see a slat open at the bottom of the door. An unseen hand shoved a tray through. He ran across the room, dropped to his hands and knees, and tried to peer outside. "Is someone there? Where am I?"

The footsteps retreated. A minute later, a door clanked below. Val rushed back to the window to try to glimpse who had left. He saw no one.

With a frustrated sigh, he picked up the tray and carried it to a table. It contained a bowl of fast-cooling porridge, hot bread, an apple, and a jug of water. Ravenous, he fell upon the food. Once he'd eaten, he prowled about his prison, running his fingers over stone walls, leaning from high windows, and rolling up rugs to examine the floor. The only exit was that door.

Briefly, he pondered leaping to his death. Maybe they would throw his body in a midden. Though, if they buried him, he would be in a worse position than now. His new prison was at least comfortable, bright, and airy. They did not intend to let him starve.

But who were they? And what did they want from him?

His existence quickly fell into a dull routine. Food appeared at dawn and dusk. After the second day, an impatient male voice snapped that he should leave the previous tray just inside the slot. Val crouched and demanded to know who held him.

"Leave the tray, or that's it for food."

Val left the tray.

Twice a day, he listened for the footsteps up the stairs, always questioning whoever delivered his meals. No one ever answered him.

On the third day, a large bowl of warm water was shoved through after the tray. Val lifted it onto the table. It contained a cloth and soap. He stripped and washed. Then he explored the chests and found fresh garments.

"Leave your old garments near the latch," the voice barked the next day.

"Who are you? What do you want from me?" he cried.

There was no answer, just the echo of fast-fading steps.

Frustrated, unable to rein in his unease, he strode up and down, shouting at the walls. It was as pointless as driving his fists against the stone. But he craved a release of tension.

This had to be a stupid mistake. Why keep him in a tower, alone, with no word, even a word of torment from his captors? Someone, somewhere would free him.

But what then? The Quisnaf would think he'd run again. Sisilia would believe he had broken his word. Gods help him, if ever they took him once more, his fate was set. They would imprison him in dreams until he didn't know who he was. How, he wondered, had Roaran managed to hold on to even a tiny piece of himself as Archanin's prisoner?

At the thought of Roaran, Val's belly churned. Maybe the gods wanted him to suffer, to lose himself, and to pay for what he'd done to Roaran. Again, he fell to pacing, tussling with his thoughts, sometimes too stirred up to sleep, until at last, exhaustion brought the relief of dreams and emptiness.

GENYA

The crisp, cool air smelt of dew. Dawn streaked like spilled dye, its pink fingers splashed across a lightening sky. Etched into the rosy brilliance, a castle's towers were stark charcoal sketches against the glowing horizon.

From horseback, Genya appraised the Falls fortress with a warrior's gaze. With the forest growing close, the castle was easy to approach. But its many towers faced in every direction, their rounded stone built into a bed of rock. A barbican reinforced the gatehouse, no doubt with a narrow tunnel to the ward that was a death trap of murder holes.

She yawned. She'd slept poorly, disturbed by fragmented dreams and visions of blood and bodies heaped on a battlefield. Kaell's warning, too, about using blood magic lingered in her mind. But she would not give it up. The power, the awe she glimpsed in others' eyes when she cast a spell excited her. Fate had put her on this path, and it would lead to glory. And when she had won Telor for Alecc, when she had destroyed every ghoul, she would earn Val's praise. Even earn back his affection.

"We should turn around," Nicky said from the mount beside Alecc, his hand never far from his blade. He had transposed his grief about Roaran into a determination to keep Alecc safe. Nicky needed purpose. To serve. To believe. Genya sneered. It was pathetic. She wondered why she hadn't seen that before.

"What?" Alecc's tone was light, but Genya knew he, too, had doubts. "When the Lord of the Falls has nice warm beds waiting? Nice warm baths?"

"And maybe Gendrick Caelan has a nice, warm welcome waiting, too?"

Genya sighed. This argument grew stale. The entire journey from Vraymorg, Nicky had tried to convince Alecc to return to the Mountains. Despite the desperate tone of the Isles king's message, it could well be a trap.

"Gendrick has too much to lose."

"You can't trust him, Alecc. He wants you dead."

"Hear, hear." Genya caught them up. "Gendrick is a snake."

"I can't just sit comfortably behind Vraymorg's tall walls while Wardorians plunder Telor."

"You're the rightful king," Nicky said. "I must keep you safe. That means keeping you away from Gendrick Caelan."

"I'll be king of nothing if the Wardorians invade. What do you think the people will say of me? That I'm a coward? That I think more of my own skin than saving my country? No." He shook his head firmly. "I know the risk, but Gendrick swore by the Isles gods no harm would come to me. I have to trust him. For the sake of Telor."

"Gendrick's word means nothing," Genya said. "His is a forked tongue."

"Roaran would say—" Nicky began.

"No," Alecc whipped up a hand. "I've had enough. Roaran this, Roaran that. I know you grieve for him. I do too. But he's not here."

Nicky's mouth twisted, but whether it was in sorrow or anger, Genya could not tell. She eyed Alecc with interest. Despite his youth, there was steel and resolution in him.

"You're too young to know real loss," Nicky said, his tone empty. "I hope you never do."

Alecc twisted in the saddle to glare. "I've not known loss?" he heaved, indignant. "My father is kept across the seas by the Quisnaf. My mother is all but a prisoner in Tide's End. I watched men I'd fought beside die hard, Nicky. I watched Archanin slaughter Roaran." He scoffed. "Not known real loss?"

Genya's mouth was stale with guilt. Hearing Roaran's name still shook her, took her back to that night when ghouls butchered him. If only she could use magic now, to shield herself, to find elation, and to be above hurt. But there was no call upon her to use spellcraft. And in its place, a restlessness filled her, as if her body craved release.

They rode on in silence. Dully, Genya listened to the clip-clop of hooves, to jangling harnesses, and to snatches of conversation from the Mountains warriors. Cold dread filled her heart. When she had lain in bed that last night in the Mountains, all she could picture was Gendrick's face, tight with rage. The king hated Alecc, as much for Rozenn's deception as for the risk Alecc posed to his rule.

Maybe hate was more intense when its roots lay in love. Maybe hate that sprouted from indifference or fear did not burn so dangerously bright. She shivered. "Nicky's right. There's danger ahead. No good can come of this."

"I know you both have doubts," Alecc said softly. "And I love you for your concern. But my father once told me that those who hold on too tightly to life, forsaking all risk, shall find that life devalued by others. Do you understand?"

Nicky's stern expression softened. "Lad, I do. A king must take risks. Roaran told me that. He also said there was no point in living if you have lost all else, including yourself."

"Roaran this, Roaran that." Alecc's grin flashed with mischief.

A challenge rang out from a tower. Men bunched on the walls. "Who are you?" The call floated down, as clear as a bird's shrill chirp in the dawn stillness.

"Are you fools?" Genya shouted. "What do the banners tell you? We're from Vraymorg,"

"Banners can be false."

"Do we look like Wardorians? Open for Alecc Caelan, Lord of the Mountains." *Rightful king of Telor.* But she did not say that. This journey was as diplomatic as military. It was not the time to press Alecc's claim to the throne. But once the Wardorians had been defeated...

Arguments broke out above. Then men moved off. Moments later, the portcullis rattled up, and the gates scraped open. Nicky led Alecc, Genya, and the rest of their warriors through into a courtyard. An older man waited at the front of a small group of armed soldiers.

He jeered as Alecc dismounted. "Well, the boy king. Crawled out from behind his witch's skirts."

"His witch does not wear skirts," Genya said, her tone dangerous. "But I'll gladly find one for you."

"Tomasin Caelan." Alecc threw the man a cheery grin. "I heard you were dead... uncle."

Genya eyed Tomasin doubtfully. His fierce reputation surely had been earned in his youth. Stoop-shouldered, his grey hair thinned, his gaunt face etched with pain, he looked anything but a warrior of repute. Deep lines grooved his mouth, and his eyes sank into hollows beneath bushy brows.

"I'm not your uncle, brat. Word is you're the whelp of that man who called himself Vraymorg. I never liked him. Arrogant." The old man glanced at the Mountains warriors with contempt. Then his glare shifted to Genya. "This castle has seen better days if it lets the likes of you through its gates, witch."

"It's not the only thing that has seen better days. Be careful, *old man*, I don't bring down its gates," Genya said. *On your head.*

"Hmmph." Tomasin snapped gnarled fingers. "Steward. Find somewhere to billet these men. You." A finger jabbed at Alecc. "Come with me, brat. The king will speak with you."

Cadan forced his way through riders to Alecc's side. He threw Tomasin a sour look as though displeased at his tone, then he dipped his head to his king. "Your Grace, is all well?"

Alecc bristled with annoyance. If he had a weakness, it was pride. To have others fight his battles belittled him. "You don't need to defend me, Cadan. Just take care of our men."

With Nicky at the rear, Genya fell in beside Alecc as they strode after Tomasin. For an old man, he moved briskly, without the aid of a stick.

"We need more guards with us," Nicky hissed. "By the gods, I thought Roaran was reckless and stubborn. But you?"

Alecc tossed him a crooked grin. "I'm my father's son. I'm loath to trust Gendrick too far, but he swore an oath before the gods. Death riders have returned to Telor, Nicky. Even Gendrick has heard the stories of oath breakers or kinslayers struck down. He won't hurt me. Not while I'm within these walls at least."

"And once we're away from these walls?" Genya asked.

Tomasin led them to a hall. Genya peered about with interest, remembering Dannon's story of guards dragging him before the Lord of the Falls, how he was very nearly executed in this chamber.

Frustration and bitterness swept through her. Curse the Quisnaf. What right did they have to abduct him? Genya would not let them manipulate her. She would fetch Dannon and make them pay—in her own time. For now, her duty was to Alecc.

The hall was empty except for four men at the far end huddled about a table, heads bent close. Genya recognised Gendrick at once. Another stout man beside him was likely the Lord of the Falls. The other two were clad like warriors.

Tomasin waved a hand. "Walk on if you dare, brat."

Irritated, Genya shoved her face close to his. "Treat him with respect, or I'll turn you into a toad."

"Genya." Alecc touched her arm. "He's just an old fool. Pay no attention. I never did."

"Old fool?" Tomasin blazed up. He shook a fist at Alecc. "Why, you insolent little bug. I would squash you beneath my heel and think nothing of it."

Alecc laughed. The four men about the table lifted their heads.

A stranger whispered something to Gendrick. The king did not reply. His scowl did not move from Alecc.

"If I were the king, I'd gut you here and now," Tomasin said. "Oath or not. Death riders be dammed." He turned on a heel and stomped out.

Gendrick came forward, arms spread in welcome. At his insincerity, Genya stiffened in alarm. Alecc's expression was carefully neutral.

"Alecc, thank you for trusting me." Gendrick's lips were set in a disarming half smile. Though he had the same Caelan cheekbones and thick, gleaming black hair, he could never be beautiful in the way Val was beautiful. Unlike Val's, Gendrick's face was etched with bitterness and cruelty. "Let us put the past behind us, for the sake of Telor."

"Indeed," Alecc said. "Wardour cannot prevail."

"You'll drink with me?" Without waiting for an answer, Gendrick poured wine into four cups. He took one, drank heavily, then passed Alecc another. "Genya." He offered her a cup of wine. "How nice we can be done with the lies."

"I'm not done with lies," Genya said. "And I suspect neither are you. This is a temporary alliance. Once the Wardorians are defeated, Alecc will kill you."

Alecc threw her a warning frown.

"We'll see," Gendrick said. "And who is this? He has the look of the Isles about him."

"Nicholas Saltman," Nicky said. "*Not* at your service, Your Grace."

"Ah." The wine cup bobbed as Gendrick's hand moved. "The strange warrior who rode with Roaran. What stories you must be able to tell."

Nicky shrugged. His expression was hostile, his body taut with mistrust.

"And your companions?" Alecc stared at the three men with Gendrick.

The stout man curled a lip in contempt. "I am Maglo, the Lord of the Falls. We met once when you were a child. Not so long ago."

Alecc's expression was grim. "If you think me a child, you underestimate me."

Maglo waved a hand at one of the armed men. "My battle captain, Jake Fisher."

The captain was an impressive man: raven-haired, slender, and tall, but with powerful muscles outlined beneath his tunic. He dipped his head. "My lord."

Gendrick introduced the other man. "Velleran Damadar."

Alecc stiffened. Nicky's eyes slitted. Genya stared with interest. An Ice lord. If not for an agreement reached between Myranthe Damadar and Archanin, Velleran would be dead. She wondered what had happened to the old hag. Myranthe, Velleran's sister, was reputed to be the most powerful sorceress this side of the Ice Sea.

Until me.

One day, there would be a reckoning between Genya and Myranthe. One day, Myranthe would pay for what she had done to Roaran. To Val. Her guardian had never revealed the details, but Nicky had told her a little.

Velleran's cool gaze flickered over Genya to settle on Alecc. "You've brought how many men?"

"Three thousand," Alecc said. "And from the Icelands?"

"Four thousand." Velleran offered an unpleasant smile.

Alecc gave a curt nod. His gaze fell on the map stretched on the table. He advanced quickly. His hands flattened the parchment as he studied it. Genya followed.

Velleran joined them. He poked a finger. "My spies tell me the Wardorians are set to sail any day. Our sentries in watchtowers will light a stream of beacons as soon as sails are sighted."

"The weather is against them," Gendrick said. "The Isles gods are good. The fleet is becalmed. But the gods will not control the wind forever."

Genya traced the map with her fingers. Alecc had a plan. It was daring and unexpected, just the sort of crazy idea Dannon might come up with.

"From the direction the fleet is headed," Jake Fisher explained, "the Wardorian fleet plans to sail up the river to the Falls."

"Dal-Kanu is their target." Gendrick stabbed the map. "This Wardorian king is not so stupid as to attack Tide's End. But if he takes Dal-Kanu, he could use it as a base, bring in reinforcements over weeks up the river."

"I don't think he'll bring his ships as far as the Falls," Maglo said. "This castle has never been taken. But the Wardorians could come ashore anywhere along the river."

"If we spread our men too thinly to cover all possible landing places," Velleran said, "we'll risk heavy casualties before reinforcements arrive. We need to be ready to move as soon as we're certain of the Wardorian king's intentions."

"There's another way," Alecc said.

Genya nodded. The plan was risky but brilliant.

"Well, please share," Gendrick said with an ironic flick of his brows. Clearly, he thought Alecc knew nothing. But Alecc was his father's son. And Val Arques Caelan was a tactician as well as a warrior.

The old bitterness turned in her gut. Val had abandoned her and judged her harshly. Oh, how she wished to banish all thoughts of him, to use blood magic, so that not even Val's neglect could wound her.

Alecc jabbed at the map. "This dam, here."

Gendrick's brows furrowed. "What of it?"

"What would happen to the river? What would happen to a fleet of ships on that river if all that water was released at once?"

They stared. Silence swirled, as thick as smoke. Jake stroked a scanty beard. Genya sniffed the tallow candles. She remembered the cloying scent of potions and spells in Rozenn's rooms. The queen burned lavender candles to mask it, but always beneath lingered the fragrance of mystery and magic.

"It's daring," Velleran said. "So outrageous, it might work."

Gendrick spluttered in disgust. "At what cost? Before the water hits the river, a torrent will swamp the land below the dam."

"Clear the land," Genya said. "Either that, or be prepared to lose Telor. How many ships sail against us?"

"Four hundred." Jake stroked his beard again. The beard gave him a disreputable, dangerous air. The man was broodingly handsome, with a warrior's build. Perhaps she might seek him in his chambers tonight. Until they rode out to fight Wardorians, boredom would be her greatest enemy.

Velleran turned to the king. "How many villages between the dam and the river?"

Gendrick shrugged. "How should I know? Do I concern myself with peasants? Just so long as they tend fields and behave, know their place, I give them no thought."

That was why he was a poor king. Nicky had said Roaran often rode the length and breadth of Telor, through every valley and hamlet. A king must know his kingdom, Roaran had said.

"Clear the villages," Alecc said, resolute. "We, all of us, will rebuild them. Get the villagers to safety and destroy the dam."

"The timing must be right." Jake drove a fist into the table. "We can't destroy the dam until the ships are in the river. Too soon, and the water floods out to sea. Too late, and they might get their soldiers to higher ground. But I think it might work."

"I think so, too," Velleran said. "Now, let's work out details."

⁕

The thud of hammers and the clash of metal rang out across the hills. Now that battle was nearing, Genya trembled with fierce excitement. Blood hot in her veins, she was ever eager to draw her sword, to join the hundreds of warriors hidden in thick forest high above the valley and its wide river.

Before combat, she always trembled with anticipation. But once the waiting passed, once she stormed into the tumult, the chaos of steel, a calmness swept through her. There was only her sword and her will, welded into a fighting machine.

She shifted her feet, leaning towards Nicky, who watched the riverbend with a glass to his eye. Genya, Nicky, and Alecc had a vantage point high above the river, above the forest, on a jutting rocky cliff. "Any sign?"

"Stop fidgeting," Nicky complained. "Go bother Gendrick."

"I might kill him—accidentally, of course." Genya glared at the king.

He was in a huddle with Jake and Maglo. Velleran Damadar commanded the men waiting to ambush Wardorian soldiers if they put ashore on the right bank. Cadan commanded the left. But with luck, few of the invaders would even make it from the swirling water.

If the dam comes down. At last report, workers had breached the wall. They now sought to widen it, to smash holes in other key places as instructed by engineers, then break open the dam all at once and let the force of the walled-up water do the rest.

"I see something," Nicky muttered.

Alecc tore the glass from him. "I'm not seeing sails." He passed the glass to Genya. "Tell me what those ghoul senses of yours reveal."

She peered through the glass. A white sail had appeared just beyond the headland. Driven by a gusty wind, the ship ploughed towards the river entrance. A second vessel bobbed in its wake then a third. She turned the glass upon the horizon. Hundreds of sails spread across the ocean. Genya returned the glass to Alecc and called to the king, "The Wardorian fleet is near."

Gendrick, Jake, and Maglo rushed to join them.

"Wait, wait." Alecc held up a hand. "We need most of the fleet to be in the river."

They silently watched the ships advance across the sea, around the headland. In the quiet, Genya could hear the swish of wind through sails, the creak of timber, and a thin drift of drumbeats. Slowly, the Wardorian fleet bunched in the river, a field of white canvas just below the Telorians' vantage point, with only a few stragglers still at sea.

"Light the beacons," Gendrick commanded. Jake nodded and ran off.

"This is foolish," Maglo said. "We have the advantage of surprise. If they see smoke, they'll know we're here."

"They know already," Alecc said. "We've not captured any Wardorian scouts, but they're watching us in the forests. They expect us to ambush them once they land. But if the gods are good, none will."

"May Khir protect us." Maglo made a sign to his god.

Without warning, the earth shook. A rumbling began farther up the river. An enormous cloud of dust and dirt shot up above the tree line.

"The dam," Nicky said. "That's the dam down."

A roaring filled the air—a terrible, dreadful sound like thousands of drumbeats rolling together. To their left, a breaker of water crested the rise like a thousand rearing horses. Then, with a deafening boom, it crashed onto the hillside. Trees splintered as a tsunami of water smashed over the land, down towards the river below. The frothing torrent flooded around the river's bend, ploughing down trees on the banks, terrifying in its unstoppable force.

Above its thunder, Genya only just heard the shouts and cheers from the Telorians. They beat spears into the ground or against the shields the Ice men carried. Though warned not to close on the riverbank until the wall of water passed, the more curious might find themselves drawn to watch the horrific chaos.

Then screams of terror broke out as the men on the ships saw their fate only moments before the merciless water swept up their vessels, tossed them up, or swamped them beneath the waves. Masts groaned and snapped; ships broke up beneath the pounding.

All the while, the helpless soldiers and sailors wailed with fear as the flood bore down upon them.

Furious excitement tore through Genya. Her blood ran hot at the destruction, at the power of the deluge, at the tide of death. A gleeful shout shot from her lungs. It was all she could do to stop herself running down the hill towards the carnage.

The curtain of water raged on. It surged up the slopes, reaching with furious fingers towards the watching Telorians. For a moment, it seemed to freeze, a curled menace poised to crash into the hillside. Then the wave plunged down in a violent spray of foam and gushed towards the distant sea. In its grip, the white-churned river bucked and thrashed, carrying broken ships, debris, and dead men away on a fierce, relentless tide.

For a long while, the river boiled, seethed, and frothed. When it at last stilled, an eerie hush settled upon the valley. All manner of wreckage scarred the river surface: trunks, split planks, broken sails, and bushes ripped from banks. Drowned bodies floated facedown.

The survivors swam through the debris to the banks, collapsing to their knees or lying prone, unable to summon the will to move.

With blood-curdling cries, the Telorians ran down the slopes to kill them. "Take prisoners," Velleran Damadar shouted.

Genya whipped out her sword. She grinned sanguinely. If it were up to her, the Ice lord would gain few slaves today.

Bloody slaughter unleashed. Telorian soldiers swarmed over the banks like ants, cutting down those who tried to fight. But few of the Wardorians resisted. The river had swept away their weapons and sapped both their spirit and strength.

A handful broke free and ran for the trees. Genya hunted them down. Quickly, the surviving Wardorians were either butchered or rounded up. Disappointed she had killed so few, Genya shoved her sword back into her belt and trudged up the slope to join Alecc and the king. Gendrick rubbed his hands in glee. Perhaps it was at the prospect of profit from the sale of so many able-bodied men or because of a victory that had cost him very little.

"All that water." Gendrick turned to Alecc. "Your plan worked. I'm grateful."

"It was risky."

The king smiled grimly. "What a victory. Hardly a Telorian life lost. The mighty Wardorian fleet destroyed. Their haughty king, if he's not among the drowned, humbled." His eyes glittered greedily. "But what if he's here and didn't die?" He called Maglo to him. "Check every face. If the Wardorian king lives, I want him in irons and brought to me."

The man hurried off.

Genya bit her lip, a shadow forming at the back of her mind. She should be elated. This was an incredible victory, a sign of the gods' favour. Singers and poets would weave pretty words about it for centuries—the day the waters crashed down. Yet something niggled at her. Something out of place.

Uneasily, she watched Telorians herd their captives up through the trees. Ice men, Isles men. No Mountains warriors.

No Mountains warriors.

A shudder of alarm tore up her backbone. She curled her fingers around her sword hilt, her gaze sweeping about. None of Alecc's guards were here.

Shouts carried from beyond the trees. Metal clashed on metal. Cadan burst from the forest, yelling. Men chased hard on his heels.

"Betrayed," Cadan cried. "Betrayed. Run."

Genya started towards him. Sunlight glinted on naked steel. With one mighty stroke, a man drove a blade into Cadan's back. His arms flew out, his mouth gaping in surprise. Then he collapsed.

Alecc had his sword out. Men sprang in to block him. Shocked, he whirled. More men advanced, shields pressed ready to slam him bodily to the ground.

"Alive," Gendrick shouted. "Take him alive. Shoot to wound only."

Shoot? Genya spun towards a line of archers with bolts nocked to crossbows. They fired low. A quarrel skimmed her shin. By then, the king's soldiers were on her, shields raised. With no time for a spell, she struck out wildly, splintering a shield. From all sides, soldiers pressed with wood. One hit her across the back. She dropped to one knee. A shield smashed into her head. Dizzy, faint, her vision jumping, she tried desperately to keep her grip on her sword and to force words of a spell up her dry throat.

"Is he down? Is he?" Gendrick sounded as giddy as a child with a present.

Soldiers gripped a struggling Alecc. Others held Nicky.

"You snake," Alecc hissed, struggling in his captors' hold.

Men seized Genya's shoulders. Again, she tried to whisper a spell, but she could not form a thought. Her skull thumped, the pain like nails driving into her temples.

Gendrick shoved his face close to Alecc's. His breaths heaved in and out. "At last you'll pay."

Then a sword hilt swung at Genya's head. She knew a moment of blinding pain, then blackness swamped her.

⚬⚭⚬

Tide's End's notorious prisons were deep in the earth—damp, squalid holes of filth and despair. Yet Gendrick imprisoned Genya, Alecc, and Nicky in a tower jutting over a sea that rippled like wrinkled blue-grey parchment. Apart from the wind, it was very quiet in their stone-lined prison, as if defeat cast a pall upon the bare chamber.

At times, they wrenched at the wrist fetters attached by a length of chain to the walls, teeth clenched, panting as they struggled. At other times, they slumped into despondency, speaking little, resigned to impending death.

"Can't you do anything, lass?" Nicky asked.

Genya shook her head. Try as she might, spellcraft did not work in this tower. She couldn't understand why. She had become so powerful, yet she was unable to help her friends.

Genya wandered to the single window, her chains scraping over the floor in a discordant jangling. The salty breeze cooled her neck. Dusk closed in. The tide crept towards the tower with darkling waters that nipped at rocks, rekindling life in sundried seaweed. As if for the first time, she listened to gulls cawing and to the arrah-arrah of a colony of gannets. Very slowly, she ran her fingertips along the sill, tracing every groove and bump in stone that was warm beneath her touch.

Now, so close to death, an intensity clung to her, as if every sensation, every emotion, was exploding within her. Never before had she heard that song in the wind, its haunting melody lifting gooseflesh on her arms. Never before had the fragrance of brine and the perfume of wildflowers seemed so lovely.

Every sound, the wind through broken stonework, the sea's gentle hum, was familiar to her, but none brought comfort. Instead, they whispered of loss, a harsh, blunt whisper that pierced her heart as surely as a blade. Death drew near. How was it possible her breaths could stop? That she could cease to be. She could not take it in.

Alecc put his fettered hands on the sill beside hers. He breathed slowly and deeply. "I've never thought about death or how I might like to die—or where. The sea tower is as good a place as any." He shrugged. "Better than some."

"This isn't the end." Genya clenched her teeth. "It can't be." She fisted her hands, trying to break the shackles. Then she let out a frustrated cry. She had to save him, for Val. She had to save them all.

"Can you try another spell?" Nicky sat with his back to the wall, arms about his knees. Dried blood from a cut in his temple streaked his weary face.

Genya was just as dishevelled. Blood matted her hair and soiled her tunic. Her body stank of stale sweat. "Nothing works," she said.

"It's as if the tower is enspelled against magic."

"Must be why Gendrick threw us in here," Nicky muttered.

"Will it be a public execution?" Alecc turned from the window. "The rope? The axe?"

Nicky lifted his head. "Don't think about it."

"I'm not afraid, Nicky. If Gendrick hopes I'll fall to my knees and beg for my life, he's mistaken."

The older man's expression softened to fondness. "I know you're not afraid."

"When will it happen?"

"Soon, boy." Nicky dropped his head onto his knees with a resigned sigh. "I don't mind so much about me. But Genya, oh, gods, Genya. And you, boy. You're too young. It isn't fair."

"It's not a matter of fairness." Alecc laughed bitterly. "I threw the dice in the game of power and lost."

"No," Genya cried. "No. We have to get free." She had to show Val her worth. She had to win his forgiveness. The gods could not be so cruel as to send her to her death without redemption.

A door creaked. From the whisper of dread down her spine, Genya knew Gendrick Caelan stood on the threshold.

Slowly, she turned. At the sight of the king, flanked by guards, anger surged through her like a current. His long tunic with its golden threads and his brushed, shining hair seemed a deliberate contrast to his dishevelled prisoners. A taunt. How she longed to throw herself at him, to strike him again and again, to bloody his garments, and tear at his hair.

Gendrick's cold gaze passed over Nicky to her then came to rest upon Alecc.

"The boy who would be king. The bastard who would take my throne." His sneering triumph turned Genya's stomach.

Alecc said nothing. He met Gendrick's stare resolutely, unafraid.

"What? No retort from that sharp young tongue? How sad." Gendrick stepped close to his prisoner. Slowly, he raised a hand to Alecc's face. With his fingertips, he stroked the young man's cheek.

"Don't you touch him." Nicky stormed to his feet.

Alecc knocked Gendrick's hand aside. "What do you want?"

Gendrick smiled slyly. "Why, nothing. I have it all. My kingdom is secure, thanks to you. I have no rivals—again, thanks to you and your naïve faith in others. And I have you at my mercy. What a strange expression that is, Alecc, wouldn't you agree? At my mercy when there is no thought of mercy and shall be none. You will soon be dead."

"What's stopping you?"

Gendrick grasped Alecc's chin.

"Get away from him!" Nicky lurched at Gendrick, only to be hauled back by a guard. "How dare you, snake. You'll answer to death riders for this." Struggling uselessly in the guard's grip, he turned his head and spat on the ground.

"I'm going to kill you," Genya said quietly.

"Little witch." The king let Alecc go and turned to regard her coolly. "You'll be the last to die. And your death will be slow. Unless you care to tell me where the queen's bastard is?"

Genya lifted her head and glared.

"No? I assume the brat is with Yvonne Maglo. Since she went missing that night. But where might the lovely Yvonne be hiding?"

Genya shrugged.

"I'll find the child. I shall suffer no bastard Cahirean rivals to live." Gendrick's dark eyes shifted back to Alecc. The king was a grim man, vicious in his need to dominate. But a sick joy curved his lips as he considered his prisoner.

"You think you've won," Alecc said. "Take your moment of triumph, Gendrick. It shall be your last. For with my death, you will bring down vengeance upon your head."

Gendrick sneered in disgust. "If you mean the little witch, I do not fear a girl. Especially one robbed of her petty spellcraft by the magic cast into the stones of this tower."

Genya laughed. "I don't need spells to kill you."

"Just a girl," Gendrick muttered. "Just as you, for all the tales that swirl about your father, are just a boy. Soon a dead boy. Make peace with your gods, boy. For soon you die, and I shall at last be rid of you."

"Those gods will never grant you peace," Alecc cried, defiant.

Gendrick patted Alecc's hair as he might a disobedient nephew. "There he is. The sharp-tongued brat." He drew his sword. "I'm saving up your death, Alecc. Tomorrow night, I think. But first—" With only a grin, he spun and ran his blade into Nicky's belly, twisting the tip up.

"No!" Genya screamed. She threw herself at Gendrick, ready to claw his eyes. But the chains snapped her back. Oh, goddess, how powerless she was without magic, how useless. The thought drained her of hope.

Nicky slumped to his knees, his scream dulled by blood bubbling from his mouth. Then he collapsed in a huddle. His eyes blanked.

Alecc leapt at Gendrick. A guard grabbed his shoulders to hold him back. He struggled in the man's grip, shouting, "You monster! You brute!"

Gendrick stooped and wiped his bloody sword on Nicky's tunic. Straightening, he flashed Alecc and Genya a sinister smile.

"And now it is just you two and the gods." Gendrick turned his head towards the window, listening to waves lapping the tower walls. "Noisy, aren't they?"

Humming, he strode to the door. The guards followed. The door clanked shut.

ROHANE

"I need him back," Sisilia hissed. "Why have you failed to retrieve him, Blaire?"

In flickering candlelight, the sorceress looked wan and unearthly, like a spectre. Dark pools circled her fevered eyes. Lank, uncombed hair fell about her lined face. Even so, she dominated the room by the force of her presence, by the force of her need.

"I cast more spells. Still nothing. I cannot find him within the Enarae."

"Mostly likely because he has died in the past," Jenna-Dairine offered. "Is it true you cannot find the dead through the Enarae?"

Rohane slid a puzzled glance to Jenna-Dairine. She had not expected the battale captain to be among an intimate group in the Regenta's chambers. Jenna-Dairine and Blaire must have been reconciled while Rohane was in Telor.

"There is something in what you say." Sisilia's gaze turned inward.

Exhausted, Rohane closed her eyes briefly. The ship from Telor had docked in Vene at dawn. She had hired a horse and ridden to Quisnaf, only to learn Val had again fled. Oh, how he had deceived her, when all along he could not be trusted.

"We'll search again." Blaire turned on two kneeling warriors. "I won't hear any more excuses. Find him."

The two warriors saluted. Trembling, they backed from the room. Rohane could almost taste their fear. Blaire rarely surrendered to anger but was dangerous when she did. The Regenta drummed impatient fingers against the table. "I don't know where else to look. How is this possible? He is not a ghost."

Jenna-Dairine sank onto a couch in Blaire's audience chamber, her legs crossed. "Let me take a few warriors to search every cavern again. Perhaps we missed something. A sign."

"He had help," Blaire reasoned. "Someone who knew their way through the caves."

"Find that someone, and we'll find him."

"Who?" Blaire kept coming back to that question. "Who would betray us?"

"Someone put the guards and a priestess to sleep. The guards saw a figure," Jenna-Dairine muttered. "This may not be what we think. He may not have gone willingly."

"Any word from our spies?" Blaire asked. "What do we pay them for? If he reached Veniva, someone must know."

"If he reached Veniva, he wasn't alone," Jenna-Dairine said. "Someone got him away."

"Or he just ran," Rohane said bitterly. She crossed the room to where Florentine lay sleeping upon a pillow and picked up the fox's lead. Florentine lifted her head and gave Rohane a raspy bark.

"No blood keeper, no priestess would betray Quisnaf," Sisilia pronounced. "It is more likely to be a warrior. We know they are intemperate, ill disciplined. They take what they want with men, they drink to excess, and their behaviour is scandalous."

Rohane bristled with indignation. She was about to take Sisilia to task when Jenna-Dairine growled, "Be careful, Sisilia. That is a very sweeping condemnation. Do you have any proof, any reason to suspect a warrior?"

The sorceress sniffed. "Only because betrayal suits their

temperament better than it does a servant of Cyrah."

"And don't our warriors serve Cyrah?" Blaire threw up a hand. "Enough of this game of blame. I am sick of it. I want to hear something useful—and soon."

Jenna-Dairine rose and slid an arm about Rohane's shoulders. "You knew him best. Did he ever say anything? Give any clue where he might go? Did he ever mention anyone approaching him, offering help? Anything like that."

Rohane shook her head. "I don't know what to suggest. But I am more than willing to join the search." Her hand slid to her sword hilt. "If he has dared defy us again—" She trembled with anger.

"I will find a way to trace him." Sisilia's eyes hazed as though she were peering at something unseen. "I have his blood. I'll try a stronger spell. It's dangerous, but so be it." With a curt nod, she swept from the room, her long gown swishing the floor, her bare feet a soft patter. The faintest scent moved with her: oils and herbs, along with the eerie aroma of enchantment.

"Rohane." Blaire grasped the young woman's arms. "Please tell me that you bring encouraging news. I have had enough doom and gloom to last a century."

Rohane shoved aside her furious thoughts about Val. "I shall cut to what you want and need to hear. Needless to say, I shall give you my impressions of this would-be king and the men close to him later, but—"

"The girl," Blaire said. "Tell us of the girl. Will she be drawn to Quisnaf? Will she come for this man, Dannon?"

"Oh, she'll come for him," Rohane said darkly. "She has sent the council a message. She demands we surrender her lover. Or she will take him by force. That is her word to us. That we will give her what she wants, or she will make us pay."

Worn out, stunned by Val's disappearance, Rohane stumbled to her rooms, guiding Florentine by the lead. Warriors called greetings. She nodded distantly without really hearing.

Val Arques could not be trusted. He was gone. Yet if she hated him, why did her throat tighten? Why did her belly pitch? Why did she feel his absence from these caverns as she might that of a friend? No, this would not do. She would raise her shield of anger. She would not allow herself to feel anything that led to pain.

Turning the key, she let herself into her rooms. They seemed still and undisturbed. But cold. Empty like her heart.

As Florentine settled upon her cushion, Rohane draped her cloak over a chair and lit a candle. Her foot brushed something on the floor—a folded parchment that had been slipped under the door. Rohane picked it up. It was thick, expensive paper, lightly perfumed. It bore Cassian's seal.

"Hmm." Rohane broke the seal, smoothed the parchment, and held it to the candlelight.

Rohane, daughter, the letter read. *Seek permission to come at once. There is no danger, no threat to me, but tell Blaire I have need of you. If they refuse to let you come, then I shall make this a formal request to the council. Your loving father.*

Rohane frowned. *Come at once, but there is no danger?* She left the letter on the table, went to the bed, unlaced her boots, and drew them off. Too weary to undress, she lay back, her head resting on her hands, resolving not to think of Val Arques.

But he followed her into her dreams, and his fate was the first thing on her mind when she woke.

GENYA

Nicky's head rested on Genya's lap, her fingers entwined in his hair. "Do you remember when you taught me to swim, Nicky?" she murmured. "Or how to track outlaws? Do you remember when we went to Tide's End and saved Caelan? You and Val argued, but then you were always arguing."

At each memory, so dear, she laughed. Because that held back her tears. Because it held back the grief. It was there, ready to consume her. But not yet. No, first came vengeance. Only then would she have time for sorrow.

As the quiet built about them and the day faded to violet twilight, night shadowed the horizon across the hushed sea. Alecc sat with her, unspeaking, his hand in hers.

"He'll come for me next," he said softly.

"Don't," Genya said. "Don't speak of it."

"We'll meet again, Genya. Beyond this world."

"A world of bitterness," she said.

"A world of hope," Alecc said.

Frowning, she turned her head to stare at him. "How can you say that? Nicky is dead. We're imprisoned in an enspelled tower, about to die."

"I have to think there's more to life, Genya, than this tiny sliver we've been shown."

At dusk the next day, Gendrick returned with two guards. The king went straight for Alecc. He pulled his prisoner to his feet, circled behind, and threw an arm about Alecc's neck, lips close to the young man's ear. "So now you die. Your mother will be sad for a time, then she will forget you. History will forget you. For you are nothing."

A prickle stole across Genya's scalp. With fascinated horror, she stared at Alecc. An eerie shadow had fallen like a hood over the young king, a shadow that shimmered as if the fates turned, as if the history of kingdoms were about to dissolve and reform. Dizzy, sick, sniffing closing death, Genya dry retched.

"Stop," she croaked. "I'll tell you what I know. About the child."

Gendrick paused. He lifted his head and regarded her. "Tell me."

"In return for his life." She knew she couldn't trust him, but she had to try. The child was far away, safe from Gendrick's rage. Alecc was not. "Swear it upon your own, before the gods of the Isles."

The king considered her for a moment. "Very well. I swear it upon my life, before The Three."

Genya's breaths heaved out. She had no choice but to trust him.

Hesitantly, stumbling on the words, she muttered, "You're right. Yvonne has the child. There was a ship. From beyond the Ice Sea. From the Circle Kingdoms."

"And?" Gendrick demanded.

"The queen called him Decallion. The child. That's all I know." *Let it be enough,* Genya prayed silently. *Let him be merciful.*

Gendrick tapped a finger on his chin. "The Circle Kingdoms. So the bastard is beyond my reach—for now." He nodded. Then with a sly smile, he pulled Alecc against him once more.

Alecc closed his eyes, releasing his breath in a sigh. He looked pale, his young face smeared with blood and grime. Genya thought wildly of how in that moment, he looked more like Val—his body beneath a ripped tunic hard with muscle, the bones of his face chiselled to an exquisite fineness.

"No," Genya jolted forward in alarm. "You promised—"

Steel flashed in Gendrick's hand. Then his knife ripped across Alecc's throat. Alecc's eyes snapped open. He gasped in pain and shock as his blood pulsed out in great torrents. His body jerked. His hazed eyes emptied.

As though savouring Alecc's death, the king held him almost tenderly against his breast, his clothes soaked with his rival's blood. A growl of triumph became a bellow. Then he let Alecc's corpse drop at his feet.

Dazed, unable to take in what she had seen, Genya crawled to Alecc's ruined body. Hot tears slid silently down her cheeks. With a shaking hand, she reached to touch Alecc's hair. Gendrick kicked her aside. He snapped his fingers at the guards. They released Alecc's body from the chains and dragged him out, leaving a trail of smeared blood in their wake.

"No, don't!" Genya screamed. "No, leave him be."

Gendrick turned for the door. On the threshold, he glanced back. "Roaran Caelan's daughter. I've saved you for last. But tomorrow, it shall be your turn." His footsteps scuffed in the stairwell.

For a moment, shock held her, blissfully enclosing her in its numb vacuum. Then a terrible high-pitched wail echoed about the chamber. Genya clenched her teeth against it until she realised it came from her.

Horror, grief, and disbelief suffocated her. Her breaths sobbed out. This could not happen. First Roaran. Now that monster had taken Nicky and Alecc from her.

She began to scream, howling out her misery, beating her shackled hands on the floor, cursing the faithless goddess. Then she drew Nicky's head onto her lap once more and rocked back and forth, weeping.

In time, she quietened. A hardness formed around her heart, a place where anger swallowed the grief and pain. Again, she thumped her fists against the stone floor. This would not be the end. She would have revenge. She would hunt down Gendrick to the ends of the earth.

"Cyrah," she cried in desperation. "Gods and goddesses of Quisnaf, of Telor, of Seithin. You let me believe I was fated. Is it my fate to die here in this lonely tower? Then what is the point of it? What is the point of me?"

A rush of wind gusted through the barred window. It was as if from nowhere, a storm blew in. Roused waves dashed against the rocks below. The starlight and glimmering moonlight vanished into darkness. Thunder rolled through the sky. When it died away, a wisp of sound, a murmur, stirred through the tower chamber. For a moment, Genya was certain she glimpsed a shape. Then it faded into shadows.

In the wake of the short, sharp tempest, an expectant stillness cloaked the room. The first moon frosted the bare floor and walls. The wind paled to a breeze, cool on her face. And Genya thought back to another night when she had fled down the cliff face, how she had summoned power into her, how she had commanded the skies.

She thought of Rozenn's lessons. The queen told her again and again that magic was innate within a precious few. It was alive in her. It flowed in every vein and filled every sinew. No petty spells could stop her. If this tower was enspelled, she must break the enchantment. Only she could do it. She was destined. She would be the most powerful sorceress ever known.

A knife. She needed a knife. But there was nothing sharp in the prison.

With sudden resolution, she lifted her arm and bit deep into the skin, the tendons, and muscle. She gasped at the pain, then blood seeped from the ugly wound. She bit again and again, teeth clenched. Blood stained her lips, its metallic taste in her mouth. As best she could, she smeared the blood on the chains.

"*Discuto*," she shouted. "Shatter. With my blood, I command that which holds me shall no longer bind me. I offer my lifeforce to enable this spell. *Discuto. Discuto.*"

Again the sky darkened, the moonlight gone. For a moment, silence shrouded the earth. Then thunder crackled, just once.

Pain shot through her—a bolt of blinding, sickening agony. It was like a dark force invaded her form, straining against her ribs, breaking her bones and pulverising her muscles. Then it exploded outwards, as if ripping her apart from within.

Genya screamed and screamed. At a shrill sound like crystal shattering, she covered her head with her arms. The chains splintered into tiny shards that ricocheted against the walls. Other pieces whirred and whisked in a wild, wild dance. Then they fell to the floor.

Moonlight, pale and pure, flickered into the tower. Waves murmured over rocks. As if in a trance, Genya walked slowly to the window. The bars were gone, their metal tiny fragments on the floor. She climbed onto the sill. The darkness was still in her. A whisper was soft in her ears, in her mind. Alecc was close. She had to go to him.

For a moment, all thought shut down. There was only the power within her. Without understanding what she was doing, as if compelled, she dived into the sea. Foaming water closed about her, pulling her down. Genya tasted the ocean's salt on her lips and in her mouth. Lower and lower, she sank. Her eyes stung as she searched through the churning sea for Val's son. Cloth brushed her arm. She snatched at it. A weight came towards her. Alecc's face appeared in front of her, his hair splayed, his eyes wide and unseeing.

A chain tethered his ankles to the reef. The currents tugged his body this way and that. A sob rose in her throat. No longer able to fight the pull of the waves, she let them take her away, up to the surface. To the gleaming moon. To terrible, peaceful blackness.

She came to lying in shallow water on a pebbly beach. A warm wind blew about her. Slowly, Genya sat up. She hugged her knees and rocked. Darkness coiled about her heart, pressing and suffocating.

Unable to move, unable to go on, she bit back a sob. She was completely, utterly alone. What did she do now? Where did she go? There was no way back. *Back to what?*

Her eyelashes were wet, the taste of her tears salty in her mouth. All that she had lost sat like a chasm within, its blackness creeping up to consume her. Roaran, now Nicky. *Oh, gods, Nicky. Alecc.*

All she had left was a man who despised her and a man held captive by the Quisnaf.

Loneliness churned in her belly. She needed Val, the comfort of his presence and his strength. But how did she summon the will to face him, to go after him? And how would he receive her? With joy or bitterness? Had his disappointment faded with the months?

Then the thought came to her. There was one other. There was the man Alecc had left in charge at Vraymorg. He would help her. It rankled to need him when she resented and disliked him, but she had no choice.

She had to return to Vraymorg and seek out Kaell. There was no one else who could help her get to Quisnaf and to Val.

ROHANE

Her father's spirits seemed impossibly high. Either he had a new mistress, or word of a battle won and spoils taken had enlivened him.

They sat together on cushioned high-back chairs in the lesser hall, just the two of them. Even so, dinner was a grand business. A fine linen cloth covered the ornate table, its thick legs carved with swirls. On the table, candles in silver holders smoked, their beeswax blending with the fragrance of frangipani from the garden beyond the flung-back doors. Inconspicuous servants wisped about, removing dishes and filling wineglasses.

In the distance, waves broke over reefs, their crash comforting like fine music. Rohane liked this room opening onto the verdant castle gardens. She never felt trapped here, not like she did in Vene's streets and noisy, riotous marketplaces that stank of fish and brine. With its close-pressed houses and stores, its temples and public baths, the city was alien and crowded.

With a contented sigh, she leaned back, wondering why her father had summoned her.

"It is so good to have you here." Cassian raised his glass. "To your health. I want to hear all the gossip from Telor. What manner of child is this boy who would be king?"

Rohane sipped wine. After the strong pepper-and-berry-scented Cahirean reds in Telor, it tasted watery.

"The first error, Father." She wagged a finger at him. "He's young, true, but there's tempered steel there. Wit. None of a boy's rashness. And the remainder of Roaran's brotherhood has stayed with him." And he was Val's son. Did that make him untrustworthy?

"He has good advisers then. Who is the one with power? Who does he listen to?"

Rohane rolled the glass in her hands. "A man called Nicholas Saltman; Alecc seemed to listen when he spoke. There's a rather decorative warrior called Cadan he trusts also."

"Decorative?" Cassian wriggled his brows. "Is that the word you young things use? Handsome?"

Rohane laughed. "Handsome, then." She sobered. "Though Alecc does not always heed those closest to him. Before I left, they advised him to ignore King Gendrick's plea for warriors to defend Telor against Wardour. Alecc would have none of it."

"The Wardorian fleet would have reached Telor by now." He paused. "And the girl? The one they say is Roaran Caelan's daughter."

"Oh, you've heard about her." Rohane drummed her fingers on the table.

"I've heard strange stories. That she killed the ghoul god Archanin. That she killed Roaran Caelan, too. Her father. Is it true she's a witch?"

"Of sorts." Rohane gulped wine quickly. "She's powerful. But it's hard to say what sort of magic she possesses."

"Is she the part of your mission you can't tell me about?"

Rohane nodded. "And don't think if you ply me with liquor, I'll reveal all my secrets. And talking of secrets." She flicked up a brow. "What is so important that you would drag me from Quisnaf so soon after my return?"

"Ah." Cassian sat back with a smug smile. "Did I tell you how it delights me to have you in Vene?"

"Three times already. You're up to something. Tell me."

He leaned forward to pat her hand. "My lovely Rohane. Clever daughter. I miss you badly when you're not here."

"Now, Father," Rohane cautioned with a soft laugh. "Not this again. You knew your daughter, any daughter you sired, would be raised in Quisnaf. That is the way of things."

"True." Cassian sighed. "But you are half Venivan. You should spend more time here, with me. I could do with your support. My noblemen are rapacious fools. Your brother is capricious."

Rohane pretended to adopt a stern manner. "You've gotten old. Sentimental. I'm a Quisnaf captain. I have duties, a place in Quisnaf."

"You have a place here."

"Father—"

"It would please me if you spent more time in Vene. I do not say *all* your time, only more. So I took steps to make that more convenient, more desirable. I have something for you, something to entice you. A reason to be more often in Vene, by my side."

"Oh?" What she wanted, not even a king could give her. Could he bring her battle sister back? Could he cleanse her blood of its curse? Could he turn a deceiving man into a man she could trust? A man she could love.

"Come." Cassian started to rise. When Rohane did not, he brushed warm fingers over her arm. "Come. This will please you."

"To where?"

"Into the gardens. They're beautiful at night."

"You think the moons will entice me? The same moons sit above Quisnaf." With a laugh, she rose. *He and his secrets. Such nonsense.*

Cassian snatched up an oil lantern and walked into the gardens. Discreet guards followed a few paces behind. Indulgently, Rohane followed, muttering, "And this enticement is in the garden? How very strange."

Cassian only smiled.

The night was soft, the velvet sky dusted with stars. A sliver of moon blinked through shifting cloud. Jasmine and gardenia blended in a rich perfume. Warm air licked her neck.

Maybe it was the wine, but Rohane knew a moment of contentment, despite Cassian's silly games. Maybe she could forget Val. Maybe she would even forgive his lies—in time.

"This way."

Cassian led her along shaded paths beneath flame trees that shed scarlet flakes. The gardens were deserted but breathed with life. Paws stirred fallen leaves. An owl hooted. Shadowed wings darted towards the moon.

The trees fell away. In a clearing, the dark-stoned tower Rohane remembered from childhood needled the sky. "This old ruin?"

She followed Cassian to the door. The king stooped to insert a key into the lock. Turning, he pressed the key into Rohane's palm. "I have a gift for you. Carefully gathered, carefully kept."

Rohane frowned at the stone steps twisting into the gloom. "Up there?"

"Go on," Cassian said, mischief in his tone.

"What are you up to, you sly old dog?"

He tapped his nose and passed her the lamp. "Go up. Just you. Take your time up there. Do what you want with my gift."

"What's up there?"

"Walk to the top chamber. Use the key."

"This is all very strange."

Cassian smiled. He seemed very pleased with himself. Smug.

When he turned away, Rohane paused for a moment, listening to the silence. Then slowly, she trudged up the stairs. Whatever foolishness this was, she had little patience with it. The room above likely held a delicate rose he'd named after her. Or a new sword. Perhaps a jewelled knife or an embroidered cloak of the finest silk from the far reaches of the world.

Rohane reached a sturdy door. She unlocked it and shouldered her way in. Someone gasped. Rohane froze. Then she took a step inside and swung the lamp about.

"Rohane," Val breathed. He was lying on his back on the bed, naked from the waist up, his wrists bound to the frame. "Oh, gods, Rohane."

Rohane stared with widening eyes. Her face flushed with heat, her throat constricting. "No," she muttered in disbelief. Then her shock flamed to anger. What game was this? No, she did not want this. "No," she shouted. "No."

Whirling, she ran for the door and down the stairs. Cassian was no longer below the tower. She paused, glanced about, then hurried across the clearing, along the path, and back to the castle.

Guards stepped aside at the open doors. A lute's soft notes thrummed. Her father sat sprawled in his chair, eyes closed to listen to the musician, a glass on the table before him.

Rohane stomped into the room. "What did you do?"

Cassian opened his eyes. He flicked a hand. "What? No thanks for my gift? It was expensive and hard to acquire."

"What did you do?"

"You're not pleased?"

"Pleased?" Rohane stamped a booted foot. "Pleased? You abducted him from Quisnaf, imprisoned him in a tower to please me?"

Unrepentant, he shrugged. "Yes."

Rohane could only glare. Then she heaved an exasperated cry. "Why?"

Cassian rose from his chair. He rounded the table to seize her hands. "I heard what was in your voice, Rohane, and what was in your heart. Hope."

"Hope." In disbelief, she shook her head. "What nonsense is this?"

"You were such a cheerful child. So sweet. Even as a young woman, when you told me stories of training or mischief you and your friends got up to, you bubbled with the joy of it all." He sighed. "Then she died. Your battle sister. You blamed yourself. The light in your eyes faded to dull resignation, as if you expected nothing of life. There was nothing to hope for, only duty."

"What has this got to do with you abducting a man?"

"When we spoke in the garden, even though you were angry at this Val Arques, I glimpsed a longing in your eyes. For a moment, you were alive again. You were my daughter, my beloved Rohane, again. Not that dull-eyed creature of duty."

"I hate him."

Cassian dropped her hands and smiled. "So you say. But even that is something. Too often, you are indifferent to everything, even pleasure."

Rohane kicked a chair leg. "I didn't want this. How could you think I did?"

Her father dismissed her words with a wave of his hand. "You want him. I procured him for you."

"He betrayed me. I despise him." Rohane huffed in exasperation. "And worse, you don't understand the damage your mischief has done. I can't just take him back. If the council learns what you did—"

"They won't find him."

"Sisilia." Fear lanced Rohane's breast. "She's using magic to trace him. Eventually, she'll succeed."

"Don't you think your old father knows a few tricks? The tower is protected with all manner of nasty spells."

"This is serious. They will not give up."

"When they can't find him, of course they'll give up." His gaze sharpened on her face. "Unless there's something you're not telling me."

Rohane hung her head. "Maybe."

Cassian returned to the table to pour more wine. "I thought so." He didn't look concerned or angry. "I always know when you're holding something back."

Rohane tapped her fingers on her thigh, wishing for the touch of her sword pommel.

Cassian pressed a cup of wine into her hands. "Here, do something with your hands. You always fidget when you're nervous."

"I'm not nervous," she grumbled. "I'm angry. You don't know

what trouble you've created. I need to take him back—it's my duty—but how? The Quisnaf council will be furious at you."

"Duty again." Cassian sniffed with displeasure. "Always duty." His hand fell on her shoulder. "I will never tell you to turn from duty, child, but I want you to be peaceful. Not at war with yourself. I want you to find something that makes this life worthwhile."

Rohane huffed again. Why didn't her father understand? The Quisnaf would search and search for Val, just as they had for centuries. Sisilia would not give up. Cassian's foolishness might cause a rift between Veniva and Quisnaf.

"He has Caelan blood," she blurted. "Now do you see?"

Cassian's hand stilled on her shoulder. In the corner, the boy began a mournful tune on the lute.

At his shocked expression, Rohane laughed bitterly. "Now do you see what you've done?"

A shadow crossed Cassian's face, a single moment of uncertainty. "You have interesting taste, daughter," he said slowly. "I foolishly wondered if his beauty drew you. Yet you would never be so shallow. So who is he? Some bastard cousin of Gendrick's?"

It's worse than that, she might have said. *He's a prince of the Isles. Centuries old.* But she would not reveal Val's secrets. They had become Quisnaf secrets. Rohane dragged her hands down her face. "How do I get him back to Quisnaf? Without dispute or even war between Veniva and Quisnaf?"

"You don't."

"I must."

"He stays where he is. Do what you will with him, Rohane. He is safely kept, well looked after. You may visit him whenever you choose."

"What do I do with him?" she wailed.

"Beat him. Berate him. Nag him. Make love to him. Whatever pleases you."

"No. This isn't right." She fisted her hands again. "I don't want this."

Cassian drained his cup. He turned to the musician. "Something lively. Play."

The tune began. Rohane recognised it from numerous feasts in both Veniva and Quisnaf.

"I don't want this," she repeated. "I don't want him."

"I misunderstood then."

"You misunderstood."

He shrugged. "Easy to fix. I'll send someone to kill him."

"No!" Rohane shouted, the protest torn from her.

Cassian laughed. "Just as I thought."

VAL ARQUES

She was nothing more than a silhouette in the doorway, framed by moonlight. But he knew Rohane's shape, the breathy fragrance of her hair, and the sound of her steps. A lamp flared to brightness. She carried it to the bed and considered him as he lay there, bound and helpless. Her expression was calm but resolved. He met her eyes, letting her see his anger.

"So it was you?" Disbelieving, he waited for her to deny it. He waited for words like, *I came to find you. Someone told me where to look. I had nothing to do with this.*

In the lamp's soft glow, her face was all planes and shadows, especially dear to him. Her long tunic clung to every curve, her cloak held together by a single clasp. Too many emotions boiled through him. Desire, longing, relief she was here… resentment.

"You imprisoned me? This is all you?"

"My father."

Understanding lashed him. Val laughed harshly. "More secrets, Rohane? You said you were Venivan. You just didn't say you were the daughter of the king of Veniva."

Rohane shrugged. "In Quisnaf, we do not define ourselves by our fathers."

"Why did he imprison me? To punish me?"

She did not answer. But her eyes dwelled on his face, their darkness unreadable.

"Rohane." Val shifted on the bed. "I didn't break my word to you. I'd never betray your trust."

Her expression hardened. Slowly, she put down the lantern. Even more slowly, she drew her knife. The light glinted on its metal and jewelled hilt.

A simple warrior of Quisnaf did not carry such a jewelled blade. And her sword. Seithin steel. He hadn't thought that through. The signs were all there. *King's daughter.*

"My father brought you here as a gift—to me. He says I must do what I wish with you. Beat you, berate you, love you... hurt you." She touched fingertips to the knife's edge.

Val fixed his eyes upon her face. "Do you want to hurt me, Rohane? Is that it? Then do it."

Still, she stared at him. A remote, ethereal quality clung to her, a shadow.

With a sleepwalker's detachment, she approached the bed and knelt, her knees either side of his hips. He could smell the exotic, rich perfume of her hair and skin, so familiar, as she leaned and placed the knife to his breast. Her mesmerised gaze fixed upon the blade. Softly, gently, she dragged the tip over his bare flesh, a cold ghosting over skin.

He met her eyes and did not look away. Intimacy thickened like desire, a strange spell that bound them with blood, resentment, and hurt. "Do what you must, Rohane. If my pain makes things right between us, then I welcome it."

Her breaths were unnaturally slow. The knife whispered down his half-naked body like a lover's caress. Val shut his eyes, unable to unravel the fury of emotions that passed between them into the other so none was pure. Not anger or forgiveness. Nor grief. Instead, there was only a tainted, sick blend of misunderstanding.

The tip paused on his groin. Rohane drew a shuddering breath. Val braced for pain.

Metal clattered on stone. Val snapped his eyes open. The knife lay on the floor. Rohane still crouched over him, so close, and yet her remote, lost expression was a chasm parting them.

"I thought I wanted to hurt you." She spoke slowly, as if unravelling the words. "I thought your pain would mask mine, that it would free me of you. But I'm not my father. I would take no pleasure in your pain."

With a shake of her head, she leaned to untie his hands. Her breast brushed his shoulder. Val wanted to pull her into his arms, to comfort her with soft murmurs and kisses.

Rohane straightened. "Go through the gardens. There's a wall. You'll find yourself in Vene. Make for the harbour. Take a ship. They'll hunt you. Keep moving, or they'll find you. Sisilia has your blood, so you can't stop, not ever."

He rubbed his wrists. "Where will you go?"

"Back to Quisnaf. Where else?"

"Come with me." Eagerly, he grabbed her hands. "Come with me, Rohane."

She stared, astonished, then laughed unhappily. "And turn my back on my sisters? Turn my back on my duty? No. I belong in Quisnaf. That is my home. Not Veniva, not some unknown city across the sea."

"Then—" Val seized a deep breath. "Then I belong in Quisnaf, too."

Rohane tore her hands away and reeled back. "You don't know what you're saying. Even if you persuaded the council someone abducted you, they will keep you deep within the caverns. There is no coming back from this. No third chance."

"I must be where you are, Rohane."

"What?" Her voice quavered. She began to shake.

"I must be where you are."

In the candlelight, her face was wan, her brow furrowed. "I don't care if you deceived me, not anymore. I just want you safe. I want you to be free, beyond hurt, beyond pain."

Val's voice was husky. "I can't be free. I belong to you, Rohane. You belong to me."

She gasped. He glimpsed a spark deep in her eyes as though a fire roared up, only to die down at once. "But you ran," Rohane cried. "You left me to be punished, and you ran."

Val sprang up. He cupped her face in his hands. "Will you listen this time? Someone hit me. I woke up on that red-soil plain with a sword and seeing a cloud of dust as riders approached." He drew his hands away and dragged his fingers violently through his tousled hair. "Oh, gods, why don't you believe me?"

She trembled. "A guard is dead. It had to be you."

"I didn't kill her. On my love for you, I didn't."

"It had to be you. Nothing else makes sense."

"Rohane—"

"It can't be so—" She rose and began to pace like a caged beast. "No, it must be more lies."

"Rohane."

A sob escaped her lips. She drew up sharply and turned to stare at him. "But what if your words are true?" she whispered. "You say you will return to Quisnaf, to face imprisonment, humiliation, all because you won't leave me. What am I to believe? That you didn't run? That you were set up? But that's so much worse."

"How can it be worse?"

"Because I doubted you," she wailed. "I'm false to the bone. Not worthy." With a terrible, anguished cry, she dropped her head into her hands, weeping.

Val pulled her to his breast. "Rohane."

"Who got you out of the caverns? Who was it?"

"Marlisa."

"Marlisa!" Rohane scowled. "I knew my father must have an agent in Quisnaf. It's what he does. She was paid, no doubt. It's her weakness. She's not wellborn."

"Will you keep your father's secret or expose his agent?"

"I don't know." She tilted her head to look at him. Tears stained her cheeks.

Softly, Val touched a tear. "How did this happen?" he murmured.

"When did I let my guard down? I thought my heart shielded. Not just to protect me but to protect you. Yet I have to be where you are, Rohane. By The Three, what a fool I am."

She stroked his cheek tenderly. "Then by The Three, we're both fools."

Pulling back, he shook his head. "You'll be hurt. Everyone who's close to me gets hurt. That's what I do. I destroy. I bring misery."

"I was already miserable." Rohane put her hand behind his head, drawing him closer for her kiss. Her lips plundered and devoured, her hands hungrily roaming over his naked skin.

She pushed him back onto the bed. Val sprawled. He rose to his elbows, considering her. An abandoned, fierce desire glinted in her eyes. With savage desperation, she drew her tunic over her head and kicked off her pants. Before him, she was naked and lovely and his.

Growling, Val pulled her onto his lap. Heat flamed through him. Beneath his lips and tongue, she tasted wild, her skin salty. He was lost in the sensation of her nipples pressed against his chest, her thighs gripping him, her wet mouth on his throat. With a shiver of pleasure, Rohane groped for the string to his pants, pushing them down, kissing him hard as he slid into her. She pushed against him, as if needing to feel more, rocking and rocking.

His fingers stole through her hair, down onto her shoulders then her back. At the rough scars, he gasped. "By The Three, your back. Oh, gods, it's my fault."

"It's nothing. Do not stop. Harder. Faster."

Val thrust deeper, his hands caressing her nakedness. At the scent of honey and heady desire, his head spun. Wanting. Taking. Giving.

Urgent, hot, surging arousal took him over. He surrendered to the force of it, his body quivering. She was what he had longed for. She was his. He was hers.

His gaze leapt to meet hers, his eyes showing her his need, the ache in him, the strength of his passion. At his intensity, he sensed her retreat, her fright. With sheer force of will, he pulled back from the precipice of desire and kissed her mouth softly, reassuringly. Her lips parted beneath his touch, her tongue tentatively finding his. The kiss lengthened.

He wanted to be gentle, but a storm of pleasure took him over. His thrusts quickened. Rohane gasped, trembled, and yowled.

"You're mine, Rohane," he whispered as she clutched at him.

She laughed, her light-brown hair spilling onto his breast. "You have it all wrong, Telorian. When a Quisnaf woman gives you her heart, that means she makes you hers."

ROHANE

His hands burned her skin. Those lovely bladesman's hands—calloused, rough, and yet so tender—moved over her breasts and through her hair then touched her face with a feather-soft caress.

The taste of him, the scent, the feel of him, just the weight of his body pressed against her overwhelmed her with sensation and desire. Too much. Not enough.

She moaned and rocked, wanting to take him deeper. Wanting more. Just more. He bent his head to kiss her neck then her shoulder blades, groaning softly. With the full length of him buried inside her, he lifted his head and stared into her eyes. At his possessive gaze, Rohane shivered. It was too demanding. Too knowing.

His intensity unnerved her. He would allow nothing short of surrender, of will and body. She wasn't ready. She could not be that vulnerable.

As though sensing her fear, his eyes softened. Gentle lips sought hers. Beneath his pressure, Rohane's mouth slowly opened. Lost in the kiss, she arched her back, bearing down on him, always down, still needing more. Her body shuddered on the edge of climax.

Val moaned. She moved back and forth harder, building

rhythm until his body trembled and jolted. A whirlwind of pleasure took her over. Then came wonderful, shattering release. Rohane fell against him. His hands moved through her hair as he whispered her name. At the sheer bulk of him, at the delicious strength in his body, a thrill ran through her. Rohane wanted that weight on her, to lie beneath this man, to feel that slow grind of flesh in flesh.

When he reached to stroke her cheek, a pulse fluttered beneath the thin skin on his wrist. Mesmerised, she watched it. For all his strength, the life in him was fragile. As soft and vulnerable as that tiny beat.

A sob choked her. She clung to him, wanting to protect him, to protect that fragile life—the way she had wanted to protect her battle sister.

His strong, warm arms folded about her. Val's lips brushed her ear. "What is it? Why are you crying?"

"I'm afraid," Rohane whispered.

"For me? Don't be, Rohane. I'm not. Not now."

"There's no future for us, Val. Not here. Not in Quisnaf. Not anywhere."

"Then come with me. I don't care where if you're there."

"You don't understand. Sisilia can use your blood to find us. They'll come for us. They'll keep coming."

"But this tower—?" He frowned.

"My father's sorcerer warded it. But the moment we leave here, she'll know. Oh, goddess. They'll send retrievers." Fierceness rose in her breast. She would guard him with her life, whatever it took. "But I'll keep you safe," she growled. "I'll kill them if I have to."

Val held her so tightly, her ribs ached. "No," he whispered. "I can't ask you to do that. Never would I ask you to side with me against your sisters, against Quisnaf."

"You didn't ask me. It's what I'm prepared to do. To keep you safe."

"If you do that, one day—maybe not tomorrow, but one day—

you'll resent me for it. Resent me because we're adrift and don't belong anywhere. You say you won't, but you will. That's the truth of it. No." He nuzzled her neck. "There's only one answer."

Reluctantly, she untangled herself from his arms. She wanted to fall beside him, to curl up next to him, kiss him, to feel the weight of his body on hers. To squirm and wriggle beneath him. But he was right. His arms represented a fantasy. Reality was something different, something colder. *Duty.*

"Don't ask me to take you back, Val. I can't."

"Then what?" He leaned on his elbows.

Only their breaths, still synchronised as if they still moved together, filled the silence between them.

"Don't ask me."

"Then I won't ask, Rohane. But I won't ask you to give up your people or your duty. I won't ask you to turn traitor, to kill your Quisnaf sisters to keep me safe. So you must decide yourself to take me back. Not because I ask but because you must."

"If only there was anything I could do."

Val looked away from her into the shadows. "There might be something. I don't know how reliable it is, but Jenna-Dairine came to me in the blood keepers' caverns. This is what I remember."

VAL ARQUES

A thousand lights burned in the cliff face. Fairy lights, Rohane had called them. Long ago. From the path leading to the entrance to Quisnaf, Val peered up, thinking them beautiful. They glowed in the gathering dusk. Beacons in the blackness.

Sunset mottled clouds at his back, as if the fading day represented freedom and the shadows ahead, his surrendered will.

"Last chance to run." Rohane grinned to cheer him, but Val sensed her unease as she walked beside him, her glance flickering left and right, her hand close to her sword hilt.

He spread his arms. "To where?"

"It's a big world, Val."

"Not so much."

Rohane glanced at the majestic stone arch at the entrance to the Quisnaf city then gestured at the sword he had carried on their journey. "Here, best give me that."

He passed it to her, at once missing its familiar weight against his hip. How quickly the illusion of freedom shattered without a weapon.

Rohane's gaze lingered. "Venivan clothing suits you well."

Val smoothed his black silk tunic with a palm. "It's rather more clothing than I've become accustomed to wearing in Quisnaf.

Maybe Sisilia will let me keep my new garments."

"Sisilia will add a few ornaments," Rohane said. "Lovely chains that peal when you shuffle along, maybe an iron collar. You'll look very pretty."

"I don't know what to say to that."

"You must be coming down with an autumn fever. From here on in, Val, say as little as possible. Drop your eyes. Try to look humble."

"I'm humble," he complained.

Rohane scoffed. "You hold your head like a haughty prince of the Isles, Telorian. Your eyes burn with defiance, and your beautiful mouth more often than not twists with irony."

"I sound horrible."

Rohane shoved his sword into her belt beside her own. "You have your moments."

"I know, I know." He threw up a hand. "Most of them bad." He sighed. "It's a lot to hope for, Rohane. A few muttered words I remembered on the edge of sleep. Maybe Blaire doesn't have a plan. Maybe I dreamt Jenna-Dairine's words?"

"You heard Jenna-Dairine say she'll cloak you. And if she doesn't, I will." Rohane laughed softly. "That means you become mine. You'll hate being at my beck and call."

He seized her hand. "What terrible tasks will you have me do?"

"I'll keep you naked in my bed. Always." Rohane sobered. "We'll outwit her, Val. Sisilia won't expect Jenna-Dairine to cloak you. I can't wait to see her face when she realises she is outmanoeuvred."

"Even though I belong to the blood keepers, Jenna-Dairine can do this?"

"She's a councillor, Val. Though, Sisilia may challenge her right to overrule the court's decision, but there's hope at least."

In the gathering night, a soft whistle sounded. A bush rustled. From dusky shadows figures emerged. Early moonlight glinted on levelled swords.

"Who are you?" a woman challenged. "State your business."

Rohane dropped his hand. Quietly, she said, "Do nothing. Say nothing. Trust me." She lifted her voice. "Rohane, daughter of Samantha. With a prisoner."

"Samantha, the councillor? Bring light," the sentry snapped.

Val heard footfall then he blinked as a lantern shone on his face. The lantern swung to Rohane. "Captain, who is this with you?"

"An escaped slave."

Val lowered his eyes. *Humble.*

"He's not chained."

Rohane shrugged. "He surrendered himself. Gave me no trouble. But I must ask you to let me pass. I am required to take him directly to the council."

"Here." Another sentry pushed forward. "Is this the one they've been searching for? Jenna-Dairine and the others?"

Rohane hesitated. "It is."

The sentry whistled. She and her companion stared openly at him.

"I'm in a hurry," Rohane tapped her fingers on her sword belt. "Let me through."

Without answering, the sentry clapped her hands. A Decan guard appeared. "Take word ahead to Persia if you can find her. To any councillor, if not. Tell them the retrieval captain Rohane has returned with the man they've sought." When the guard ran off, the sentry's hard gaze shifted once more to Val. "You don't know the half of the effort spent searching for him, Captain. He should be restrained."

"He's contained," Rohane snapped.

"Wait here for the escort. Word is he's valuable."

"I have no time." She shoved Val forward. When he stumbled, Rohane grabbed his elbow and dragged him beside her to the gates between the arch. Reluctantly, a sentry hauled them open. Rohane took Val through. The guard's eyes burned his back.

The valley closed about them. Cliff lights twinkled. More and more torches appeared, lighting pathways or stairs. More sentries touched hand to brow and let them pass.

Rohane marched him on confidently. The crisp air smelt of dew. At a hoot, Val turned his head. An owl watched from a stone balcony, unafraid.

Persia emerged from a gaping cavern with a handful of the Decan Watch. Torches blazing at her back rimmed her head with golden light. "This is interesting." She dropped her hands to her hips. "Not quite the message I expected to receive tonight."

"You're not needed," Rohane said rudely. "I'm bringing him in."

Persia glanced from Rohane to Val. "It seems you succeeded where everyone else failed. That must be why Branwyn calls you 'girl wonder.'" Her tone was faintly ironic. "They're in the hall. Not the council room. At least Blaire is. Your mother, too. And Jenna-Dairine."

"Jenna-Dairine?" Rohane arched a brow. She remembered how Jenna-Dairine had been in Blaire's chambers.

Persia laughed. "Oh, yes, they are reconciled. Didn't you notice?"

"Nobody tells me anything," Rohane grumbled.

"Jenna-Dairine has forgiven Blaire for whatever she thought she held against her. Blaire, also, has foolishly forgiven all slights."

"Foolishly?"

"Walk on," Persia said gruffly.

Rohane shrugged and dug a hand into Val's back. "Move."

Persia fell in beside Rohane. "Where did you find him?"

"It's a long story."

"I can't wait to hear it." Her chill blue eyes shifted to him. "I knew the Telorian was trouble. But this is the end for this one. He'll be fortunate ever to see daylight again. Sisilia will keep him very, very close."

Rohane gave another meaningless shrug. Val admired her control. Every emotion, all her fears for him, remained hidden behind a mask of indifference.

469

They reached the hall. Guards threw open the doors. Val remembered how this enormous chamber had blazed with colour and light at the feast, laughter and voices had swept to every dark corner. Now it sat still, silent, and gloomy. Dismal torchlight flickered.

At the far end, he glimpsed Blaire, her beautiful head held stiffly. Samantha and Jenna-Dairine were with her. A fourth woman had her back to him, but he knew her. *Sisilia.* Alarm shuddered through him.

Persia on her heels, Rohane brought Val forward. "Humble, remember."

Val bowed his head. He could feel the women's eyes upon him, even before Sisilia turned. Her brows arched.

Blaire exhaled slowly. "Thank the goddess, Rohane. Where was he?"

Rohane's hand still rested upon his shoulder. "I can't tell you."

"What?" Jenna-Dairine's voice was harsh with disbelief.

Persia sniffed with disgust. "Can't or won't? What about him? Can he tell us?"

"He doesn't remember," Rohane said. "My father's guards found Val beaten and wounded in an alley near the seafront in Vene. My father recognised his Quisnaf garments and sent word to me."

Blaire frowned. "What do you mean he doesn't remember?"

"Cassian's physicians believe someone forced a potion on him. Val was dazed, bewildered, hardly knew his name." She thrust a parchment at Blaire. "Here, my father sends word of it in greater detail."

Blaire took the paper and frowned at Val. "Is this true?"

He met her probing gaze. "All I remember is walking through a passage towards the bathhouse. Next, I was lying bleeding in a street."

"So you don't know who abducted you?" Jenna-Dairine pressed. "Where they held you? Anything?"

"I remember smoke, feeling sleepy. Then nothing."

"Who helped get you out of Quisnaf? Who is the traitor?"

"Jen." Blaire laid a hand on the woman's arm. "He doesn't remember."

A slow hand clap began. Heads swung towards Sisilia.

Val glanced at her uneasily. She'd said nothing as Rohane told their story. Now she began to laugh, a mocking sound that hunted through the hall like an arrow.

"Lies," she said. "Pretty lies from his pretty lips."

Rohane's chin jerked up. "Oh, yes, and what do you think happened? Maybe you abducted him, to set him up again." She poked a finger at the sorceress. "You're devious and single-minded, Sisilia. You don't care who you hurt as long as you get what you want."

The sorceress sneered.

"Rohane, say no more." Blaire threw up a hand.

"I won't stay silent," Rohane spluttered. "Val explained to me what happened before I found him in the desert. It was all her doing. The abduction. The death of the guard. She wanted Val in her clutches."

"Rohane, I said shut up," Blaire said. "You do well to remember you are accusing a councillor of Quisnaf and the high sorceress of the temple."

"Whatever it takes, Sisilia," Rohane said. "That's how you think, isn't it?"

"You are a meddlesome child." Sisilia dismissed Rohane with a wave of her hand. Her cool gaze fell upon Val. "I'd hate to think you lied to me, Val Arques." Sisilia's voice was silk laced with menace. "We had an agreement, you and I. We still do."

His heart skidded against his ribcage. He met her violet eyes. The fires of Cyrah's temple ghosted in their pale light.

She smiled. Then a flash of light jagged from her fingertips. Pain shot down his spine. Val collapsed to his knees, gasping in shock.

"Stay."

Val strained to move. Invisible bonds held him on his knees as surely as shackles.

With deft fingers, Sisilia loosened the clasp about her cloak. "I think some might like to meddle in our agreement, Val Arques. So I will set that right. You are uncloaked. I will cloak you. And that will be an end to it."

"No, stop her," Rohane screamed, starting forward. "Someone stop her."

Sisilia leaned over Val. Unhurriedly, she draped her cloak over his shoulders.

"She can't," Jenna-Dairine hissed. She lurched as though to attack.

Samantha grabbed her by the tunic to hold her back. "Hush, it's done," she said. "A councillor may do this—if a man is unclaimed."

"Val." Shaking with anger, Rohane crouched beside him. "Are you hurt?"

"I can't rise." Sisilia's spell bound him to this spot, immobilised his limbs.

"She guessed," Jenna-Dairine muttered. She turned a stricken face to the Regenta. "Blaire, she knew what we plotted."

Sisilia laughed scornfully. "Of course I knew. Did you think you or our beloved Regenta could trick me with petty schemes? Such nonsense. I serve the goddess. She will not be denied. You'd best not try and stand in my way again."

With another sneer, she regarded Val and Rohane. "Step back, Captain. You need no longer worry about his protection. His care falls to me. He wears my cloak, after all."

Val could only watch in horror as Rohane straightened. Her face was grey, her expression bleak. "I don't know what you're intending, but I'll find a way to stop you."

"Will you, *Captain?* Your duty is to do nothing. You understand about duty, don't you, Rohane? It's all you have, after all."

Drawn by Blaire's shouts, guards ran in. The Regenta waved them back.

"She can't do this." Rohane's breaths were quick and sharp, her jaw tight.

Samantha put her hands on her daughter's shoulders. "Hush. Be calm."

Through a veil of shock, Val heard her only vaguely. It was as if time had paused, as if he were caught in its lull and could not even blink. Dimly, as though from far away, he took in the cool silk cloak touching his bare arms, the dread shifting in his belly, and Sisilia's smirk as she bent to whisper words freeing him from her spell.

Sisilia carried a torch to light their way. With heavy steps, his mind numb, Val followed. Sisilia's cloak rubbed against his neck, a silken fetter.

What had just happened? That spark of hope that ignited at the thought Jenna-Dairine had a plan had guttered as easily as a candle flame. Now he was adrift, bewildered by the bitter turn of fate. Lost.

Sisilia took him to the temple, through its ornate, tiled rooms, and along a corridor. He shivered not with cold but foreboding. Every sinister shadow yawed. Even the light from burning braziers mocked him.

At the end of an unfamiliar passage, doors stood open. A slender young woman rose from a stool and waved a lamp. Cool blue eyes passed over him to her mistress. "My lady." Torchlight lit thick coils of red-gold hair as she bobbed her head. "What is this? Who is he?"

"Mine." With a flurry of her whirling cloak and swirling gown, Sisilia brushed past.

The girl gasped in bewilderment. "I don't understand." She

stumbled after the sorceress. "Yours? What does this mean? Is he a new slave? Are we to bleed him for spells?"

Sisilia strode into a spacious chamber. It was far from what Val had expected—light and airy and just as luxurious as Blaire's rooms. Sheepskin rugs covered tiles. Embroidered tapestries decorated the walls. Cupboards with linenfold panelling, chests, and chairs with the seat and back made of leather all caught his eye. Yet for all its beauty and comfort, this was a prison. With his every step, Sisilia's cloak grew heavier and heavier until he could hardly breathe.

"Come."

The sorceress led him through curtains into a smaller chamber. This was more the sorceress's den he expected. Leather books stinking of dust lined shelves; bottles, sachets, and ampoules were scattered over stained benches. Roots and herbs hung from roof beams. From wall crevices, candles blazed.

The room threw him back to Myranthe's vile lair. He could nearly smell the odours of her potions and his unwashed body and hear scraping iron when he shifted his fettered ankles.

Val quickly shuttered that memory behind a wall in his mind.

"You'll sleep there tonight." Sisilia pointed to a cot half in darkness in a small room off her lair.

Val cast a resigned look about for chains. "What? No restraints?"

"There is no need," she replied, her tone distant. "Our agreement still stands." Sisilia turned to the hovering servant. "Fetch him something to eat. And a blanket for the bed."

Hands on hips, the woman gaped in disbelief. "Am I to serve him? A slave?"

Sisilia's face darkened. She menaced with a pointing finger. "You'll do as I say, Anna. Do you hear?"

The woman looked ready to argue again. She slid Val a hateful glare. "How long is he to stay?"

"As long as I say. I cloaked him."

"Cloaked?" Anna's mouth opened and closed.

Sisilia sighed. "If caring for him is so distasteful, fetch one of the slaves. Instruct him on how to see to this man's needs."

"He's the one all the fuss is about, isn't he? The one who has the council in a lather. The Telorian."

"Yes, the Telorian." Sisilia sounded weary. "Just do as I ask."

Anna flounced off.

Val walked into the inner chamber and sank onto the cot. A trembling ran through him. He hunched his tight shoulders.

"I have work to do." Sisilia turned to leave.

"Wait. Please."

She spun back, eyebrows raised.

"What… What do you expect of me?"

"I need your blood. I thought we were clear about that."

Still stunned by how events had turned in a heartbeat, Val swallowed hard. "And?"

Sisilia flicked a hand. "You'll offer your body to the blood keepers so the required children are born. They shall seek my approval for when and where, as you now belong to me. As for you, I shall tolerate no defiance, no argument, no refusal. In return, you will be well fed. Clothed in fine garments. You will walk always with your head high, proud that you wear my cloak. Only I or a councillor may command you. Not even a battale captain may now tell you what to do. She shall ask me."

"I see."

"You may bathe as often as you choose. I know that sort of thing is important to you. Anna will take you—once she stops sulking."

"I see."

She huffed. "Is my blunt answer distasteful? Yet I am the only one who does not lie to you, Telorian. I have always told you the truth, told you exactly what will happen, even if you do not want to hear it."

"So this—" He glanced about the small chamber, empty of all but the bed, a table, and a stool. "Is my life now?"

"You may wander about my chambers at will. If you do as I say,

I shall not mistreat you. I have no interest in cruelty for cruelty's sake."

Anna returned with a tray and a blanket. She plonked both on the bed. "Stew. Eat."

Val looked at the bowl with disgust. The smell of cooked meat turned his belly. He didn't feel hungry. He hardly felt anything. Only cold.

"He's shivering." Anna put a hand on his cheek. "He's as cold as ice."

Sisilia hastened to Val. She touched fingertips to his face. "You're right. Like ice."

"Is he sick?" Anna recoiled. "If he's sick, I don't want to catch it."

"It's shock." For a moment, the sorceress stared at Val coldly. Pitilessly. Then she snapped her fingers. "Fetch that spiced wine from the fire."

With a disgusted sniff, the girl disappeared again then returned with a cup. She passed it to Sisilia. The sorceress pressed it to Val's lips. "Drink. Do you hear me? That is a command. This contains herbs that will help you. Drink."

He did, surprised by how warmth curdled through his body. The shaking subsided.

"Now lie back," Sisilia said. "You'll sleep now. I need your body to be strong, healthy. Otherwise, you are useless to me." She started towards the larger room. "Anna, you may go. I must study my charts. I have no need of you tonight."

Anna thrust her hands to her hips again. "What you said before about training one of the slaves to tend to him—well, it won't do. You are the grand sorceress. You cloaked this man, the first you've so honoured. No slave is worthy to tend to your possessions. I am mistress of these chambers, your apprentice. No one else shall touch your person or your things. I shall deal with him."

"Contrary as always. Do what you will. You always do."

Anna rumbled a reply. Val did not hear it. He plunged into welcome sleep.

ROHANE

"Maybe Jenna-Dairine told," Rohane muttered. She sprawled on Blaire's couch. It was near dawn, well after Sisilia had taken Val to her chambers.

"It wasn't Jen. Why are you so quick to accuse her?"

Rohane screwed up her face in a grimace. "Why are you so quick to trust her? She's been hostile since you became Regenta."

From her chair opposite the couch, Blaire smiled faintly. "Sisilia warned me about Jenna-Dairine. Said she'd try to overthrow my rule. Said she'd seen it in the sacred fire."

"Well, then—"

"Sisilia's visions aren't always right. She's been prophesising about a fleet of ships coming to attack us for years. And yet, nothing."

"It doesn't mean she's wrong about Jenna-Dairine."

"You don't understand. She came to me. Jenna-Dairine. To seek reconciliation. Once more, we are friends, just as we were as girls. Do you remember, Rohane? The four of us. You, me, Trevin, and Jenna-Dairine. Four councillors' daughters, destined for greatness, with dreams of glory and honour." She laughed, the sound harsh, broken, and bitter. "Look at us now."

"Hmm," Rohane said.

The Regenta arched a brow. "I thought you admired Jenna-Dairine."

"I do," Rohane said. "As a battale captain, she is exceptional. She is fierce, relentless, determined."

"Loyal?" Blaire asked.

"To Quisnaf, undoubtedly."

Blaire frowned. She considered Rohane keenly. "But not to me. Is that what you think?"

"I don't know—" Rohane broke off with a gasp.

The earth shook, one violent rumbling. A pot rolled from a shelf. A wine carafe tumbled from the table, splintering blood red on tiles.

A fist hammered upon the door. "Regenta, there's trouble."

Blaire sprang up and flung open the door. Persia stood in the passage. "*She*'s at the gates. Beyond the arches. She can't get in, but she's shouting, hurling magic."

"Who?" At another deep rumble, the room quaked. Blaire clutched at a wall. "This is *her*? Roaran's daughter?"

Persia nodded. "Sisilia will meet you on the arch."

"I'll come at once." Blaire headed into the passage.

Rohane scooped up her weapons belt and strapped it low over her hips. She followed. "She didn't waste any time. I've barely been back in Quisnaf a week."

Blaire paused. "You said she'd come. You said she'd come with anger and vengeance in her heart. And it seems she is here. Genya Caelan is here."

⁘

Rohane strode after Blaire and Persia to the arch between two cliffs marking the entrance to Quisnaf. On the wall above the gates, she leaned upon the balustrade, considering the two women below— Genya Caelan and the dark-haired warrior she had called Kate.

Against the gathering dawn, Decan guards and warriors raced

to take up positions inside the gate. Others pressed close on the wall walk or stood in groups to whisper and wonder. Excited children dodged around guards. A sentry gave chase to one and dragged the girl back with a harsh admonishment.

Sisilia led a group of hooded women, their gowns scarlet, onto the wall. Marks of the goddess in ash from a sacred fire darkened their brows or cheeks. The air smelt of magic. Rohane found the scent hard to describe: cold like winter, sharp and dank, but with an underlying cloying sweetness of dying daisies.

Genya hurled another spell. The arch beneath Rohane's feet trembled and shuddered. The gates, though, stood intact, unbroken and immovable.

"Let me ride out and take her on." Persia shoved her hands onto her hips. Defiant. Ready always to answer a challenge with steel.

"She'll simply throw you back with one sweep of her hand," Blaire muttered. She turned to Sisilia, who was watching Genya with an intense interest. "What magic is she using?"

"Seithin."

"Seithin," Blaire said. "But that is dangerous."

"I do not think so." Sisilia sniffed. "Mere theatrics." She looked at Blaire. "Shall I deal with her? I have called a number of sorceresses from the temple."

"No." Blaire wrinkled her brow. "Let's start by talking to her. Rohane, I want you with me."

"She was nothing but suspicious of me in Telor," Rohane said. "But I will come."

"Foolish child," Sisilia muttered as she followed Blaire and Rohane down the stairs. "She does not know how to control her gifts. This witch pup must learn her place."

Guards flung open the gates. Blaire led Rohane and Sisilia outside. An excited murmur rose at their backs.

At the sight of the three Quisnaf women, Kate grabbed Genya's arm and leaned to whisper. The girl shrugged off her companion's grip and walked forward, unafraid. Rohane admired her daring.

Perhaps this child was too young to know real fear. Youth often meant overconfidence—or stupid, reckless arrogance.

"Rohane," Genya hissed. "You deign to face me. Where is my guardian? Where is Dannon? You hold them both."

"So we do," Blaire admitted readily. She cast the girl a long look, frowning as if disappointed Genya lacked Roaran's curling hair, as black as midnight, and his dark-blue eyes of the gloaming. Indeed, with her fair hair, her long muscular legs and bulky shoulders, Genya might be mistaken for a Quisnaf warrior. Or a Quisnaf sorceress. Magic rippled off her like a shimmer of light across sand. Her eyes, tainted with sorcery, shifted purple then silver then black as Rohane had often seen Sisilia's change. "Who are you?"

"I am Blaire, daughter of Jennifer. Regenta of Quisnaf."

"Am I meant to be impressed?"

Blaire shrugged. "And you are Genya Caelan, daughter of the Seer King. Welcome. We've been expecting you."

"Welcome?" Genya spat. "I cannot enter your cursed gates." She sounded surprised. "How are you denying me entry?" She took a step forward, fists curled.

Kate put a warning hand on her arm.

"Only those who are wholly human may pass freely," Blaire said. "Unless we open our gates to you." She gestured with a sweep of her arm. "And we do. Come forward, Genya Caelan."

The girl considered Blaire suspiciously. "I just want my guardian. My lover, too. You have no right to keep me from them."

"Won't you come inside?" Blaire asked calmly. "Or do you prefer to rattle our city a little longer?"

Genya hissed out a breath. "I will destroy your city. I will bring it down. It's only a matter of time before I breach your gates."

Sisilia laughed. The sorceress had watched Genya like a snake sizing up prey. Now that laugh rang out coldly, scornfully.

Genya whirled to face her. "You laugh? Did you not feel the earth shudder beneath your feet?"

"A child's tantrum," Sisilia mocked. "Let me show you how it is done." She flicked a hand. Light jagged from the sorceress's fingers. A force lifted Genya Caelan and flung her back. The girl lay coughing in stirred dust. Kate rushed to help her up. Genya furiously brushed off her hands and rose.

With a laugh of pleasure, Sisilia again waved her hand through air. Genya fell to her knees. Struggling to rise, she hissed, "Release me."

"Regenta?" Sisilia twitched with mischief.

"Release her."

The sorceress flicked a wrist. "Oh, if I must. But we shall have no more tantrums."

Genya pushed to her feet. From her hunched shoulders, her drooped chin, and wary eyes, Sisilia's demonstration had knocked the cocky assurance from her. But Rohane was not fooled. This young woman was dangerous. They must win her and win her quickly.

"You are welcome in Quisnaf, Genya Caelan," Blaire said coolly. "Come. Let us show our hospitality. You must have had a tiring journey. You and your companion." She looked pointedly at Kate.

Genya glanced at her companion with what Rohane thought was dislike. "This is... Kate."

Blaire smiled. "Kate. Please. Come this way."

GENYA

The woman calling herself Regenta led them through a lush valley. Birds chirruped, and water in a blue-green river glistened and trickled over pebbles. None of it comforted Genya. The Quisnaf sorceress's magic had startled her. The woman presented another obstacle.

When they took a stone staircase onto a ledge then into a cavern lit only by torches, Genya wondered who would choose to live in caves. Though torches blazed everywhere, the darkness settled like a shroud.

"It's like the Icelands, only summer." Kaell peered about with interest but held himself warily.

Ahead, guards flung back wide bronzed doors. Genya walked in after Blaire. The room beyond was spectacular. Candles sparkled in every corner and crevice as if the room were painted of moonlight. Ornate pillars of stone fluted against a domed bronze ceiling. A veneer of multicoloured marble covered the walls. Genya's boots squeaked over a mosaic floor, but deeper within, patterned rugs spilled beneath exquisite marquetry tables and chests.

Blaire waved a hand at a divan. "Would you sit?"

Impatiently, Genya did, leaning against a ridiculous fluffed pillow. Kaell took up a watchful stance close by. Women carried trays of food and drink to wooden tables.

Blaire gracefully sat opposite Genya. She wore a fixed smile, but even beneath her pretence, Genya thought she was an elegant creature.

"Would you take tea?" Blaire fluttered a hand at a table as Rohane, the sorceress, and a fourth woman joined them on the couches. "It comes from the Shadow Kingdom, beyond the Ice Sea."

"Yes, tea." Genya thought she had heard of it. *Something you drank.*

Blaire nodded. A woman stepped in to pour steaming black-stained water into cups from a spouted ceramic pot. Blaire sniffed and sipped. Genya took her cue from the Regenta. The tea was pleasant enough.

"Your... companion?" Blaire raised a brow at Kaell.

Kaell nodded. "Thank you."

A woman took him a cup.

Genya sipped again, watching the four Quisnaf women over the rim of her cup. She would not make this easy for them. They had taken something belonging to her, and if they did not give Dannon back, they would pay. In blood. In pain.

Blaire smiled. "I should introduce my companions. Rohane, you know. The councillor Samantha. And this"—she swept a hand again—"is the high sorceress, Sisilia."

Sisilia offered Genya a cold look. "Child."

Carefully, a tremble of anger in her hand, Genya put down the cup. "I am no child."

Sisilia dismissed that with a gesture of contempt. "You have a child's rashness. You waste magic as though it is as common as water."

"Is it not?"

The woman's eyes gleamed. Genya remembered the force that had thrown her back. It had shocked her and humbled her to find someone more powerful than she. Half with fear, half with fascination, she shivered.

"It is rare. Dangerous in inexperienced hands. Did *he* teach you?" Sisilia leaned forward eagerly. "Roaran? Did he show you the mysteries of the Enarae?"

"I did not know him very long." That roiling of sadness and guilt turned in Genya's gut. Her betrayal had cost her heritage, of not only what Roaran might have taught her but also that simple joy of coming to understand her father.

"How sad," Sisilia said. "How formidable you might be if he had lived long enough to train you. Formidable and less careless."

"Where's Dannon?" Genya was done with the niceties. "Why do we sit here drinking tea instead of fetching him? Where's my guardian? I demand you bring him to me."

Blaire sipped tea. "First, I must ask you what you know of what occurred in Telor. Troubling news has reached us."

Genya looked down. "Gendrick betrayed us. Alecc Caelan is dead." Her voice cracked. *Oh, gods, Alecc.* "Nicky Saltman, the man who rode with Roaran, too. I was Gendrick's prisoner. I barely escaped." She pressed her lips into a tight line. "I want vengeance. That's why I'm here. I need Val. I need Dannon."

She needed Nicky. Genya had expected him to always be there. She'd loved him like a father. Tears welled. Guilty tears. She remembered with shame how she had dismissed him as pathetic. Angrily, she swiped away the tears, refusing to let others see her grief. She would put it aside until the day she could have revenge.

"My dear." Samantha rested fingers lightly on Genya's arm. The girl did not shake off her grip. The councillor's concern seemed genuine.

Rohane shifted uncomfortably on the couch. "We were wrong not to tell him. Val. After all, Alecc is his son."

"No," Genya cried. "It would break him."

"He has a right to know."

"Not yet," Blaire said. "If he hears of Alecc's death, he'll try to return to Telor. We can't have that. He's much too valuable."

"He belongs here," Sisilia said. "As does this child." She grabbed Genya's hand. Her skin was dry but cool. "I could train you. I could teach you how to take a terrible vengeance against Gendrick Caelan."

Genya ripped her hand away. "I came for Dannon. I want him and my guardian, Val Arques. Whatever purpose you have for him is no less urgent than my need for his help to take down this vicious king."

Sisilia's intense stare bore into Genya's eyes. "The seer did not prepare you." She turned in disbelief to Blaire. "She does not know."

Blaire shifted uneasily. "This is not the time—"

"Prepare me for what?" Genya peered from the Regenta to Sisilia.

Frowning, Blaire rose. With solemn steps, she crossed the room to a chest and knelt to unlock it with a key dangling from a wrist chain. For a moment, she rustled among papers then straightened and carried a scroll to Genya. "You may read."

Mouth dry, her pulse unsteady, Genya took the scroll and broke the seal. The four Quisnaf women seemed to still, waiting and watching. Kaell edged closer to peer over her shoulder.

The first paragraph was in Quisnaf, then the writer switched to Telorian. The handwriting was beautiful, with swirls, dashes, and flourishing *t*'s and *f*'s. Genya traced the words with a finger. At first, she could not take in the meaning. Then slowly, it sank into her. "No," she muttered in disbelief. "No."

She read on quickly with growing dismay. At the sight of the signature, written in what looked like faded blood, she jolted. *By my hand,* it read. "*Roaran Caelan.*"

"No!" she cried, storming to her feet. "He would not do this."

Sisilia scoffed. "And yet you declare you know him hardly at all. Can you truly say what he might or might not do?"

Kaell snatched the scroll from Genya. Frowning, he read. "Good gods. This can't be true."

Genya thrust her hands to her hips, glaring at each of the Quisnaf women in turn.

"But this says—" Kaell stared at her in horror. "This can't be right."

"It means nothing." Genya snatched up the tea cup and drank quickly.

"It says," Blaire said quietly, her gaze dwelling upon Genya, "that if Roaran should ever have a daughter, he promises her to Quisnaf."

A flare of anger tore through Genya. She stamped her feet, shouting, "He had no right. I am not subservient to his will, especially words written even before I was born."

"It is signed in blood, Genya Caelan," Sisilia said. "It matters not what you wish. The goddess shall have her way."

"No!"

"You could find a place here, Genya," Blaire said gently. "You would flourish in Quisnaf. I am told you are skilled with the sword. Our battales would gladly welcome a warrior of Roaran's blood. And think what you might learn from our seers and sorceresses. Not since Seithin at its strongest has any city possessed such magic as we do now."

Genya fisted her hands. "I do not care what Roaran promised. I am here because *she*"—she glared at Rohane—"promised me Dannon. *She* promised word of my guardian. Bring them to me now."

Blaire compressed her lips, her pale eyes hard. "You did not keep your part of the bargain. Dannon in return for another. Someone we sought."

Blood pulsing in her eardrums, Genya glanced at Kaell. One word now, and she would have Dannon returned. It would cost her nothing. After all, she cared little what happened to Kaell. She bit her bottom lip. But what of Val's pain? He loved Kaell. *Loved*.

A memory came to her then of Val in the ward at Vraymorg, at how he had hugged Kaell but had only harsh words for her. She

THE SWORD AND ITS WOMAN

tried to shove aside temptation and bitterness. But the fury that had run through her in that distant Vraymorg ward, as hot as metal in a blacksmith's furnace, rekindled.

She would rid herself of her rival. Besides, whatever happened, it was Val's fault. He had abandoned her, giving Kaell the love that was rightly hers.

"I kept my part of the bargain."

"Well?" Blaire asked. "Where is he?"

Genya let the anger move through her body. Slowly, so very slowly, she lifted her arm and pointed at Kaell. "There."

Puzzled, Kaell frowned. "Genya? What is this?"

"You dare play games with us?" Sisilia hissed. "Who do you think you are, little witch?"

Bile soured Genya's throat. She had not expected betrayal to again taste so foul. But she would not back down. "A dangerous spell trapped him in this woman's form. But despite his appearance..." She hesitated. This was her last chance to step back, to say she had made a mistake. "This is Kaell. The one who you seek."

It was done. She could not retreat. She would have Dannon back. And Val would turn to her for comfort. His love would not be split with Kaell.

"Seek?" Kaell's hand stole towards his sword belt. "I don't understand."

A look passed between Rohane and Blaire. Blaire gave a faint nod. At once, Rohane sprang on Genya, knife drawn. She locked an arm about the girl's neck, a knife to Genya's throat.

Kaell started forward.

"Stop," Rohane cried. "I'll kill her."

He whipped to a halt. "What do you want?"

Blaire beckoned to her guards at the door. "I want you to fall to your knees and surrender."

Kaell shifted his weight. "Why?"

"Do it, or I order Rohane to cut her throat."

Unconcerned, Genya remained still. She could haul the knife away with a spell, force Rohane back. But she understood that the Regenta was using her, that Blaire wished to take Kaell alive, without struggle.

Kaell dug his teeth into his lip. The thought of surrender would rekindle his every fear and bring back memories of how Archanin had held him, tormented him, and abused him. For a heartbeat, pity threatened to plunder her bitterness. She shoved it down, seeing again in her mind how Val had put his sword into Kaell's hands and hugged him without ever looking at her.

Rohane pressed the knife into Genya's throat. "I *will* hurt her."

"All right. All right." Kaell threw Genya a helpless look and knelt. He placed his sword on the ground.

"Take him," Blaire said.

Guards pounced, dragging Kaell to his feet and grabbing his arms. As steel clamped about his wrists, he grimaced in pain.

Rohane released Genya and stepped away, shoving her knife into its sheath.

"He'll be fairly treated," Blaire told Genya. "Until he's tried." She shook her head. "So strange the way he looks. You must explain about this spell later."

"I kept my word," Genya muttered. "I brought him to you. Now keep yours."

Kaell's eyes rounded in surprise. "Genya? What is this? Brought?" Bewildered, he stared at her. Then he blinked. His jaw tightened as if he realised she had betrayed him.

"Take him," Blaire said again. "We'll interrogate him later."

Kaell thrashed briefly against the hands holding him. "What do you want with me? Why are you doing this?"

Her heart hard with spite, Genya sneered. "You can thank Val for this."

Kaell shook his head. "I don't understand."

But Genya would say no more. With a grim smile of satisfaction, she watched the guards drag him away. Kaell staggered with his head bowed, as if the shock of her duplicity had broken his spirit.

Blaire was watching her with a tight frown. "It little matters, but why do I sense you're using us for your own personal vendetta, Genya Caelan?"

Genya shrugged. "He's the one who killed your warriors. That's all you need to know."

"And yet..." Blaire said. "When someone tells me I don't need to know something, it rouses my curiosity. Is there anything you wish to tell me?"

KAELL

They forced him down a stairwell, then another, into welling darkness. Bewildered by Genya's betrayal, he barely realised where they were taking him until his escort reached a metal door. It was tall and thin. Keys jangled. The sound snapped him from his bewildered daze. At the sight of the tiny dark crevice cut into rock, he recoiled. "No."

A frenzied struggle seized him. Bucking, twisting, he flung his captors off and desperately tried to scramble away. Women leapt at him. Kaell thrashed his body, kicking out with wild fury. Hands snatched at him, and punches flew. One pummelled his belly. Winded, he collapsed to his knees, gasping. An arm fell about his throat. A knife's tip forced his chin up. "Still."

Kaell's every instinct screamed to resist. But his captors held him firmly.

"Genya!" he managed to cry as they hauled him up. The word held all his fear, his disbelief. Her treachery cut like steel ripping apart his chest. "Genya."

They bent his head to force him into blackness. Rock pressed into his back. As the door clanged shut, horror shook him. His captors had entombed him in a space so tight, he could not turn. Nor could he straighten his back or lie down. Sitting was impossible.

The heavy, dead darkness settled like a black pall prickling down his spine. Not even a sliver of light crept beneath the door. If he lifted his hand to his face, he could not see it. In the suffocating stillness, there was no sound except his heavy breaths. Desperately, he ran his fingers over the rock beside him. Already muscles cramped in his neck.

Panic kicked in his gut, useless, blind, and desperate. Kaell shoved a shoulder against the door, but without space to draw back and build momentum, it was hopeless. All he could do was scream out his terror and his frustration. All he could do was beat a fist against rock until his knuckles were wet and aching. In the end, all he could do was collapse against the rock, head bent, and sob.

GENYA

She followed Sisilia through shadowy passages deeper into the caverns. The only sounds were torch flames hissing in the stale air, Sisilia's long gown swishing on stone, and Genya's quick breaths. The darkness moved with her, as if condemning her. She shrugged off remorse. Kaell's life in return for Dannon was a price she would pay again and again. But what of Val? This was his doing. If Val knew pain, *he* had caused it.

And yet, at the thought of what was happening now to Kaell, she shuddered. The interrogation cells in Quisnaf would be gruesome places. And Kaell was stubborn. Snared by tangled thoughts, she hardly heard Sisilia speak. "What?"

The sorceress cackled. "Feeling guilty, child? Betrayal is hard the first time. It gets easier."

It's not the first time, she might have said. *I'm an old hand at betrayal. I know its bitterness all too well.* Genya pressed her lips tightly. "He means nothing to me."

Sisilia shrugged. "Maybe. I don't really care. You made a choice, and it is done."

"What… will they do to him?"

Sisilia paused then turned. "Do you want me to tell you comfortable lies or the truth?"

Genya stiffened her resolve. She wanted lies. Sweet lies to appease her guilt. "The truth."

"Something unpleasant. He killed two Quisnaf warriors. You will discover there are codes in Quisnaf, unspoken laws. One of them is vengeance. We always hunt down those who do us wrong. Always."

At the sorceress's remote, cold tone, hairs rose on Genya's arms.

"I could show you Roaran's room," Sisilia said abruptly. "It's kept exactly as it was."

Genya shivered. If she closed her eyes, she could see Roaran's ruined body on that wheel. That had been the first betrayal. She tapped her fingers against her thigh, desperate to shut out the memory. Desperate for the release of magic, the feverish power that blocked all remorse, all guilt.

Sisilia turned her cold eyes upon Genya. "We made him, Genya Caelan. Forged him with truth and blood and magic. When Roaran Caelan was first brought here, unwillingly, he could not understand what he was, so he feared it. We gave him purpose."

Genya tried to imagine Roaran walking these dark passages. He would have been younger than she. Alone. Afraid.

Sisilia lowered her eyelids in a slow blink. "My ancestor, a sorceress called Racinta, trained him. I have her writings. Her words about Roaran Caelan are carefully kept. They are a rare treasure that survived the Great Fall. I could show them to you."

"What do I care?" Her indifference was a lie. She wanted badly to read them. The Quisnaf knew more of her father than she did.

"You had so little time to know him." Sisilia gave a perceptive nod. "So little of this prince, this lord of magic. If only he'd had the chance to teach you."

"Archanin trained me," she growled, stung. "Do you think to sway me, to seduce me to Quisnaf with talk of my father?"

"Trained you how? To draw upon the same darkness that empowered him? Yes, that Seithin blood magic is strong.

Intoxicating. But beware, Genya Caelan. It will change you. Every time you surrender to its seduction, you will lose something of yourself. Until it claims you." She sighed. "Roaran could have sought this power. But he knew its dangers and chose not to."

At Sisilia's warning, her neck prickled. To cover her fear, Genya snapped, "Was too afraid to, you mean."

Whenever she used blood magic, the growing chasm of darkness within her deepened. It yawned and beckoned and whispered. Yet she'd never felt so enlivened or untouchable as when she used magic.

"And you…" Sisilia's eyes gleamed knowingly. "You are not afraid."

"No."

"If I told you there was another way? Other magic? Magic that will not scar your soul?"

"My soul? Roaran, too, had spoken of a soul. What do you mean by it?"

Sisilia pressed a hand to Genya's chest. Her touch burned. "We who serve the goddess believe it is the essence, the eternal part of us that lives on. The part that we can blacken with our deeds."

At Genya's sneer, Sisilia withdrew her hand and sighed. "I see you are more like him than you know. Roaran, too, believed in nothing."

Sisilia turned and walked on.

Genya hastened after her. "I would like to know more," she blurted. "Of this other magic. I would like—" She paused, not wishing to admit her longing or that Sisilia's words kindled her interest. To need something made her weak. It could even allow Sisilia to manipulate her. She ran her tongue around the inside of her mouth. No, surely, she had wit enough to hold her own against this fierce woman, no matter how powerful the sorceress was. "I would like to read your ancestor's writings about Roaran."

Sisilia stopped and turned. "Then I will show you, child."

"But first… Dannon."

The sorceress flicked an impatient hand. "Ah, the lover. How sad. One day, Genya Caelan, you will learn that knowledge is of greater value than love. Well, we are here." She bent to turn a key in a lock then nudged the door. It squeaked open.

Genya walked in, breath trapped within, her throat dry, and her heart thrumming.

Dannon looked up from a book. For a long moment, he stared, bemused. Then he said simply, "Genya."

Sisilia shut the door behind her.

DANNON

Neither moved or spoke. For a long moment, they stared at each other.

"You came," Dannon said at last, his voice breathless with wonder.

Genya took a hesitant step towards him. "I came."

The candle upon the room's single table guttered. Carefully, his thoughts in turmoil, Dannon turned and walked to the table. He put a new candle on the holder and struck a flint to light it. When it flamed, he faced Genya, half expecting her to be gone, a figment of his imagination and his loneliness.

She hadn't moved. The expression on her face mingled hope with fear.

"Let me hold you," he said.

As if released, she ran into his arms, her lips seeking his. The kiss was long and tender. An exploration. A reclaiming. An acknowledgement. Dannon let its sweetness engulf him, his thoughts on hold, his astonished joy that she had found him across the seas coursing through him like a river of honey.

"Oh, goddess, Dannon," Genya murmured, her hands moving over his shoulders, his back, his chest. "I've been so alone. No one understands. Val won't speak to me. And then Alecc. Nicky. Oh, the gods take Gendrick Caelan."

Dannon drew back slightly. "What do you mean? What's happened?"

She frowned. Her lips parted in surprise. "You mean... no one told you?"

A shiver of warning ran through him. "Told me what?"

Genya dropped her head. "Nicky," she whispered. "Alecc. Murdered."

Dannon's hands fell to his sides. In horror, he rocked back. "No."

"Gendrick Caelan executed them. He shall pay in blood," Genya said. "I have sworn an oath to Cyrah to kill him."

Dannon could not speak. He could hardly take in what she'd said. Oh, the gods were cruel indeed. Merciless. Shuddering, he turned his back. "How?" he wheezed. "Tell me."

Her voice unsteady, fisting her hands, Genya told him of the battle and Gendrick's betrayal. When she spoke of finding Alecc's body in the sea, an icy fury gripped Dannon. "There's no one left," he muttered. "They're all dead. The Brotherhood."

"Cadan... I don't know. I saw him fall..." Her words trailed off. "Gendrick—"

"Shall die." Genya lifted her head to stare into his eyes. "Will you help me? I need you now. There's no one on my side, no one I can turn to. Even Val has deserted me. He's so judgemental, so condemning. He can barely look at me."

The words took a moment to sink into him. *Judgemental. Condemning.* Puzzled, Dannon frowned. "I don't understand. What have you done?"

She glanced at him then quickly looked down. "Why must I have done something?"

"Genya." He touched her arm. "Did something happen? At Vraymorg. After I was taken prisoner by Felix?"

"Surely you heard," she muttered, still without looking at him. "The Quisnaf could not be so cruel as to tell you nothing?"

Dannon shifted uncomfortably. "I know Roaran died. Gethin and Neil, too. I know Cadan survived. And Val." He spread his arms, gesturing at his chambers. "I am told only what they want me to hear. And I can do nothing but accept it. For the most part, I'm kept in this room." His gaze sharpened on her face. "Is there more to know?"

She reached a hand to his cheek, frowning. "Your face."

Unease stirred in his belly. "Does it displease you?" He was a wreck of a man. A wreck of a warrior. Who or what was he now? What had defined him—his ability with the bow and with the sword—was gone. He was lost, without purpose. *Useless.*

Genya traced a scar that ran from the corner of his eye down onto his jaw then touched fingertips to his eyelid. When he winced, she dropped her hand in concern. "Does it hurt?"

"It's still tender," Dannon admitted.

"Can you see from that eye?"

"A little." He shrugged. "Felix poured something toxic into my eyes. Elena saved my sight." It wasn't just his face that bore witness to what he had endured in that miserable prison. His body, too, was twisted.

With a shudder of shame, he retreated into himself. What would she see? The man who had been her lover was broken, his body scarred and marred.

"Elena?" Genya echoed.

"A healer. She tended to me." Without conscious intent, he smiled. There was a warmth to Elena that drew him and surely drew others, too.

Genya was watching him. Her lips were stretched tight, her eyes narrowed. "You like her. This Elena."

"Yes." He grinned and punched her arm teasingly. "Jealous? There's no need. She was kind to me, that's all. I'm grateful to her."

"Grateful," Genya said. "Grateful." Shoulders shaking, she turned away.

Dannon touched her arm. "You came for me. I didn't dare

hope. I thought I had been abandoned here."

To his surprise, Genya gulped in a sob. "I'm the one who's been abandoned. Oh, goddess, Dannon." She spun and hurled herself against him, pinning him with her arms. "You don't know what it's been like. First Val was taken from me. Then Alecc and Nicky."

Again, Dannon frowned. "What do you mean Val was taken from you? Where is he?"

Genya made an astonished sound. "You didn't know?"

"Know what?"

"He's here, Dannon. Val is in Quisnaf."

Bewildered, Dannon could only stare. "I had no clue." He seized a breath. "Why have they taken him? And why do you say he abandoned you? Is there something I don't know?"

"Nothing," Genya said. But just for a moment, her eyes flickered.

And Dannon knew she was lying to him.

KAELL

Time passed, but he could not measure it beyond beats of agony. Every strained muscle in his back and thighs ached. His head pounded from sleeplessness and thirst.

As he struggled to hold himself up, exhausted and despairing, his thoughts turned always to Genya. Why betray him? They were not close, but he'd sensed she no longer resented him as she had. Though... what if she had been forced to give him up? Oh, how he wanted to believe that. But deep within, he knew she still resented him because of Val.

Long hours crept by in misery. When his shoulders cramped, Kaell groaned in pain. His legs could hardly hold him up, but the tomb-like space wouldn't allow him the release of sleep. Hunger gnawed in his belly. The thirst was worse. He tongued his cracked lips. When his bladder burst, Kaell sobbed at the indignity. Closing his eyes, he rested a hip against the door until it hurt. Already, he hated the sound of his rasping breaths and the stench of sweat and fear.

Footsteps padded over stone. Kaell snapped his eyes open. A slit of light appeared at his feet. Someone shoved a cup through a grate. He stooped as best he could to scoop it up. The light disappeared. Kaell sniffed. *Water. Oh, gods, water.* He drank, groaning in pleasure as it soothed his dry lips, stale mouth, and parched throat.

Legs like jelly, he pressed against a wall. Almost at once, his head swam with dizziness. A haze thickened his thoughts.

The door opened, and Kaell fell forward onto his hands and knees. He peered up into a blur of faces and blinding torchlight. Then, with a moan, he passed out into welcome darkness.

⁓∞⊰∞⁓

He woke gasping, blinking away cold water flooding his eyes and dripping from his sodden hair and down his face. Rough rock bruised his back. He was naked, his spreadeagled hands and ankles fettered to the wall.

A short young woman holding a bucket grinned. "There he is. Though I'll admit I'm having trouble with the 'he' bit."

"Long story," Kaell croaked.

"That's what we're here for, lovely. Stories." Kaell flinched as she touched his cheek with her fingertips, regarding him with blue eyes so pale, the colour mirrored a frozen sea. Her hair, though, was bright gold, a molten stream that disappeared down her back.

Kaell shot a look about at a stone-walled chamber lit by candles and a red-ember fire. A prison, no doubt. Close, airless, and hot.

"You're very young to be a torturer. Who are you? Are you responsible for throwing me in that awful hole?"

"Questions, questions. Which to answer first? I'm called Malgaria. It's a common enough name in Quisnaf. The name of one of the founders of our great and glorious city. They call me Mad Mal." She cackled. "That's good, isn't it? Mad Mal." Her laugh died away. "That tight little hole in the rock is meant to soften you up."

"It was unpleasant."

Malgaria tilted her head. "Yes, you look nicely rattled, I must say. Shadows beneath the eyes. Hungry. Wary. Not afraid, though." She flashed another smile. "Not yet."

"What is this place?" A useless question. He knew. *Knew.* But he did not want to accept it.

The woman waved a hand. "This little chamber has one purpose only. To cause you pain. See those racks?"

Kaell shivered. They held whips, knives, and thumb screws.

"All manner of instruments we will come to understand—together." Malgaria unfolded a serene grin. "And in the fire? A nice long poker warming up. Nothing like the smell of burning flesh."

Kaell swallowed hard. "Why am I here?"

Malgaria raised her brows. "Really? You don't know? Blaire wants your confession. And if that's what the Regenta wants, then that's what she will get."

"To what? I don't understand."

She wagged a finger. "Naughty. If you're going to be like that, let's get acquainted. How shall I begin our conversation?" When she slid her hand along his arm, Kaell could not hold back another shudder.

"Shall it be the knife? Maybe the whip. No, you do not readily show fear, so perhaps the poker?" She walked to a table laden with more vicious instruments and unhurriedly drew on gloves.

Kaell watched her with sickening dread. *No, no, no.* Violently, he tugged at the fetters about his wrists.

"Do you know," Malgaria began conversationally as she drew the poker from the embers, nodding at the metal's red glow. "It's so rare to be permitted to come to know a captive slowly and intimately. Blaire prefers to have the truthsayer assess them, but the poor old dear is gravely ill in Veniva. A pity for you. Though even when she's away, Blaire sends me prisoners who must not be permanently damaged. 'Do not touch his face,' she says. 'Do not mar the perfection of that body. It's worth gold, blah, blah, blah.' Just hurt him a bit as a warning. Or a punishment. But you." She turned back with a cheerful grin. "No restrictions. 'Do whatever it takes,' she says. 'Just bring me his confession.'"

Kaell pressed his back into the rock, following the poker with his eyes. "To what?"

Malgaria waved the red tip close to his face. Kaell recoiled from the heat.

"Of course, I do hope you don't confess at once." She stroked his face with her empty gloved hand. "But you will in the end. They always do. There can be no executions without confessions. Our lovely Regenta likes to feel that righteous glow when she orders your death."

"Execution?" Kaell stammered. "For what?"

"Now, now. You're being naughty again. I think I'll stab you in the eye. You'll only need one to stumble to the block or the gallows." She jabbed metal at his face.

Kaell whipped his head aside. The poker's red tip scorched his ear. At the sharp burst of agony, he screamed.

"Missed. Let's try that again."

"Stop!" he howled. "I don't know what I've done."

Malgaria rocked back, lips pursed. Her dark brows shot up in a quizzical curve. "Dear me, do you really mean to say no one told you your crime? It's so hard to get good guards these days." She sighed dramatically.

Kaell panted. His ear throbbed. "What am I to confess to?" he rasped. "You're going to have to tell me, because I don't have a clue."

Malgaria rested the poker against the wall beside his head, its heat flaming his cheek. She leaned in. "Do you mean you're guilty of so many nasty crimes you cannot remember how you wronged us? My, my, what a wicked creature." She looked pleased. "I am to extract your confession to murder."

"Murder," he echoed in disbelief.

"Murder." She nodded. "Two Quisnaf warriors. Matilda and Morgan. Though I doubt to a wicked creature like you, their names will mean much."

Kaell squeezed his eyes closed. A memory snapped of snow drifting across a bleak hillside, of a cave. "Oh, gods," he whispered.

Malgaria tilted her head to consider him. "Well, well. You do remember."

"Yes."

"And do you deny it was you?"

"I left them in a cave, bound but alive. I threw in a knife so they could free themselves." A deep weariness weighed upon him. *Confess and die.* Would it be so bad? His life had stretched longer than he deserved anyway. It should have ended in a vile room in the Waste Mountains with rich wall hangings and climbing plants. That was where Archanin should have killed him, before Kaell's life was marred by bitterness and resentment. By anger. "I didn't intentionally leave them to die. But if that's what happened, it was my fault. So yes, I confess. I accept whatever punishment your Regenta considers just."

"That's it?" Malgaria leaned in again, her gloved fingers tracing the burn on his ear. "A pity. I longed to play with you." She sighed. "Ah well. Blaire shall be pleased. Now, what more can you tell me? How did it come about? Were you acting for someone? The Damadars, perhaps? The council never quite trusted them."

"No. It wasn't like that." Kaell thought back. "My lord was their prisoner, and I came for him. Morgan and I fought. I won." He lifted stiff shoulders. "I left Morgan and Matilda tied up, but I also left a knife. That's all there was to it."

"And your lord—"

"Val Arques Caelan."

"Did he help you?"

Kaell shook his head. "He didn't want me to hurt them."

"Val Arques, you say." She turned and heaved the poker into the embers. "I know this man. I should like to have him naked here before me, shackled to that stone. Helpless. I think he would prove a challenge like none other."

"No!" Kaell gasped in horror.

She spun with a predatory smile. "Do not fear, pretty boy-girl. Your lord is safe from me. He shares our Regenta's bed, after all. And he is of late under the protection of the high sorceress, Sisilia."

Relief flooded him. "I did not know that." Kaell snatched a breath. "So what now?"

Malgaria tangled a lock of Kaell's damp hair in her fingers. "You can rest here a bit. I shall tell dear Blaire you confessed. And she shall order your death. Decide the manner of it. She's good at that sort of thing, at least."

"Who told?" Kaell mumbled bitterly. "How did you know it was me who came after them in the Icelands? Was it Genya?"

Malgaria only smiled and left him.

❦

Candles burned low. The fire died to ashes. Slumped in his chains, Kaell slept. It was an exhausted sleep, too thick for dreams. He woke, aching, hungry, and thirsty, hearing voices.

Malgaria carried a flaming torch into the chamber. She was not alone. At the sight of Blaire, Kaell straightened his weary shoulders and lifted his chin.

Torchlight sparked off the Regenta's ashen hair. Her blue eyes seemed to dance and glitter, enlivening the straight lines of her perfectly carved face. She wore leather pants and a jerkin over a light-blue tunic. A knife and sword poked from a belt tightly circling her waist.

The danger in her drew him, fascinated him. How easy it was to imagine her on the battlefield, coolly, precisely delivering death.

Blaire was cold fire, from the smouldering ghosting behind her oval eyes to the restless, driven way she compelled herself forward. Yet when she stopped before him, she was completely still, that energy contained and simmering.

"I'm honoured you came yourself to pronounce sentence."

"Your confession surprised me." She laughed without humour. "It certainly disappointed Malgaria."

The interrogator's eyes glinted with mischief. "I shall take my disappointment out on someone else, Regenta. You know how I like to play."

Blaire's gaze held on Kaell. "What if I said I did not come to condemn you?"

"Oh?"

"That I came instead to ask for your help."

Kaell blinked in surprise. "I would say that makes no sense. I've willingly confessed my crimes." He laughed sourly. "I have others. Believe me, my death is long overdue."

Blaire's expression changed. Beneath her furrowed brow, her eyes held a shadow. Sorrow suited her, he thought. Those perfect features, sharp cut like marble, could only be framed by melancholy.

At Blaire's nod, Malgaria freed him from his chains. He slumped. The interrogator caught him and helped him to the chamber's only chair. She threw a blanket about his bare shoulders, poured water into a cup, and thrust it at him. Blaire watched all with a remote, almost blank stare.

"You've chosen well, Regenta," Malgaria said. "He wasn't afraid."

"How can I help?" Kaell sipped water.

Again, the Regenta nodded to Malgaria. The interrogator walked briskly to open the door to peer into the passage. "We're alone, Regenta."

Blaire faced Kaell. "Very soon, something will happen that I am powerless to stop. Not now. Perhaps it's my own fault." She laughed bitterly. "You say you have many sins. Mine is pride. I am prideful, I know."

"What will happen?" Kaell asked.

"Very soon," Blaire said, "they will come for me. Perhaps tomorrow. Perhaps the day after. Perhaps in a week. But whenever it happens, I will be arrested and condemned to die." Her blue-eyed gaze settled on him. "I need you to play a dangerous game."

"My life is a dangerous game," Kaell said.

VAL ARQUES

H e lay in the darkened bedchamber just beyond Sisilia's
workroom, not bothering to light a candle. Fractured,
sluggish thoughts turned over and over on nothing. He
long ago lost track of time. Most of the time, he dozed, lingering
on the edge of sleep, tormented by wisping nightmares.

A lamp puffed to life in the workroom. Through the open door,
Val blinked at its brightness. The sorceress untied her cape and
dropped it over a table. Footsteps moved towards the bed. "What?
Still abed?"

"I'm awake."

Sisilia spluttered in disgust. "So you just lie there in darkness,
feeling sorry for yourself?" She glanced at the tray on the table.
"And you did not eat. Again. Must I force you?"

He shrugged. "Force me; don't force me. What does it matter?"
This was his life now. A dark room. Snapped commands. That
dreadful march to the temple so Sisilia could take his blood. When
he considered the future, all he could see were the years and years
under her control—until he obeyed without question, his will if
not broken, then moulded.

"Oh, I see."

He frowned. It should bother him that she could mock his

misery, but what was the point? The world had become meaningless. Even his limbs felt weighted, as sluggish as his mind.

Sisilia sank onto the bed. "I could rid you of despair," she said. "If you wish, I could take away your past, take away your memories. You would not remember your pain."

"If I have no memories, then who am I?"

"That, indeed, is the question." She grabbed the untouched bowl of pottage from the stool. "How pitiful that I must feed you."

"I don't want anything." He rolled onto his side, away from her. "Just leave me alone."

"Oh, stop this nonsense."

Val didn't bother to reply.

"I'll have you whipped. Beaten. That might snap you out of this inertia."

"What do I care?"

She grabbed his shoulder to turn him. "Are you so weak? You think others have not suffered as you do? I should leave you to rot, but I need you healthy."

"Everyone needs something of me. Samantha was right." He coughed a bitter laugh. "She told me it was my fate to be hunted, sought, held."

Sisilia sat back. She scratched her chin with a long-nailed finger. "She always was clever. Well, what of it? If that's your fate, then that's your fate. Stop wallowing in self-pity. It is unbecoming."

"Just leave me alone."

She did.

ROHANE

Val curled on the bed in a darkened room. He had not even bothered to light a candle. Rohane stepped inside with her lantern. Her shadow fell on the wall. "Val?"

His head shot up. At the sight of her, he groaned in despair. "Go away. I don't want you to see me like this."

"What's wrong with you?" Rohane took a step closer. "Sisilia says you might hurt yourself. Is it true?"

"If the high priestess says it, then it must be so."

"I'm asking you, Val."

He hesitated then sighed. "No. I won't hurt myself."

Rohane put the candleholder on the bedside table. "Why are you like this? I thought you had more courage."

"Courage," he muttered. "What's the point of it? Tell me that, Rohane. What does *courage* get me?"

Rohane sat on the bed. Gently, she stroked his hair. "It will get better. I promise."

"How?" he cried. "How?" He grasped her hand. "I should have listened to you when you said we should run. There must be somewhere we can go. Beyond the Ice Sea, to the legendary Circle Kingdoms even—far, far away. Just us."

For a moment, she was tempted. Her father would help. They

could take a ship anywhere. But what of duty? It would always come back to that. For it had been his solace for centuries, just as it had been hers since she had killed Nessa. No, neither of them was free to do as they chose.

The candle guttered and died. In the darkness, he was nothing but a huddled shape. He made no move, no sound. At length, her hand fell away. "Sisilia won't let you go. The Quisnaf will never let you go."

The stillness settled about her words.

"Rohane," Val whispered. "What do we do?"

She struck a new flame. "I'll think of something. I promise." It hurt her heart to see him so despairing. "You have to take it, put up with it. It's not as bad as being kept by the blood keepers. Sisilia promises you can come and go as you please, with an escort. She says I can see you—often, if you like." She leaned and kissed his lips as softly as she might brush her fingers down silk. "We can… do this. I can make love to you, comfort you."

"I don't need that, Rohane," he whispered. "I need…"

She heard the loneliness, the yearning in his voice.

"Will you… will you just…?"

She put her arms about him and held him.

⁓ ∞ ⁓

The sorceress ground roots in a mortar. The shadowy chamber stank of sulphur from a potion bubbling in a pot upon the fire. Florentine padded about the chamber, sniffing.

Rohane brushed her fingers through a crumbling dried herb hanging above her head. "He needs more than me."

Sisilia did not look up. "What? Am I to let a whole bevy of women see him?"

"No." Rohane swept her hand over the gnarly bench surface. "Let him swing a sword about. That's my suggestion. It reminds him of who he is, gives him something to hold on to."

"Will that mean no more pathetic looks? No more despondent sighs? No more searching his room to make sure he hasn't palmed a knife?"

"He won't hurt himself." At least, she didn't think so.

Sisilia peered up with a frown. "He has scars."

"From a long time ago. Think about what I said, Sisilia. He forgets himself in swordplay."

Sisilia stopped her grinding. She put down the pestle and looked at Rohane. "If it means no more moping about in his room, I'll think about it."

VAL ARQUES

Val wandered about Sisilia's workroom, an excitement in him. Iron pots sat on red coals. The putrid stink of bubbling potions mingled with the peppery aroma of herbs and wood smoke. He picked up stacked clay vessels, put them down again, then brushed aside a dangling aged bone strung up like a wind chime.

In the two weeks since Rohane or Anna had begun taking him to the training caverns, the darkness shadowing his mind had slowly lightened. Oh, clever Rohane. She knew just how to draw him out of his despair. It still came upon him sometimes when he lay alone in the night, staring at the shadows upon the ceiling. But he could shake it off when he woke.

Sisilia took a mortar and pestle from a shelf to grind an ugly thorned plant. Curious, Val edged closer. These past few days since he had ventured out of his room, Sisilia didn't seem to mind him watching. Most of the time, she forgot he was there, so intent was she on whatever potion she prepared.

"It's the thorns that are potent," she muttered. "They will take a seer easily beyond the Enarae."

"Hmm."

"Once ground with bone and dream root and—" She snatched

up a knife and grabbed his hand. With a quick nick, she sliced his palm.

"Ouch. You might have warned me."

"In there." Sisilia pointed at the mortar.

Obediently, Val held his bleeding palm over it.

"Good boy." The sorceress took up a spoon to stir. "Now, why are you here, bothering me? Isn't it the time when Anna takes you to the training halls?"

"My reward." He grinned like an eager boy.

"Yes, you've behaved. But I am fed up with you stalking about. Off with you."

"Anna is late today." He looked hopefully towards the doors. "I wonder where she's got to?"

Sisilia sniffed in disgust. "Warriors. You're all the same. You care only about sweating and stomping about, making that dreadful clanging. Such a racket. It gives me a headache. Oh." She frowned at a sudden thought. "Your ward has been asking for you. I think I forgot to say."

Val jolted in surprise. "What?"

Sisilia bent over her potion. "That child of Roaran's blood. Genya. The fool girl is here and has been demanding to see you."

Shocked, Val stared at Sisilia. His thoughts slammed together, all too fast. Bewilderment then resignation. "I forbade her to come." He heaved a sigh. "Of course she disobeyed me. She always does."

Sisilia's hand paused on the spoon. "You sound angry."

"Do I?" He was aware of a churning in his gut. Even now, he was not ready to face Genya. Not ready to forgive. Half the brotherhood was dead. Roaran was dead because she'd chosen to believe Archanin's lies without considering who it might hurt.

"Shall I arrange a visit?"

"No," Val said. "I don't wish to see her."

"Very well." Sisilia bent over her task. "At first, she told Rohane she would not come. It seems the lure of the other man proved too much. The fool girl thinks she is in love." The sorceress sniffed in disgust. "What do the young know of love? They think it is sunny meadows and fragrant flowers, all sighs and caresses. Love is winter. It is cold and painful. It is hard."

"What other man?"

"The one they brought back with you."

"I don't—" He frowned. Memories took shape. A man's groans from the second cabin on the ship. Samantha's curious absences. Whispered words to guards at the door. Careful glances to make sure he did not listen.

And Genya had travelled this far because of a man.

"Oh," he gasped, hardly believing his conclusion. "Dannon. But I don't understand. I thought him safely in Telor. How can he be here?"

Muscles in Sisilia's shoulders strained as she ground the thorns into the bloody paste then reached for a clay vessel beside her.

"Sisilia, how is it possible Dannon is here?"

"What?"

"Dannon?"

"Is that his name? I've had nothing to do with him beyond testing his blood. Now, that was surprising. The truth of who he is will have to be uncovered. No, do not glare at me. I do not know the story of how he is here. Ask Rohane."

Rohane. Val frowned. She'd known about Dannon and kept it from him. He shrugged it off. Rohane would have her reasons. Did he really blame her for choosing to keep Quisnaf's secrets?

Val dug his fingertips into his temples to rub away a tiny grain of disquiet. He had to trust Rohane. He had to believe she was completely on his side… or he was completely alone.

GENYA

"What do you mean he won't see me?" Her hands curled into fists. To hold back the tears, she squinted at the fire in the greeting chamber. A cool wind whipped in, the first sign of winter in this exotic land of heat and storms.

Firelight gleamed on polished wood. Bunched candles burned through shadows. Genya did not fear the shadows without. But those within tormented with dark thoughts, stirred up by the bleak night.

I do not belong here. The truth in that shuddered through her mind. Quisnaf was strange and unknowable. *Hostile.* Yet Sisilia's words returned to her again and again: *I could train you. I could teach you how to take a terrible vengeance against Gendrick Caelan.*

How she longed for the solace of magic, to feel its power burn through her veins, banishing all else. How she longed for the knowledge that Sisilia promised to share.

Blaire's eyes dwelled upon her. It was a careful contemplation, as though the Regenta sought to untangle a knot of complication about Roaran's daughter. Genya didn't want to be understood, at least not by this cynical woman. She found Blaire repellent. Whatever warmth found its way into these stone caverns and whitewashed passages waned in the Quisnaf Regenta's presence. When Blaire's gaze passed over her, Genya shivered, wanting to reach for comforting steel.

Samantha, though, oozed warmth and charm. She clasped Genya's hand in sympathy. "I'm sorry, child. The obstinate man holds on to whatever grudge he imagines he has a right to."

"Two weeks," Genya muttered. "That's how long I've been in your goddess-forsaken city of darkness. Two weeks, you've shown me every hall, every valley, every field, every ornate chamber. Again and again, I've asked to see my guardian. 'Soon,' you said. 'Patience.' Now you tell me he won't see me. *Won't.*"

Blaire shrugged. "We could bring you together, but it will be against his will."

"I grant him his right to hold a grudge." Genya kicked her chair leg. "But will it ever soften? Will he punish me forever? Obstinate, you say? Why, he is the most stubborn, irritating—" She bit down on the complaint, surprised by the strength of her resentment. For all his words about debts and vows, Val had abandoned her. He had walked away, leaving her to deal with Nicky's bewildered grief and her own guilt, her fears for Dannon, and her sorrow about Alecc. She hadn't deserved that burden.

Anger knotted in her gut, a tight, hard ball ready to burst out. How dare he? How dare he judge her so harshly then leave her alone and now refuse to see her? Yet Val would never turn his back on Kaell. Oh no.

"Did he ask?" The words choked in her throat. She swallowed. "Did he ask about me, at least? Ask how I fared?"

A silence fell. When Genya looked at their faces, she knew the answer.

Samantha squeezed her hand again. "I'm sorry."

"The goddess take him," she muttered. "I'm tired of his righteous, sanctimonious judgement."

"He is stubborn," Blaire said. "He has not easily accepted his life here."

Genya whirled with an accusing glare. "You swore to me he is well, that you have not mistreated him."

"Genya, Genya." Samantha grasped her shoulders. "Val Arques is precious to us. Very precious. But I will not lie to you." She nodded to herself. "Too many people in your life, I think, have lied to you. You shall not find that here, only truth. I know you are strong enough to hear it. Val Arques came to us as a guest. That entitled him to freedoms not enjoyed by other men in Quisnaf. But he broke the rules. He ran—"

"Ran? Then he is not content. I demand you bring him to me at once."

Samantha dropped her arms with a heavy, resigned gesture. "It has become complicated. The sorceress Sisilia cloaked him."

"Cloaked?" Genya tossed her head. "I don't understand."

"It is a tradition, a sacred law even, in Quisnaf." Blaire's cool blue eyes passed over Genya like a whip. "A woman of a certain rank may bring a man under her protection. He becomes her responsibility."

"Her possession? No, no, no. I must speak with my guardian. I must see him."

Blaire exchanged a look with Samantha. "I will tell you where he will be. Approach him if you wish. But let it be understood you may receive a frosty reception, for he is adamant he will not meet with you."

"So you say." Genya stormed. "Maybe you're lying to me."

"I do not lie," Blaire said coldly. "A lesson for you, child. Be very careful whose word you challenge here."

That word again. *Child.* Irritably, Genya glared at Blaire. Then she laughed. The sound rattled about the chamber without warmth. "I shall challenge whoever I choose. I am the daughter of a seer, the daughter of a king, the daughter of a great bladesman."

"How sad." Blaire's look pierced right to her heart then beyond. "That you define yourself only as a daughter and a daughter of men."

She took two steps towards Genya. It was as though a fire sparked through her. Her lips were slightly parted, her eyes gleaming with eagerness. "Let us show you your true worth, Genya Caelan. So that you need not say, 'I am the daughter of this man and this man.' So that you say only, 'I am Genya.'"

VAL ARQUES

Ringing steel echoed through the passages. Val's heart lurched with joy. The sound comforted him like rain pattering on a roof while he lay in a warm bed. Eagerly, he followed Anna through double doors into the cavernous tournament chamber big enough to hold three ships. Stairs led down from double doors past tiered benches to the rectangular arena where he had fought Jenna-Dairine.

Blades of a variety of hilts and of all lengths—some curved, most two-edged—hung on wall racks. At the far end were targets for archers. In the centre of the arena, pairs of young warriors drilled beneath the watchful attention of a weapons instructor, the light from lines of candles on the floor and in wall crevices flashing off steel. A few young women performed the sort of shadow combat his masters had taught him—a solitary repetition of patterns against an imaginary opponent.

The odours of sweat and leather—the odours of discipline, determination, and purpose—the clang and din of steel at once put Val at ease.

Anna found a seat on the benches. She yawned. "You have an hour."

Val strode through the benches to the arena then paused to

watch the women. Tension seeped from him as blood might seep into the sandy ground. He walked onto the square and selected a blade from the racks, testing its weight with a swish. Then he found a space half in shadow. His toes sank into gravelly sand. The hilt was smooth and worn in his curled fingers.

Slowly, he began moving back and forth, carving out a series of steps in a familiar dance. *Lunge, recover, step, lunge, retreat.* His arm moved a heartbeat before his legs when attacking, a heartbeat later when defending. *Step back, parry, lunge.*

The rhythm of swordplay stilled all thought. Gradually, he surrendered to instinct, aware only of his body, its position, how it reacted, any stiffness.

Picking up the pace, his cleaving sword dealt imaginary death, his dance becoming faster and fiercer but controlled. *Lunge, recover, lunge. Retreat. Step, lunge.* Soon, sweat trickled down his neck, matted his hair, and left damp patches on his tunic—a trophy of effort, of achievement.

Val switched from shadow combat to patterns, practising every attack and parry. It was only then that he realised the loud ringing had stopped and a crowd had formed to watch.

The weapons instructor waved a hand. "When will we have footwork like that?" she lamented. "Pay attention, girls. This is the only warrior who lasted in the arena against the Quisnaf champion."

Uncomfortable, Val broke off. "I am sorry. I thought only to quietly practise by myself. I did not intend to disturb you."

The woman shook her head. "Do not stop. These lazy girls might learn something."

Val, though, was done. He ran his fingers through his damp hair, hoping Anna would take him to the baths. He sought her in the stands and saw her chatting with two strangers, apparently indifferent to the fuss below.

"Good to see you're ready for me." A different voice carried from above.

Val whirled. Torchlight from the passage framed Jenna-

Dairine in the entrance. She ran lightly down the steps, paused to whisper to Anna, then strode purposefully towards him. She wore loose pants and a sleeveless shirt but no sword or even a knife.

When she reached him, she grinned. "I enjoyed that. It also gave me a chance to watch you, to glean your patterns."

"I use patterns only when I train. Otherwise, I have none."

"Every warrior has patterns. Yours are very complicated, I'll grant you that." She trod to the weapons rack and picked out a sword. "Shall we see?"

A gasp of awe ran through the young warriors. Some nudged each other or whispered behind their hands. The weapons mistress swept them a withering look. "This is a rare chance, students," she said. "Pay close attention. Jenna-Dairine, daughter of Kathryn, is champion of Quisnaf. Apart from the contest at the Blessing, she rarely honours a man with the offer of swordplay."

"Almost never, in fact," Jenna-Dairine said softly to Val. "Not unless it's an official challenge so the goddess may have her sacrifice."

"What's this then? Couldn't sleep?"

"Something like that. I do, in fact, sleep like a baby after swordplay. Shall we?" She kicked off her sandals, tossed him a helm from the rack, and gestured towards the centre of the arena.

Val dragged the helm down over his tangled hair. As he followed her, he reassessed his surroundings. A large space. No obstacles, just so long as the spectators kept their distance. Sand afoot. The ground flat. No chance for tricks, then. Just steel against steel. Will against will. Just as he preferred it.

He laughed softly.

Jenna-Dairine frowned. "What's that laugh about?"

"Oh, nothing. I came here tonight seeking that concentration of thought that banishes all else. The prospect of fighting someone as talented as you... well..." He shrugged.

"I know that longing to banish thought." With a vicious grin, she cut at his head with her blade.

Val fell back a step as he whipped up a parry. That single clash of steel sounded impossibly loud until he realised every other sound had vanished. Breaths were held. Shuffling feet stilled.

Jenna-Dairine circled, still smiling. It was a detached smile, hazy like a sleepwalker's. He was not fooled. A warrior might seek this dream state, as though stepping apart from the world into a cocoon of cold purpose. It made her more dangerous, not less. Despite her glazed eyes, her every taut muscle and tensed fibre screamed readiness.

She fell upon him with a storm of strokes. Some battering. Some swinging. Some stabbing. Val answered most with the blade, the rest by leaping clear. He watched her other hand, remembering how she could lull an opponent with just her touch. That, too, was a weapon.

Jenna-Dairine struck low, still content to only use the sword. Val fended her off with a sweeping swish. A high, cleaving stroke hissed through air at his head. Steel clanged as he blocked. They exchanged fierce blows then, one on the offensive then reeling back as the other took over the assault. Hew, hack, slash. Metal screeched in the echoing chamber.

Breathing hard, they broke apart and stalked each other carefully, seeking openings.

Dimly, Val heard the weapons instructor explaining what she guessed were the tactics, what her students might imitate. In the lull, Val took his chance to attack, charging with flurried metal, forcing Jenna-Dairine to retreat. He pursued her with steel, thrusting short then disengaging. She took the blow high near the hilt. Val yanked his blade clear.

Again, they circled. His nostrils prickled at sweat that drenched his clothing and soaked through to skin. Jenna-Dairine's hair tangled onto her forehead. Her sleepy gaze passed over him and snared him in an intimate spell. The world shrank to their rushed breaths. To the glint in her eyes. To the scent of blood and death. Only this. Only them.

Val broke the mood with a low thrust. Jenna-Dairine's parry

crashed down, the impact of her heavy stroke shuddering through his shoulders. With her other hand, she pawed at his arm. One touch, and he was hers, to do with as she chose.

Desperately, he recoiled from her hand and from her hunting sword. Two weapons. With no shield to block one, he backed up fast, as if fleeing racing wildfire. Jenna-Dairine prowled like a wolf, loping and bounding after him, herding him towards the wall. Her breath rasped. Sweat streamed down her neck. The air was steamy, hot, and expectant.

Stone pressed his hip. Trapped, Val could only take stance to parry and riposte as she thrust, aiming low to wound. His arm served him truly, directing his leaping, flashing blade that was the instrument of his trained hand and will.

The students began to shout, fired up, as Jenna-Dairine pressed her advantage. Val kept her at bay—just. He glanced sideways, seeking a chance to escape to open ground. But Jenna-Dairine kept the right distance to cover him if he tried to dart left or right.

Impatiently, she cut high. Val rolled aside. The sword crashed into the wall. Snarling, she whirled, but he had slipped away. She plunged after him. Val weaved this way and that, not engaging but keeping beyond her reach.

"Fight me," she snarled.

He just laughed and edged sideways. Enraged, she ran at him, sword raised. At the unexpected opening, Val's heart slammed against his ribs. All he had to do was drop to one knee and drag the blade across her exposed belly.

He did not.

Jenna-Dairine's sword clanged on his helm. Her hand groped for his arm, fingers tugging on his sleeve as he drove his elbow up into her jaw. She howled in pain. Her sword swung wildly. Val dipped beneath. Abandoning his weapon, he flung himself at her legs. Unbalanced, Jenna-Dairine fell backwards. Breath blew out of her in a gasp. Her sword skittled over sand.

A moan rose from the spectators. "Hit him," the instructor shouted. "Get up."

Val pinned Jenna-Dairine's wrists with his hands, his knee to her hip. "Do you yield?"

"Bastard," she hissed, thrashing and bucking beneath him. The only sounds were their harsh breaths and her curses. Stunned warriors gaped. Even their instructor had nothing more to say.

Then Jenna-Dairine stilled. For a heartbeat, Val was confused. Her head lifted towards his. He jerked back, but not before her lips brushed his. It was the faintest of touches, but it burned like a cut. All thought stalled. A strange weakness washed through him.

"Get off me," she whispered. "Kneel."

Dazed, he let her go and rose to his knees.

Jenna-Dairine scrambled up, snatched her sword, and circled behind. She fisted his fringe to yank back his head. Steel tickled his throat. Long blonde strands of her hair brushed his arm as she bent. Damp cloth pressed against damp skin. She put her lips close to his ear, her breath warm on his jaw. "No man has defeated me with the blade. It excites me that you did. I want you in my bed, Telorian. And soon."

She drew back the sword and walked off, leaving him huddled in the sand, head bowed. A silence held a moment. Then clashing steel again rang out as the weapons mistress instructed her students to resume drills. They kept away from him, though glances fell hot on his back.

Val could not move. Slowly, his wits reformed. He grew aware of his body and where he was. Sand ground into his knees through his pants. Sweat dampened his armpits and trickled down his brow. Dully, he registered Anna's hand on his shoulder. She spoke words he couldn't understand. With a worried look, she hurried off.

Still, he could not rise. His lips burned. His limbs tingled as though they had cramped. Then a sound pierced the surface noise of shuffling feet, grunts, and shrieking metal. A slow hand clap.

Val turned his head towards the sound. Stunned, he blinked, unable to take in what he saw. Halfway up the tiered seats, one knee drawn up on her seat, Genya watched him.

"How low you've fallen." Slowly, she rose and strolled into the arena, her boots crunching over sand.

Tangled emotions churned in him. Relief she was safe. Guilt, yes, that. He had left her. He knew that. But he could not look at her without seeing Roaran's broken body. Without seeing Neil swinging from a rope. Without seeing the chains about Kaell and Alecc.

"What was that? You've lost your edge. You had an opening— I saw it. You didn't take it. Then you pinned her, and suddenly, you back off and kneel? Let her put steel to your throat? You'd never let anyone put steel to your throat."

Val struggled for control of his limbs, managing only an embarrassed shrug. He did not want her here. He did not want her to see him a captive, diminished because he was subject to others' wills. He did not want her to see his shame.

"She…." He sought the right words. "Jenna-Dairine has magic. Her touch…"

"Then you don't let her touch you," Genya snarled. "Gods, you've been around magic your entire life. You know the danger."

Their eyes locked. What he glimpsed in hers serrated his gut like sharpened iron. Genya stared boldly, defying him to challenge her presence, ready to answer anger with anger. But beneath her defiance, like a glimmer far within, he sensed longing. A tiny flare of hope that he might be ready to forgive her.

If he should soften, if he should hold out his arms, she might fall against him and sob as she had as a young child. And the tears would flow readily—hot tears of contrition and shame.

He nearly did. He nearly said, "It's all right. I understand. You made a mistake. I forgive you." Yet the words did not come. And still did not come. There was only suspicion that she was not sorry. That if time repeated, Genya would choose the same path.

He *would* forgive her. In time. He must. Beneath his disappointment and sorrow, he loved her. Val would surrender his life to save her. But he was not ready to forget.

"I needed time," he muttered. "I asked for time. Why won't you give me time?"

Those dark-blue eyes, too much like Roaran's, blazed. Her slouch and stormy face bespoke resentment. The training ground seemed colder, and it was not a cold carried by drifting wind or rising from the earth.

"You refused to see me." Her face collapsed with hurt.

Again, he nearly buckled, nearly pulled her into his arms and stroked her hair, comforting and assuring.

"I'm not ready. Every time I look at you…"

"Forgive me," she pleaded.

Again, their eyes met, trapped by the bond of time. Of the past. Of love. Of misunderstanding and pain.

"I want to."

Her breath caught. She took a hesitant step towards him. "Then…"

"I want to," he repeated. "But when I look at you, I want to shake you, to rage against what you've done. I see *him* in you. Roaran. And I'm afraid, Genya."

"What are you saying? Am I never to be forgiven?"

Val shook his head. "No. I just… I can't. I'm not ready. I will forgive you, Genya. But not yet. It's all too raw. I cannot."

A silence closed in. She did not move. She said nothing. Then, as if a fiery anger ran through her, her expression changed. "Cannot?" Disbelief sharpened her tone. "Cannot?"

"Genya…"

"I came all this way. I came for you."

"I didn't ask you to. I asked you to leave me be. It would not be forever. I just needed…"

"Time." She waved a hand. "You said."

"You made a mistake. I know that. And Archanin is dead. But whenever I shut my eyes—" He saw their bodies. Gethin. Neil. Roaran. Val could not suppress a shudder.

"Do you know what I see every time I shut my eyes?" Her voice was flat, her face a stranger's. Her stance was as taut and tense as an arrow against a string. "Fields of death. Scorched earth. Heaped bodies. Blood. Even without Archanin, ghouls have ravished our land. And what did you do? Nothing. You left me to face it alone. You left me with Alecc, a boy who was expected to know how to become a king. You left me with Nicky, who was lost to grief, his life fragmented. You left me with them, to fight alone. You abandoned me."

"Genya—"

"And for what? To play the whore? Oh, I know what you do here—"

"Genya." Val whipped up a hand. "Be careful, or we'll both say things we can't take back."

"It's disgusting. You're disgusting. You bed women to get them with child. Women you don't know. Women you don't love. I know men and women do that, but not you."

"Why not me?" he cried bitterly. "Do you think I'm so righteous? You expect too much of me."

"I expect very little. And I get less."

"Genya…"

"Why didn't I see it before? You never loved me. All you did was prepare me to do what the gods willed. Face Archanin. Die. I was nothing to you but someone to be sacrificed in the fight against ghouls."

"That's not fair!" Anger surged through Val. "You sided with a ghoul god, Genya. You didn't care who died. Just so long as you had what you wanted."

Genya's lips parted slightly. "I said I was sorry."

The anger was still in him. Words shot out—words he at once regretted. "Sorry? You were never sorry. Never once. You'd do it again if it suited you. No child I raised would betray their friends like that."

She reeled back, staring. "So now you disown me? Who are you to judge me? You don't know what I've done to save Telor, to save the Mountains." There was a furious edge to her voice and an angry glitter in her eyes.

"Genya." Oh, goddess, what had he said? "I didn't mean—"

"I hate you!" she shouted. "It's you who should beg me to forgive you. You no longer have my love. You have my scorn." With that, she turned and ran.

GENYA

Muttering, fists curled, she stomped through the caverns to the rooms she shared with Dannon. Furious thoughts pursued her. *That stubborn, stubborn man.* That he, *he,* should judge her. "Whore," she whispered. "Whore." He would be sorry. She would make him sorry.

A shadow peeled off a wall ahead. A figure blocked Genya's way. Genya drew up hard, tensing, her hand on her knife hilt. "Out of my way."

The figure moved into the light. It was a woman with long auburn hair tied in one plait that swung over her shoulder and a petulant, full-lipped mouth. A tattoo swirled up her neck. She wore loose pants, a tunic, and a sword belt. Genya looked at the woman's long blade in the belt then slowly lifted her eyes to the stranger's face. "You don't want to start something with me."

The woman grinned and held up her hands disarmingly. "I want only a few minutes of your time, Genya Caelan."

"Oh, you know my name. Should I be impressed?"

The stranger laughed. "Everyone knows. It's no big secret. At least, not anymore."

"I see." Genya hunched her shoulders. "Well, you have my attention. Who are you, and what do you want?"

The woman laughed. "You're fierce. That's good. You're going to need to be."

Genya frowned. "Why?"

"Because there's something coming. Something big. Something dangerous." She offered that open smile again. "I just want to make sure you're on the right side."

"I'm to take a side? That sounds like you're expecting a fight."

The woman's smile faded. "No," she said. "I'm expecting war."

Genya's blood quickened. "War? With who?"

The figure curled a finger. "Come with me. There's someone who wants to meet you."

"Why should I go anywhere with you? And who are you, anyhow?"

"My name's Branwyn," the woman said. "I am nothing more than a messenger, bid to bring you to *her*. Someone who can give you everything you want and more. Someone who wants to help."

Someone who could give you what you want. Genya shivered with temptation. She touched her blade. If she went with this Branwyn, she was in no danger. Not with her sword and her command of magic. "Lead on. Let's hear what your mysterious leader has to say."

With a sly smile, Branwyn turned and started back down the passage. Genya followed. Very soon, Branwyn came to a door. It opened onto stone steps leading down. Surprisingly, torches flamed in cressets upon the walls.

Branwyn shut the door behind Genya and led her down. They both had to bend their backs to enter the narrow, cramped tunnel at the bottom. For a moment, Genya thought of the rock and dirt above her head and shuddered. Her breaths echoed loudly in the hush.

The tunnel ended. Before her was a rock-encased chamber with more torches smoking from sconces. A few low couches, tables, and chairs were scattered about the room. Racks of weapons hung from the walls. Upon one table, pebbles held down the corners of a map.

A few armed women slouched on divans behind a hooded figure. She was seated at a table, her face shadowed. "Thank you, Branwyn."

With a nod, Branwyn retreated back towards the tunnel. The woman waved a hand at a chair opposite. With a curious glance about, Genya sat.

"Who are you, and what do you want from me?"

"I want you on my side, Genya Caelan."

"Oh?" Genya raised her brows. "In this so-called war? And why should I take your side? Just who are you?"

"Someone who is going to save Quisnaf. Who is going to get rid of the rot and restore it to its previous greatness."

Genya frowned. "I thought Quisnaf was all-powerful as it is."

The woman shook her head. "Blaire has left us vulnerable. She is determined to undermine our laws, laws that have kept us strong for centuries."

"Your internal problems are nothing to do with me."

"Roaran intended you to be here, to be part of Quisnaf. He knew you would find a place here. Don't you want that, Genya Caelan? To belong."

Genya shrugged. "I am not bound by any contract between the Quisnaf and Roaran."

The woman leaned forward.

Genya strained to see her face, but the hood's folds kept it hidden.

"I want to offer you a place in the new Quisnaf order. I want you by my side."

"Why would I want a place? What's in it for me?"

"Unlimited magic," the woman said. "You would have a position where you were respected. You would learn the secrets of Quisnaf sorcery and have more power than you can ever imagine. Think about it, Genya. You are alone. There's nothing in Telor for you anymore."

A shiver of longing tore through Genya. Unlimited magic. Quisnaf magic. Power. Respect. "It's not enough."

The woman clasped her hands together on the table. "I'll help you take down Gendrick Caelan. Blaire won't lift a finger to help you, but I will. I will send you back with ships and a battale of warriors. And there's more."

Genya's breath snagged. An entire battale. Ships. In her mind, she began to see how Tide's End would fall. How she would drag Gendrick out of his palace by his hair and put her knife to his throat. "More?"

The woman paused. "I'll not only give you the Cahirean, but I'll give you Val Arques."

Another shiver ran up Genya's backbone. She imagined Val on his knees while she was enthroned before him, his fate hers to determine. "Who are you that you can offer so much?"

"If I show you my face, you cannot leave here unless you are one of us."

Genya stared at her. All her anger at Val knotted in her stomach. All her bitterness at Gendrick. All her longing since Alecc and Nicky's death for companionship, for solace, for comfort. This stranger was right. She was alone. Even when she was with Dannon, loneliness ached through her.

"Show your face," she said.

ROHANE

They took him from the prison at dawn, his hands tied at his back, his feet bare. Crisp dew frosted the grass. A glorious pink-hued horizon shimmered beyond the cliffs, its splashes of rose a delicate flush in the grey sky. Rohane thought it was a good morning to die.

As the guards escorted the prisoner through spectators to the scaffold, his steps dragged. She wondered what he was thinking, wondered at the revelation that this woman was actually a bonded warrior called Kaell, transformed by magic.

Kaell walked with his head unbowed, gaze straight ahead, as if apart from the crowd that had gathered to watch his execution. But for all his resolve, Rohane guessed the fear was in him. In the faintest tremble in his limbs. In the clamour of his heart. In the nausea roiling in his gut.

The knot of guards escorted him up the stairs to a platform. The noose hung from a crossbeam upon the gallows, limp in the still, heavy air. Unresisting, Kaell let the black-masked executioner put the rope about his neck.

Rohane glanced out over the small clearing bounded by mountains. Shrill, clear, and beautiful, birdsong accompanied the coming day. She looked over the crowd. Some were warriors;

others were scribes, sorceresses, or servants. Her gaze settled upon Samantha and Blaire near the scaffold, their cloaks pulled tight, though the night had been mild and the dawn only a little colder. As her eyes met Blaire's, the Regenta nodded.

The executioner drew very near. With no warning, she swung the crossbeam out, sweeping Kaell off his feet. His body jerked once, sharply, the drop calculated to break his neck. In the gathering hush, the faintest breeze fluttered the folds of his tunic.

His body swayed slightly then hung limply.

Rohane wandered back into the caverns, her mind troubled by what she had just seen. A bonded warrior executed in Quisnaf. A warrior who served the gods.

Oh, goddess, who should tell Val? Perhaps it should forever be kept from him. Perhaps he never needed to know. But was that fair?

Her thoughts in turmoil, she walked through the underground tunnel and took the stairs to Blaire's chambers. It was the secret way to Blaire's rooms, more private than the official entrance through the temple.

As she rounded a corner, Rohane rocked to a halt, her breath on hold. Blaire's door stood open. Cautiously, Rohane edged closer. A rustling sound came from within. Rohane crept to the door, noting the broken lock, and peered inside. A cowled figure bent over a table, their back to her as they examined unfolded parchment.

Rohane's hand slipped to the knife in her belt. "Stop," she cried. "What are you doing here?"

The figure turned. Rohane got a glimpse of a pale chin and pale hair a second before the figure rushed at her. Rohane snatched at them, but they shoved her, knocking her against the door. The figure ran off towards the stairs. Recovering her balance, Rohane started after them. At the top of the stairs, she paused. The tunnel was empty. Nor could she hear footsteps.

She listened, but there was nothing to tell her which direction the figure had gone. With heavy steps, Rohane returned to Blaire's rooms. She crossed to the table where she had seen the figure and examined the top parchment. A sinking feeling gathered in her belly.

"Rohane?"

She turned and found Blaire stood in the doorway, frowning.

"Someone was here," Rohane said. "They were reading this." She tapped the parchment with her fingertips. "The proposed new laws regarding the status of men in Quisnaf."

Blaire's face was ashen. "The Order," she whispered. "Then they know."

"They'll use it against you."

For a long moment, Blaire stared blankly at Rohane. Then she muttered, "It would have come out. When I presented the new law to the council. I just didn't want it to be so soon. Not when things are enflamed. When there's danger." She blinked. "Did you see who it was?"

"No. They were cowled." Rohane took a step closer and touched Blaire's arm. "We have to hunt them out. Don't you see? We can't wait for the Order to make the next move."

"I don't even know where to start looking."

Rohane bit down on her frustration. She flung her arms wide. "Then what do we do?"

"We wait," Blaire said.

GENYA

That morning, Genya summoned the strength to tell Dannon the details of Gendrick's betrayal. He listened with consternation then fury. Then he wept silently, his fist grinding his palm, his teeth clenched.

"For Nicky and Alecc to be murdered so brutally," he muttered again and again. "Oh, the gods are cruel indeed. They are fickle and vicious. Not to be trusted. They take from us again and again."

"What of Cyrah?" Genya asked.

"They are all the same," Dannon said bitterly. "Pitiless and malicious. We are but puppets dancing on their strings."

He listened to her complaints about Val, nodding in agreement when she called him judgemental. "He's stubborn, all right," Dannon said. "But what is the cause of the dispute between you? You haven't explained why he's so angry."

"Do you think I deserve it?" she cried. "Is that what you think?"

"No, no." Dannon shook his head in bewilderment. "I just wish you trusted me with the truth. I sense there's something you're not telling me."

"There's nothing," Genya muttered. "Besides, soon, it won't matter." Not Val nor his harsh condemnation. Soon, petty disputes and concerns would be beneath her. Soon, she would know the comfort and protection of the most powerful magic, magic that cocooned her from hurt.

Genya remembered the woman she had met in the hidden chamber. They had sat together as night gathered, talking of the woman's plans and her dream for Quisnaf. A shiver of excitement tore through Genya. "Things are about to change."

He frowned. "What do you mean 'change'?"

She leaned in, her tone lower. "It's secret. You can't breathe a word of it."

"Of what?"

"Of what's about to happen in Quisnaf. There's a new power rising. Someone with vision. Someone who will restore this realm to its past glory. And there's a place for me, for us, in that new world."

Dannon frowned again. "Do you mean rebellion?" When she said nothing, he touched her shoulder. "Genya, if someone is about to try and overthrow Blaire, we have to tell the council. Samantha, maybe. This is dangerous."

"No." She shook her head furiously. "It's not dangerous. It's necessary."

"But—" He rubbed his chin. "How do you know this? What's going on?"

"I was told. No, do not ask me by who. It's secret, like I said. I was just warned to be ready."

"Why tell you this? What's it to do with you—an outsider?"

Another shiver of exhilaration took off down her spine. "They're going to teach me magic," she whispered in awe. "Not like Rozenn taught me. Something different. Something incredible. I'm going to have real power. The sort of power that will let me destroy Gendrick." *The power to punish Val. Oh, how he'll be sorry for all his harsh words.*

For a moment, Dannon said nothing. In the stillness, a distant chime resonated, its tone sweet. Then he shook his head. "At what cost?"

Genya grabbed his arm. "It's meant to happen, Dannon. I believe in her, you see. She's going to restore Quisnaf so that it's strong again. She's going to root out the decadence, the corruption, the weakness that is enfeebling this land."

He sat back, his hands clenched in his lap. "Who is this she?"

Genya only smiled.

⁓⧓⁓

Guards arrived with a summons from Blaire. Comfortable, sleepy in Dannon's arms, Genya ignored their knocking. Though it was surely late afternoon, even twilight, she did not want to ever rise from this bed. The knock on the door sounded again.

"Leave me alone," she shouted.

"Genya Caelan, the Regenta insists we take you to her."

"Go away."

Another knock came. "We cannot."

Reluctantly, Genya pushed herself to her feet. Dannon murmured then rolled over. Tenderly, Genya touched a lock of hair on his brow. There had been joy in their reunion, solace and true companionship—all she had been denied for so long. Did she love him? She wanted to. She wanted love's heady joy, passion, and affection. But not its vulnerability.

No, better to rely on magic. Magic was truth. Magic was power.

Genya straightened and found her clothes. Once dressed, a thin cloak clasped at her throat, she threw open the door.

A guard bowed. "Sorceress, if you please."

They fell in around her, escorting her through torch-lit caverns then into the valley, shadowy with dusk. Insects hummed a loud chorus, but beneath, a hush held, as if heralding change. *Tonight. Would it be tonight?* Genya hid a tremble of excitement.

At the end of a road of marble, the temple loomed atop stone steps. Flames leapt from braziers, scarlet fingers against the gathering darkness. When she hesitated, her palm brushing sun-warmed stone on the balustrades, the guards waited until she was ready to move on into the domed building.

Despite her tangle of emotions, her anger at Val, and that tingle of anticipation, part of her recognised the beauty of the temple with its shining marble walls and floors. The sight of the towering, imposing statue of Cyrah lifted hairs on her arms. Genya wanted to lean against the stone and run her hands over the goddess's gown.

Remembering Dannon's words and his bitterness at the gods, she wondered what it might be like to trust an omnipresent deity, to surrender her will and even her resentment. Neither Nicky nor Val had seemed particularly interested in gods. Genya had never thought to ask what they believed. It had been enough for her, as a child, that her grandfather, Archanin, called himself a god. Then she had killed him, along with her need to believe in something greater than herself.

Quickly, she walked on between pillars that buttressed like roots against the roof. Tapestries and murals covered the walls. Leafy vines in pots curled up trellises. Scents of cinnamon, cloves, and vanilla were warm and welcoming, unlike the cold, empty air of the Mountains.

What a strange place this was. An uncomfortable place of sharp contrast. Beauty and cruelty. Passion and discipline. Law, order, and barbarism. Yet it no longer seemed alien. No, she could find a place here. Indeed, a high place had been offered to her.

The guards stopped at ornate doors of wood, bronze, and iron. At their knock, Blaire opened the door. She waved Genya inside. The Regenta's face was tight, her lips pinched.

Blaire's distress clamped fear about Genya's heart. Blaire could not know what was about to happen. Careful plans had been made. It would unfold soon, without warning.

The Regenta led her into a columned room, its corners shadowy at dusk. More embroidered tapestries decorated walls. Woven silk rugs spread underfoot, a testimony to Quisnaf's wealth. Compared to the Mountains castle Genya had called home for the past few months, these caverns were lavish and far too comfortable for a martial society. Yes, the decadence must be rooted out and Quisnaf set upon a rightful footing again.

At their approach, Samantha and Rohane rose from couches, the two women's expressions ill at ease. Blaire gestured at a chair. Genya took it.

"Wine?"

Genya nodded. A girl stepped from a discreet place near the wall to pour. Blaire waved her away and passed Genya a cup.

"I asked you here because I have news. Ill news." Blaire moistened her lips with her tongue. "This morning, we executed your companion."

For a long moment, Genya stared at her, not understanding. Then coldness cut through her. "Kaell," she whispered.

"It was quick."

Genya hardly heard her. Her gaze held on nothing. Though she'd cared little for Kaell, the shock of hearing he was dead sat like lead in her belly. She shook off a pang of guilt. Surely she should be pleased. Except it was all too late. Her anger at Val was too deep, too raw, and too wide for her to care that she no longer had a rival for his affection.

"We must tell him," Rohane implored Blaire. "Val Arques. First his son, Alecc. Now the young man he trained. Raised."

"No!" Genya thumped down her wine glass. "No. Do not tell him. Not yet. Not about Alecc, nor Kaell." There would be a time when Val would learn of their deaths. A time of her choosing. A time when she could hurt him with the truth.

"He has a right to know," Rohane insisted.

"Not yet," Genya insisted. "You must let me do it when I think it's right. He loved Alecc." She would not think upon how Val had loved Kaell and how her betrayal had taken him from her guardian.

Blaire ground a fist into her hand. "Alecc Caelan's death is a setback. Though truly, Gendrick Caelan shall answer to his gods.

Death riders are returned, delivering justice. His fate is sealed. He shall wither, suffer, and die in agony."

"No," Genya said in a quiet but resolved voice. "He shall not answer to the gods, either his or yours. They shall not cheat me. Gendrick shall answer to me."

ROHANE

When Genya left, the three women sat quietly drinking wine, each lost to their thoughts.

"I do not know if she is to be trusted," Rohane muttered, breaking the silence.

Blaire shrugged. "She's Roaran's daughter. Roaran was always a friend to Quisnaf. For his sake, we have to give her the benefit of the doubt."

"She's very young," Samantha said. "Headstrong. If we could win her to Quisnaf, we could temper that passion, direct it."

"What reason has she to be loyal to Quisnaf?" Rohane asked. "I think she will bear watching—"

A furious knocking sounded at the door. A breathless guard ran in. "Regenta." The woman dropped to one knee. "There's trouble."

Blaire waved the guard up. "What trouble? What's happened?"

"There's fighting. Warriors attacked a group of temple guards in the bathhouse. Another group attacked some of Persia's battale in the valley."

"What?" Samantha shot to her feet. "Is it still going on?"

The woman shook her head. "They attacked at dusk, killed the guards, then slipped back into the darkness. No one saw where they went."

"It's happening." Abruptly, Blaire turned her back, her bowed head in her hands.

Rohane went to her. She touched Blaire's shoulder. "You think it's the Order? You think they're making their final move?"

"Don't you? The signs are there. They've been gathering strength, growing more daring."

"Or it's nothing," Samantha said. "Only a small group of troublemakers. They'll slink back to whatever hole they crawled out of."

Rohane tapped her fingers on her sword belt. "I'm sick of this. I'm going to find them."

"Rohane, wait—"

But Rohane was already out the door.

The first thing that struck her was the absence of guards. The next was the silence. It clung to the temple like a pall. Uneasily, Rohane crept into the nave, stepping over the bodies of two sleeping priestesses. She bent and shook one. The woman muttered but did not wake.

An acrid smell rose off the burning candles. A wave of dizziness washed over her. Rohane shook it off and hurried on, down the temple steps into the valley. A shard of moonlight silvered the trees, their branches still in the breathless, heavy air. Rohane glanced up at the mountains. There were no lights. Scalp prickling, she crept forward along the valley, taking the stairs near the gates and arch to the walls. No guards were upon the walk, no sentry at the entrance to Quisnaf. Where was the watch?

A scream cut the air then cut off. Though the winter night was heavy, warm, and sultry, Rohane shuddered. Something was badly wrong.

Then a foot turned a stone. A shape flitted through the trees. Rohane started after the figure then drew up hard. In the distance, a bright light flared from the valley wall, as if someone had lit hundreds of lamps within a cavern. As if someone were meeting.

A shiver took off down Rohane's spine. *The Order? Would they make their final move tonight?*

At her back, shouts broke out. Steel clanged. Rohane whirled in time to see two groups of women fighting in one of the clearings. A scream then the sounds of more scraping, battering steel carried from within the caverns above her.

Drawing her sword, Rohane started forward. Something hit her hard between the shoulder blades. She stumbled, pain shooting through her back. An arm dropped about her throat, squeezing. Struggling to breathe, Rohane elbowed whoever was behind her and kicked a shin. A woman grunted. The arm fell away. Rohane whirled. A cowled figure groped for the blade in their belt. Rohane thrust her sword tip to the woman's breast. "Stop."

Reluctantly, the woman threw up her hands. Rohane peered beneath the hood but did not recognise the stranger's face. "Why did you attack me?"

The woman did not answer.

Rohane prodded her with the sword. "You should have killed me at once. That was your mistake."

The woman shrugged. "You're on *her* no-kill list. When I saw you there, it was opportunistic. I thought I could take you alive. Knock you out."

"Who is this *her*?"

Another scream split the air, chilling in the heavy silence.

For an instant, Rohane glanced towards the sound. The woman knocked her sword aside and fled. Cursing, Rohane started after her. Then cold, hard reason took over.

She had to get back to Blaire and Samantha. She had to warn them.

VAL ARQUES

He spun awake into darkness streaked by thin light beneath the door. Sounds, familiar and alarming, pummelled him. Shouts. Clanging, scraping steel. Running footsteps. Cries of pain and fear.

Val bolted up. By the pale light of the candle he had left burning, he groped for his pants and cloak. He was half dressed and across the room when the door was flung back. Sisilia stood in the threshold. At the sight of him, she stilled, her eyes slits of displeasure. "Where do you think you're off to?"

Val drew up. "I hear fighting, sword strikes. Is there danger?"

"It's happening." Sisilia nodded slowly. "Sooner than I thought."

"What's happening?"

"The Order is making its move."

The Order. A memory flickered of symbols painted on stone walls, an assassin's knife coming at him in the darkness, shuttered glances, tight lips, and meaningful nods.

"I... do you mean..." Alarming thoughts jammed together. If there was fighting, Rohane and Genya were out there somewhere amid bloody chaos. He had to help them. Val started to move past Sisilia.

She gripped his arm. "You will not leave this room."

"Let me pass." Val shrugged off her hand. "I must find my ward. And Rohane. Make sure she's safe. Blaire, too. If it's the Order, then she's in danger."

"And you care about Blaire?" Sisilia's green eyes glittered like polished stone.

"Of course…" He broke off, staring. "You don't?" Frowning, he followed that thread. Val gasped. "Oh, by The Three. Are you one of them?"

"Silence," Sisilia snapped. She filled the doorway, blocking his way. "None of this concerns you, Telorian."

Val started to shoulder past. He was bulkier, taller, and stronger than her. "Let me go. You can't stop me."

Her hand came up. One minute, he was on his feet. The next, he sprawled on the ground. Winded, Val forced himself to his knees, shocked she had used magic to stop him.

Sisilia drew manacles from a pocket and flung them at him. "Put your wrists in those."

Val's chin shot up in defiance. "No." He'd had just about enough of commands, harsh hands, and restrictions. She could not keep him here, not when those he loved were in danger.

Her face darkened. Again, her hand whipped out. Val plunged back. Something tightened about his throat. He gasped and spluttered. "Can't… breathe."

"Wrists." Her tone was unsympathetic.

Choking and wheezing, he groped for the manacles and shoved his wrists through. Sisilia spat a word. They snapped shut just as the invisible band about his neck loosened.

Val sucked in deep, painful breaths. He rose again to his knees, furious at his helplessness. *Genya. Rohane.* He had to get to them. "Don't do this, Sisilia. I beg you. If you don't care about Blaire, then at least let me find Genya. I must know she's safe. I must make certain no harm comes to Rohane."

Sisilia considered him without pity. "I am commanded to keep you from trouble. The Order will come for you soon enough. *She'll* come for you. You are a prize of war, after all."

Val threw out a hand against the wall to rise. Sisilia's magic had sapped him of strength. "She?"

Sisilia shut the door.

ROHANE

Rohane stormed into Blaire's chambers in the temple, dragging the door shut at her back. In her frantic return through the valley, through the caverns, the chaos of revolt had swept aside the unnatural quiet. The temple throbbed with the cacophony of pounding footsteps, clanging swords, cries, screams. In every passage, in halls, and even in the gardens, slumbering women lay as if someone had cast a spell over the entire kingdom.

Blaire fastened a weapons belt sheathing a sword of Seithin steel and a curved dagger about her waist. "My personal guard?"

"Gone." Rohane dragged a hand down her face. Whoever this was, they had coordinated their attack. "My mother?"

"Seeking out the other council members."

A fist pounded the door. A panicked voice cried, "Regenta, are you safe?"

Rohane flung open the door.

A temple guard stood in the entrance, breathing hard. "Regenta, bladeswomen are in the temple. There's fighting. I was sent to warn—" The woman's body jerked. She slumped violently against Rohane, an arrow protruding from her back.

Rohane glanced quickly into the passage. A group of warriors stormed towards Blaire's chambers. Rohane dropped the dead woman, dragged the door shut, turned the key, and backed up to join Blaire. "They're coming."

Blaire grabbed her arm, her expression hard. "Are you with me, Rohane? Are you at least with me?"

"I've always been with you," Rohane said. "Just as I was when we were girls. The four of us, remember? You, me, Jenna-Dairine, and Trevin."

Blaire shot her a lopsided grin. "Then let's not make this easy."

A spear butt struck bronze. "Open the door, Regenta," someone commanded. "There's no point hiding in there."

Rohane gripped her sword, her eyes held on the door. An axe thudded twice. Metal buckled. Warriors pushed inside through the ruined door, weapons drawn. They flung themselves at Rohane and Blaire.

Rohane took the first attack high on her sword. Her opponent's weapon trapped, she kicked the woman back. The warrior reeled. But a second assailant was already on Rohane, with a third coming at her from the side. A shield crashed into her head. Rohane staggered. Desperately, she shook her head to clear it and gripped the sword tightly.

"Put it down, Captain," a woman ordered.

Rohane backed up a step, her blade levelled at her attackers. Her vision hazed in and out. "Why should I?"

"Because we hold the Telorian. We'll kill him if you resist."

A pang of fear took hold of Rohane. *Val.* She shoved it aside. *No, Val is immortal. Blaire is not.* She glanced from the women circling her to Blaire. The Regenta fought furiously against a horde of warriors charging her from all sides.

Rohane tightened her grip on her hilt. "Val can take care of himself."

With a roar, she charged them, reaching within for the berserker rage. Her sword slashed up and down. Then a red fog overtook her. Her mind narrowed only to the sword, to her opponents, to the killing. With battering steel, she thrust, cut, and skewered. A woman shrieked. Rohane yanked her sword out of bloody, torn flesh. No longer consciously in control, she sought a new target, her strokes a cacophony of rage. Her body moved in rhythm with the blade as it hacked, cut, and swung. A second figure before her fell. Then another crumpled in a bloody heap. She rounded on the next, thrusting. Iron slid between ribs then slid out. A woman dropped, her breath hissing out in pain. A crimson splash of blood blinded Rohane briefly. She swiped at her face, glimpsing more warriors storming through the door.

Distantly, she was aware of Blaire screaming, her sword flashing. Then, like rabid dogs, a knot of warriors fell on the Regenta, knocking her to the floor.

"Drop the blade, Captain, or she's dead."

The words slowly pierced Rohane's rage. *Blaire. In danger.* Bit by bit, the red mist dissipated from her mind. She glanced from their attackers to Blaire writhing in her captors' grips, then back again. Frustrated and angry, she bellowed and flung her blade to the ground.

Women grabbed her arms, pushed her down, and held her on her knees. As her vision righted, Rohane began to recognise faces. Evolet from Joanna's battale. A Decan guard called Beatrice. One of Persia's bladeswomen. Elizabeth, whom everyone called Zo Zo for no good reason.

"You have Blaire? Good. Quickly, now. Bind her."

As her hands were tied, Blaire stared at the speaker in astonishment. "Evolet. You? Whatever did I do to you that you should turn on me?"

The woman sneered. "It's what you didn't do, *Regenta*."

"It's not too late. We can end this madness."

Evolet walked to the door. "We've got her," she called to someone outside.

Rohane strained to see who it was.

"Bring her to the temple."

That voice. Shock then pain cut through Rohane. In disbelief, she stared at the door, her heart pierced with dread.

Jenna-Dairine strode in. But for a splatter of blood on her arm, the heavy sword in her hand stained and dripping, she looked immaculate, with no sign she had been fighting.

"You." Blaire sobbed the word. "Jenna-Dairine, you? Do you hate me that much?"

The battale captain's heavy gaze settled upon Blaire. She blinked once, slowly. A lip curled at the corner. "And that says it all, doesn't it, Blaire." Jenna-Dairine's voice was thick with contempt. "This is not about you. You're just part of a sickness, a sickness that's been allowed to fester in Quisnaf for too long."

"Quisnaf is strong," Blaire said. "We have never been stronger."

"No. You have weakened us," Jenna-Dairine said. "With your new laws, your plans to cut the battales from four to three. It can't happen."

Rohane still gaped. A bitter laugh burst from her. "Oh, goddess. You belong to the Order? You, Jenna-Dairine? But that's madness. You don't believe in that sort of nonsense. You and I and Blaire, we laughed about it when we were girls, called it archaic."

Jenna-Dairine swung on Rohane with a smug smile. "Belong to the Order?" She chuckled. "Oh, sweetheart. Don't you see? Don't you see it yet? Rohane, dear, I *am* the Order."

VAL ARQUES

al spent a restless few hours pacing, thinking. Imagining
the worst. At every sound beyond his room, he stiffened
with alarm, his heart unsteady. At every scrape of steel,
his stomach lurched. The fighting sounded intense, not just
another skirmish. And Sisilia had muttered about the Order. By
The Three, who lived? He couldn't bear to think of who might be
dead.

At last, two Decan guards unlocked his door. Without resisting,
he followed them through corridors and into the temple. "What's
happened?"

The guards answered with hard-faced stares and shoves.

Val forced down his frustration and fear. Until he understood
what had occurred, he had to keep his wits about him.

"Inside." Another hefty push forced Val through doors into an
unfamiliar chamber, a formal room of polished wood, gleaming
tiles, and pale marble. Women milled about—warriors,
sorceresses, healers, and scribes. A line of dishevelled prisoners
crouched beside a wall, some bound by rope, others by chain, their
faces weary or tight with despair.

The odour of sweat, the tang of blood, and a buzz of excitement
filled the chamber. These were the victors then. He shuddered.

Nothing was more dismal than watching those who won the battle gloat.

Hands dragged him forward. His escort dropped him on his knees beside a huddled woman, her arms lashed at her back. Foolishly, Val tried to rise, only to be held down. He peered through his tangled fringe at his fellow prisoner. Long pale hair fell about her bloodied face.

"Blaire." He released a breath. "Are you unharmed?"

She turned her head. No tears marred her cold beauty. Instead, her lovely violet eyes smouldered with fury.

"She's unharmed, Val. So sweet that you care."

He looked towards the voice. Jenna-Dairine leaned forward from a tall-backed chair in front of him. A wave of power and exultation thundered off her. The truth of what had happened hit him like a blow. The new queen. Enthroned.

"It's you." He stared in disbelief. "You're the Order?" Anger lumped in his belly. What had she done? Who had she hurt?

He swept a glance along the women under guard, his mind sifting who had stood against Jenna-Dairine and who fought with her.

Wrists manacled, her expression blank with shock, Samantha looked through him. Aine, stony-faced and hard-eyed, raked her captors with a wilting grimace. With surprise, he recognised Persia among the prisoners.

As for those who'd sided with the rebels... A shudder crept at his neck at the sight of Sisilia at Jenna-Dairine's shoulder. Sorcha, too, had chosen the conqueror. No surprises there; he'd come to understand how rigid she was.

At movement behind Jenna-Dairine, guards parted for a woman. Val gasped. Relief shot through him. "Genya!"

A sword hilt poked from a shoulder strap; her clothes showed no sign of blood. Genya paid him no heed, only moved through the crowd of women towards Jenna-Dairine. Slowly, as though through a haze, Val's mind filtered where Genya stood—at Jenna-

Dairine's right. Unguarded. Unrestrained. She looked easy, comfortable, and untroubled.

"But…" Shock slammed into him. "Oh, by The Three," Val whispered in horror. "Genya, did you side with her? With this so-called Order? How is that possible?"

Genya's eyes passed over him with a remote, detached look. He might have been a stranger in a city square who had accidentally jogged her arm.

Val turned pleadingly to Jenna-Dairine. "Why is she here? I don't understand any of this. What has happened?"

"Surely it's obvious." Jenna-Dairine swept her hand to the prisoners along the wall. "Do those wits of yours at last fail you?"

"A coup," Val said flatly. "Rebellion."

She shrugged. "Such a word. A political word. Not the truth. The Order fought to win control. Quisnaf is weak. It is sick. She"—Jenna-Dairine stabbed a finger at Blaire—"is part of that sickness, she and all her councillors who destroy our traditions, who water down our laws. No, Telorian. Not rebellion. A restoration. Regeneration."

"It is so," a few women shouted. "She speaks the truth. We need strength. Order."

"Praise the goddess," Sorcha said, making a sign.

Val looked helplessly at Genya. "Why? Why involve yourself? What have you done?"

She regarded him coolly. "Now you ask? Days ago, you could not bring yourself to see me, to speak with me. So no, you don't get to ask. You no longer have the right to pretend to care."

"I do care," Val said.

Genya laughed—a cold laugh, a stranger's laugh.

The doors pushed open. More guards appeared, dragging in a line of straggling captives, Rohane among them.

Val's belly lurched. She was safe, thank The Three, but a captive, her arms bound to her body with rope. What did that mean? Would they execute those who defied them? *Oh, no. Please, no.*

He followed her with his eyes, willing her to see him. At last, as the guards threw her down, Rohane caught his gaze. Her face grim, she shrugged.

"Rohane." From the blood on her face, on her clothes, in her hair, she had fought. He supposed even a berserker must eventually be overwhelmed by sheer numbers.

"Val…" Rohane offered him a weak smile. "Are you unharmed?"

Jenna-Dairine crouched before Rohane. She brushed her fingertips over her prisoner's cheek. "Ah, sweet, silly love. Good to know that berserker heart beats the same as anyone else's."

Rohane turned her head aside sharply. With a laugh, Jenna-Dairine rose. She walked along the line of captives, nodding.

"You." Her finger poked at Persia like a knife. "You fought against me, Captain. I thought we were allies. I know there is respect between us, Persia."

Persia lifted her head. Blood stained her face. Her left arm hung limp. Despite her exhaustion, her shock at defeat, she glared at Jenna-Dairine. Val had never liked Persia, but he admired the fight in her. "I am loyal to my Regenta."

Jenna-Dairine waved a hand. "That means you can be loyal to your new Regenta."

Persia looked at Blaire. "My Regenta still lives."

Jenna-Dairine yanked a knife from her belt. She went for Blaire. "Not for long."

"No," Val cried. He jerked up, only for the guards to force him back down. As he struggled uselessly, they held his arms.

Jenna-Dairine considered him with a sneer. "Another foolish man taken in by her beautiful face. She's weak, Val. Weak. Not able to lead us. A weak Regenta must be overthrown. She must die. That is the Quisnaf way."

"No." He rocked his head back and forth. "You were friends…"

"I carry his child," Blaire blurted.

Torchlight flashed on Jenna-Dairine's blade. "Do you think that will save you?"

"Wait." Sorcha whipped up a hand. Her face seemed frozen, stunned. Quickly, she hastened to Jenna-Dairine and whispered in her ear.

The battale captain listened impatiently. Then she huffed. "That precious Caelan blood. The high priestess says the child of this bloodline must be born, no matter the mother's errors."

Blaire lifted her head, defiant. "My only error was trusting you. I should have listened to Sisilia. She warned me."

Jenna-Dairine raised a brow at the sorceress. "A curious game, friend."

Sisilia stared back blandly. "I glimpsed this night in the sacred waters. In the flames, too. I told Blaire you would betray her. It was my duty. I also knew from my visions she would not listen, that she would be taken in by your offer of renewed friendship."

"You're very naughty," Jenna-Dairine mocked with a wagging finger. "You could have brought us all down."

"I think not."

"It's as well you're useful, Sisilia," Jenna-Dairine said. "You're certainly not loyal."

The sorceress's lips twisted downwards in disdain. Val knew that look. Any of his actions she deemed stupid drew that expression of disapproval. Sisilia was sharp-witted but arrogant. She had no patience for those she thought less intelligent than she.

"I am loyal to the goddess. I am loyal to Quisnaf. At the moment, I judge you better able than Blaire to serve Quisnaf. That is all. It's hardly personal. I certainly don't like you any more than her."

The doors flung back. At rushed footsteps, Val glanced over his shoulder. A panting guard wearing a Decan badge dipped her head. At Jenna-Dairine's gesture to approach, she hastened forward and dropped to one knee.

"Report."

"Councillor, the seer and warrior caverns are ours. The potion that put most of the city to sleep worked like a charm. Everyone ranked a captain or above is taken or dead."

"Not so," Jenna-Dairine said. "Joanna is missing."

"Dead."

"Did you see the body?"

"Not personally," the guardswoman stammered. "I was told…"

"Then personally see it," Jenna-Dairine's voice rose a notch. For the first time, Val heard tension in her tone.

"Yes, Councillor."

"And?"

The woman snatched a steadying breath. "The only resistance is a small group of warriors holed up in the armoury."

Val considered that. Only a few hours had passed since he'd woken to the sound of swordplay. This struggle had been quick and brutal. Well planned.

"Who leads them?" Jenna-Dairine's tone was sharp and matter-of-fact. Val realised he had discounted that part of her—the ability to command, scheme, and manoeuvre.

"Marlisa, daughter of Margaret."

"You didn't offer the greedy cow gold," a guardswoman jeered. Laughter broke out.

Gold. So Marlisa's penchant for wealth was well-known.

Jenna-Dairine turned on Persia. "Your lieutenant oversteps herself. I don't suppose you'd order her to surrender?"

Persia's lips parted in a sneer.

"I thought not." Jenna-Dairine faced the guardswoman again. "What's to stop you overwhelming them?"

"They're well armed, as you might expect," the guard answered. "The armoury has one entrance. They have at least one archer with them. She took out four of us when we attempted to get through the door."

"Make sure they can't leave. Wait them out. Starve them out if necessary."

The guardswoman nodded. With a quick touch of hand to brow, she departed.

"Why am I here?" Val asked.

"We'll get to you," Jenna-Dairine replied with an ominous smile, sprawling in her high-backed seat, legs thrown over a chair arm, her body and voice relaxed.

One by one, guards forced prisoners to kneel before her. From each captive, she sought a blood oath. When it was given, she flicked a disinterested hand. Those who submitted walked free. Those who did not, guards led away.

"And you, Aine, daughter of Georgina, councillor of Quisnaf? Will you save your life and offer your pledge to your new Regenta?"

Aine lifted a blood-stained face. She said not a word but spat at Jenna-Dairine.

Calmly, Jenna-Dairine wiped her face with a cloth. She swung her legs down and leaned forward. "Be sensible. Think, woman, think."

"I will never bend my neck to a usurper. You are a self-serving creature, Jenna-Dairine, daughter of Kathryn. Your actions here tonight will rip Quisnaf apart."

Jenna-Dairine scoffed. "My actions here tonight will save us, Councillor. I shall restore the old laws, those weakened over the centuries by councils too afraid to do what must be done."

"You are mad. You think to bring back the Right of Overlord?" Aine shook her head. "You will lead us into wars we cannot win. We shall be overwhelmed."

The Right of Overlord? A shiver trembled through Val. He wrapped his arms about his drawn-up knees.

"It is a new dawn." Sisilia's tone was ringing and imperious. "A would-be conqueror will come against us, but now victory is assured."

"You're as deluded as she is. I am content to die rather than see my beloved Quisnaf torn apart."

Guards took Aine away.

Persia was next. Guards dragged her forward on her knees. Once they cut her hands free, she rubbed her bruised wrists, eyes downcast. Val thought she looked ill and in pain. Blood seeped through her tunic near her breast.

"Persia, Persia, Persia." Jenna-Dairine sighed. "Do you know how much I've always admired you? So calm. Decisive. I remember my mother calling you a leader sculptured by temperament. A strange thing to say, but I grew to understand it. I used to aspire to be like you."

Persia grimaced but did not look up.

"Give me your oath." Jenna-Dairine rose and stood over the battale captain. "Let me spare you."

"No."

"As stubborn as you are dutiful. I have need of you, so I cannot accept your answer."

"You cannot change it."

Jenna-Dairine's smile was smug. Val wondered how he had thought her warm that night they talked in the garden. When they'd traded sword strokes, he'd glimpsed arrogance, even ruthlessness—not always a bad trait for a warrior.

"You have two children within this valley. A son and a daughter." Jenna-Dairine turned to a scribe. "Fetch them."

"No!" Persia sprang up, only to be shoved back down by the guards. Her breaths came fast. "No, you can't involve them."

"Your daughter is twelve. Is that right? The boy, fourteen. Let's start with him. I'm told you're fond of the child."

"Please." Persia's face paled. Compassion rushed at Val. Despite his anger, he would do anything to save Genya, even give his life willingly, without a moment's hesitation.

Genya stood talking softly to Sisilia. She was half in shadow, a shoulder to the wall, watching events unfold with an almost amused interest. This new coldness, this spark of cruelty, frightened him. This wasn't the child he knew. What had happened in those short months they had been apart? Was her defiance his fault? He'd pushed her away because he was afraid, always afraid, of what he might say to her out of anger, bitterness, and sorrow.

"Your oath," Jenna-Dairine snapped. "Or the boy dies first. Then the girl."

Persia hesitated. A guard pressed a knife into her hand.

Val's breath stalled. She need only cut her palm, draw blood, and say the words. Persia lifted her eyes to Jenna-Dairine. Her lips were set in a stubborn, hard line. Slowly, she curled her fingers about the knife hilt.

Then she smiled—and plunged the knife into her own breast.

"No!" Jenna-Dairine screamed, lurching for the dying woman.

Persia fell forward. She gurgled blood and died.

Shock and sadness tore at Val like a jagged blade. He understood Persia's sacrifice. Unless she was a monster, Jenna-Dairine had no reason to harm Persia's children if she was dead.

Shoulders stooped, Jenna-Dairine stood over Persia's body. In the hush, her heaved breaths were like thunderclaps. Her eyes looked wet. When a single tear smeared her cheek, she did not bother to swipe it away.

"She was once my captain," she muttered. "Take her away." She sat down heavily, staring upon nothing. Then her gaze shifted first to Rohane then to Val, as if choosing between them. Her eyes snared him. "And now for you."

Guards threw him to his knees before Jenna-Dairine. They held his shoulders. Val almost chuckled at the idea that he might give them trouble. No, Jenna-Dairine held power over him. Rohane was her prisoner, Genya her ally. He would offer whatever oath she wanted to keep both of them safe. Yet why should Jenna-Dairine bother with his oath? He already belonged to Sisilia; that had been made abundantly clear. She answered for him.

Val dug his knees into a thick rug. He hunched his shoulders. From the gathering chill, it must be close to dawn. This ridiculous ceremony had lasted all night.

"We have a matter to settle." Jenna-Dairine swung her legs back over the chair arm.

Val's gaze held on a smear of blood on her boots. Persia's blood.

He sighed. Exhaustion washed through him. He wanted Rohane and Genya safe and this terrible night done with. "You want my oath? Cut my hands free."

"Don't be stupid. You're nothing more than a slave. Your oath is unnecessary."

Val flicked up a brow at Rohane.

She shrugged, mouthing, "I don't know."

"What then?"

For a moment, Jenna-Dairine did nothing more than tap her finger on her chin. Then she gestured at Genya. Without looking at Val, Genya came forward.

"Sisilia." The sorceress stepped closer. "You must surrender him." Jenna-Dairine flicked a hand at Val.

The sorceress scoffed. "I think not."

Jenna-Dairine sighed heavily. "The girl has a blood claim—"

Sisilia turned to scowl at Genya. Puzzled, Val again glanced at Rohane, who shook her head in bewilderment.

"—and intends to hold to that claim."

"Stop." Sisilia clenched a fist against her thigh. "You said nothing of this, Jenna-Dairine. What game are you playing? The man is cloaked. That is an end to it."

"I know my rights." Genya wore a strange predatory smile. If this were a game, Val recognised she was at its centre.

Sisilia scoffed. "She is not even a sister of Quisnaf."

"That is not so," Jenna-Dairine said. "She offered her oath both to the goddess and to me today."

Sisilia growled and tapped her fist against her chin.

"What is a blood claim?" Val asked.

Jenna-Dairine looked down at him with a serene smile. "She is your ward? You have been as a father to her."

"You know that," he growled.

"Well, then." Jenna-Dairine spread her arms. "A mother or daughter is responsible for a man in Quisnaf. She may decide to surrender that responsibility to another who then cloaks that man.

But until she does that, he belongs to her."

"Belongs," Val echoed bitterly. A sour laugh caught in his throat. "Belongs." He shot a dismayed look at Sisilia.

The sorceress's eyes glittered with fury. "I can do nothing," she spat. "A blood claim takes priority."

Val glanced at Genya. She stared back, impassive. "So you own me." Disbelief rippled in his voice. "What do you intend to do with me?"

Genya offered a sweet smile. "Oh, don't think I haven't imagined all sorts of unpleasant things. However…" She shrugged. "I shall make a gift of you—a present to my new Regenta."

Blood pounded through his skull, his thoughts thick and dull. Vaguely, as if from far away, Val heard Rohane gasp. Sisilia tensed, her gaze levelled like a drawn sword on Jenna-Dairine.

Genya dropped to one knee before Jenna-Dairine. She bent her head and kissed an offered hand. "My gift to you, Regenta. A token of my loyalty, of everything we will achieve… together."

"Yes, everything we will achieve." Jenna-Dairine's hand rested in Genya's fair hair. "You understand, I think, my vision for Quisnaf."

"I understand." Slowly, Genya rose. "And I welcome your offer of a place here, in the new order."

"You asked to speak with him," Jenna-Dairine fluttered a hand. "You have my permission to address my property."

Genya turned. "Yes, I have something to say."

Val stiffened his shoulders and lifted his chin, preparing to face accusing words. He was not blameless. He would listen to her accusations and accept she had that right and that maybe even her words held truth.

"Alecc is dead," Genya said.

Something shattered in Val's mind. He heard the words but did not take them in. All he did was stare at Genya.

"Did you hear me? Your precious son is dead." Her voice broke. For all her bitter words, her face twisted with grief. And she would grieve only if she spoke the truth.

Alecc. Dead. The words, their meaning, wound their way through him with gathering pain. It was as though a whip flayed him inside, leaving him raw and empty. Breath died somewhere. He could not think because thought was no longer part of him. There was only pain.

Blackness rushed him. How long it held him, Val didn't know. He realised he'd slumped to the ground. Someone held his head. A voice—Sisilia's—instructed, "Take slow breaths."

"Alecc. No, no, no." With a cry, Val brushed off her hands and sat up. His belly clenched. Every part of him was exposed, uncovered, and aching. Then a sob burst from him.

"You cry for him." Genya's face contorted with anger. "Oh, how your tears rip my heart. Where were your tears for me? Well, you shall cry and cry, for your precious Kaell is also dead. Executed."

Horror then blessed numbness swept over him. Dimly, he heard Rohane shouting his name then pleading for Jenna-Dairine to let her go to him.

Sisilia still crouched at his side. "He will slide into despair again." She shook her head. "You foolish child. It was agreed to keep this from him. You yourself said it would destroy him."

Kept from him? He could not take that in either. How long had Genya known? When had Kaell died? Sorrow pressed on his chest, the weight unbearable. *First Alecc. Now Kaell.*

"Rohane," he wept. "Please. Where are you?"

She yelled words he could not make out. She tried to stand, only for guards to hurl her back against the wall.

"You cry for Alecc." Genya's voice was as bitterly cold as a Mountains winter. "Now you cry for Kaell. Will you cry for her?"

Genya whipped out her knife. In too few strides, she reached Rohane and pulled her up. Val rose fast. He lunged for Rohane. Guards grabbed his shoulders.

"What are you doing?" Jenna-Dairine stormed to her feet, arms extended in protest. "I need her."

Genya laughed wildly. She put the blade to Rohane's throat. "Tell me why I shouldn't, Val. Nicky is dead. Alecc, too. You can't look at me without disappointment or even disgust in your eyes. What have I got to lose?"

Val struggled violently in the guards' grip. "Don't," he begged Genya. "Please."

"Beg!" she screamed. "Go on. Get on your knees and beg me to spare her."

Val dropped at once to his knees. "Genya, what's happened to you? This isn't you. I don't understand. She's done you no harm."

"Get away from her," Samantha shouted, her voice broken with anger and fear.

At Jenna-Dairine's gesture, guards closed in on Genya. She threw up a hand, chanting. Blue light sparked from her fingertips. It shot through the air and hit the guards in a cloud of blue smoke. They fell back, groaning. Genya's cold gaze returned to Val.

"You love her." Genya hurled the words like an accusation. They pierced like a sword to his heart.

"I love you, too. I never stopped."

"Liar," she spat. "I'm going to make you suffer. I'm taking everything from you."

"No," he cried, throwing himself against the guards as Genya's knife flashed across Rohane's throat.

For the briefest moment, amid the spouting blood, he glimpsed Rohane's eyes, wide and brimming with shock. Then, with a thud, she collapsed to the floor.

Val slumped like a discarded cloth toy, his spirit thrashed, shattered, and broken. Destroyed. His mind could not accept what he had just seen.

Around him, as though released from a spell, everyone seemed to move at once. Sisilia and Jenna-Dairine both rushed to Rohane. Guards bustled about, lost. Samantha was screaming. And screaming. And screaming. Then a sound like a blow cut off the scream. Now he heard weeping. Not his.

"She's dead." Sisilia straightened with a sigh. "Fool child, do you know what you've done?"

"A waste of a good warrior." Jenna-Dairine's tone was dispassionate.

Sisilia shook her head. "No, you don't understand. She just killed the King of Veniva's only daughter." Hands tore down her face. She wailed, "Oh, by the goddess. What has she done?"

Val heard her words but felt nothing. All he knew was darkness, a hollow pit that closed in about him, that consumed him.

"You need to know what it's like, Val," Genya said. "If I can't have your love, then no one shall, especially her."

In an empty, flat voice, he asked, "What more can you do to me?"

Genya smiled viciously. If he were not dazed, how that smile might sting. But now he puzzled at it in a detached sort of way, wondering why she smiled. Why she wanted to hurt him. How Rohane could be dead.

Genya turned to Jenna-Dairine. "Leave me with him. You promised."

Jenna-Dairine nodded. She looked to the guards and gestured to Samantha. "Bring her."

The room emptied, and Genya faced him. "Remember how Archanin offered you a choice?"

He sat back on his heels. A torrent of anger, sorrow, and disbelief engulfed him, consuming him. Part of him wanted to shake her. The other part wanted to curl his knees to his chest and sob. "I remember."

She nodded slowly. "Now, I offer you a choice."

Val swallowed. "What... choice?"

Genya crouched beside Rohane's body. "How strange to think you love her. What is so singular about this one woman? I thought you immune to such nonsense, your heart always shielded."

He shivered. "What choice?"

Careless of the blood soaking into her garments, Genya pulled Rohane's head onto her lap. Her fingers brushed Rohane's cheek.

Part of Val, the tiny part that still functioned, wanted to scream, *Do not touch her. How dare you touch her.*

"I can bring her back to life."

"What?" His heart kicked against his ribs.

"If that's what you want."

"You mean—" His mind tore back to that night when Genya had killed a young man, only to restore his life.

Genya was watching him closely, as if to absorb his every reaction. "Oh, Val, really. I am a death rider's daughter, after all."

He gasped. Sudden hope shook him.

"One kiss, and she is restored. But…"

Breath on hold, he waited.

"Not restored to you." Genya laughed. "A kiss, and she lives, but she must stay close to me always, or she will lose her sight. So choose. Rohane alive, but lost to you. Rohane dead and still lost to you."

"Do it," he said. Dull misery and despair emptied him. He was no longer a man alive but a shadow. "I don't care if I cannot be with her. I only want her safe, well. Happy."

"Good gods." Genya's brows shot up. "You do love her. Who'd have thought that cold heart could feel anything?"

"Genya…"

"I know what you're thinking." Her mouth twisted. "You think your beloved will choose blindness if it means staying with you. Think again. Quisnaf is a harsh place. Harsher than even you realise. They do not tolerate cripples. Once blind, she will find no place here."

"Do it," Val said. "I only care that she lives."

With a sneering glance at him, Genya bent her head and put her lips to Rohane's. For a heartbeat or two, nothing happened. Then Rohane stirred. She spluttered a breath. Violent coughs racked her chest.

She lives. She lives. A flame of joy flared in Val.

Rohane sat up. "I was… I don't understand." She cast a bewildered look about.

Genya rose with ponderous slowness, watching Val.

"She killed you." Val's voice shook. "Then she restored your life. She is Roaran's daughter. The daughter of a death rider."

"What?"

Val began to laugh, a wild, lost, and crazed laugh. A perfect revenge. How could Genya do this? To him. To Rohane, whom she hardly knew. It wasn't fair. It wasn't right.

Despairing, he watched Rohane struggle to understand what he had said. He wished he had words of comfort. He had none. He had nothing. No more tears. No hope. He had moved beyond sorrow to a terrible, bleak, and empty place where his spirit floundered in darkness.

Rohane's eyes shadowed. She blinked twice rapidly. "Is it true then? What they say about a death rider? The legends. If I should…" Bemused, she shook her head.

An explosion of laughter rocked Genya, ringing with sneering triumph.

Val had never thought she could do something to make him hate her, but in that moment, as she stood over Rohane laughing, he loathed her.

"You still don't see," Genya jeered. "He does. He knows."

"What does he see?" Rohane looked in bewilderment from Genya to Val.

"That I've taken you from him. He cannot leave here, certainly not now Jenna-Dairine owns him. But you must go where I go. And I will leave Quisnaf."

Val sobbed—a sound soaked in pain. He drew Rohane against him, desperate to hold her and breathe in her scent.

To his surprise, she pulled away sharply. "Who are you?"

Horror ran cold through him. A memory flashed of the boy Genya had restored, how he had lost six months and forgotten that time just before he died. Oh, by the gods, it couldn't happen again.

"It's perfect," Genya taunted Val. "A perfect revenge for your scorn. You can never be with her, with this woman you love. Because she doesn't even know you."

Rohane was watching him, still with that puzzled frown. "I don't understand. Am I meant to know you? Yet I swear by the goddess, we've never met."

Val struggled to speak. Sorrow choked in his throat. "You've taken everything," he murmured to Genya. "Is that what you want? Then I guess you've won."

Doubt shadowed Genya's face. Victory could be hollow. He knew that. Vengeance never tasted as sweet as its first tantalising sniff promised.

A strange pity for Genya moved through him. Unexpectedly, something so small and delicate had found its way through his misery.

Genya's gaze fell on him. She must have seen something in his eyes, for she stiffened, her face darkening with anger. "Do not look at me like that. How dare you pity me."

Snarling, she grabbed Rohane's arm and dragged her from the room. The door closed on Val, kneeling and broken. Alone.

Val rose to his hands and knees. For a moment, he stayed like that, unable to move, his tormented mind fractured by pain. *Kaell, dead. Alecc. Rohane gone.* Then his misery burst out of him. He howled, beating a fist against the floor.

The door flung back. Fast footsteps approached. Sisilia stooped to throw an arm about his shoulders. "Hush now."

He hardly heard her. He could only sob and thump the floor with a bleeding knuckle.

She pulled his head to her breast, her fingers stroking his hair. "Hush. Hush. It will pass. Everything passes. You and I, we've lived longer than most. We know that."

At last, he grew quiet, his sobs turning to sniffs. Val wiped his nose and eyes with the back of his hand. He was trembling, unable to move, barely able to think. From deep within, he found the strength for words.

"You offered once," he said, his voice as bare and broken as his spirit. "To rid me of despair."

"I did," Sisilia said.

"You offered to rid me of painful memories."

She grimaced and spread her hands in a gesture of regret. "It is a high price to pay. You would forget who you were. You would forget everyone you've ever loved, every place you've ever been."

"Yes."

She arched a brow. "Is that what you want, Val Arques?"

Val thought about Kaell. About Alecc. About Rohane and the lost look in her eyes, her blank, puzzled stare as she had gazed at him.

"Yes," Val said. "Do it."

KAELL

Dying, he remembered, but not death. The rope had jerked. In agony, he had spiralled through layers of darkness. Then the sound of voices chanting reached down into the emptiness, dragging him up into a hazy, dulled awareness.

For a time, caught in an eddy between living and dying, he dreamed. Sometimes there were sweet scents—a thread of orchids from the valley's scent gardens or a drift of candlewax. Sometimes there were sounds—his own serration of breath echoing in his head, its wheeze, and its laboured release. Then the voices came again, ebbing and flowing.

Life spilled into his body with an agonised gasp, a pounding in his skull, and a needling sting in his limbs. His mouth tasted stale. The weight of his head was heavy against a pillow. Cloth brushed his back. Fingertips whispered on his cheek.

As if emerging from fog, he came to in a shadowy cavern. A lamp's light hurt his eyes. Instinctively, he lifted an arm to shield them. His breath caught. It wasn't his arm.

Panic filled him. He began to flail about. Someone grabbed his shoulders, holding him down.

"Shh," a woman murmured. "You're safe."

The word slowly penetrated his spiralling mind. *Safe. Alive.*

"What's happened?" His voice came out as a croak. He struggled to focus on the face of the woman bending over him. Her smile was gentle, her pale hair caught up in a long plait.

"Blaire's plan worked." The woman nodded to herself. "We have brought you back from the dead. Given you a new body."

"What?" Bewildered, Kaell shifted on the bed. "What do you mean?"

"Kate is no more."

"Show me," Kaell said urgently.

The woman turned away, walked across the room, and returned with a mirror. Kaell took it from her. He peered, bewildered, at his face. It was that of a young man, his skin sun bronzed, his hair light brown, and his eyes dark.

For a long moment, all he could do was stare. Then a slow shudder went through him.

"So it begins," he said. "Blaire's plan to take back Quisnaf."

The woman's gentle smile unfolded. "So it begins."

WHO'S WHO IN THE SHADOW SWORD WORLD

QUISNAF

ROHANE, a cursed berserker warrior and retrieval captain.

BLAIRE, Regenta of Quisnaf.

JENNA-DAIRINE, One of Quisnaf's four battale captains and daughter of the previous Quisnaf Regenta.

SISILIA, Sorceress of Quisnaf.

SAMANTHA, Councillor of Quisnaf and Blaire's loyal ally.

PERSIA, Battale captain.

MARLISA, Persia's lieutenant.

ELENA, a healer of Quisnaf.

SORCHA, the high priestess of Cyrah, servant of the temple.

QUISNAF OF OLD

SABIN THE REBUILDER, the warrior who restored Quisnaf after an earthquake nearly destroyed it when the God of Fire escaped his prison centuries ago.

SORGANNE, the first sorceress of Quisnaf who fled the city of Seithin to help establish Quisnaf.

THE SWORD BROTHERHOOD

CADAN TIERNAN, Roaran Caelan's captain. The younger son of a lord, Cadan turned to piracy until Roaran redeemed him.

GETHIN MAELSTROM, a legendary warrior of the past.

NEIL CULLY, the warrior-priest who served King Rollo.

ALEYN AIL, the king's shield to Dashel the second.

IVAAR, JACK, ORAN, warriors of the Sword Brotherhood.

THE MOUNTAINS

VAL ARQUES CAELAN, the second son of Rhoslyn and Teynan Caelan. Teynan was Lord of the Isles when it was called Avanti. Val Arques became Lord of the Mountains. As custodian of the Mountains fortress Vraymorg, he was addressed as Vraymorg.

KAELL, the Seithin-born 19th warrior bonded to the ancient gods. His duty is to take up the sword against the inhuman followers of a bloodthirsty god.

ARN TRANTER, Kaell's captain and friend.

OLIER, Kaell's second captain

EWEN, Vraymorg's trusted servant.

FELIX HILLBORN, a noble of the Mountains, his brother AALART, a new captain at the fortress of Vraymorg, his sister MARGARET.

THE ICELANDS

ROLLAND DAMADAR, Lord of the Icelands.

VELLERAN, the son of Lord Rolland and Vivianna, princess of Adorean. The new Lord of the Icelands after his father's death.

HEATH, Lord Rolland and the Mad Mother's eldest son. The Damadar enforcer, Heath was also a fire dancer whose duty was to fight in the Icelands' notorious fire halls and kill opponents as sacrifices for the gods. In The Sword Brotherhood, Heath is a death rider with no memory of his previous life.

MYRANTHE, eldest daughter of Lord Rolland and the Mad Mother. The most powerful sorceress outside of Quisnaf.

GRIFFIN, younger son of Lord Rolland and the Mad Mother.

JUDITH, younger daughter of Lord Rolland and the Mad Mother. The Quisnaf trained Judith in the art of seduction.

THE FALLS

MAGLO, Lord of The Falls.

YVONNE, his wife, now lady-in-waiting to Queen Rozenn.

THE VAREE AND THOSE WHO LIVE ACROSS THE GORGE

DANNON BLOODTAKER, Varee battle (or host) captain who becomes overlord. Dannon takes up his role with the Sword Brotherhood in the third book of the series.

CONROY, overlord of the Varee.

THE MAGE, the magic man and priest of the Varee.

SHAHVEN, a Varee boy apprenticed to the mage.

NATASHA, sister to Shahven and Dannon's some-time lover.

JULIETTE, a wood witch and healer, now an ally to Roaran Caelan.

ELOISE, Robert's daughter and Dannon's wife (deceased).

SLOANA, a warrior of the Sisters of Cyrah.

CAHIR

ROZENN, Queen of Cahir. Wife to Gendrick Caelan.

ALECC, her son and heir, now Lord of the Mountains.

DAL-KANU

CATHMOR, The former King of Telor, once wed to ANNATISE of the Downs, betrothed to AZENOR of the Isles. Upon Cathmor's death in battle, Gendrick Caelan took the throne.

CAEL-CARREN, Cathmor's uncle.

THE ISLES

KING HATTON, Lord of the Isles. His children, Gendrick, Aric and Azenor. His brother, Tomasin. King Hatton was also killed in the battle that delivered Gendrick the throne.

GENDRICK CAELAN, Hatton's eldest son and heir. He became King of Telor after defeating King Cathmor in battle.

ARIC CAELAN, Hatton's second son and Commander of the Isles. Now a death rider with no memory of his former life.

AZENOR CAELAN, Hatton's daughter, once betrothed to Lord of the Henge, SHERRIN CROSS, and later betrothed to KING CATHMOR.

PAIRAS MORGAN, Aric's captain and heir to The Rock.

AIDEN SALTMAN, Aric's second captain. Upon Gendrick's ascension to the throne, he becomes the King's captain.

AINGEAR, High Priestess to The Three, the Isles gods.

ETHNE, a young sorceress in service to the gods of the Isles.

KINGS AND WARRIORS OF OLD

ROARAN CAELAN, son of Karolus of the Isles and Marginet of Quisnaf. Known as the seer king. He came to throne upon the death of Rainer Caelan, the son of Dace Caelan. After his murder, an Icelands sorceress stole his body and transformed him into a death rider, the gods' most feared weapon.

GENYA CAELAN, Roaran's daughter, created by taking part of his soul, and part of Kaell's soul.

DEKARNE CAELAN, a warrior of Quisnaf, Dace Caelan's daughter, and Roaran's queen.

RYOL CAELAN, Dekarne and Roaran's son, who became Lord of the Isles after the civil war that followed Roaran's murder.

DEVARSI CAELAN, Rainer Caelan's daughter who became Roaran's ward when her father died in distant Quisnaf. In return for freeing Archanin from his otherworldly prison, the ghoul god helped Devarsi seize the Telorian throne from Ryol after Roaran's death.

THE MAZART, the Wardorian sorcerer, emperor and tyrant who destroyed Seithin and ruled the known world until killed by Dace Caelan in the ruins of the desert city.

DACE CAELAN, a legendary king and bladesman, and Val's beloved cousin.

NICKY SALTMAN, once a warrior of the Isles, restored to life by Roaran Caelan after Nicky died saving Ryol from an assassin sent by Devarsi. He served as lord's sword to MORGAN THE DAMNED, ruler of The Rock, and Dekarne Caelan's bastard son.

CAELAN, the son of a Cahirean princess and the god Ghani-Jai, who established the kingdom of Telor. Known as the gormel slayer.

SISKA, Caelan's queen and a Quisnaf sorceress.

CALLANDARRAN, Raggamirron's brother who was executed centuries ago.

THE GODS

ARCHANIN, God of Seithin, banished centuries ago, along with those of the Seithin who chose to follow him into exile. The other gods condemned his followers to become like him, drinkers of blood. Members of Archanin's council, called the Nobles of the

Night, include LASTENARRON, RAGGAMIRRON and TARTHALAN, MAUD THE MALICIOUS, NATHANIEL, and the LADY YAMA.

KHIR, the god of battles. An old god of Telor.

CYRAH, a goddess of war worshipped by the Quisnaf and the outcast Sisters of Cyrah.

KUTRON, Telorian and Cahirean god of the wind and sky.

AZAIRR, a god of fire imprisoned deep in the earth beneath Quisnaf. With Roaran's help, Rainer Caelan killed Azairr with an arrow made of ice, only to die moments later.

THE THREE, the old gods of Avanti, as the Isles was once known.

RACHEL, A minor goddess and guardian of the Hawkwood, a forgotten gateway to the Enarae.

FROM THE AUTHOR

Thank you so much for reading *The Sword and its Woman.* The fifth in the series, with the working title, *Kingdom of the Broken,* should be published in 2024.

If you have a moment, it would be really helpful if you could leave a short review on Amazon or Goodreads or both! I'm a new author and reviews help other readers discover the Shadow Sword series. Thank you!

I love hearing from you, even if it's to tell me off for what I put Kaell through.

Feel free to drop me a line at writersjhartland@gmail.com, on Facebook at www.facebook.com/the19thbladesman/, or at my website www.sjhartland.com.

ABOUT THE AUTHOR

S. J. Hartland is an emerging author of epic fantasy who calls the Darling Downs, Queensland, home.

She lives in chaos with two labradoodles, Lily and Coffee.

Susan is an Australian journalist, and a former fencer, who watches too much TV, spent too many holidays wandering around obscure castles, and is obsessed with anything medieval.

The 19th Bladesman (2018) was her first published novel. The *Last Seer King*, the second in the Shadow Sword series, was published in 2019, followed by *The Sword Brotherhood* in 2020. The fourth in the series *The Sword and its Woman*, was published in 2022.

The first in a new series, *Blade Lord*, was published in 2021.

Find out more about the two series and the characters at www.sjhartland.com, or drop her an email at writersjhartland@gmail.com.